Red Sky Over America

Ladies of Oberlin, Book One

By

Tamera Lynn Kraft

Published by Mt. Zion Ridge Press

M Zion Ridge Press
Books off the Beaten Path

Mt Zion Ridge Press
295 Gum Springs Rd, NW
Georgetown, TN 37366

https://mtzionridgepress.wixsite.com/

Copyright © 2017 by Tamera Lynn Kraft
ISBN 13: 978-1-949564-02-0

Published in the United States of America
Publication Date: September 1, 2018

Editor-In-Chief: Michelle Levigne
Executive Editor: Tamera Lynn Kraft
Cover Artist: Gwen Phifer

Cover Art Copyright by Mt Zion Ridge Press © 2018

Ladies of Oberlin

Book One: Red Sky Over America
Book Two: Lost in the Storm
Book Three: The Aftermath

Other Books By Tamera Lynn Kraft

Alice's Notions
Resurrection of Hope

Dedication and Acknowledgment

I dedicate this novel to my sister, Ellen Marie "Sis" Lalu, who died of lung cancer. Before she passed away, she was able to read this novel. As one of my biggest fans, here's what she posted on Facebook.

"You will not want to miss a novel called RED SKY OVER AMERICA. I had the distinct pleasure & honor to read this book before it published. I was blown away on several levels. I cannot wait to read more of what she might have to offer us. Look out for this one. Writer is Tamera Lynn Kraft. Some of you might know her, but someday all of you will know her name. She is awesome."
I love you and miss you, Sis.

I would like to acknowledge and thank the Oberlin College Library Archives for their help as I researched this series of novels. They went above and beyond in their assistance with this project. I also was assisted by the Maysville Historical Museum in Maysville, Kentucky, the Rankin House Museum in Ripley, Ohio, and the Underground Railroad Freedom Center in Cincinnati, Ohio.

Chapter One

October 1857, Oberlin, Ohio

America Leighton's hands trembled as she read the letter. It was worse than she thought. She stood frozen in place, staring at the words, hoping somehow they would change.

They didn't.

The grandfather clock chimed, and she glanced up. Five o'clock. She didn't want to be late. Placing the envelope in her book, she tucked it in the pocket of her hooded cloak, pushed open the post office door, and rushed outside. As she passed the historic elm on the edge of College Park, the wind burned her cheeks, just what she needed to get her thoughts off the mail she'd received.

Two riders on horseback galloped toward her, rustling the yellow autumn leaves and stirring up a cloud of dust and brown grass. Dirt clung to their long wool coats buttoned tight against their chins. They wore their wide brim planters hats low on their brows. If their attire wasn't enough, the revolvers holstered around their waists and the shotguns perched in their gear showed what they were.

Slave catchers.

America drew in a short breath. She diverted her attention and walked on to Ladies Hall a bit faster than usual, but the hope they would leave her alone trampled under horses' hooves as the men rode across the grassy lawn and stopped in front of her.

The older man tipped his hat. "Ma'am, we're deputies from Maysville."

Cold air turned her breath to steam. *Remember to act natural.* She forced her voice to keep an even tone. "You're a long way from home."

The younger man wrinkled his forehead. "Aren't you Miss Leighton?"

America pressed her tongue across the back of her teeth and nodded. She didn't recognize any of them.

He turned to the other man. "George, this is Colonel Leighton's daughter."

The older man smiled, and his front gold tooth glimmered. "Ma'am, the name's George Mills. This is my partner, Pete Fowler. Pleased to make your acquaintance. I've had the occasion to buy horses from the colonel in the past. He has a good eye for horse flesh."

"So why are you gentlemen clear up here in Northern Ohio?" She didn't need to ask.

"We've been hired to retrieve some property." Mr. Mills adjusted in his saddle. "What about you? You're a long way from Kentucky."

"I attend Oberlin College."

Mr. Mills raised his eyebrow. "I didn't know Oberlin was a ladies' school."

"It's not. I attend classes with men."

He leaned back in his saddle. "Didn't think the colonel would allow his girl to attend one of those schools."

Mr. Fowler cleared his throat. "Maybe you could help us, Miss Leighton, you being a Kentuckian and all. Have you seen any fugitive slaves around these parts? We're looking for an ebony skinned girl about sixteen with a scar across her right cheek, and a copper colored young buck, tall and thin."

Taking a couple of steady breaths to keep her tone even, she gazed straight at them without flinching. "No, can't say as I have." They couldn't have given a better description of Chance and Milly. If only they would ride off.

"Don't fret about it," Mr. Mills said. "We'll find them. Ma'am, if you do see any Negro runaways, you'll let us know? We're staying at the hotel."

Her heart skipped a beat. "I'll do that."

Mr. Fowler tipped his hat, and they rode off.

America leaned against the elm and watched them. Everything inside urged her to dash off to the boarding house where Milly and Chance stayed, but she waited until the men were out of sight. As soon as they disappeared from view, she hoisted her skirts up and ran to warn the couple to hide.

*****

An hour later, she made her way to her dorm room. She hated being delayed. If they arrived at the church meeting late, she'd have to sit in the back where she couldn't get a clear view. Perhaps Brother Woods would preach tonight. Butterflies fluttered in her stomach.

She stopped to catch her breath before hanging her cloak on one of the hooks behind the door and plopping onto the second of six cots lined against the wall to the left. The narrow dorm room, only half as wide as her bedroom in Kentucky, may not have been as nice as the house where she'd grown up, but it had become her home.

The fire blazing in the wood box stove on the opposite wall was enough to warm the room, but she couldn't shake the chill inside her.

She cupped her hands and blew into them.

Lavena Falcon looked up from the pine writing table near the window and nodded her greeting.

"It's cold out there," America said.

In appearance, Lavena was America's opposite in every way. While America had to deal with strawberry blond hair, freckles, and a fair completion that burned in the summer if she didn't carry a parasol, Lavena's Mediterranean complexion and eyes darker than a moonless night gave her an exotic look to go with her extraordinary perspective.

Her roommate headed toward her, barely missing the small cedar chests at the foot of each cot. She grabbed a yellow afghan folded at the foot of the bed and wrapped it around America's shoulders. "Are you all right? You look winded."

"I ran into some slave catchers looking for Milly and Chance," America said through chattering teeth. "I ran the whole way to the boarding house to warn them."

Lavena splayed her hand across her chest and sat on the bed across from her. "Are they safe?"

America nodded. "After I left the boarding house, I stopped at Professor Calhoun's office. He'll spread the word to the rest of the escaped slaves to be mindful."

"Thank God." Lavena grabbed a brush off the table next to her and ran it through her thick black hair. "It seems like more slave catchers come up here every year. It's only a matter of time before they capture some."

When America could move without shivering, she pulled her father's letter out of her book and ran her hand across the lettering on the envelope.

Lavena began braiding her hair. She never pinned it up, said men didn't have to fool with their hair, so she wouldn't be bothered with hers. "What are you holding?"

"A letter post from home."

Lavena pointed to the novel and delivered an I-told-you-so grin. "I mean the book. You're finally going to read it? I told you a month ago you should."

America shrugged. "I know, but I don't have time." She wouldn't admit she resisted reading the popular abolitionist novel. From what she'd heard, it portrayed slave owners like her family as scoundrels. "I don't see why it's so all-fired important to read a work of fiction anyway."

"*Uncle Tom's Cabin* should be required reading for everyone loyal to the cause." Lavena tied the end of her braid with a ribbon. "You'll no doubt be familiar with some of the things in there, you being a slave owner's daughter."

America let out a heavy sigh. Why did everybody have to bring up her father as if he were single-handedly responsible for all the evils of slavery? "It's just the way things are in the South. He's not a wicked man."

Specks of light flashed across Lavena's eyes. "He traffics in human flesh and misery and puts his fellow man in bondage."

"He's still my father." She grabbed a small wooden box containing her belongings, threw the letter inside, and slammed it shut. It's not like he was as bad as some of the slave owners. He treated his slaves almost like kin.

"So, what's it say?" Lavena pointed to the box.

"Same as always. He wants me to come home during winter break." America glanced away hoping Lavena wouldn't notice the apprehension on her face. She wasn't about to let her friend know her father insisted she quit Oberlin College and return to Kentucky for good. With less than a year until graduation, she didn't dare visit him now. Her resolve might falter.

"You're not planning to go there, are you?"

"I should. I haven't been home in three years." America chewed the inside of her cheek. As much as she missed Papa, could she risk ever going home again?

"The man owns human beings." Lavena stood with her hands on her hips, stretching all of her four-foot-eleven-inches until she looked almost as tall as America. "He's against everything we stand for."

She blinked away the warm tears forming behind her eyes. "He may be wrong, but he's still my papa. I want to see him."

"Then why haven't you gone before?"

Her throat closed as she stood, folded her afghan, and held it against her, trying to hold off her conflicting emotions. "He doesn't know I'm an abolitionist."

Lavena gasped. "You never told him."

"You don't know what it's like to oppose Colonel Beauregard Leighton."

"All the more reason to keep your distance."

"Don't worry. I'm not going home." America set the afghan on her bed and smoothed out the covers. No matter how much she wanted to see her family, she didn't have the courage to oppose him now any more than she did when she lived in his home.

"A wise decision." Lavena grabbed her coat off the hook and threw it over her shoulders. "The hour is late. We'd better hurry."

"Where are the others?"

"They went to a lecture. Professor Perkins' wife is speaking about exercise and healthy living. They're meeting us at First Church."

"Betsy too?"

"No, she left early to sit with her gentleman friend. I hope she doesn't drop out of school and marry him before she graduates."

"She'll make it." America wrapped herself in her cloak. "Who's speaking today?"

"A senior theological student," Lavena said. "Brother Woods."

America's voice rose almost imperceptibly. "William Woods?" Brother Woods sat in the front row of her theology class, and they'd spoken a few times, but he rarely looked her way.

"I do believe you have an interest in the man." Lavena raised her chin and narrowed her eyes in full-lecture mode. "If you're not careful, you'll sell yourself in bondage and never make it to graduation day."

Heat flushed her face as she turned toward the door. "We have a class together. He's an inspiring student. Besides, not every lady on this campus considers marriage slavery."

"True." Lavena opened the door and flashed a smirk in America's direction. "Is that what you're going to do? Marry Brother Woods and become a meek little housewife?"

"May I remind you, until I graduate in August, I'm not allowing any gentlemen to call on me?"

"I meant no offense."

"You know my first priority is the mission field." America stormed out of the room leaving her friend to tag behind.

Lavena called after her. "I know your only desire is to finish school and fulfill God's call on your life."

America stopped at the bottom of the narrow stairway and blew out a breath to calm herself.

Lavena rushed to catch up with her. "I spoke out of turn."

"I know you like to tease." Lavena was her dearest friend. She could never stay angry with her for long. "I shouldn't get my dander up."

"It's all right." Lavena gave America a rueful half smile the way she always did when she realized she'd gone too far with her banter.

America tilted her head. How did her friend know she was interested in William Woods? She was certain she never mentioned his name. She opened the door at the bottom of the stairs.

A gust swirled leaves into the air. The wind howled, threatening not to be contained by the closed door. Dark clouds released their pent-up fury, plummeting freezing rain to the ground. Normally snowstorms gave her a cozy feeling inside as they blanketed the hard ground, but this tempest reflected an approaching gale having nothing to do with the weather. It might sweep away any chance of making things right with her family.

****

America arrived at the crowded church and tried to remove her drenched cloak without getting her skirt any more soaked than it already was. She and Lavena scooted through the throng looking for seats near the back of the vast building. First Church seated fifteen hundred people and was the largest church in the country, but when students and townspeople filled the sanctuary, there weren't enough pews for everyone. Some men in the back stood allowing the women to sit. Lavena was about to refuse, but America pulled on her sleeve, and she accepted the offer.

Brother Woods stepped up to the massive podium on the raised platform. The murmur and rustling of the crowd hushed. His bass voice bellowed with power and authority, much like Father Charles Finney, fiery evangelist and president of Oberlin College.

America leaned in gazing into those eyes of his. They bored into her soul. Her stomach fluttered every time he looked in her direction.

He cast an inspiring presence in his black wool sack suit with a white shirt buttoned at the collar, the one he always wore when he preached. He was shorter than most men, only a couple of inches taller than America, and thin, but with broad shoulders and muscular arms, he always appeared larger than his short frame, but it was more. He carried an anointing and passion few preachers – or men - possessed. He drew everyone's attention, especially hers, by simply walking into a room.

He grabbed hold of the sides of the pulpit. "Could one man end slavery in Egypt and cause Pharaoh to let go of those he held in bondage? Moses did. Why can't we, being many, go to the pharaohs in our nation and demand they let God's people go?"

He delivered his sermon with conviction, but it wasn't as easy as he said. Slavery was wrong. She'd known it from the time she was a little girl and her slave nanny, Aunt Ruth, told her stories about Moses and the children of Israel, but it was the way things were in the South. Confronting her father wouldn't change anything.

The "amens" drew her attention back to Brother Woods.

"Many of these men are not evil. They are deceived. They don't see what they do is a stench in the nostrils of God."

Her face flushed. It was as if Brother Woods knew her father.

"We need to offer them mercy and show them the errors of their ways so they can repent and turn to the Savior for forgiveness."

If only she could convince Papa of the injustice of slavery. She'd tried a couple of times, but it always ended with him reminding her, as a woman, she couldn't possibly understand the financial considerations involved.

"Furthermore," Papa would then say, "I treat my slaves well. They're better off than most free Negros in Kentucky."

Brother Wood's voice rose in volume. "If they will not repent, we must defend these poor men and women caught in the clutches of their masters and rescue them from their bondage."

Her heart sank. How could she share the gospel in foreign lands when she didn't have the courage to stand for what was right in her own home?

"You may say this can't be done, but would you have thought it possible for Moses to confront Pharaoh as he did?"

She let out a heavy sigh. She couldn't risk going home. Her father would never listen to her.

"With God, nothing is impossible."

Lord, is it possible?

"Shall we rise against this great wickedness or will we compromise everything in this Word," he held up his Bible, "to keep peace in a nation enslaving its brothers?"

She knew God was directing her to somehow convince her father to free his slaves, but she couldn't. If she made the journey to Kentucky this winter break, she'd risk everything. Her father wouldn't listen, and he might keep her from returning to Oberlin, but it was more than that. She adored Papa, but she didn't have the courage to resist his strong determination. If she went home, she would compromise her convictions and God's call on her life.

As Brother Woods preached, the urgency to go home and change her father's mind grew stronger. She shook her head. No. This time, God was asking too much.

Chapter Two

America sat with her back straight on the bench at Wellington station ten miles south of Oberlin. A light dusting of snow from the night before covered the ground, and the footprints of the other ticketholders had smudged and dirtied the snow around the station. Two elderly women sat beside her, and dozens of men in wool overcoats closed in around. She was fortunate to get the last seat outside.

The coldness pressed in on her chest. This was a mistake. Her father wouldn't listen to her. If she were to go home, Papa might not allow her to return to Oberlin. It wasn't too late to change her mind.

She stood and walked toward the tracks. She had to escape the murmur of her fellow college students chatting to each other about visiting families on winter break. Her eyes fixed on the rails leading northeast in the direction of Cleveland, the vastly populated Lake Erie seaport where the train would come from.

The clacking of wheels, the clanging of the steam engine and the smoke rising into the clouds forewarned of the approaching train before she saw it. She placed her arm across her knotted stomach. The coal black iron horse rolled along the rails, and with brakes squealing, crawled to a stop.

Glancing across the street at the stagecoach, she longed to be on it when it returned to Oberlin. She had spent a month arguing the matter with the Lord before she had surrendered. She would obey no matter the cost. She squared her shoulders, grasped her carpetbag in one hand and her novel in the other, and strode in the direction of the train.

"Sister Leighton." A voice from behind startled her.

She turned around. William Woods gazed at her, his eyes the color of buckeyes, the brown two-toned nuts common in Ohio. Those eyes, full of passion and fire, drew her in.

"Please, let me help you with that." He flashed a grin, causing her knees to weaken, and grabbed her bag.

His hand brushed against hers as she released her grip. A curl fell into her face, and she tucked the unruly ringlet under the flap of her bonnet. She chided herself for being so flustered. What would Lavena say? "Thank you kindly," she managed to squeak out.

Green flecks darted through his brown eyes. "You don't remember me, do you?"

"Why yes, Brother Woods, I do." She couldn't stop thinking about the words he spoke so passionately at prayer meeting two weeks ago or the other times their paths had crossed, but she didn't want to appear forward. "I believe we attend a couple of theology classes together, and we have spoken with each other a few times."

A dimple bored into his right cheek. "Lead on."

She nodded and climbed aboard the train. Holding down the folds of her yellow dress, she scooted in the first available seat, a burgundy cushioned iron wrought bench large enough for two people to sit comfortably. Brother Woods handed her the carpetbag. She held her book under her chin and squeezed the bag under the bench. With her tongue sticking out of her mouth, she gave it one last push.

While adjusting her wool dress, she slid onto the bench, and opened her novel. She read the first few words, but sensed Brother Woods lingering over her. She looked up.

He shrugged. "There doesn't seem to be any more seats. May I sit with you?"

"Of course." She scooted closer to the window. "You were so kind to help me with my bag. I'm obliged to return the favor."

He deposited his saddlebag and hat under the bench. "Please call me Brother William. After all, we do go to school together."

"Brother William it is. You may call me Sister America."

He chuckled.

She scrunched her nose. "Why are you laughing?"

"I'm sorry. Sister America has a funny ring to it, like Uncle Sam. Are you ever called by a nickname?"

She let out a sigh. "My papa calls me Merry."

"Would you mind if I call you Sister Merry?"

The whistle blew. "Please do."

The steam engine hissed, and the train jerked. America closed her book and looked out the window at a man strolling through an open field leading a black stallion behind him. He turned and gave his animal a piece of apple. Her father often treated his horses in the same way. He cared for all of his livestock, but slaves were not livestock. They were people created in the image of God.

William cleared his throat. "A powerful story, isn't it?"

America glanced at the book's cover already worn around the corners. "You've read *Uncle Tom's Cabin*?"

"Yes. Mrs. Harriet Beecher Stowe is a prophet for this age." The color of his eyes now appeared more sage than brown. "I've never read anything convincing me more of the need to end the abominable practice of slavery. No matter the cost, we must do all in our power..." He stopped midsentence. "I'm sorry, Sister Merry. Forgive my outburst."

"Please, don't apologize. You so eloquently captured the feelings

God has placed in my own heart."

"That surprises me a bit."

"Why?" She exhaled an audible sigh at having to defend herself again to those who had heard about her father. "I go to Oberlin College and believe in the principles of equality and abolition just like you, and I am a servant of God called to the mission field. You do me a disservice by suggesting I would feel differently."

"I'm sorry. It's just I've made inquiries about you."

She lifted her eyebrow. "Inquiries?"

William offered a slight grin. "Remember over a year ago when we prayed together on the steps of First Church?"

America nodded. She would not tell him just how often she remembered that moment.

"I felt a bond with you, and I thought we might have an opportunity to talk about our shared interests." He glanced at his hands, fingers intertwined, in his lap. "I assumed since your father owns slaves, your viewpoint might not be as adamant concerning this issue as mine."

She had wondered why he'd never approached her with more than casual conversation since that day. She'd felt an attraction to him but had come to the conclusion it was unreciprocated. "Brother William, you assumed wrong."

"Forgive me." Lines creased the corners of his eyes hinting at a repressed smile.

"Of course." How could she be upset with somebody who believed in the cause so fervently? "Why are you traveling to Kentucky over winter break? Isn't it a little like marching into the enemy's camp?"

"I suppose that's what I'm doing. I've decided to face the lion in his den. During school breaks, I'm an itinerant preacher. I've secured revival meetings in three churches, and I hope to preach in others as well."

He'd lost his senses. "Are those churches acquainted with your abolitionist views?"

"Some aren't. I assured them I would preach the Word of God. And so I shall."

"You're crazy. You can't preach against slavery in Kentucky. More slaves are bought and sold there than in any other state in the Union."

"What better place to implore slave owners to repent and free their captives?"

"They're going to lynch you."

He flashed a bemused grin. "If I'm not willing to die for this cause, what good am I? Let's not talk about me. Why are you going to Kentucky?"

America bit a jagged nail on her pinkie finger. "To visit my papa."

"There's more to it?"

"What makes you think so?"

"I can see the concern on your face."

"I haven't been home since I left to attend Oberlin three years ago." She leaned into the seat. "My father didn't approve. He wanted me to attend a woman's college, one not so liberal in its ideas about women's suffrage and abolition. He reluctantly gave his blessing, but now there's so much in the newspapers about Oberlin's radical activities, he wrote insisting I end my studies and return home."

"Will you abide by his wishes?"

"No. I hope it doesn't alarm you I would challenge him like this. I do honor my father, but I've been called to missionary work, and I have to put God's wishes above all else. Besides, Oberlin is the best place to be trained in the field."

"True. I also endeavor to do missionary work. So why are you going home?"

"To implore my father to free his slaves and to give me no further resistance about my education."

William snorted. "And you say I'm crazy."

America allowed the edge of her mouth to curl. "Brother William, have you never heard it said, 'Nothing is impossible with God'?"

*****

William grinned. Sister Merry looked adorable the way she gawked out the window as they pulled into Maysville.

"Look." She pointed to the large white building with columns. "There's the Mason County Courthouse. They built it after the county seat moved there from Washington, and there's Maysville Academy. My brother went to school there."

The train roared across Limestone Creek Bridge. As the breaks squealed, she let out a noisy sigh, ran her tongue across her lips, and leaned back in her seat.

William placed his hand on hers. "What's wrong?"

"I suppose I'm a little nervous about confronting my father."

The glow in her sea blue eyes sparked a warmth his heart. An abolitionist and a slave owner's daughter. America Leighton was an unusual woman. She would make a fine help-meet for a man planning to devote himself to preaching the gospel overseas. He could see himself with a wife like her by his side. "The Lord will give you the strength and courage you need."

She delivered a smile lighting up the train car. "Thank you."

He'd made a decision. He would ask her permission to court her when they returned to Oberlin. It was obvious to him, especially after their conversation on the train, they were like-minded. Her strawberry blond curls, half a dozen freckles dotting her nose and cheeks, and eyes as blue as Lake Erie did cause heads to turn, including his, but her appeal went far beyond looks. He didn't know many women willing to stand up to their fathers. Most Southern women would compromise their values. Yet she was willing to risk society's disfavor and her father's ire to rise against the evils of slavery. He rarely met a man so bold in the faith, let alone a woman. She was remarkable.

Graduation was still nine months away, and a courtship now would be difficult, but there was no better time. Once he finished his schooling, he wanted no delay in fulfilling his missionary call to China.

He stroked his jaw. He had a desire to ask her for a proper courtship now, but perhaps he needed to wait until they returned to school. She had enough on her mind.

The train slowed as it rolled into Maysville Station and came to a halt. William grabbed their bags, and Merry followed him onto the station platform twice the size of the one in Wellington. She lifted her chin and gazed through the sea of faces. Probably looking for her father.

"Aunt Ruth, Uncle Joe." Merry waved at a man and woman standing near a Riddle Carriage. Riddle was the company known for making coaches for presidents and rich business owners. It must have cost a fortune.

"Miss America." A thin copper-skinned woman with gray curly hair motioned to her. "You sure are a sight for sore eyes."

William carried the bags over to the buggy.

"Aunt Ruth." Merry hugged the woman. "So are you."

The man towered over them like a giant. His skin was the color of coal, and his muscles threatened to rip through the sleeves of his worn jacket. "Miss Merry, Colonel Leighton sent us to fetch you."

"How's Papa?" Merry asked.

"Oh, he be all right," the man said. "He sure enough excited to see you."

"Well, then, fetch my luggage and we'll be off." Her voice was condescending.

William clenched his jaw.

Merry skirted past William without even a glance in his direction. Her father's slaves must not have been important enough to her for a proper introduction.

He cleared his throat.

"Oh, forgive my manners." She waved a dismissive hand in the direction of her servants. "Brother William, these are my father's slaves."

"Do they have names?" He couldn't keep the edge out of his tone as his stomach soured. She'd only been in the South five minutes, and she was already acting like a slave owner's daughter.

A scowl crossed her face. "This is Uncle Joe and Aunt Ruth. Aunt Ruth raised me after my mother died."

"Brother Joe, Sister Ruth." William extended his hand, determined to show them more curtesy than their mistress. "It's an honor to meet you."

Joe paused and wiped his massive hand on his trousers before reaching out to William, but he kept his eyes focused on the ground. "Likewise."

If there was only a way William could show this man he had nothing to fear from him. "Let me help you with Sister Merry's bag." He couldn't help delivering a glower in her direction as he placed the carpetbag on the back of the buggy.

"Thank you for your assistance, Brother William. I must be off now." Merry turned before he could reply and let Joe help her onto her seat like a spoiled princess.

William crossed his arms as he watched her buggy roll down the dusty road lined with whitewashed storefronts and houses. Maybe he needed to rethink pursuing a courtship with her.

Slave owner's children liked to spout their views on abolition, but he rarely met one who didn't compromise when it meant going against their family's way of life, especially if freeing the slaves brought financial hardship. He should have known Merry would be no different than the others. When would he ever learn he couldn't trust a woman who'd been raised in the South, especially one whose family owned slaves?

Merry turned toward him, and when she saw him staring, she at least had the decency to blush. He delivered a half smirk but wouldn't look away. Merry whirled back.

He gazed in her direction another moment, seeing if she would try to catch another glimpse of him, but she didn't. Soon the buggy turned down another road, and he lost sight of her. It was for the best. It would be unwise to have anything to do with her, especially not with what he really planned to do in Kentucky.

Chapter Three

As they rode west down Third Street, America glanced back. William stood at the train station watching her with that stony expression and disapproving smirk of his. She flushed and spun back around. She enjoyed talking to him on the train, but since they'd arrived at the station, she couldn't shake the feeling he was judging her. He acted like Ruth and Joe were her slaves instead of her father's.

If he were this arrogant and patronizing, maybe it was better she found out now. Not that he ever indicated any intention of wanting a courtship.

Joe turned at Limestone Road.

America's skin crawled as if her carriage seat had been infested with fleas. Why didn't she think to tell Joe to wait until the next road to turn? She didn't want to see it, but she couldn't force herself to turn away. The building at the corner was still there. The two-story, roughhewn log cabin besieged Maysville.

Chained men and women brought here for auction, and escaped slaves drug back from across the river were held at this pen until they could be sold at auction or returned to their masters. It wasn't the only one. Another slave pen afflicted the landscape at Captain Anderson's farm near Dover, only a couple of miles from her father's horse ranch.

She'd never been inside one of them, of course, but her slave nanny told her about this one. Before Papa bought Aunt Ruth and Uncle Joe, they had stayed there waiting to be sold. Ruth had told her men, women, and children were packed in like hogs in a slaughterhouse, sometimes for months at a time. It took weeks for Ruth to get the stench of the place out of her nose.

It should be torn down, even Papa said so, but the locks on the doors and the man standing guard showed it was still in use.

The buggy rolled on until they'd passed the city limits. She tried to get the image of the slave pen out of her mind as woods, farms, and rolling hills passed by too quickly. Beams of sunlight shining through white fluffy clouds brightened the Indian summer day. The red, orange, and yellow leaves revealed the warm day was a deception. Winter weather would appear on the horizon soon enough.

The storm America would soon face loomed in her thoughts. She had to find some way to gain her courage and resist yielding to Papa's commands no matter how much she loved him.

Ruth interrupted her thoughts. "What's wrong, child?"

"It's been a long time."

"Three years," Ruth said. "Don't know why you been staying away. Master's fit to be tied about it."

"I have my reasons." Her voice had a harsher tone than she meant.

Ruth looked down. "Yes'um, I forgot myself."

America bit the inside of her cheek. She wasn't even home yet, and she was talking to Ruth like she was nothing but a slave in her father's household. "Aunt Ruth."

Ruth turned but kept her eyes lowered. "Yes'um."

"I'm sorry. I shouldn't have been cross with you."

"It be all right, miss. I expect riding on that train done wore you out."

"I still should have treated you with consideration." America flustered. She didn't know how to say it. "What I mean is, y'all don't deserve my disrespect."

Ruth's eyes shot up, and Joe's back stiffened.

"Landsakes," America said, "you raised me, and I treated you like slaves."

Ruth's lips pressed tight, holding back what she wanted to say. "That's what we is. We Colonel Leighton's slaves."

"It's not right."

"Maybe not." Joe spoke in an easy way, but he paused, taking time to deliberate each turn of phrase. "No use fretting what should be."

"Do you ever think of running off to Ohio?" The words escaped America's lips before she could stop them, and she clapped her hand over her mouth. They had to suspect her motives for asking such an outlandish question.

Joe's head jerked. "I don't know where you get such notions, ma'am." His voice remained calm but took on the syrupy sweet tone slaves used to appease their masters. "This be my home. Why I want to run off? The colonel own me."

Ruth wiped the palms of her hands on her dress, but she kept her eyes fixed on the clouds blocking the bright glare of the sun as if a stray glance might reveal her feelings.

America leaned back in her seat. Why had she never seen? She lived with these people all her life. They raised her, but they were guarded, fearful, even with her. She wouldn't allow this any longer; she would talk to her father. Something must be done.

*****

Joe dared not say another word on the ride back to the ranch. He was partial to America. She treated him, and his, better than most white folks. She even taught his daughter, Naomi, to read, and if Colonel Leighton found out, he would pitch a fit.

Law said slaves ain't allowed to have book learning, and master always done what the law said–at least when it come to coloreds, but Joe had a hard time refusing Naomi, especially when she enjoyed it so much.

Naomi took to reading like a catfish to water. America often gave her books. Sometimes, at night, Naomi read out loud. He especially loved when she read about Hawkeye in *The Last of the Mohicans*. Joe enjoyed hearing the stories about other men and their adventures... free men.

He needed a swallow of water to get rid of the lump in his throat. It scared him having the master's daughter talking about escaping over the Ohio, like she knew something. Sure, he'd thought about it, especially now, but he wouldn't cross over. He needed to stay put and keep his family safe. A heaviness swept over him. He'd failed to do that with his oldest son.

Joe reached for his wife's hand. Sure one fine woman he married. Never once brought it up like it was his fault, but he knew better. He should have tried some way to convince the colonel not to do it.

It had not gone well the last time he tried to talk to the master about something. Colonel Leighton had just bought them at auction. Ruth was about to birth Amos, their oldest. The colonel had dealt with them better than their last master from Virginia. He told Joe if they worked hard, he'd treat them right. He even asked Joe's opinion on some horses he had wanted to buy.

One day, they'd gone to buy livestock in Flemingsburg, but the horse dealer had asked too much. The horses weren't prime breeding stock like the man said. Joe had looked Colonel Leighton straight in the eye and told him he was being cheated. Master told him he had no right to question a white man's word and beat the skin right off him.

He'd asked the master's pardon, told him he was right to whip him. He had no business going against a white man. He was nothing but a slave. He'd forgotten his place.

Now Naomi. He couldn't help her any more than he did Amos. What kind of man don't keep his family safe? He grasped the reins tighter. A black man ain't no kind of a man unless he's free.

*****

The buggy drew closer to the two-story brick federalist house where America grew up. Nothing had changed since she left, except the willow tree outside her window was a little taller. She used to climb that tree as a child when Papa had adults over for a party. She could hide in the tree and hear the conversations without anyone seeing her. When her father found out, he took a switch to her and threatened to cut the tree down if she ever did it again. She never did.

She wasn't ready to see him yet and instructed Joe to pull the carriage up to the barn standing a couple hundred feet behind the house. A sorrel in the farthest pen whinnied and nodded her head. "Red." America strode to the mare and stroked her mane. "It sure is good to see you, girl. I missed you."

"She sure enough missed you." Joe pulled the carpetbag down from the buggy. "Expect you'll have time with her later. Miss Merry, I gots to get you to the house. The colonel says me and Ruth was to bring you up yonder soon as you get in."

America gave Red one last pat. She couldn't put it off any longer. "I'll see you later, girl." She trudged down the dusty path around the house and entered through the front door. She hung her cloak on the hook in the foyer and placed her carpetbag on the walnut foyer table by the door. After wetting her lips, she took a step into the parlor.

It hadn't changed, the same flowered wallpaper with yellow and pink roses. When she was a little girl, she imagined herself as a princess in the middle of a rose garden. Once she counted the flowers to see which color had more roses. There were ten more yellow than pink. Her favorite color became yellow, the color of roses and sunlight.

The burgundy settee faced the fireplace. The balloon back chairs on either side were the same colors as the wallpaper, one chair pink and the other yellow. She swiped at her eyes. Papa once said her mother had gone clear to Philadelphia to buy the furniture and pick out the wallpaper. America didn't remember a time when the room didn't look exactly like this.

The pianoforte Papa insisted America learn to play sat in the middle of the parlor. She'd hated the lessons at first, but her father believed every accomplished young lady should know how to play an instrument. Later, after she'd changed teachers, she'd been grateful her father insisted. She enjoyed playing hymns.

Papa stood near the stone fireplace. He only came up to Joe's chin, but not many men were taller than Colonel Beauregard Leighton. His beard and hair had begun to turn gray. The salt and pepper look gave him a distinguished air. When he saw her, his eyes lit up. "Merry." He picked her up and swung her around. "My Merry." He pulled her in tight.

America melted into his strong chest. "Papa." She could smell the aroma of his pipe tobacco. She missed that. A rush of emotion lodged in her throat.

He squeezed a moment longer before letting her go. "You've finally come home. We've done killed the fatted calf, and Ruth and Naomi are fixing you a meal fit for royalty."

She bit her bottom lip. "Papa, we need to talk."

"So we shall, but not yet. First, we'll have a feast with you and your brother. Tomorrow will be time enough. I'm mighty glad to have you back."

She shouldn't put it off, but she thanked God she would get one night's reprieve to enjoy time with her family.

Papa turned to Ruth who stood by the kitchen door. "Don't just stand there gawking, girl. Get a wiggle on. I expect dinner on the table by six."

Ruth stiffened and dashed out of the room.

"I don't know what's with my Negros lately," Papa said. "They've been getting uppity ever since I sold Amos."

America opened her eyes wide. "You sold Amos?"

"I did. Amos fetched a good price with his knowledge of horseflesh. I got top dollar for him."

"Papa, Amos was Uncle Joe and Aunt Ruth's oldest son. How could you take him from his family?"

"Some of them Republican ideas you're getting from Oberlin no doubt. Remember, Merry, that boy belonged to me to do with as I saw fit, and I saw fit to sell him."

"Papa–"

He snapped his fingers. "Enough."

Her stomach churned. "Yes, Papa."

He put his arm around her. "I had Naomi get your room ready. You must be tired after such a long train trip and the dusty ride from Maysville. Go lie down, you hear? I'll send Ruth to fetch you when supper's laid out."

America wrapped her fingers around the oversize bannister and climbed the tall staircase feeling every bit the chastised little girl being sent to her room. She closed the door a little harder than needed, grabbed a pillow off the bed, and held it tight against her. Home for a short time and already yielding to her father's iron will.

*****

Joe sat at his table eating Johnnycakes with Naomi, and his son, Obadiah. Their one room cabin would never have wallpaper on the walls or a wood floor like the master's house, but he couldn't complain. It was better than most slaves' quarters. The master's son, Luke, helped Joe and his sons build it. It even had a real window.

Invisible hands twisted Joe's insides akin to his wife wringing out his shirts on wash day. Where was Amos now? Did his new master treat him as well as the colonel had?

"It'll be good to have Miss Merry home," Naomi said. "Maybe she can talk to Master Leighton."

"Don't you trust her," Joe said a little harsher than he meant. "I know she's been a friend to you and all, Naomi, but white folks side with their own. She'll do what her pa wants."

Naomi looked at her feet. "I know."

Obadiah jutted his jaw. At sixteen, he was almost as big as Joe, but he hadn't learned to hold back the reins. "Did you talk to the master yet?"

"No, son. Leave it be."

"Leave it be?" Obadiah slammed his fist on the table. The sound reverberated through the cabin. "Naomi's gonna be sold in less than two weeks 'less you get the gumption to stand up to him. Ain't it bad enough losing Amos?"

"What good did it do you going against him then?" Joe said. "You got a beating, and Amos still went to auction."

"Maybe if you'd done something." Obadiah charged toward the door like an angry bull and stormed out, slamming it behind him.

Joe understood why the boy was angry, but getting mad never did no good, and the Good Lord commanded forgiveness. Joe did find it a might hard to forgive the master when he set out to sell his children on the auction block.

Chapter Four

"Miss Merry." Naomi's voice arose through murky dreams.

America hadn't intended to fall asleep. She squinted, and Naomi came into focus. She leaped out of bed and threw her arms around the slave girl. "It's so good to see you again."

Naomi stiffened and backed away from the hug. "Master asked me to come fetch you for supper. It's laid out."

"Why are you acting so peculiar?"

"I don't know what you're jabbering about."

"Something's afoot. Uncle Joe and Aunt Ruth behaved as if they were afraid of me. I know I haven't always treated..." America swiped her hand across her mouth. "Now you're as jittery as a moth flittering around a candle. Are you going to tell me why you're so afraid?"

"I'm no different. I'm treating you like the mistress of the house."

America sat on the bed and motioned her hand to the chair. "Sit down."

Naomi slid into the wooden rocker.

"Does this have something to do with Amos being sold?"

"I expect partly."

"I know you're my papa's slave, but I always thought we were friends. You used to trust me." *The book.* "I almost forgot. I brought you a present." America rummaged through the carpetbag on top of a trunk at the foot of the walnut sleigh bed until she found it and placed it lovingly in Naomi's hands. "It's called *Uncle Tom's Cabin.* It's a great piece of literature about a slave family who escaped to freedom. I thought of you when I read it."

Naomi rubbed her fingers across the lettering and brought the book close to her chest. The corners of her mouth turned up. She sprang at America and embraced her. "I missed you."

"Me too." America pulled back. "I need to know what's going on. Why did Papa sell Amos?"

"Master lost all his foals and some of the mares over the summer. All the horses were ailing. Amos said the ranch needed them foals. The master figured since he had Luke and Obadiah's help, he could do without Amos, so he sold him at slave auction. Some folks in South Carolina bought him, and we ain't never gonna see him again."

"Oh, Naomi, I'm so sorry." Things had to be bad for Papa to sell any of the slaves. He never did agree with slave owners separating families on the auction block.

"It's a might worse," Naomi turned away and straightened the covers on the bed.

"How?" America placed a hand on Naomi's shoulder "What else happened?"

Naomi faced her. "Colonel Leighton's gonna sell me at auction in a couple of weeks. He figures it'll pay off the rest of the note."

"No, it can't be. Are you sure?"

"He's gonna, and there's nothing we can do about it. Riley's trying to get the money in time. You remember Riley?"

"Isn't he the free colored man who owns the farm down the way and is sweet on you?"

Naomi nodded. "Master said when Riley got enough together, he could buy my freedom. We planned to jump the broom, figured we'd still be close to my ma and pa. Riley's been scrimping and saving and doing odd jobs for white folks willing to pay, but it ain't enough." Naomi wrapped her arms around herself. "No telling where I'll end up now. Only way Riley can get it in time is if he steals it, and he's not gonna do that, him being a preacher at the African church and a God fearing man."

"I'll talk to Papa."

"Won't do no good. Gonna be real hard on Ma and Pa. Do you know why my ma named me Naomi?"

"I supposed because it was a good Christian name."

"That's only part of it." Naomi swiped at the tears forming in her eyes. "She figured since Ruth never left Naomi's side in the Good Book, if she named me Naomi, I'd never be sold off." She let out a heavy sigh. "Guess it didn't work out."

"We still have two weeks." America tapped her fist against her mouth. "Don't give up hope yet."

"I'll try not to, but I'm afeared. Some of them masters ain't like the colonel. Mama told me the stories about how they buy us Negro women so they can breed us like the colonel breeds his mares. Or they send us to the cotton fields down in Georgia or the rice fields in the Carolinas where we're beaten and worked half to death by some overseer."

America bit her bottom lip. "I know, Naomi, I know."

A knock sounded, and Ruth peeked her head in. "You best get downstairs. Supper's on, and they're waiting for you."

America nodded and hurried through the hallway to the banister at the top of the stairs. Luke stood at the bottom of the steps. Her brother hadn't changed much with his reddish-brown hair, blue eyes, and crooked smile. She sprang down the wide staircase and flew into his arms.

He whirled her around and set her back on her feet. "So, my little prodigal sister has returned."

"Why is everybody calling me that? I just went off to school, and I've written letters."

Luke raised an eyebrow. "You haven't been here for three years. Why did you stay away so long?"

"I'm wondering if I should be here now."

"Of course you should. This is your home."

"A lot's happened while I've been gone."

"It has been a long time."

"I need to have a talk with Papa about Amos and Naomi."

Luke groaned. "So, you heard?"

"You can't think this is right?"

"Sis, now's not the time to argue abolition with him. We lost a lot of horses to glanders disease this summer, and the bankers are at the door. If he doesn't get the money to pay them soon, we'll lose the ranch, the horses, the slaves, everything. He had to sell Amos."

"What about Naomi?" Heat shot up the back of her neck. "You know why some men buy slave girls."

Luke stroked his chin. "Maybe, but there's not much else he can do. He'll have to sell her too. Amos fetched a good price, but it's not enough. Uncle Joe and Obadiah are needed for the ranch. We only require one household slave, and Aunt Ruth's too old to fetch a good price."

"He could sell some of the horses."

"Not if he wants to get back on his feet again. He needs those horses to breed."

"What about the races in Maysville?"

"Our best racing stallion up and died. We don't have another one good enough to win."

"I'll talk to Papa." She pressed her tongue against the back of her teeth. "There's got to be another way."

"I'm warning you." Luke pointed his finger at her. "Father's under enough burdens without you adding to them. He's not in the humor to indulge your fancies. He's trying to save the ranch."

America brushed past Luke on the way to the dining room.

Luke called out. "Don't do it, Sis."

Her shoulders stiffened as she entered the room with dark oak-paneled walls. The bay window lined with gold draperies to the right allowed plenty of light. A buffet made out of black oak rested against the wall to the left and displayed her mother's china with a yellow rose pattern.

America sat rigid in one of the press back chairs at the heavy bog oak table large enough to seat ten. Papa entered the room and took his place at the head.

Naomi dished out fried chicken, mashed potatoes, and green beans onto their plates. Nobody said anything. Despite believing this business would ruin her appetite, the smell of Aunt Ruth's chicken made America's mouth water.

Papa glanced from Luke to America and back to Luke.

America picked at the food in front of her waiting for grace to be offered.

Papa bowed his head and said the prayer. "Dear Lord, we're grateful for the bounty you set before us. Thank you for sending my Merry home. Help us to show love to one another and not to get caught up in foolish squabbles. Amen." He grabbed his fork and pointed it at Luke. "Something going on between you two?"

Luke cleared his throat. "What makes you think that, sir?"

"The air is thick with it. Y'all haven't seen each other in three years. Whatever argument you're having, put it aside. Now!"

America shrugged. "I'm sorry, Luke."

Luke looked like he wanted to say something but swallowed his words. "Me too."

"Good," Papa said. "I expect I'll find out what's going on sooner or later. For now, we're going to have civilized dinner conversation. Merry, tell us about school. Have you met any interesting gentlemen?"

"Papa, I'm not going to school to find a husband."

"I know. You're going to become a missionary or some fool thing. When I ponder about you wanting to go to another country to preach to a bunch of heathens, well, I'm out to sea."

America ate a bite of mashed potatoes.

"Even if you do want to go God knows where, you could find a gentleman suitable enough to marry along the way."

She dropped her fork onto her plate. "Papa."

"All I'm saying is you're twenty-one years old, and you're not getting any younger. If you don't want to end up an old maid, it might be a good time to start looking."

"We've been through this before. I'm not opposed to marriage if God brings along a man called to the mission field as I am." William was called to the mission field. She shook herself. No point daydreaming about a future with him. "But I need to finish my studies. You know if I marry before I'm done, I won't be allowed to graduate."

Papa pointed a chicken leg in her direction. "Would that be so bad? If you're so determined to act on this course, you could marry a missionary and travel with him."

"I thought we were going to have a civilized conversation, not talk about why I'm not married yet. Luke's not married, and he's five years older than me. He's not forced to sit here and explain himself."

Luke wiped his chin with his napkin. "That's one of the things changing around here."

America caught the glint in his eye. "Luke?"

"The nuptials are in June."

"Wonderful, who?"

"Virginia Foster."

America scrunched her nose.

Papa raised an eyebrow. "Getting a little high and mighty, aren't we? Miss Virginia is a fine girl from a prosperous family."

She swallowed. "I'm happy for you, Luke." As much as she tried to say it with a lilt in her voice, it came out shrill.

Luke nodded slightly. "You don't seem too pleased, dear sister."

She forced a smile and calmed her tone. "Anyone who has won your heart is all right with me. I'll call on Miss Virginia and welcome her as my sister."

"You can visit Miss Virginia after you get settled and rest a couple of days," Papa said. "Then we'll have that talk."

"Yes, Papa." This wasn't going at all as America had hoped.

Chapter Five

For two days, William rode into Cumberland Plateau of the Appalachian Mountain Range near the Virginia border. He pulled up his reins and stopped for a moment to gaze at the mountains ascending from the rolling hills. The magnificence of nature displaying the glory of God contrasted with the ugliness of slavery he would find here.

He rode on to a clearing in the forest where his first meetings would be held and trotted his horse to a two-story brick house sitting near a white church with a bell tower and a picket fence nestled in a grove of maple and elm trees whose leaves had changed colors. The mixture of red and yellow made a spectacular sight.

In the tobacco field to the left, three young white men worked alongside colored children clearing the land for winter. Some of the children had a mulatto tone to their skin suggesting their father might have been white, a common occurrence in the South.

A copper-toned boy with kinky brown hair and a narrow face and nose stopped working and stared at him with bright green eyes. He nodded, but the boy lowered his eyes and plunged a hoe into the dirt.

William strode to the house and knocked. A colored woman, taller than him, with an orange scarf around her head opened the door. She had a smooth bronze complexion and high cheekbones and stood with her chin tilted up as if she were one of those statues he'd only seen in books. Her flawless skin showed she'd never worked in the fields. He'd rarely seen a prettier woman, black or white, but even with her outward beauty, a sadness cast over her countenance.

He tipped his hat. "Ma'am, I wonder if you could tell me, is this the home of Reverend T.J. Hull?"

"Yessir. Can I tell the master who's calling?"

"My name is Brother William Woods. I believe he's expecting me."

The woman slammed the door in his face.

A thousand thoughts darted through his mind and jumbled together. Why would she do that? Maybe they'd heard he was an abolitionist. If so, was he in danger? Should he wait or make a run for it while he could? He brushed his foot against the leaves rustling along the doorstep. There wasn't really a choice. God had led him here, and he would face whatever may come. He leaned against the door post at the corner of the porch.

The door opened. A stocky middle-aged man appeared. His curly blond hair, narrow Roman nose, green eyes, and square chin made his bushy handlebar mustache look out of place, as if he'd stolen it from another man's face. "Good day, Brother Woods." He shook William's hand heartily. "I'm Reverend Hull. I've been expecting you. Come in."

Did the boy in the field get his green eyes from Reverend Hull? He paused a moment then followed the minister inside. He chided himself for jumping to conclusions. Of course, they weren't related. After all, even if Reverend Hull owned slaves, he was a man of the cloth. "When the lady closed the door so abruptly, I feared there may have been some misunderstanding."

"Lady? Oh, you mean Mildred, my house slave."

A blond curly-haired girl with green eyes, about thirteen years old, took William's hat and coat. She also had a narrow nose and square chin.

"Thank-you, ma'am." William turned to Reverend Hull. "You have a very hospitable daughter there."

Reverend Hull's brow furrowed. "Tabitha is Mildred's daughter. She's one of my slaves."

William coughed ferociously and put his hand over his mouth. A moment later, he was able to give what he hoped was a neutral expression. "Forgive me. It was a dusty ride. I ingested a fair portion of the road."

"Not at all, sir. Mildred!"

The woman hastened into the room from a side door. "Yessir, master."

Reverend Hull placed a hand around her waist and squeezed her closer to him. "Get Brother Woods a glass of water."

Mildred pulled away, gave him a half-smile, and hurried through the door.

William took a half step back and bumped into the foyer table with his thigh. Had he just walked into a preacher's home or Satan's lair?

"We've had some trouble with those foul abolitionists." Reverend Hull twirled the corner of his mustache. "Some men came here from New York passing out their propaganda pamphlets. They had the gall to secretly communicate with our slaves. They were trying to start a slave rebellion or get them to run away, I'm sure of it. We whipped them and run them out. They can consider themselves blessed we didn't lynch them."

William's clenched his jaw. He rubbed it to keep Hull from noticing. He'd never been the violent sort, but he had an overwhelming urge to yank this man by the collar and give him the thrashing he deserved.

"Those snakes might try to sneak back, so I told Mildred not to let any Northerners in. That's why she shut the door in your face."

Mildred brought William a glass of water, and he gulped a swig.

"You can meet my family later." Reverend Hull motioned for him to enter the parlor. "Mrs. Hull and my daughters are visiting neighbors. My sons are out in the fields with the slaves. We have a farm here to help make ends meet."

William took a deep breath and tried to gain control of his ire. He trailed after Reverend Hull through the main entrance and struggled to keep his attention on the décor. Anything to focus his thoughts away from the obvious.

The room was nicer than he expected for a Kentucky preacher. Two eight-by-eight pane windows offered a view of the tobacco fields behind the house. Bentwood chairs, a rocker, a sofa, and a parlor table lined the walls around a stone hearth fireplace. A pianoforte rested against the far wall next to the doorway to the rest of the house. A flowered rug covered most of the wood floor.

"Have a seat. We're pleased to have you do your meetings here. Not many get out this way." Reverend Hull opened an old wooden box. "Would you like a cigar?"

William sat erect in a nearby chair. "No, thank you. I don't smoke."

"You should take it up, son." Reverend Hull clipped off the end of his cigar. "There's nothing finer than men talking over cigars."

"I'll keep it in mind." William struggled to keep his voice calm. "Sir, Tabitha doesn't look colored."

Reverend Hull cleared his throat.

William rubbed the back of his neck. "She looks very much like you."

The reverend twisted the corner of his mustache. "You insult me, sir. Mildred and her children are my slaves."

"Oh." He let out a quiet exhale. "So they're not your biological children?"

Hull's face turned red. "Of course they are!" His voice lowered. "You have no right to stick your oar in. What I'm doing happened in the Bible all the time. Abraham and Jacob both had slave concubines."

William swallowed back his outrage to keep it from spilling out in his tone. "Does your wife know?"

Hull drew his fist to his mouth. "You leave my wife out of this. She's a fine woman, and if I was taking up with some white woman, she'd chew on me for supper." He lit the cigar and glowered at William. "Mildred's my slave and a fetching Negress. I'm not doing anything wrong. Do you cotton my meaning?"

William gazed at the rug by his feet. He wanted to kick it to the other side of the room, but he offered a silent prayer instead. Now was not the time to confront if he wanted his message to be heard beyond these four walls. It would be better delivered from the pulpit. "Yes, sir, I understand what you're saying."

"Good." The preacher pointed his cigar in William's face. "I would have never had a Northerner here if you hadn't assured me you'd preach the Word and nothing else. See you do, and stay out of things that are none of your affair."

William repositioned himself in the chair.

"Let's change the subject." Reverend Hull leaned back and puffed his cigar. "So, you're a college man."

"Yes, sir. I'm in my last year at Oberlin College. I graduate in August."

"Oberlin's too liberal for my taste." Reverend Hull blew smoke out of his nose and mouth until it circled around his head. "I'm planning to send my oldest to college, maybe some place like Transylvania University in Lexington. It's expensive though, more than a poor tobacco farming preacher can afford."

Photographs in ornate frames of Reverend Hull and his family caught William's attention. Not something they came by cheaply. "Some colleges do cost dearly. Fortunately, Oberlin is within the budget of a working man."

"I got it all planned out." Reverend Hull leaned forward. "If I sell my oldest slaves, Micah and Tabitha, that should pay for Isaac's education and living expenses with some to spare."

William gulped down the rest of the water. "How old are they?"

"Micah's ten. I figure he's old enough to be away from his mama now, and he's strong. Tabitha's thirteen. I should have sold her off a couple of years ago, but she's such a pretty little thing. Anyway, no reason they won't fetch fair prices at the slave auction in Maysville."

Tabitha entered the room. "Supper's on."

"So," Reverend Hull said. "Are you ready for some good Southern cooking?"

Please, Lord, put a guard over my mouth until the right time. "I'm ready." America was right. They were going to lynch him after his first sermon.

Chapter Six

America rode her sorrel to the Foster plantation on the outskirts of Dover. Negro children huddled in front of a wooden shack. The boys around eight to ten years old stared at her with round dark eyes. She didn't want to come this way, but it was the only clear path to the house. At least the tobacco crops had already been harvested. After they plowed the ground under, the children wouldn't have to work fifteen hours a day again until spring.

The slave quarters were little more than rows of shacks made of rotting wood and patched with mud. They wouldn't be able to stay warm through the winter months with the conditions they lived in. Every two shacks were connected by one fireplace heating both houses. The chimneys were made with tabby, a mixture of shell, lime, and water. Some masters provided it because they didn't want to pay for brick. Shutters protected one small glassless window in each house. If brick was too costly, glass was more so.

Most of the slave yard was clean of debris, but garbage was piled in one corner. The stench assaulted her nose. Only two outhouses stood in the yard servicing at least fifty slaves and adding to the foul odor. A stick fence and wide dirt road blocked the slave quarters from the rest of the plantation. America's horse trotted along that road on the way to the big house.

Keeping her eyes fixed straight ahead, she ignored the glare the slave children gave white folks, a mixture of fear, hopelessness, and controlled hatred. The hopelessness disturbed her most. Her jaw hurt from grinding her teeth. She'd almost forgotten how plantation slaves were treated. Since she'd been away, the horror struck her in a new way. How could a man treat other human beings, even children, like animals? No, not quite. They treated their animals better.

At least her father's slaves were well fed and clothed, and they didn't work any harder than he did. Why would her brother even consider marrying a spoiled plantation owner's daughter?

The swoosh of a whip and muffled cries caught her attention. She cringed as she rode past an overseer beating a slave on the side of the road. The girl looked maybe fourteen or fifteen years old, thin the way most slaves were. America didn't remember ever seeing a robust slave on the Foster Plantation. They weren't fed enough.

The slave lay whimpering on the side of the dirt path, hands above her head and blouse pulled up to expose her back. Modesty wasn't a luxury afforded to slave girls. "Please masser, please."

The sound of the lash pierced striking America's heart.

A groan. "Ohhhh, masser."

"Don't you cry out to me, Missy. Trying to get out of work. I'll show you." The overseer brought the lash down again.

America looked away. She was a coward, but she couldn't bear to watch the girl's suffering. There was nothing she could do for her. She nudged her horse to gallop up the hill until she was beyond hearing range.

The excess of the white columned, two-story colonial anchored between rows of tulip trees rested on top of the hill littered with yellow leaves looming over the poverty of the shacks as a castle would tower over peasants' hovels in England centuries ago.

Six windows decorated the front of the house so the owners could survey the landscape. Each massive window was made up of twenty panes across and twenty up and down. Three chimneys shot out from the roof, one on either side and one in the middle. They were made of brick, not tabby. Chairs and a swing rested on the spacious covered porch.

America knocked on the front door. A mulatto man with gray hair dressed in a waistcoat too big for him answered.

"Miss Leighton to see Miss Virginia Foster," America said.

"Yes'um, come in. I'll go fetch her. She be down straight away."

America gave the man her riding jacket and followed him into the parlor. It'd been a long time since she'd been in a room so affluent. A pianoforte stood in the corner near a window. She glided her fingers across the keys but resisted the temptation to play a tune.

She sank into the plush flowered sofa and leaned forward to warm herself in front of the ornate marble fireplace. A lot of slave labor must have paid for that marble. America leaned back into the soft cushions, then adjusted and sat straight. She twisted in the seat a little and tugged on the skirt of her bloomer outfit.

She probably shouldn't have shown up dressed in the new style of clothing. She had made it out of yellow and green flowered calico. It was a day style dress only coming to her knees, but under the dress, she wore matching bloomers - wide legged trousers gathered at the waist and ankles with a ruffle at the bottom for modesty. Although some women felt the outfit unladylike, America loved how it gave her the freedom to ride a horse astride and do other things her long skirts impeded.

Lavena had convinced her and all her roommates to sew them. Well not all of the ladies. Betsy said she would never be caught wearing trousers. Although this rational style dress with the full-length bloomers and knee-length skirt was being enthusiastically embraced in the North and East, at least in larger cities, many in polite society still frowned on it, preferring corsets, hoops, and fourteen pounds of undergarments. It probably wasn't a wise decision to wear bloomers here in Kentucky, but it was such a nice day, and she hated to ride sidesaddle.

Virginia appeared at the doorway wearing a pink satin hoop dress. A set of pearls lined her neck. Her chestnut brown hair was done in ringlets and kept back with ornate ivory combs.

America had worn fancy hoop dresses when she lived in Kentucky, but since she left to attend Oberlin, she'd packed away her finery for practical apparel, cotton and wool day dresses, and the Turkish bloomers she wore today.

"Good-day, Miss Leighton." Virginia's lips pressed to form a tight smile as she scrutinized America from head to toe. "This is an unexpected pleasure. I thought you were still in Ohio."

"Please." America rose to her feet. "We needn't be so formal. When you marry Luke, we'll be sisters."

"All right, America. You may refer to me as Virginia." She motioned to the flowered settee. "I'm so glad you came to visit. Lucas didn't tell me you were home."

"I just arrived a couple of days ago." America sat beside her. "When I heard about the upcoming nuptials, I wanted to see you and give my best wishes."

"Why, thank you kindly. I'm so glad you came for a visit. I know we've had our differences in the past, but I so hoped we could be sisters, for Luke's sake."

America let out a sigh of relief. "I had hoped the same thing."

Virginia fanned herself. "You simply must be one of my attendants at the wedding. We can set the date after your graduation so you can attend. Please, say yes."

"Yes, I would be honored." America tried to keep the astonishment out of her voice. The Virginia she remembered would have never changed the date of her wedding to accommodate anyone.

"This calls for refreshments." Virginia stood and stepped to the doorway. "Fanny, bring lemonade." She turned to America. "Papa has lemons brought clear from Georgia. I do love lemonade."

Virginia adjusted her full hoop skirt before easing back into the sofa. "What's it like in Northern Ohio? I hear they're rude and uncultured."

"Not at all. Some in the North consider the practices of the South unseemly."

"I can't imagine why they would think such a thing."

Fanny, a light brown-skinned girl with brown eyes and curly hair slipped in with a tray of glasses and a pitcher of lemonade. She couldn't have been more than ten years old. She kept her head lowered as she set them on the parlor table and poured the lemonade. Her hand trembled, and she spilled a little on America.

"You stupid fool." Virginia sprang to her feet and raised her hand to slap the girl.

Fanny didn't even flinch.

"No!" America grabbed Virginia's arm. "Stop, it's all right. She only spilled a drop. It's already drying."

"Fanny." Virginia's voice lowered a notch. "Wait for me in the kitchen."

The girl skirted out of the room.

"Please don't punish her," America said. "She meant no harm."

Virginia shot America a caustic glare and circled her like a cat waiting to pounce. "Lucas warned me about you. He told me how y'all want to end our way of life and how you go to college with Negros. He even told me, how you want to go oversees to preach to savages. Why your papa would allow it, I can't imagine, but I'm willing to overlook it for Lucas' sake."

America had never hit anyone in her life, but she wanted to slap this pompous brat.

"What I'm not willing to overlook," Virginia said, "is you coming into my home and interfering with me and my slaves. I won't have it."

"Maybe I should leave then." America started toward the door.

"Maybe you should," Virginia called after her.

America grabbed her jacket off the hook and slammed the door on the way out. She mounted Red and galloped down the path, past the slave quarters, and onto the road leading home. She shouldn't have come. Nothing ever changed in Kentucky.

She reached the path to the house, paused at the fork, then nudged her horse onto the trail leading the other direction. Urging Red to full gallop, she rode to the Ohio River where it bordered the Leighton Ranch. Pulling back the reins, she fixed her eyes on the brick home at the Ohio side of the river on the hill overlooking the town of Ripley. The rows of stone steps leading to it called out.

She dismounted and tied Red to a nearby bush. She dug a worn Bible out of the saddlebag and carried it with her as she strolled along the riverbank. When she passed by a felled tree, America sat and thumbed through the pages. A tear fell slid down her right cheek. *Lord, what am I going to do? If I proclaim the truth and stand up for what I know to be right, Papa and Luke will turn against me. They won't listen no matter what*

I say.

Papa's letter marked the place in the book of Hebrews, Chapter Ten, where she'd left off reading the day before. She came to Verse Thirty-five, she read aloud. *Now the just shall live by faith: but if any man draw back, my soul shall have no pleasure in him.*

It had always been difficult to go against her papa. Colonel Leighton was a formidable man who made her feel guilty when she defied his wishes. Her stomach would knot until she appeased him. It's the way they interacted for as long as she could remember. She would capitulate -- until she decided to go to Oberlin College.

Her knees had wobbled when she confronted him. Even then, she didn't go against him. She just persuaded him to let her go. She wasn't sure she would be capable of opposing him for long, but this time she had to.

America mounted Red and rode home. It was time to do what she came here for.

Chapter Seven

America burst into the parlor. "Papa, anyone home?"

Ruth rushed through the kitchen doorway. "Landsakes, miss. What's all that shouting about?"

"I need to talk to the colonel. Is he home yet?"

"None of them is. I expect them shortly."

America sank onto the settee. She had prepared to meet her father head on. Now he wasn't here.

"Can I help?" Ruth moved to America's side. Worry lines framed her face.

America stared into Ruth's compassionate eyes. She didn't remember her mother. Ruth was the one who bandaged scraped knees and comforted her when Papa's scoldings wounded her spirit. Ruth was the one who cared for her and saw to her needs when her father was fighting the war in Mexico for a year. Ruth had been her mother in every way that counted.

She didn't really miss her mother. Elizabeth Leighton had died from a cholera epidemic when she was only two. She glanced at the painting over the fireplace. The woman had her strawberry blond curls, but she was a stranger, just somebody Ruth described as full of fire and faith.

Did her mother have the courage to stand up to the colonel? Probably not.

"This isn't something you can fix. I'm not little anymore."

"Maybe not." Ruth put an arm around her. "I'm mighty good at listening."

"Oh, Aunt Ruth." She rested her head on her nanny's shoulder. "I shouldn't even be talking to you about this. I've believed slavery was wrong as long as I can remember, but I've always thought there's nothing to be done about it. It's the way things are."

"That's a fact."

"It's not true." America lifted her head and faced Ruth. "Evil triumphs in this world because we don't confront it. I've compromised by not proclaiming the truth."

"Just how do you expect to do that?"

"I'm going to tell Papa what he's doing is a sin against God. Selling Amos was wrong, and sending Naomi to the slave auction would be even worse."

Ruth lips pressed together.

"I have to call evil what it is. My papa needs to repent and free his slaves. It's the only way."

"The master's not gonna free us, and you shouldn't be going against your pa. Ain't no call for it when there's nothing can be done."

America gazed into Ruth's soft brown eyes. "I have to try."

"I've been praying the Good Lord finds a way to keep Naomi here with me." Ruth eyes darted to the whip hanging on the wall by the kitchen door. "He didn't see fit to rescue Amos, so I'll bear up under it the way our people has for hundreds of years."

"Don't you see? God's heard your prayers." America took Ruth's hands in hers. "I've been away three years. The Lord spoke to me to return now."

"You listen to me, child. You're a fool if'n you figure to come in here and change things by going against your pa. Things ain't like that. You raising false hopes ain't doing nobody no good. You drop this foolishness."

"Are you telling me to disobey God?"

Ruth's shoulders slumped. "No, child, I'll never go against what the Good Lord tells you, but it's bound to end poorly."

"I know." America's voice thickened. "God didn't promise me it would turn out well, but He told me what I must do, and I'm set on doing it."

"Then may the Good Lord help you, child. They'll be back soon, and I got to get supper on. I'll be praying." Ruth headed to the kitchen, but before she left the parlor, she turned to say something. Before she could, the front door opened, and Papa and Luke sauntered through the foyer into the parlor. Ruth darted through the kitchen door without another word and closed it behind her.

"I won't be here for supper, sir," Luke said. "After I wash up, I'll be going to the Foster plantation. Mrs. Foster invited me to sup with them."

"You give her our regards," Papa said. "Merry, did you have a chance to call on Miss Virginia?"

America swallowed. "Yes, we visited."

"Good. I'm pleased to know you two will be getting on."

"I'll take my leave." Luke whisked over to America and whispered in her ear. "Keep in mind what I said. Don't vex him with this." He warned her with a parting glance as he made his way outside.

Her father planted himself on the settee. "Sit, Merry. We have some long overdue matters to discuss."

America's stomach tightened as she sat beside him.

"I've been considering," Papa said, "if sending you off to Oberlin College was the best course of action. I might have given you my permission too hastily."

"Papa–"

He raised his hand. "Now you hush and hear me out. Once I have my say, I'll listen to your side of it."

"Yes, sir."

"I'm concerned about you, darling. I knew when you came to me that Sunday five years ago, you had the call. It was hard to take in when you wanted to go to some college in Ohio, but I accepted it."

America parted her lips but couldn't think of what to say.

"All right," Papa gave her a half grin and a shrug. "I had my concerns. I felt it would be more proper for you to go to a woman's college in Kentucky where you could learn womanly arts, but I relented and allowed it."

He retrieved his tobacco pouch and pipe from the parlor table. "Then, a year into college, it troubled me to receive the letter saying you weren't coming home for winter break, and you spring this foolishness about wanting to go to heathens and foreigners and be some kind of missionary. Mighty hard to swallow, but I did. I figured you met a gentleman at school who had the call to go overseas, and you were figuring on a proper marriage, but, now, you're into your last year and no gentleman has come to my door to ask for your hand. I hope I'm wrong, but it's plain to me, you plan to go off on your own."

America chewed the inside of her cheek. "You knew I had the call."

Papa filled his pipe with tobacco and packed it. "Most ladies who have the call marry preachers. They don't go to heathen lands alone. It's not proper."

"But –"

"America, hush. I told you I'll have my say."

Her heart raced as she swiped her tongue across her lips.

"You've been gone near on three years, and I've heard things about Oberlin since." He lit the pipe and drew a puff. "The newspapers say it's full of them abolitionist rebels. It's been reported they allow Negros to attend classes with whites. I can't believe I sent you all the way to Ohio to go to school with coloreds. Some even say you not only go to classes and church with them, you even eat in the same dining hall. Now is that the truth of it?"

"Yes, Papa, it's true. All of it."

"It's not decent. I'm not going to forbid you to go back since it's your last year, but I'm not happy about this. I'd like you to tell me what's going on in that foolish little head of yours."

"Oh, Papa, you don't understand." She squeezed her nose between her thumb and forefinger to hold back her tears so he wouldn't see her cry.

He set his pipe down and placed his hand on hers. "You're right there, daughter, but I know it's important to you, so tell me your side of it."

She let out a prayer for the right words to say as she pulled her hand back from his. "Slavery is wrong. It's an injustice to imprison a man who has committed no crime, and to make that man work for you without any compensation, or to sell his children without thought of how you're breaking apart his family. It's a sin to own a man who is your brother in Christ and treat him like you would an animal."

"Treat him like an animal?" The vein in her father's forehead pulsed. "Is that what you think of me? Do you consider me one them slave traders and plantation owners who whips their slaves for any offense?"

"No, Papa. I know you treat them well, but it's still a sin."

He stood and leaned against the fireplace. "I do treat my slaves well. I only remember two beatings I've ever given. One was to Joe after I first bought him, and he admitted he deserved it and asked my pardon."

"Papa, don't you see? He's afraid of you."

"It's a healthy fear. He knows who his master is."

"What was the other time?"

He stabbed the log with the poker. "Obadiah interfered when I took Amos to auction to be sold."

"Do you think it right to sell him from his people?"

"America, his kin doesn't own him. I do." Papa tossed the poker aside. "I didn't sell him until he was full grown, and I had no choice." He picked up his pipe and tamped it before drawing in smoke. "So, you want to talk about right and wrong, do you? I give Joe and Ruth a home, don't I?"

She nodded with a slight jerk of her head.

"I provide them and their children with doctoring, food, and lodging. Luke even helped them build a cabin nicer than some free Kentuckians have. Is it wrong I ask them to work the ranch they live on? I work as hard as they do."

"I know." America felt a familiar hand on her brain gently squeezing, her papa's words trying to convince her the evil he did was good.

"Then is what I'm doing really wrong?"

"Yes, Papa, it is."

He set the pipe down and sat beside her. "What if I did free them? Where would they go? How would they live? Who would care for them if they were sick? You've seen how free coloreds in Kentucky live. Do you really think they'd be better off?"

"You could hire them. They could work for pay."

Papa snorted. "Are you trying to ruin me, child? Let me tell you a few facts of life." He pointed his finger in her face. "I've put a mortgage on this ranch to buy horses, and most of them up and died. I don't have funds to hire out. I don't even have enough to pay the creditors. All I have left is four mares and two studs I plan on breeding next spring, not even a decent race horse among them, and a few slaves. The slaves cost more than the horses, and you want me to let them go?"

America swallowed. If only he would listen. "Yes."

"If I do, we're ruined." He massaged his forehead with his thumb and index finger. "Those slaves are the only assets I can afford to get rid of. If I don't sell Naomi soon, I'll lose the ranch. Is that what you want? You want me to lose everything I've worked for all these years? I'll have nothing to pass on to you and Luke."

"Papa." America's voice quivered betraying her newfound resolve. "I don't want you to lose the ranch, but isn't it better than to lose your soul. Think about what will happen when you sell Naomi. What if some man decides to abuse her? What would you do if a man owned me and sold me to someone who would beat and misuse me?"

Papa slapped her across the face. She drew her hand to her cheek.

He grabbed hold of her shoulders and spoke in a controlled rage. "You go too far, child. You're a white lady. You're not like them. If you were, I'd take a horsewhip to you instead of my hand. God made them to serve us, and I'll not lose my ranch on account of a few slaves."

The fire in his eyes made her mouth grow dry. This was the master the slaves were afraid of.

Luke stormed in, slammed the door, and gave America a fierce look. "You've done it now. I can't believe you."

Papa spun around. "What did she do?"

"She almost ruined everything. Virginia's fit to be tied. America marched into the house like she owned the place, and she wore britches."

"I don't even own britches. I wore the Turkish dress I have on now."

"America." Papa relit his pipe and eyed her clothes. "Do you really consider what you're wearing proper attire for visiting?"

"It gets worse." Luke crossed his arms and glared at America. "Virginia was giving orders to her household girl when Merry interrupted her and went on a tirade about slavery."

"I didn't." Her tongue swiped between her lips as if it couldn't stay contained to the inside of her mouth. "Papa, she was set on beating a young girl for accidently dripping lemonade on me. She said I was uncultured and unladylike. She insulted me, and I left."

"Virginia's thinking about calling off the wedding." Luke started pacing. He always wore out the rug when he was trying to keep his anger from exploding. "She doesn't know if she wants to marry into a family who would treat her so poorly."

"Good." The word thrust forward with little concern for America's will to hold her tongue. She gazed into her father's scorching glare and flinched, expecting him to strike again.

He stepped back and drew in from his pipe. He lowered his voice. "America Elizabeth Leighton, I've heard enough for one night. Perhaps you should retire to your room for now. Tomorrow at church, you can pray and ask God if you've honored your father by your actions today. You can also entreat Him about the wrong you've done in trying to break your brother's engagement."

"But Papa, I--."

"Enough! Go to your room. When you've had time to consider what you've done, we'll thrash this out. If you still need correction, I'll dispense it in the woodshed."

She stepped back. "You wouldn't."

"I've coddled you. It's been a long time since I've taken a switch to you, but I can remedy that. You may be of age, but you're still my daughter, and you're under my roof."

America gaped at him. Did she really know him? She tried to find the right words, but there were none. She ran up the stairs to her room and slammed the door. Standing in front of the ornate full-length mirror, she touched the red handprint on her cheek. A sob escaped her lips as she winced from the sting, but the quivering in her stomach bothered her more.

Maybe she'd misunderstood what God wanted. Maybe she was wrong for going against her father.

Chapter Eight

William trudged up the warped wooden steps into the small white church, his jaw set and shoulders squared. Two men with long scraggly hair and unshaven faces sat on the wooden bench in the back. The taller man wore grass-stained wool trousers. The shorter one wiped his nose on his blue flannel shirtsleeve. Both had guns tucked in their belts. William raised an eyebrow. God's house was not the place for pistols.

Reverend Hull headed to the men, and they stood and shook his hand. He turned to William. "Brother Woods, this is Horace and Gus."

William shook their hands. "Horace, Gus."

"They're the law in this county."

Horace, the taller and scrawnier of the two, grinned big enough for William to see his buckteeth and reel a little at the garlic he must have recently eaten.

"Yep," Horace said. "You'll have to excuse the side arms, Brother Woods. Me and my brother's on duty. You never know when we might have to go after some of them godless abolitionists been causing trouble round these parts."

"Then there's them slaves always trying to meet on Sunday," Gus said. "They say they're having church, but we break it up anyhow. I can't abide them singing, praying Negros."

"Don't want them plotting against their masters." Horace sniffed. "It's against the law for them to have a meeting in this county. When we catch 'em, we give 'em a good whipping. They take heed the next time."

William swallowed down the lump in his throat. "I would imagine they do. Nice meeting you." He would be dead by the end of the day. He knew some might give him chase after the sermon he planned to deliver, but he never thought they would have firearms. In church?

Only one thing to do. If he were to die, he would give this sermon everything he had. No sense his last message being in vain. By the end of his admonition, they would be on their knees repenting or they'd be gunning for him. William believed he might die a martyr's death in the mission field but not here or this soon. He made his way past the wooden benches filled with people to the front of the church and sank onto the front bench beside Reverend Hull.

Considering the great sin making its way from the pastor of the church to the lawmen sitting in the back, this seemed like a regular Sunday meeting. The church had a country feel to it, a log building with a piano on one side, a Franklin stove on the other, a pulpit, and an anxiety bench in front. Familiar hymns were played, offering collected, and men, women, and children in their Sunday best prayed in earnest.

One little girl in braids tied off with ribbons matching her ruffled yellow dress sat on the front bench across the aisle. She closed her eyes and sang off key at a volume drowning out those around her. The towhead boy beside her, probably her older brother, tried to sing louder but couldn't manage it. William kept his focus on them instead of glancing to where Reverend Hull led the congregation in singing, but occasionally his eyes wandered to the front.

Hull acted like he was praising God with his hands raised and his eyes lifted. He even did a little jig during a faster song as if the Spirit of God moved him, but no amount of outward devotion would cover his black heart.

Mrs. Hull played another song on the piano, *A Mighty Fortress Is Our God.* William raised his bass voice to cantillate the last hymn prior to him standing before the congregation. How appropriate this song would be played, since it might be the last he ever uttered. The words strengthened his resolve. He sang the last two verses, his voice thick with emotion.

And though this world, with devils filled, should threaten to undo us; We will not fear, for God hath willed His truth to triumph through us. The prince of darkness grim-we tremble not for him; His rage we can endure, for lo! His doom is sure, One little word shall fell him.

That word above all earthly powers, no thanks to them abideth; The Spirit and the gifts are ours through Him who with us sideth. Let goods and kindred go, this mortal life also; The body they may kill; God's truth abideth still, His kingdom is forever.

William marched to the front with the sermon he was about to deliver burning in his heart. He repeated the last phrase aloud. "'God's truth abideth still, His kingdom is forever.' As the preacher before you today, God's truth is what I shall deliver. You can kill His messengers and prophets, but His truth remains, and His kingdom shall stand."

Voices of agreement came from various places in the congregation.

"Amen," Reverend Hull shouted. "Preach on, brother."

"My text is Isaiah Chapter Five, Verse Twenty. 'Woe unto them that call evil good, and good evil; that put darkness for light, and light for darkness; that put bitter for sweet, and sweet for bitter!'"

"Amens" resounded, but that would soon change.

William's voice thundered in his own ears. "When I say evil, I am referring to the foul stench of iniquity in your very midst. Slavery."

An *Amen* stopped in midstream coming out as amm--, then a clearing of a throat. A bearded man rubbed his hand across his forehead.

The young woman beside him, heavy with child, grabbed hold of his arm.

Reverend Hull's face turned red. There would surely be reprisals as soon as he recovered from the shock. In the back of the room, Horace crossed his arms and gave William a glower to strike him dead if it could have carried out its intent. Gus looked too flabbergasted to do anything.

An eerie silence pervaded the room. Every eye focused on William. "Some of you have become so blinded, so deceived, you would force yourselves on these young women you have taken into bondage and engage in fornication and illicit adulterous relationships. You call this evil good, because you say that poor unfortunate girl is my possession to serve my needs. Woe to you who call evil good."

The mother of the girl in the yellow dress gasped and covered the child's ears. All heads turned to Reverend Hull. Hull's mouth dropped open. Mrs. Hull frantically fanned herself. With her pale complexion and blue lips, the woman looked as if she might swoon. An elderly woman near the front tapped her cane on the floor.

William preached with fire coming from his soul and passing through his lips. He only had a faint recollection of the words he used, knowing God called to account the sins of the congregation. He felt it odd nobody moved, nor uttered a word. He'd assumed they would articulate their displeasure. Apparently, he'd left them speechless.

"As God spoke through Moses to Pharaoh, He speaks through me now, 'Let my people go.' As he spoke to the church of Laodicea, he speaks to you now, 'As many as I love, I rebuke and chasten. Be zealous, therefore, and repent.' God is imploring you to free your slaves."

William stepped back and waited. Nobody spoke or moved. It was fortunate the weather was too cold for flies, for surely, they would have found their way into some of the open mouths he viewed.

A bearded man stood and made his way to the front. Two men sitting behind followed, and they knelt at the anxiety bench. William started toward them when Gus and Horace stood and approached him. Gus drew his gun first, then Horace.

The crowd scurried to the side of the room. The men at the anxiety bench stood. Reverend Hull nodded to the lawmen.

William glared into Gus' eyes with fervor. "Will you shoot me now for telling you God's truth?"

Sweat beaded Gus' forehead. He lowered the gun.

Horace fidgeted and aimed higher. He jumped, dropping his firearm and holding his hand as if it had been burned.

William took a step forward when the men at the anxiety bench grabbed his arms and shoved him out the side door. He pulled free from them. "Stop, what are you doing?"

"I'll get the horses." The youngest, a scrawny sixteen-year-old kid with peach fuzz on his ruddy face, sprinted to the corral.

The man with a full beard turned to him. "You fool. God delivered you from their hands. Are you gonna just stand there and wait 'til they recover?"

The third man, heavier than the bearded man by about fifty pounds, glanced over his shoulder. "We gotta get out of here."

The youngest one brought four horses already saddled, William's gelding among them. At least William had thought to pack his supplies in the saddlebags that morning. He suspected he wouldn't be returning to the preacher's house after this morning's sermon.

The bearded man mounted. "We'll ride to my house. It's closest."

William didn't know if he wanted to run like a coward, but it did seem like God sent these men to rescue him. He mounted his bay and galloped after them. A rumble clamored behind, and he glanced back. Dirt and dried leaves shrouded Gus and Horace as they rode their horses hard.

The bearded man called out, "Hurry, we'll lose them in the woods."

Bullets whizzed past William's ears as guns fired. He gripped tighter on the reins and galloped on the path through the trees behind the three men who saved his life.

*****

America sang *A Mighty Fortress Is Our God* with the rest of the congregation. She'd sung this song many times before, but the words impacted her for the first time. She gave her father and brother a sideways glance. *Let goods and kindred go.* Could she? She would have to if she stayed on this course. Papa had ordered her to pray. *God, if you want me to go through with this, show me what to do, and give me the courage to obey You, even if it means going against him.*

Reverend Thornton, a short stocky man in his early thirties, gazed across the congregation and his eyes rested on America. Clearing his throat, he opened his Bible. "Today's text is found in Isaiah Forty-Three, Verse Two. 'When thou passest through the waters, I will be with thee; and through the rivers, they shall not overflow thee: when thou walkest through the fire, thou shalt not be burned; neither shall the flame kindle upon thee.' "

Was this her answer? She felt the heat from the flames of oppression. She leaned forward, paying heed to Reverend Thornton's sermon.

The message ended with Peter and John standing before the high priest saying, "We ought to obey God rather than men."

The call to the anxiety bench was given and America hastened her way to it. Let Papa assume she went there to assuage her guilt. She needed God's strength to walk through this fire.

A hand rested on her back. She glanced behind her to see who was praying for her. No one. The unseen hand supported her, comforted her. She wiped her eyes and strode toward her father and brother waiting for her at the back of the church.

No words were spoken on the ride home or during the lunch America prepared. The slaves had the day off on Sundays so they could attend the African church service held after the normal meeting let out. After supper, her brother dismissed himself to go to Virginia's house.

"Luke," America said.

He flashed an icy glare in her direction.

She gulped regretting her hasty words to Luke even if her words to her father were well thought out. "I'm sorry for what I said about Virginia. I only want your happiness, and if she pleases you..."

One side of Luke's mouth turned up as he strolled to America and gave her a hug. "Don't worry about it, Sis. She says she might call off the engagement at least once a month. She won't really do it."

America forced a grin. "That's good."

Luke jerked his head toward Papa and whispered in her ear. "Besides, you have other things to fret about."

He let her go and scooted out the door before she could say anything. He was right, but she could still feel the unseen hand giving her the courage she needed.

"America." Papa's voice interrupted her thoughts. "I see you prayed at the anxiety bench today."

"Yes, Papa."

"Did you repent of going against me in this foolish crusade?"

She swiped her tongue across the back of her teeth. She knew she wasn't about to lie. "No, I prayed for strength to stay the course."

Papa crossed his arms. "You offer no apology, no remorse for declaring I'm wrong in supporting my family."

"Slavery is a sin."

"You want to side with slaves against me, and you'll be treated as such." He marched over to the kitchen doorway and grabbed the horsewhip hanging on the wall.

America's heart dropped to her stomach.

He strode to her, whip in hand, his face set only inches from hers. "You're not going back to Oberlin. You'll stay under this roof until I can arrange a proper marriage, and you'll give up these abolitionist notions."

She stepped back. "No, Papa, I won't. I'll return to Oberlin, and I will declare God's truth about slavery."

"How do you propose to get there? It's a long way without train fare."

She squeezed her eyes shut. Her father had promised to pay the train fare home. Without a train ticket, she would be unable to leave. "I'll ride Red. It's a long way for a lady on horseback, but I'll get there. God will help me."

"You won't be riding Red. She's my horse."

"No, she's not. You gave her to me for my sixteenth birthday."

"You are a woman. Your property belongs to me until you marry. If you take Red, I'll have you arrested."

Tears threatened to flood her eyes. She pinched her nose to hold them back. "Papa, why? Why are you doing this?"

Her father looked at the ground for a moment, his forehead furrowed, and shook his head. "Child, you've been deceived by those abolitionist rebels in Oberlin. This is the only way I know to help you. I love you. I know you don't believe it now, but someday you'll see what I'm doing is for your good."

His words felt like fingers inching up her brain trying to mislead her. She rubbed her temple. "You're the one who's deceived. I'll find a way to get back to Oberlin if I have to walk."

He let out a groan and threw the horsewhip across the floor. "I won't let you do it. I'll fight for you, and I'll do what I gotta do."

America let out a slow breath. "As long as I'm alive, I will fight against those who own their fellow man."

Papa glowered at her for a moment before answering. "Get a hickory switch and wait for me in the barn. I'll not have you disrespect me in my own home."

America squared her shoulders and marched outside.

Chapter Nine

William swatted his gelding as it galloped on the path through the woods. A dust cloud stirred around the pursuing riders. Maybe he should stop. He didn't want to put his rescuers in danger.

The man with the full beard who had called him a fool earlier shouted over the throng. "Jack, you and Hugh lead them away. I'll meet you at the cabin." He motioned to William. "Follow me."

William chased him into the forest. He ducked, barely missing a low hanging branch, then tilted his body to one side to keep from smashing into another one. A third smacked him in the side, but he managed to stay on his horse.

The lawmen pursued Jack and Hugh on the path around the bend until they were out of sight. The bearded man pulled his colt to a stop. William reined in beside him.

"Cal Tucker." The man extended his hand.

William shook it. "Cal, I appreciate the help, but we can't let them do this. I won't risk those men's lives because of me."

"Preacher," Cal said. "You got no call to fret. Gus and Horace are cousins. They aren't gonna harm kin. They're only after you."

"Where's this cabin you want to take me to?"

"Not more than a hoot and holler from here." Cal trotted his horse on the trail leading along Big Sandy River.

William loped behind Cal. *Please God don't let the lawmen guess where we're going.* They rode on the path along the base of the mountain range. On the other side of the river bordering Kentucky and Virginia, mountains presented their autumn foliage with splashes of orange, red, and yellow. If William hadn't worried about the pursuers catching up with them, he would have stopped to drink in the breathtaking display.

Cal motioned up ahead to a log house nestled at the bend. They urged their horses on. A huge barn hidden in a pine grove towered a hundred feet away. William followed Cal inside the cabin.

"Welcome to my home," Cal said. "The clan will be by shortly. We meet every Sunday after church."

William rubbed his hand across his chin and sat on a wooden bench at the oak table in the center of the main room. "You most likely saved my life." He glanced at the door half expecting the lawmen to burst through it. "I won't stay here if it endangers your family."

"Gus and Horace won't be coming around any time soon. You stay put, and I'll make some coffee."

Cal threw a log on the fire. The fireplace was large enough to supply heat to the whole cabin and, with the crane, trammel, and pot sitting over hot coals, it also served as a cooking hearth. Two rockers sat on the rug in front of the fireplace. An oak hutch on the fireplace wall near the table contained dishes and cookware. Curtains sectioned off two rooms on the other side, and a ladder led to a nice size loft.

"I was mighty glad to hear your sermon today, preacher." Cal placed the coffee pot on the cooking coals. "You're an answer to our prayers."

William raised an eyebrow. "How so?"

"The two fellers with us were my brothers, Hugh and Jack. We've been meeting here after church every week along with some of our kinfolk."

"You have? Why?"

"We had a notion Reverend Hull's got some things mixed up in his preaching. Don't seem like some of the stuff he says is in the Word, so we've been meeting and studying for ourselves. We all get together in the barn out back, Sundays and Thursdays, to read and pray. Been doing it now for little over a year. Course Reverend Hull don't cotton to it."

"What teachings troubled you?"

"He said there's no need for our slaves to be churched cause, like animals, they don't got souls. They don't have any hope of an afterlife, so they don't need religion."

William interlaced his fingers on the table in front of him. "All men have souls, slaves too, and when they die they'll either go to Heaven or Hell."

"Hull says God made them to be our slaves. He says it's foolish for them to pray and trust in the Lord because God made them to serve us. We're their masters, not God. Maybe I'm not understanding my Bible right, but I don't think he's right. They need God as much as we do."

"Yes, they do." William sipped his coffee. It gave him a chance to consider his words before he said more. "God wants free men and slaves alike to turn to Him for salvation."

"That's what we figured." Cal plunked down on the bench, stroked his beard, and stared at William. The gaze lasted until it became awkward, but William willed himself to not look away.

Cal broke the gaze. "We're letting our slaves have church in the barn. We told them they could invite others as long as they're mindful who they ask. It's against the law for Negros to gather for a meeting in this county even if it's church."

William breathed slowly to keep from showing his anger. Hull and the men of this county would pay dearly on judgement day for hindering these slaves from seeking the Lord.

"We got twenty or so meeting every Sunday morning," Cal said. "More come out every week. What you said today though really got in my craw. In your sermon, you said we're wrong even owning a few slaves. Men like Abraham in the Bible had slaves, and we treat them right and let them go to church."

"Men in the Bible also practiced bigamy and had concubines, but that doesn't make it right." William rubbed his hand across the back of his neck. "All men are God's creatures, and slaves are men. Moses' wife was an African, and his sister was punished with leprosy for speaking against her. Did you know Jesus had African blood in his linage?"

Cal's brow furrowed. "That can't be. They're cursed."

"Africans are not the cursed people the Bible refers to in Genesis. I'll explain more later, but consider this. Jesus broke every curse by his death and resurrection." He paused waiting for Cal to take in what he said.

A clamor of voices and footsteps sounded outside. William's heart skipped a beat. The door flew open, and three women burst through.

An elderly lady with clear blue eyes peering out of her weather-beaten wrinkled skin swung her cane as she strode to the rocking chair by the fireplace. A plump middle-aged woman and the young woman who sat with Cal during church, heavy with child, assisted her.

The plump woman removed her bonnet. "I'm mighty glad you brought him here, son, but where's your brothers?"

Cal kissed her cheek. "Don't fret, Ma. They're out giving Horace and Gus a good chase. Should be along shortly."

"Preacher, we'd be mighty pleased if you'd teach us from the Word," Cal's mother said. "We've got some kin waiting out in the barn."

"I'd be honored."

Cal introduced the elderly lady as Granny Price, the matriarch of the family. Next, he presented Mrs. Price, his ma, and Emma, his wife. "Best we get out there."

William accompanied Cal and the three women to the barn. A group of thirty, men, women, and children, huddled around. The girl in the yellow dress and her brother sat near the doors.

Granny Price pressed through the assembly as they parted like the Red Sea for her. She slid into a rocker placed in the middle of the barn floor. Each of the others, after greeting William, sat on hay bales, barrels, horse blankets and feed sacks they spread on the ground around her.

While they were getting settled, Jack and Hugh joined them.

"We lost them by the river," Hugh said. He was a ruddy youth who needed a haircut.

Granny Price nodded to Cal, and he held his hand up to silence the group. "Preacher Woods has been troubling me with his words, but he knows God's Word, and we need to heed what he's got to say. If he speaks true, we need to free our slaves."

"It don't make sense," Jack said. He was the heavier brother who looked like he had a healthy appetite. "That's what he said at church today, but we treat them good, and we let them have church."

"Maybe," Cal said. "We've been praying for God to show us the truth, so we need to hear Preacher Woods out."

The clan of faces gazed at William. He swallowed hard. They expected him to deliver God's Word, not his own opinion. Weighing what he would say, he opened his Bible.

Granny Price rose from the rocking chair she'd perched in, hobbled over with her cane, and patted William's hand. "Don't you fret none. You speak what God gives you. We'll listen. If'n the Lord needs to take us to task, so be it."

William rubbed his jaw. "Thank you, ma'am."

For two hours, he taught the Word of God and finished with a plea for the freedom of the slaves. He scanned the faces in the room. Hopefully he wouldn't need to make another quick exit.

Cal knelt on the ground covered with straw and bowed his head. Others followed his example.

Granny stood and faced William. "You told us the truth, and I thank thee. We'll free our slaves this very day. If they choose to stay, we'll pay them room and board and whatever else we can and treat them as brothers and sisters in Christ." She swung her cane around and pointed toward the crowd with it. "If anyone here's not of the same mind, let him stand and face me."

William held his breath looking for any dissention. None stood.

"Then, it's done. Preacher Woods, you're staying in our home for as long as you're here."

"Dear Lady, I accept. It's rare to find brothers and sisters in Christ so hungry for the Word of God."

Jack stepped over to William. "Your words are troubling, but I'll free my slaves like Granny says."

The crowd left, and Granny, Ma Price, and Emily went to the cabin to cook dinner.

Cal placed his hand on William's shoulder. "Would you walk with me a spell?"

"Of course."

They strolled a path leading along the river. The water surged over smooth stones before cascading down. So peaceful for an area racked with turbulence sweeping the nation.

Cal lit a cigar. "Would you like one, preacher?"

"Thank you, but I don't indulge. Please, call me Brother Woods. I don't have my preaching certificate yet."

"Well, you preached two fine sermons today."

William flushed. "God is gracious."

"Preacher... Brother Woods, how long were you planning to stay around these parts?"

"Why?"

"You're welcome to lodge here. We'll fix you a fine place in the loft."

William didn't want to bring danger to these people, but he had a mission to fulfill. "I don't want to impose."

"You aren't. I'm asking 'cause I hoped you might teach us more while you're here."

"Of course. I planned to stay for a two-week revival, but I'm expected at another church when the time is done."

"Did you reckon you'd be here the whole two weeks after the sermon you delivered today?"

"After spending time with your Reverend Hull, I didn't expect to be anywhere by sundown but at the end of a rope."

Cal's lips chuckled around his cigar. "I expect they still have that rope waiting."

Chapter Ten

After spending the day mending fences, Joe dragged into his cabin and rubbed his aching back. He groaned as he leaned down to light kindling in the fireplace. He tried to sit, but stood again, struggling to find a way to ease the pain. He'd be spending another night with the hot water bottle.

If it got much worse, he might have to ask the Colonel Leighton for some laudanum, but he'd hold off as long as he could. Not smart to let the master know you're getting too old to put in a good day's work.

Obadiah stormed in and slammed the door. Joe pretended not to notice. His youngest son looked like a man but wasn't quite there. He was out to sea when it came to using a little wisdom. He wanted to prove something, make things right, but some things couldn't be fixed by charging like an angry bull.

Joe poured water in a tin cup and gulped it down. He didn't want another argument right now. He wanted to grab something to eat and get some sleep. It would be another hard day tomorrow.

"You ain't gonna talk to him, are you?" Obadiah plunked on the wooden bench. "Do you want to see Naomi sold?"

"Have some respect, boy. I'm your pa."

"Then act like it. Get some sand in you. You act like you're afeared."

"I am." He sat on the bench next to Obadiah. "But not of getting whipped. I would have taken a beating if it would have saved Amos. Did you causing a fuss help him?"

Obadiah stared at his boots.

Joe placed his hand on Obadiah's shoulder. "Didn't do no good at all."

"Pa, we got to do something."

"I'm gonna. I got me an idea, but you don't need to know nothing about it."

The vein in Obadiah's neck pulsed. "Ain't I your son?"

"I would have stopped Amos from being sold if I'd known in time. You gotta trust me."

Obadiah stood and turned away. "I did. Then Colonel Leighton sold my brother, and you didn't do nothing." He started to slam his fist on the table, then stopped, and wiped his hand across his face. He plunked back down on the bench. "I'm sorry, Pa. I'm afeared for Naomi."

"I know, son, and you're not wrong, but sometimes you gotta think things through. You can't just get mad all the time. That'll get a black man killed."

"Better to be killed and still be a man."

Joe stood and squared his shoulders. "It's foolishness, Son."

Obi's glare said it all. He was disgusted by his pa's cowardice.

Joe let out a sigh. He had to try it this way first even if Ruth was against it. If he didn't, Obi might never respect him again. "I guess I'll talk to the master."

"You said it ain't gonna do no good."

"Even so, I'm her pa. I gotta speak my peace."

"Pa, wait." Obadiah stepped in front of the door. "There's no need."

"I'm not doing it because of what you said."

"Then why?"

"I got to stand up for my family... for Naomi. I got to show you I'm a man even if I am a slave. It's what the Good Lord wants."

"I'm tired of hearing what the Lord wants. He's a white man's God."

Joe blew out his frustration. His youngest didn't have the sense God gave a mule. "Don't talk like that, Obi."

"God didn't save Amos from the auction block, and He's not gonna keep Colonel Leighton from beating the skin off you like he did me, and what if Naomi gets sold? You still gonna forgive and grovel at his feet? Yessur, master. Whatever you say. When is it enough?"

"The Good Lord sees what we're going through. We got to trust Him no matter what. If He don't deliver us here, He'll have a place waiting when we cross over to the other side. Someday we'll be free." Joe scooted past his son and opened the door. He stepped through it and paused. "If your ma and Naomi get back before I do, tell them to have the ointment ready."

Obadiah slammed the door behind him. Still angry as ever.

Joe strode fifty feet to the main house. With every step he prayed, *Lord, spare Naomi.* He knocked on the back door.

Ruth answered. A frown creased her forehead. "What're you doing here?"

"Now woman, you know what I'm doing. Figure I best get to it."

"No. Use your head, Joe." Ruth's voice took the tone of a shrill whispered yell. "Your back's ailing enough without you getting whipped, and for what? He ain't gonna listen."

"Maybe not, but if he does, it's a better way than we got planned." Joe drew her in his arms and kissed her. "I'll be fine. Now, go fetch him."

Ruth wiped her hands on her apron and walked off.

Joe brushed his foot along the dried autumn leaves. Storm clouds drifted overhead. The downpour would cause his back to ache even more.

Colonel Leighton came to the door. "You want to talk to me, Joe?"

"Yessur."

"Then you best come on. Looks like it's gonna rain."

Joe stepped inside the kitchen and wiped his feet on the rug. He took off his hat and twisted it in his hands. Now he was standing before the master, and he didn't know how to start.

Ruth stepped over to the stove to finish fixing supper on the master's fancy cook stove, but she didn't act like she was cooking much, more moving pans around with her ear tilted toward him.

"Well, get to it," Colonel Leighton said. "It's late. If you have something to say, speak plain."

"Yessur, it's about Naomi being sold." Joe kept his eyes focused on his hat. "I don't cotton to it."

"You don't cotton to it? Joe, since when do I need you to cotton to something before I do it?"

Ruth flashed Joe a furtive glance begging him to stop, but he'd gone this far. He dropped his hat on the floor and reached down to pick it up. "Sir, I've been a good slave. I've worked hard for you all these years."

"Yes, you have."

"It ain't fair you sold my son. Please, master, don't sell Naomi. She's my little girl. I've done everything you've ever asked of me. If you gotta sell someone, sell me."

He heard Ruth's gasp over the rain pounding against the roof.

Colonel Leighton steepled his forefingers against his mouth. "It's business, boy. I wouldn't do it if there were another way. You'll just have to bear up under it."

Ruth wasn't trying to be secretive anymore. She turned from the stove and shook her head.

Joe ignored her and looked directly at Colonel Leighton's eyes. He dropped the slave voice and became weighty with his tone. "This ain't right. I've done good by you. You can find another way to save the ranch."

Thunder crashed.

Colonel Leighton drew close to his face and stabbed a finger into his chest. "You've gone too far, boy. Naomi's mine to do with what I see fit." He marched to the doorway of the parlor and grabbed his whip off the hook on the wall. "Go out to the barn and take off your shirt and coat. I'll be out directly."

Joe lowered his eyes to the twisted hat crumpled in his hands. The slave pitch returned to his voice. "Please, master, I didn't mean no harm."

"Get out to the barn, boy!"

"Yessur." Joe shuffled out into the deluge. Torrents of rain drenched his clothes and sent a chill through him. He knew what would happen, but he had to try for Obi's sake. Now there was only one way to save Naomi.

*****

A few days later, Joe drove the wagon down the mud road leading away from the Leighton ranch and tried to avoid the puddles. Ruth sat by him glancing over when she thought he didn't see her. She still fretted about his back. It did trouble him some, but she didn't need to go on about it. He did what he had to do.

When he'd gotten back to the house, Obadiah had the ointment and bandages ready and had boiled some water for his tin hot water bottle.

"I'm sorry, Pa," Obadiah said. "I'll try to trust God like you want."

It had been worth the beating for him to hear his son say that. He'd done a lot of praying for the boy lately. Amos and Naomi always turned to God when things went south, but Obadiah struggled with his anger.

Joe pulled a little on the reins. The bend in the road and fir trees up ahead hid anyone who might be further along the way. If anybody saw them, it would hard to explain not having a pass. The beating Colonel Leighton gave him would be nothing compared to what would happen if they were caught.

He pondered on having Naomi write up something, but it would be better to wait. None of their children knew why they went on these weekly wagon rides. Naomi would know soon enough, but it was best not to tell her yet.

Two riders wearing raincoats approached on horseback. Joe's stomach knotted as he pulled up to a stop. The moonlight revealed their bushy mustaches and thin faces. He let out the breath he was holding. They raced in Maysville against Colonel Leighton's horses a few times. At least they weren't from Dover. Master usually only went to Maysville a couple of times a year during racing season, and they wouldn't have an occasion to tell him about this any time soon.

The taller man spoke. "What are you doing out this late, Joe?"

Joe grinned as wide as he could. "Master wanted me and Ruth to take Reverend Thornton one of her fresh baked apple pies."

Ruth uncovered the pie they'd brought along in case they were stopped and waved it in front of them.

The other man leaned forward and sniffed. "Ruth, you make the best pies this side of the Ohio. I'm gonna have to make Colonel Leighton an offer to buy you one of these days. He's a lucky man."

"Thank you, sir," Ruth said. "Next time we're up in Maysville, I'll ask the master if I can fix you one."

The tall man leaned toward them in his saddle. "Boy, you see to it you go right home after you deliver that pie. Wouldn't want no slave catchers coming along bothering you for being out this late."

"Yessur." Joe nodded his head and plastered on his best slave smile. "I'll see to it."

The man stroked his chin. "You know, I think I might just talk to Colonel Leighton. It's not very smart him sending his slaves out after dark like this."

"It be all right," Joe said. "I asked the master if we could take the preacher this pie. He enjoyed Ruth's baking last time he was at the house."

"Well," the other man said, "you be mindful."

"Yessur. I always mindful. Master taught me good."

The men rode off.

Joe wiped his face with his bandana and grabbed hold of Ruth's hand.

Ruth pressed her lips together. "You think they'll say something to Colonel Leighton?"

"It'll be a spell before they see him again. We just got to trust the Good Lord to make them forget by then."

Ruth nodded.

Joe gave the reins a flick and drove the wagon to the parsonage. He helped Ruth down and winced, leaning over to suck in air. Sensing Ruth's glare, he forced himself to straighten and grinned to hide the grimace his pain caused. Ruth's scowl showed him he hadn't been entirely successful. He marched to the cabin perched near a grove of apple trees and a little white church and knocked on the door.

Reverend Thornton, a plump man with a full head of blond hair, answered. Relief swept over his face. "You're late. We were worried."

"We was stopped," Ruth said. "They believed us about the pie." She handed the dish to Reverend Thornton.

"Come on in. It's cold out there." Reverend Thornton smelled the pie before handing it to Mrs. Thornton.

Mrs. Thornton, a woman every bit as plump as her husband, cut them each a piece and poured them some coffee.

"Good thing you thought of making those pies." Reverend Thornton ate a bite. "Not only does it give you a reason to be out without a pass, it makes our weekly visits much more pleasant."

Joe gulped his coffee to settle his nerves and looked Reverend Thornton in the eye, the only white man with whom he dared to do so. "We got trouble. We need your help."

Chapter Eleven

America sat at the pianoforte practicing the hymn she planned to play Sunday. She couldn't seem to focus on the notes. Each time she ran through it, she missed the key change on the tenth measure and played B flat instead of B natural.

A week had gone by without her or her father saying more than two words to each other. She prayed he would change his mind about Naomi and about Oberlin, but God didn't seem to be in a hurry to answer either prayer.

She heard footsteps and glanced up.

With a scowl twisting his mouth, Papa motioned to the settee. "America, we need to talk."

Her shoulders stiffened. He only used her Christian name when he intended to scold her. She moved to the settee and sat beside him. "Go ahead."

"You can't shut me out forever, child. We ought to have this out."

To keep from seeing the disapproval in his eyes, she kept her focus on the collection of horse figurines setting on the mantel over the fireplace. There were six horses in all, each one unique. "I don't see there's any more to say."

"Merry, please. Can't we settle this?"

She almost diverted her eyes toward him. She hated when he was angry with her. "I'm willing to hear what you have to say."

He stood and strolled to the fireplace. Her favorite black ceramic horse sat on the mantle near the center.

"You're my little girl. I love you, and I only want your happiness."

She looked at him. "If that's all you want, you have it in your power. Don't sell Naomi, free your slaves, and give me the money to buy a train ticket to Oberlin in February."

He shook his head. "I can't."

She turned her gaze back to the mantle. The black horse with a white star painted on its forehead reminded her of her father's favorite stallion. This figurine had been there all her life, long before her father purchased his horse. "Papa, please. I have to return to graduate or I won't be accepted by the American Mission Society to go overseas."

"There's no way I'll allow you to go to a heathen country on your own. Get this missionary nonsense out of your head. The sooner you realize it's over, the better off you'll be."

America's chest tightened, but she brushed aside the ache in her heart for now. "What about Naomi?"

"I will not let your radical views ruin us."

She tried to force out what she wanted to say, but the words caught in her throat.

He held out his hand. "If I could see any way out of this, don't you think I would take it? Joe and his family have served me well, but I must sell her if we're to keep the ranch."

A warmth rushed through her. Perhaps she could find a compromise her father would accept. She allowed her eyes to roam from the horses to Papa. "If I could come up with a way, you would relent?"

"Yes, but I see no way around it."

"And the train ticket?"

"No!" He brushed his hand against the back of his neck. "I will not let you return to that school. It turned you against me."

She stared at the horse. "No Papa, it didn't. I love you, but I can't look at something I know to be wrong and call it right, even for you."

"I'm not at fault here. Someday you'll understand. Until then, it is my duty as your father to protect you from such foolishness."

Her mouth gaped. "You believe it foolishness to stand up for what is right and to fulfill God's calling on my life?"

He grabbed the black horse with the white star and threw it across the room.

America flinched as glass shards splintered across the floor.

The vein in Papa's forehead throbbed. "Your calling is what God created every young lady for, to be a wife and a mother."

An image of William sitting on the train beside her flashed through her mind. He wouldn't even know why she didn't return. He'd think she betrayed the cause and her calling. So would Lavena and her other roommates. She couldn't bear the thought of it.

Glass slivers lay next to the figurine's head and one black leg remaining intact. Too many pieces to glue back together. "And He created slaves to serve their masters?"

"Yes."

"Papa, you're wrong."

He strode to her and leaned his face into hers. "I won't listen to any more of this. You'll stay put at home and not fill your pretty little head with matters that don't concern you."

America placed a hand over her stomach to squelch the urge to be sick. What made her think she could ever convince her father of anything? She needed to prepare herself. She would never see Oberlin or William again. What was worse, there would be no escape for Naomi. She shouldn't have ever come back to Kentucky. She had failed.

*****

Colonel Leighton rode Orion, his black stallion, to Dover. He shouldn't have lost his temper, even if his daughter was defiant. She wouldn't even look at him, just kept her eyes locked on the blasted ceramic horse. He'd hoped to come to some kind of understanding with Merry. She always was opinionated for a female, but she used to listen to reason. Now she set her resolve in her opposition to him. One more reason to keep her away from those radicals at Oberlin College.

She might not have agreed with slavery in the past, but she had been practical about it. She understood, her womanly emotions clouded her judgment, and accept he knew best. That blasted school turned her head. Maybe he'd been too lenient with her. He knew she'd taught Naomi to read when she was younger, but he turned a blind eye to it. It seemed such a little thing, and it made her happy.

Other times, she went out of her way to help the slaves, like when she snuck off with Mr. Ricker's youngest slave and took him to Doctor Adams' office. Mr. Ricker didn't want to spend the time or money to treat the slave child with a hurt leg, but he was lucky she'd done it. The leg had been infected, and if it hadn't been for her, he'd have lost a slave. The colonel had punished her, but secretly he couldn't have been more proud. Ricker was a fool.

The colonel had been wrong for letting her get too friendly with them instead of maintaining the master-slave relationship. He could see that now. Luke understood they were different, inferior, but she never did. Slaves were like children who, when they disobeyed, needed discipline. Turning them loose to run amuck wasn't the answer. The slaves would suffer. They wouldn't know how to care for themselves. The way the free black men in the area lived convinced him he was right. They barely scratched out a living. Besides, the economy would suffer.

After resigning from the cavalry, Colonel Leighton had bought the ranch and purchased Joe and Ruth at auction in Maysville. He had needed help, and it made more sense to invest in a couple of slaves than to hire transients.

He knew he'd made the right decision when his wife died. The couple helped him raise his children. He didn't know what he would have done without them, especially the two years he was called up to fight in the Mexican War. Luke was attending Maysville Academy at the time, so the colonel had asked Elizabeth's sister, Sarah, to stay with Merry while he was away, but Sarah was a flighty girl, too busy receiving gentlemen callers and going to dances to be much help.

America was only nine years old at the time. If Joe and Ruth hadn't rallied when Sarah ran off and eloped with that rich Northern dandy, he didn't know what would have happened.

Since the colonel's children were grown, Joe and his family worked as hard as he and Luke did to help him make a go of the ranch. Most slaves did only what was required to keep from getting in trouble. Joe and his sons went beyond the call of duty.

He didn't like this anymore than Joe did, but once glanders disease killed most of his horses, it was only a matter of time before he lost everything. Selling a couple of slaves was the only option. He didn't like selling children away from their parents, but Amos and Naomi were full grown. They weren't children anymore.

He understood why Joe and Obadiah spoke against it, but they went too far. They had no right to challenge him. He had to whip them to maintain his authority. God had given him charge of them just as He had given him the responsibility to care for their needs.

Now his daughter had become rebellious because he hadn't taken her in hand early on. He'd find her a husband so she could concentrate on womanly matters, then she wouldn't have time to spend on this abolitionist foolishness. He spurred his horse on.

Colonel Leighton stopped in front of the cotton mill and tied Orion to the hitching post.

The owner, Harland Boidae, met him at the door. "Colonel Leighton, it's good to see you."

He nodded his greeting. "Is there somewhere we can talk privately?"

"Is this about the matter we discussed last week?"

The colonel cleared his throat. "That and more."

Mr. Boidae led him into the back office where a mahogany desk and banker's chair stood in the center of the room. A matching bookshelf sat against the side wall. A set of *Encyclopaedia Britannica* caught his eye.

Colonel Leighton stepped to the shelves. A book on warfare he'd found helpful was there. Strange, Harland would be interested in military matters. The collection of books on the history of the United States and the law books didn't surprise him. A man going into politics would be interested in those subjects, but to see the novel, *Uncle Tom's Cabin,* and various abolitionist books caused him to scratch his head.

He would have suspected Boidae of being a closet abolitionist if he hadn't noticed materials defending slavery on the next shelf. A collection of *The Debow Review* and *Duties of Christian Masters* by Reverend A.T. Holmes were within easy reach.

On the middle shelf, sat a book on China and a few books about running a textile mill. Most of the volumes were leather bound. The man must have spent a fortune on his library.

Colonel Leighton turned toward Mr. Boidae. "An impressive collection."

"I believe a good library makes a man, and an appropriate wardrobe." Mr. Boidae's grin showed a full set of perfect teeth as he opened the mahogany cigar box resting on the desk. "Cigar?"

Colonel Leighton took a cigar, bit off the end, and lit it as he considered the man before him. He prided himself on being a good judge of character. Mr. Boidae had a difficult time growing up, but he'd persevered. In the last few years, he'd shown himself to be a gentleman and a good businessman.

Colonel Leighton sat in one of two bentwood chairs and enjoyed the fine quality of the cigar he puffed. The aroma filled his nostrils. Normally he smoked a pipe, but Mr. Boidae was known for having cigars made with premium tobacco.

Boidae had good taste in a great many things. He dressed impeccably. Today he wore a burgundy frock coat with a green and burgundy diamond pattern satin vest and matching cravat. His hair, beard, and nails were well trimmed, his boots were polished, and his teeth tried to outdo the sun with their brightness. Maybe that's why Boidae showed them off with his substantial smiles. His charcoal tooth powder certainly worked.

He successfully ran his family cotton mill since his father had taken to his bed. The South needed mills to gain financial independence. Now Mr. Boidae had his eye on a political future, and his business sense and practical outlook on slavery would benefit Kentucky, but the man's smooth politician's smile grated on him.

"I know you're a busy man," Colonel Leighton said. "I'll get right to the point."

"I appreciate it, Sir." That insufferable grin again.

"Should you decide to run in sixty, I'll give my support for your campaign for the US Senate seat, but I'd consider it a favor if you'd hear me out."

"Whatever you want, it's yours."

"This isn't a condition of my support." Colonel Leighton leaned forward. "It helps to have the right wife by your side especially when running for office."

"True." A grimace crossed his features. "Unfortunately, I haven't found a lady worthy of marrying."

"My daughter, America, is home from college."

Boidae's steel-blue eyes darted. "Will she return to Ohio after winter break?"

"No." Colonel Leighton hated this. It felt like he was negotiating the sale of his daughter. "She's twenty-one now. It's time to stay home and find herself a husband."

The slightest grin touched his lips. "Is that so?"

"Not just any man will do. America's bright, and she has an interest in God's work. She'd even considered becoming a missionary."

Mr. Boidae puffed on his cigar. "Colonel Leighton, are you aware I'm president of the Mason County Missionary Society?"

"Yes, I'd heard. Would you do me the honor of coming to supper at my house Sunday? Perhaps you and my daughter could speak of your shared interests."

The smile widened. "I can think of no better way to spend a Sunday afternoon, and please, call me Harland."

Colonel Leighton breathed a sigh of relief. Harland Boidae would make America a good husband. She might even end up as a senator's wife. There she could have influence for these causes of hers but would have Harland's practical views to keep her in rein. As her father, he had to do what was best for her. Eventually, she'd forgive him. After all, he was her father. She might even thank him once she came to her senses.

Chapter Twelve

William helped Reverend Billy, the African church preacher, set upside down pots at the doors and corners of the barn. "How come you set these out every service?"

"This be so if any slave catchers around, they won't hear us. God makes it so the pots catch the sound." Reverend Billy turned a pot over and groaned as he stood.

William reached out to help. "You all right?"

"I better than all right. I'm blessed and highly favored of the Lord. I wear stripes on my back for preaching the Gospel just like the Apostle Paul."

William cleared his throat. "I want to thank you for letting me preach to your congregation these last two weeks. I'm honored to be a part of what God's doing among you."

"The Good Lord sent you, for sure. In two weeks' time, you got half the masters in this county freeing their slaves and offering them work for a share of the crops. As powerful a miracle as freeing the Israelite children from the Egyptians."

"God already had moved on their hearts. He just used me to present the Word."

"I know, but you obeyed Him," Reverend Billy said. "About that other matter, I'll give them who needs it the routes and names you gave me so they can cross over this winter."

"I wish I could do more, but it's best if they wait until the river freezes."

A man and woman entered, and Reverend Billy put his finger to his lips. "We'll jaw some more on it later."

William nodded and walked to the back of the barn. He watched eager faces as Negroes, both slaves and free, piled inside.

Cal had decided it would be better for the Negro church to continue to meet on Sunday mornings when their masters attended church with Reverend Hull. It was the only safe time for them. The clan met afterwards.

In a way, it was fortunate Reverend Hull didn't have a slave balcony in his church. Since he didn't believe slaves had souls, he didn't want them there.

Some masters took precautions to keep their slaves locked up Sunday mornings, but most didn't bother. Men from the church took turns patrolling the woods. Since the patrols didn't know where the meetings were held, the slaves usually were able to avoid them.

Reverend Billy, a man who had bought his own freedom, had been caught a number of times while leading the armed men away from his congregation. He'd been whipped and accused of trying to incite an insurrection of violence among the slaves. The last time they caught him, they nearly beat him to death and threatened to lynch him if it happened again.

Mildred, Reverend Hull's slave mistress, ambled into the barn carrying a toddler with seven children ages three through thirteen trailing behind her. The children had various mixtures of their mother and father, except the toddler who showed no relation in appearance to Reverend Hull.

Reverend Billy had told William she'd never come to the Negro meetings before. She took a great chance coming there today. William prayed God would use him to speak to her heart.

She sat in the corner with her children, away from the others, and leaned against a stall as if she hoped she could blend into the planks and remain unnoticed. Surely, she knew she was safe here.

Reverend Billy sauntered to the back of the barn. "It's time."

The congregation shouted "amen".

"It's time to steal away to Jesus."

Again shouts of agreement.

"Slave catcher can't keep me away from the Good Lord when I steal away to Jesus."

One older Negro woman with a yellow scarf tied around her head started singing. Others joined in, and the soulful praises of the Negro church filled the air. *Steal away, steal away, steal away to Jesus. Steal away, steal away home. I ain't got long to stay here.*

William enjoyed the music they used to praise their Lord. Unlike many white Americans, he loved the variety of styles. He imagined when he made it to the mission field, the Chinese would add their own flavor to worship as well.

Reverend Billy raised his hand. The singing stopped. "Brother Woods be here to give you the Word."

Amens sounded.

"This man, he may be white, but he love our people, and he love our God. You pay heed to his words."

"Yes, Lord," the singer shouted. The others joined with shouts of their own.

William stepped forward and delivered his sermon on the saving power of God. He preached how God would give them freedom in Heaven if they turned to Him, but he spoke of another freedom as well, the freedom we have in Christ here on Earth where there is neither Jew nor Gentile, male nor female, slave nor master.

He ended his message with an invitation to anyone who would like to accept Christ as their Savior to step toward where he waited to pray for them. There was a slight rustling noise, but nobody moved. He waited and watched Mildred.

She blinked her eyes and wiped a tear from her cheek while pressing against the stall. The struggle to make a decision was evident on her face.

Her oldest boy stood and reached a hand in her direction. She clasped it and pulled herself up. Tabitha joined them. Mildred's children trailed behind like ducklings following a mother hen as she stepped between the people sitting on the ground and made her way to the back.

A giddiness rushed through William as he led them in prayer, and they all gave their lives to Christ.

A shout ring gathered in a circle around Mildred and her children. They called out testimonies and praises, rocked back and forth, and danced around. Shouting, laughing, and singing overflowed with intensity.

A tall slender woman with skin the color of coal twirled and swayed in the middle of the group. Her voice filled the building with *Every time I feel the Spirit in my heart, I will pray* and, like a chorus, the group followed her. She tumbled to the floor in a limp heap.

The Spirit of God moved in a way William had never experienced before. Of course, he'd heard of the camp meetings around the turn of the century where crowds of people, both black and white, were overcome with frenzy, but he'd never seen it. These uneducated slaves entered into the throne room of God. Reverend Hull wanted to keep them out, but he never would.

This would be a hard road for Mildred if she decided to scorn Reverend Hull's attentions. Hull didn't seem like the kind of man who would be refused without retaliation. Hopefully she and her children would make the trip across the river. Either way, God would need to be a present help in time of trouble.

After the Negro service let out, William ate lunch and reviewed his notes. His final message for the Price clan's church would begin soon. They were good people even if they were former slave owners.

Many in this county wanted to serve God but didn't understand the truth about slavery. Cal had been one of them and had become a close friend in only two weeks. If only everyone could embrace the truth as he and his clan had. He leaned back in his chair. They'd broken through his attitude toward the South. Perhaps not every slave owner was evil.

His musings rushed toward the train depot in Maysville. Merry seemed to recognize the evils of slavery when they talked on the train, but once she arrived in Kentucky, she proved her words only gave lip service to the cause. His jaw tightened. As much as he was attracted to her, he couldn't risk becoming entangled with a slave owner's daughter.

Cal's voice interrupted his thoughts. "You can stay if you want. We need a preacher who'll speak the whole Word of God."

William shrugged. "I'd like to, but I'm needed elsewhere."

"We've been pondering starting a church, one not run by Reverend Hull and his cronies."

"I can help find you a preacher. I'm on the committee of the Western Reserve Abolitionist Mission Society. They'd be interested in the work here."

"We'd appreciate their help. Figured we'd build a proper church soon as we get the spring thaw." Cal placed his hand on William's shoulder. "We best go in. They're all waiting for your last message."

William clasped his Bible in his hand and entered the barn. He stepped over two boys wrestling with each other and scooted through the crowd, careful not to step on any fingers or toes as he made his way to the back.

He looked out over the faces of these hill folks, each one eager to drink in more of God's Word. Three new families had joined their meetings. At this rate, the barn would soon be full.

William opened the Bible and cleared his throat.

A crash resonated as the door burst open. Reverend Hull stood in the doorway with Gus to his right and Horace to his left. Behind them, what was left of Reverend Hull's congregation, about fifteen men, brandished firearms.

William's chest tightened. *Lord, keep these people safe, and give me wisdom.*

"This meeting is an abomination." Reverend Hull's voice echoed. "Have care for your souls. Don't listen to this heretic."

A murmur carried through the crowd. A few men rose to their feet.

Cal stepped in front of William. "You got no call to bust in. You're on my property, and I don't recollect inviting you."

Reverend Hull looked past Cal and William and addressed the crowd. "Listen to me, all of you. Leave now, and I won't expel you from the church. Come back into the fold." Nobody spoke or moved.

The vein in Hull's neck bulged. He raised his fist in the air. "You've been warned!"

Everyone in the barn kept their gaze fixed on Cal waiting for his lead. Hugh and Jack took positions on either side of their brother.

Cal's hands drew into fists. "You got no right."

Gus and Horace stepped forward and pointed their pistols. The little girl in the yellow dress cried out.

Cal stepped closer to Gus until he was inches from his face. "You gonna shoot me, cousin?"

Gus spit. "I won't let you go against the preacher and our way of life. It ain't right."

The crowd outside muttered, budged closer, threatened to bombard through the door.

Sweat beaded William's forehead. "Stop!" He skirted around Hugh and Jack. "I'm the one you're after. Leave these good people alone. I'll go with you."

Gus snickered. "You're dang right you will. We got a rope on the oak tree out yonder with your name on it."

Chapter Thirteen

America's father stood at the door outside the church with a rueful grin on his face. What was he up to?

"Merry, we're having company for supper."

"Who?"

"Do you remember Harland Boidae?"

"Mr. Levi Boidae's son."

He nodded.

Mr. Boidae had always greeted her at church and, on occasion, had asked her to dance at church socials. A few months before she'd left for Oberlin College, he'd asked to escort her on a buggy ride, but she'd refused. She had no interest in misleading him. She would have refused even if she'd planned to stay in Kentucky. He was always smiling and friendly and was popular with everyone she knew, but something about him made her ill at ease. "Yes, he's a few years older than me."

"A fine gentleman too. Levi retired a couple years ago and deeded the cotton mill to his son."

America skirted out the door and called over her shoulder. "I don't see what his accomplishments have to do with me. We barely know each other."

Papa rushed to help her into the buggy, climbed up, and started down the road.

America listened to the hoof beats of the horse leading them closer to home. Indian summer had ended with the last thunderstorm. The crisp smell and nip of late autumn was in the air. School break rushed by as quickly as yellow leaves swirled across the path.

This was a mess. She'd struggled to accept she might not be able to return to Oberlin or become a missionary. Through many sleepless nights, she yielded to the knowledge that, unless God performed a miracle equal to the parting of the Red Sea, marriage and a life in Kentucky could be in her future but not with Mr. Harland Boidae. She stirred up the courage to tell her father.

"He makes a fine living at the mill," Papa said. "It's an important industry for a prosperous Kentucky. Not many mills in the South have been able to make a go of it."

"I'm happy for him." America turned away.

Papa flicked the reins. "He's a decent man and would be a good provider, and he's the head of the missionary society for all of Mason County. He's God fearing and has the reputation of a gentleman."

America's tongue swiped her lips. "Please don't do this."

"You're the one who's so all fired up about missionary work. I thought you'd appreciate I kept that in mind. He's been fond of you since you were young. I told him you were home. He wants to court you, and I've given my blessing."

"No, Papa."

"You're being stubborn and willful."

"I am not. I could never marry him."

"I know you're fretting about finishing college." He pulled back on the reins and brought the buggy to a stop. "You're not going back to Oberlin. You need to get it in your pretty little head. Why won't you let Harland court you? He would make a fine husband."

A gaggle of geese honked above her as they flew south in formation. "You really don't understand, do you?"

Her father's face softened. He clasped her hands in his. "No child, why don't you tell me?"

"It's not only Oberlin. Papa, he owns slaves. I could never agree to marry a slave owner."

"Merry, I own slaves."

America could no longer hold back the tears. "I know, Papa. I know."

*****

Silence permeated the stale barn air. Nobody took a breath. "There's no need for this." William set his jaw resigning himself to his fate and made his way to the door. "I'll go with you." He stepped over the girl in yellow to approach Reverend Hull.

"You're not all we're after," Reverend Hull said. "These meetings have got to stop. They're a sin against God, Kentucky, and our way of life."

Granny brushed past William, hobbled to the door, and drew close to Reverend Hull's face. "I've been around these parts a lot of years. My pa was friends with Daniel Boone. You gonna tell me about Kentucky and our way of life? You ain't telling me nothing." Granny spit. "I've been on speaking terms with God since before your ma and pa was born, and I'm not the one sinning here."

Gus holstered his revolver.

Granny stepped back and glowered at the mob outside the door. "How 'bout the rest of you? I knowed most of you before you came to be. I helped birth some of you." She pointed to a young man in the back.

"Tom, your misses and young'un wouldn't be alive if it weren't for my midwifing and prayers to the Good Lord. You gonna tell me I'm in the wrong?"

Tom glanced at his feet, mumbled, and moped away. A few men shrugged and followed him.

"What about you, Sam? You said you'd be in my debt for the rest of your born days. You gonna turn on me now?"

Sam, a husky man, whispered with four others. They strode to their horses and rode off. A few more sauntered away as the crowd dispersed.

Reverend Hull ran after some, grabbing them by the arms. "You're not going to desert me because of one old lady? Stay the course, men."

Most didn't answer. A few waved him off.

A heavy balding man with a long beard and a coat made out of animal hides said, "I ain't going against Granny Price. That's like going against God Himself. You're on your own."

Reverend Hull's eyes darted about following the mass exodus like a spooked thoroughbred. His hands curled into fists at his sides, but he said nothing.

Soon Gus and Horace were the only ones left, but their stance didn't exude their earlier bravado. Gus lowered his eyes and stuck his hands in his pockets. Horace leaned his weight from one foot to the other and holstered his gun.

Granny grabbed Gus' ear and led him inside. "Going against your Granny and kin like this. Horace, get over here." Horace scurried to Granny's side. She dropped her cane, grabbed his ear with her other hand, and motioned to William. "Beg this man's pardon. Tell him you're not gonna cause him no more trouble."

Gus' eyes watered. "Yes'um. I beg your pardon, preacher. Sorry we troubled you."

"Me too, preacher," Horace said. "I'm mighty sorry."

William cleared his throat. "I forgive you."

Granny let go of their ears, grabbed her cane, and swatted them both with it a few times. They yelped but didn't make any attempt to avoid it. "Now you two, clear out before we go round and round."

Gus tripped over a hay bale on his way out. Horace helped him up, and they scurried out the door.

Reverend Hull's face turned red, and he rasped out his words. "You think you've won? You haven't. Not one person in this room will be allowed back in the church. Y'all know what that means. Your neighbors will treat you as heathens."

Granny chuckled. "Don't want to come back no how. We're starting our own church. You're welcome anytime, but we'll be getting ourselves another preacher."

Reverend Hull pointed his finger at Granny. "This isn't over."

Chapter Fourteen

America dabbed her cheeks with her handkerchief as her father nudged the horse pulling the buggy. She watched him out of the corner of her eye but pretended not to look his way. At times, he seemed deeply wounded by what she said. His shoulder sagged.

She would be tempted to offer some small gesture like a touch to his hand or a kiss on his cheek, but he would grunt or twist his mouth suggesting it wasn't hurt stirring inside, but anger. When his nostrils flared, she turned away from his gaze and watched a squirrel scurrying across the path.

Dear God, show me what to do. This supper would happen. There was no way around the colonel's orders.

Should she challenge Harland with her views on slavery and hope he changed his mind about her being a suitable mate? Maybe she'd simply and firmly reject his proposal of courtship. Either way, her father would consider it willful disobedience.

Papa didn't say a word when the buggy reached the house. He didn't even take time to help her down, just rushed through the door. "Ruth! Naomi!"

America climbed down from the buggy and slipped through the doorway in time to see the slave women come to the parlor.

Papa tossed his hat onto the foyer table. "No church meeting today. You're staying here."

"Master." Ruth's hand covered her heart. "Did something happen?"

He took a step toward her. "You questioning my word?"

"No sir, never. Just wondering is all."

"You're staying put so you can cook your finest meal, fried chicken, mashed potatoes, and gravy, with apple pie for dessert. Merry's suitor is coming to supper. We got to make a good impression."

"Yessur, it'll be the tastiest meal I ever cooked. Come along, Naomi." She tugged at her daughter's sleeve.

Naomi followed her out the door, but she shot a glance back toward America.

America turned to her father and let out a short breath. "He's not my suitor."

Papa waved his hand. "He will be. We've worked it all out."

She forced out a whisper. "I shall decline."

"I forbid it," he shouted. He wiped his hand over his mouth and softened his tone. "It will be a fine match, and after a proper courtship, you will marry him."

"No, Papa. I may not be able to return to Oberlin, but I won't marry Mr. Boidae."

Her father groaned and placed his hands on his head.

"Sir." Her brother's voice startled her.

"Luke," Papa said, "I thought you were at Virginia's."

Luke shrugged. "We had another argument." One eyebrow lifted. "Looks like I walked into one between the two of you."

"You have a stubborn sister," Papa said.

"She comes by it honest."

Papa snorted.

"I have a suggestion." Luke placed his arm around America. "Why not allow Sis to decide for herself? She might find Mr. Boidae suits her fancy after all."

"Thank you." America crossed her arms. "He decidedly does not."

"Maybe not," Luke said, "but for Father's sake, why not give the man a fair chance. Allow him to court you for a spell."

Papa stroked his beard. "I could agree to that. Merry, I'll drop the entire affair if you allow Mr. Boidae to court you until you get to know him better."

America bit her lip. "How long?"

"Not long. Until Christmas? A month will give him the chance he needs to win you over."

Maybe it would be the solution. If she allowed this, she would gain time to figure out what to do. "I won't deceive him. I'll let him know from the start what my intentions are."

Papa's eyes flashed, but he gave a reticent smile. "The man is mesmerized by your charms. I have no doubt he's up to the challenge. If he isn't, he's not worthy of you."

America strode toward the staircase.

"Merry," her father's voice called out from behind her. "Put on one of your fancy hoop skirt dresses you used to wear before you left for Oberlin."

*****

Merry stormed up the stairs and into her room. The door closed a little harder than needed. Colonel Leighton needed to mention the habit she'd obtained lately of slamming doors. It might be acceptable at that liberal college up north, but here in his home, it was not. That hadn't gone as well as he had hoped, but at least Merry agreed to the courtship, thanks to Luke. Harland would win her over. He packed tobacco into his pipe and sat on the yellow chair by the fireplace.

Luke sat on settee. "Sir, we need to talk."

"I agree. You'll need your own home when you marry Virginia. Mr. Peterson's going to loan us the use of his slaves to help build a suitable house come Spring. Of course, it won't be as nice as I'd hoped, but when we build the ranch back up–"

"Sir," Luke interrupted. "You should have talked to me first."

"I assumed you'd be pleased. You don't want to bring your new bride to live here, do you?"

"Mr. Foster has offered me a job."

Colonel Leighton drew his fist to his mouth. "You don't need a job. You'll inherit this ranch."

"I know, but Virginia's his only child." Luke clasped his fingers together and released them. "He wants to leave the plantation to her husband. He's offered me the position of managing his estate, so when the time comes, I'll know everything there is about running it. If I consent, he's going to have a house built for us on the plantation. He even promised to give us a few household slaves to manage it."

Colonel Leighton swiped a hand over his face. A small house wouldn't be good enough for Foster's daughter. It would be a massive dwelling. The man was offering a bribe to steal Luke away from him and the ranch. "You aren't considering his offer. What about everything we've worked for?"

"That's what Virginia and I have been arguing about. I told her I wanted to raise horses, not manage a plantation."

Colonel Leighton sank into his chair. "And?"

"She says it would be different if the ranch wasn't in trouble." Luke's Adam's apple bulged. "The plantation has thrived even through the financial panic, and there's no reason to believe it won't continue to prosper. You've always taught me to be practical when it comes to business."

"Son, we'll build the ranch back up. This is temporary. You'll see." The pleading tone in his voice disgusted him. "There's something to be said for doing work you enjoy. You love raising horses."

"Mr. Foster gave me until Spring to make up my mind. I have to consider Virginia's feelings in the matter."

Colonel Leighton gripped the sides of his chair. His tone firmed, commanding respect. "I raised you to be the head of your household. You need to take a firm hand now."

Luke paced to the fireplace and back. "I'm sure Virginia will abide by whatever decision I make, but I plan to do what's best for both of us."

"By throwing away the work you love? A supportive wife wouldn't want you to do that."

"She is supportive." He strode again to the fireplace again and leaned against it.

Colonel Leighton rubbed a vein in his forehead. "If you do this, you might as well start wearing hoop skirts because she'll be wearing your trousers."

Luke stormed out of the house, slamming the door behind him.

First Merry, now Luke. Colonel Leighton hadn't seen the storm clouds coming, and now they were threatening to blow his family apart.

Chapter Fifteen

Angry words whispered in the corner of the church caught Joe's attention. He turned to see what the ruckus was. Bart and Izzy, a slave couple who attended the church, were in one of their frequent arguments. Todd, their ten-year-old son, leaned against the wall next to them, his arms crossed and his eyes lowered. He acted like he wanted to crawl under the floor boards.

The African church preacher, Riley, strode next to Joe. "I'm powerful glad you're early. Looks like they're at it again."

Joe glanced at Riley and nodded. "Miss Merry's new suitor is coming to call for supper. Ruth and Naomi's at home fixing a spread. Figured it'd be best to stay out of the way."

The words in the corner grew louder. "I ain't gonna quiet down," Izzy said.

"They need to stop bringing it into God's house." Riley tilted his head, raised one eyebrow, and offered a sideways glare. When he gave the *preacher look*, nothing to be done but do what he wanted.

Joe snorted. "You want me to talk to them?"

"Sure would be nice if you could stop this before anyone else gets here."

Joe sauntered to Bart's side.

Izzy flung her arms around. "You ain't no kind of man."

"Now, Izzy," Bart said.

"If you was, you wouldn't let it happen."

Bart stuffed his hands in his pockets. "What do you want from me, woman?"

Joe got between them and kept his voice at a whisper. "What's wrong with you two? Bringing this into the house of God. Don't you got the sense God gave a mule?"

Izzy stormed out the door.

Obadiah leaned on the wall next to Todd. "Come on. You can sit with me."

Todd nodded.

Obadiah placed a hand on Todd's shoulder and led him to a bench near the front of the church.

Joe was grateful to Obi for helping, but he wished Ruth was here. She was the only one who could handle that contentious woman. He didn't know how Bart put up with her.

Sweat beaded Bart's forehead. "You're right, Joe. Sorry I brought this here."

"You should be. What is it this time?"

Bart glanced down at his feet.

"If you don't want to tell me, fine, but you need to settle it somewhere besides church." Joe turned to go.

"She's right." Bart's voice could barely be heard. "I ain't no kind of man."

Joe stopped. "What are you jabbering about now?"

"I can't hide it no more. It's eating me up inside. Izzy's got call to blow up like she does."

"Spit it out then."

Bart brushed his foot along the floor. "My master's got a hankering for Izzy."

Joe took a step back, bumped a church pew with his knee, and let out a moan.

"Been flitting around her since his pa signed us over to him."

Joe sank onto the bench and rubbed his sore knee. Outside the window behind Bart, Izzy knelt in a bed of yellow leaves, sobbing.

Bart held his hands out. "He's a bad master. Cruel."

Joe shook his head. "I don't want to hear this." He couldn't bear it when there was nothing he could do.

Bart's body sagged low, his bones turning to mush. Something of a man must have remained. He still had the power to stand on his own. "I told her to make him happy, to do what's needful. Told her to make sure we get something out of it."

Joe drew his fist to his mouth. "You gave her to him to get favors?"

"He could take her anyhow," Bart said in a whiney tone as if that excused it. "He likes it better when she don't resist him, when she acts like she wants his attentions."

"How long?"

Bart's voice choked up. "Just about every week for close to two years."

Joe stood and turned away. Things like this happened all the time. It wasn't his never mind. He spun around and grabbed Bart's shirt. "You're her husband. You're supposed to take care of her."

"I do. I see to it we get something from it." Bart pulled away and drew himself up. His backbone made a reappearance, but he still wouldn't look Joe in the eye. "He treats us good cause Izzy makes it nice for him. She could be like the other slave girls he takes and just bear up under it, but I tell her to be smart. We get meat to eat every week, and we gots ourselves a good home, even has a wood floor. It ain't so bad."

"You call yourself a Christian? No wonder Izzy acts like she do.

She's got cause."

"That ain't the worst part." Bart's voice cracked betraying the last morsel of shame he had left. "Two nights ago, Todd busted in on them. He saw."

"Oh, Lord, have mercy."

"Master liked to have whipped my hide off for it. I was supposed to stand guard outside, but I hate hearing the sounds of... You know."

Red spots flashed before Joe's eyes. He pushed Bart into the wall and stormed out of the church past Izzy. The dull ache in his back throbbed. He dropped to the ground under the big apple tree near the top gasping to catch his breath, but he couldn't take his eyes off Bart's wife still weeping at the bottom of the hill in the bed of yellow leaves.

Lord, why you letting me know about this? What am I supposed to do? I got my own kin to fret about.

He needed to sort this out alone. If he saw Bart again before he calmed down, he might give him the beating he deserved. Worthless, no account, not keeping his family safe. Joe folded his arms across his knees and rested his head on them. He didn't keep Amos safe.

Izzy pushed herself to her feet, dusted the leaves off her dress, and hiked into the church. The singing from the congregation trailed up the hill.

Oh, we are pilgrims here below, Down by the river.

Joe couldn't go back. Not now. He rubbed his eyes.

Oh, soon to glory we will go, Down by the riverside.

Reverend Riley got excited enough during the message for his voice to carry enough so Joe caught parts of it, the part about letting go and letting God. Then the shout ring started. The service would end soon. He let out a gasp as he got to his feet and rubbed the lower part of his back. He grabbed a yellow apple, threw it, and let out a heavy sigh. He sauntered down the hill, but by the time he arrived at the church, everyone had left.

Obadiah sat on the steps waiting for him but didn't say anything. They climbed into the wagon, and left for home. The silence didn't last long.

"Todd didn't say hardly two words to me," Obadiah said.

"That right?"

"Every time I see him, he wears a body out jabbering about anything and everything. He looks up to me."

"You're a good friend to him, Obi."

"Not this week. He sat beside me in church, but he wouldn't say nothing. I asked what was going on, and he just shrugged his shoulders."

"Maybe he didn't want to talk." Joe looked straight ahead, but out of the corner of his eye, he could see Obadiah studying him.

"Where were you during church?"

"I went for a walk," Joe said.

"During church?"

Joe kept quiet.

"You never miss church less'n you're sick or Colonel Leighton needs you. What did Bart say? What's going on?"

"Leave it be."

"Leave it be?" Obadiah's pinched lips showed he wouldn't. "Pa, you act like I'm a young'un, but I'm a man. You don't tell me nothing. Give me a chance. I could help."

Joe pulled up on the reins and gazed at his son. "I'm grateful for how you helped with Todd today, but I need to sort this out on my own. A man knows when to back off."

Obadiah ran his hand through his hair and groaned. "All right, Pa." He threw his hands up in one final plea. "I just wish you'd trust me."

"I do, son. I'll tell you all of it, but not yet."

They rode on, and Obi didn't say any more.

Joe wanted to talk to Obi or Ruth about what happened, but he couldn't. It ate him up inside, but it wasn't any of his never mind what a white man did with his slaves. Nothing he could do about it. He let out a sigh already knowing what to do, but the cost of doing the right thing was too high.

Chapter Sixteen

America glanced at the mahogany mantle clock moving its gears at an alarming speed. Half past four. The minute hand moved with a click, but the hour hand must have advanced with the same rate of speed. She wanted to stop it altogether, but even if the hands ceased moving, time would continue to race ahead.

Another click of the minute hand. Twenty-nine minutes to the hour. It would soon strike five. Why did she agree to this farce? No matter. She would summon her courage and state how she viewed slavery. After that, no doubt, Mr. Boidae would run for the hills. Even if he remained after this evening's meal, she would only have to endure this courtship until Christmas when she would end it and never see him again.

What concerned her more was the swiftness of the calendar. The next slave auction was only six days away. Half the remaining balance on the mortgage would be due the following Monday, and her father was still resolute in his plan to sell Naomi.

A knock jostled her back to the present moment. A glance at the clock. 4:37.

"Miss Merry?" Naomi's voice seeped through.

"Come in. It's unlocked."

Naomi entered the room. "I figured you might like me to help you with your hair since you have a gentlemen caller."

"He's not my caller."

"The master said --"

"He forced me into this. He wants me to marry this man."

Naomi shrugged. "Maybe it won't be so bad. He might be a good man like my Riley."

America plopped onto the bed. If only it were William wanting to court her. "He's a slave owner."

"Don't matter. Your pa done made his decision. The only thing you can do is bear up under it best you can."

The minute hand clicked. 4:38. "Oh, Naomi, what are we going to do? The slave auction is only six days away."

Naomi sat on the bed next to her. "There's nothing we can do." She closed her eyes and let out a slow breath. "Riley only raised half of what Colonel Leighton agreed to. He won't get the rest in time. I just got to pray to the Good Lord my next master won't be too far away. If he's close, Riley still might be able to buy my freedom."

She grabbed hold of Naomi's hand. "If he's from somewhere like

Alabama or Mississippi or even Texas?"

Naomi's eyes lowered. "I should be grateful. Most of my kind are sold and shipped away from their kin while they're still young'uns. At least the colonel waited 'til me and Amos was growed." She opened the trunk where America kept her fancy hoop dresses. "Did you want me to smooth out one of these for you to wear?"

Another click. 4:39. "No." America looked in the mirror and admired the yellow wool dress and matching jacket she kept back for Sundays in Oberlin. It didn't have the extravagance of layers of satin and silk material, but the bright color made it pretty in a simple way, and it would be more suited for missionary work. Besides, she didn't have to trap herself in corsets and hoops to wear it. If it wasn't good enough for Mr. Boidae, that was too bad.

Click. 4:40.

America sat at the dressing table. "You can help me with my hair if you would like, but you don't have to. I'm happy with it the way it is."

Naomi smiled. "Before you went off to school, I used to love doing your hair." She grabbed the brush and combs and fixed America's hair in ringlets.

4:50.

If only Riley could find a way to come up with the money. It would be wonderful for Naomi to stand alongside her husband as they ministered together. America always longed for that. She tried to dismiss thoughts of William flooding her mind. It wasn't like they were engaged or even courting. Nothing might have ever been between them even if she returned to Oberlin. Even so, a deep longing to see him again swept over her.

4:58.

She might not be able to escape, but she had to figure a way out for Naomi.

4:59.

Naomi placed the last comb in, but America drew no closer to a solution for either of them.

"You look fine, miss," Naomi said.

The clock chimed a faint bell tone five times.

America let out a sigh. "I guess I can't put this off any longer."

She descended the stairs. A condemned man climbing to the gallows couldn't have dreaded the staircase more. With each step, she drew closer to the inevitable. Maybe she would slip and break her leg. That would put a stop to this farce in a hurry.

She reached the bottom without incident. Harland Boidae and Papa waited at the end of the staircase. Papa scrutinized her dress and raised an eyebrow, but she ignored him. She wasn't going to change.

Mr. Boidae was a fine-looking gentleman, but looks didn't matter to her. Tall and well built, he wore a black frock coat and trousers with a colorful red silk vest and matching cravat. He kept his blond hair and full beard neatly trimmed.

"Miss Leighton." Mr. Boidae bowed his head slightly. "You look lovely this evening."

"Thank you," America said.

"May I escort you to the supper table?" Mr. Boidae extended his arm.

America paused before slipping her arm through it. "Mr. Boidae."

"Please call me Harland."

She glanced over to see her father's beam. "Harland. You may call me America."

Harland escorted her to the dining room and pulled the chair out for her. Papa grinned. Luke winked at her. They were insufferable. Harland looked away for a moment, and she used the opportunity to stick her tongue out at Luke. Her brother smirked.

Harland placed his napkin in his lap. "I was pleased to see you home from Ohio. I thought you had until August before you finished your studies."

"I do," America said.

Her father gave her the glower he delivered when she and Luke were little to warn them correction would be forthcoming.

"I'm confused," Harland said. "Perhaps I was misinformed."

Papa cleared his throat. "She would go back in February if she were to finish, but I have decided to keep her home with me. She isn't returning to Ohio."

America swallowed a sip of water to keep from challenging her father's declaration. Naomi and Ruth dished supper onto the plates.

"I understand you were studying to be a missionary," Harland said.

"Yes, I had planned to do mission work."

"I also have an interest in sharing the Gospel in foreign lands. I'm the director of the Mason County Missionary Society."

"I've heard." So, he was trying to gain favor with a common interest, but no amount of missionary work could make up for him owning slaves. "What does the Mason County Missionary Society do?"

"We endeavor to send money to those going abroad," Harland said. "I plan one day to take a missionary trip overseas to see for myself what good our funds have done."

"Tell me." She forced a tight-lipped smile. "Do you support any missionary work in Africa?"

"No, I don't believe we do. Most of the work we support is in China."

"That's good." America placed her napkin on her lap. "It would be awkward to sponsor a work sharing the Gospel of Christ with the very ones you hold in bondage."

Harland sprayed the gulp of coffee he had drunk, and Luke rushed to his side and swatted him on the back as he fought to gain control.

"America!" Papa snapped.

Harland suppressed his coughing and took a sip of water.

"I apologize for my daughter's bad manners." Papa's glower caused her to gulp.

"Not at all." Harland wiped his face with his napkin. "I should have guessed since you attended Oberlin. You're an abolitionist?"

America nodded.

"I agree with abolitionists in principle. It's not right to abduct Africans and place them in bondage. I'm glad the practice has been outlawed for a good many years."

America snorted. "Yet you own slaves."

Harland gestured with his hand as if he were giving a speech. "I own American slaves, not Africans. My servants were born here as were their parents. If they weren't at my mill, they would be owned by someone else, perhaps a master harsher than me."

"Then you condone slavery," America said.

"No, I don't, but we live in a fallen world, and there are certain practices to which we must adjust ourselves. I certainly wouldn't force a man to own slaves. Each man must do what his conscience dictates until the need for slavery ceases to exist. It's only a matter of time before the South realizes slavery is an institution which must come to an end, maybe even in our lifetimes."

"Here, here," Colonel Leighton said. "Finely stated, Harland."

America rolled her eyes. "You're telling me you believe slavery to be wrong, yet you own slaves? Doesn't that make you a hypocrite?"

"Maybe." Harland flashed a rueful grin. "It's the best I can do with the world we live in. God understands. I do believe in the gradual freeing of slaves. The problem is what to do with them. They'll never be accepted here. I support the principles of the American Colonization Society. I hope to see freed slaves returned to their native Africa in my lifetime."

America had heard of these efforts by some, but she didn't think much of the idea. "As you say, these freed slaves were born in this country as were their parents. Is it right to ship them off to where they don't know the land or the language?"

Papa cleared his throat. "America, we will not bore Harland any longer with your views of abolition." He gave her a look she knew not to defy. "This is not pleasant dinner conversation."

"I'm not offended in the least." Harland cleared his throat and wiped the corners of his mouth with his napkin. "Perhaps it would be best to wait for a more appropriate time to discuss it. America, I hear you enjoy riding horses."

She nodded. "It may not be the most lady-like endeavor, but yes, I do enjoy riding."

"I take pleasure in it too. May I escort you tomorrow? I'm riding by the river. Then we could go into town and have lunch. I'll have my household servants prepare it."

She hated to admit it, but Harland was more agreeable than she had anticipated, and she had agreed to give him a month. Besides, if she followed her father's orders, he might be more receptive to any plan she might propose to delay Naomi's sale.

Time was running out.

Chapter Seventeen

America stood just inside the barn doors and brushed Red's coat with the same intensity she would beat a rug. The mare tilted her ears back and sidestepped in protest, and America softened her strokes. She didn't want to go on this outing with Harland.

He wasn't a bad sort for a slave owner, not what she expected. His understanding of the wrongs of slavery was beginning to blossom. How could she fault him? She was raised in the South, and even though she knew slavery was wrong, the full impact of it didn't weigh on her until after she'd been in Oberlin for a time. Harland hadn't had the same opportunity.

Still, she dreaded telling him he had no hope of winning her hand. Returning to Oberlin and becoming a missionary was her first priority even if her father opposed it. Too cold for a horseback ride anyway.

At least she was wearing sensible clothes. Harland probably wouldn't approve of her Turkish bloomers, but if he wanted this outing to happen, he'd have to accept her mode of dress. She didn't like riding side-saddle, and these clothes allowed her to ride astride. Maybe one look at her outfit would be enough to deter him.

A man's voice. "Miss Merry."

She spun around.

Naomi blushed. Riley stood beside her with a sheepish grin. He appeared skinny even in his heavy tattered wool coat.

"I'm sorry." America set the brush down. "I forgot you were meeting Riley this morning. I'll leave."

"Don't fret, miss." Riley wiped his hands on his patched overalls. "We can go somewhere else. Colonel Leighton said I could spend a spell with Naomi before she's sold."

"Isn't there any way you can come up with the money before Saturday?"

"I don't see how." Riley stuffed his hands in his pockets. "I only got half, and I don't see how a poor colored farmer can get me no more. Even if I was to sell my farm, wouldn't get more than a couple hundred for it. Colonel Leighton says I gots to have it all."

"My papa only needs four hundred to give to the bank next week. He doesn't need the remainder until January. Maybe he'd accept half."

"I pondered on that," Riley said, "but I ain't got no way to get the rest."

"Miss Merry. I know you're trying," Naomi said, "but there's no way out."

"There has to be." America gazed at the horses in stalls at back of the barn trying to find a revelation from God, but all she could see were two roans, a grey mare, and Orion, her papa's favorite black stallion. Papa bought him for next to nothing at a foreclosure... She had an idea. "Riley, you're a man of God."

"Yes'um."

"Do you have enough faith to risk the money you already have?"

"What you got planned, miss?"

"My papa's a businessman. Why not make him an offer?"

"I done told you. He won't take four hundred, and he won't wait 'til I get my hands on the rest."

"He'll wait," America said. "Tell him if you don't get the rest by January twenty-second, you'll forfeit your claim to Naomi, and he can keep the money you already gave him."

"I'll still lose her." Riley grasped hold of Naomi's hand.

"That's where the faith comes in. Papa will agree to it. The way he figures, if you don't come through, he'll have the money and Naomi. The banknote isn't due until the twenty-ninth, and there's an auction every Saturday. He'll still have time to sell her."

"I'm willing if I can have her with me 'til then. Ain't nobody else I want to jump the broom with, even if it only be for a short spell."

Naomi tapped a knuckle against her teeth. "A whole lot of money to lose."

"You're worth it." Riley tugged Naomi toward the door. "Let's go see him."

America accompanied them to the pasture on the hillside a few hundred feet away from the barn. Her father and Obadiah worked repairing a section of fence blown down during the last storm.

Riley cleared his throat. "Sir."

Papa stuck his mallet in the loop on his trousers. "Boy, you got some business with me?"

"Yessur." Riley took off his straw hat.

Obadiah dropped the fence post he was holding and stepped to Naomi's side.

Papa wiped his hands on his bandana. "Speak plain."

Beads of sweat lined Riley's forehead. "Well, sir, I got me half of what you need for me to buy Naomi."

"Then you're wasting my time. Come back when you got the rest, boy."

"Papa, hear him out," America said. "You said you would agree not to sell her if we could come up with a way for you to save the ranch. We think we've found it."

He snorted. "Not with half, you don't, but go ahead and speak your mind, boy. I'm listening."

"Yessur." Riley stared at his hat. "I'll give you half today and take Naomi home with me. If I don't give you the rest by January twenty-second, you can have her back. You'd still have time to sell her."

"If I take her back, what happens to the four hundred you already gave me?"

Riley flashed a grin almost extending beyond his face like he was trying too hard to be amicable about it. "Well, sir, then you keep the money and get Naomi besides. You can't lose."

Papa glanced toward America. "I don't know."

America pleaded with her gaze.

Papa stroked his beard then nodded. "All right, you got yourself a deal. Bring the money Saturday. I'll have the note ready for you to put your x on, and you can take Naomi with you then."

"Yessur." Riley extended his hand. When Papa didn't respond, he wiped it on his jacket. "Could I take her on Sunday? We gonna jump the broom during Sunday meeting."

"It won't matter if you're hitched or not when January rolls around. Slave marriages aren't binding. If you can't pay the note, I'm taking her back."

Obadiah brushed a clump of muddy yellow leaves aside with his boot and grabbed Naomi's arm pulling her part way behind him.

"Yessur." Riley took a step in front of them.

"See you remember, boy."

"Yessur, Colonol Leighton, I will."

Papa turned to Obadiah. "Boy, if you don't want to see the end of my whip, you best be minding that attitude of yours and get back to work."

"Sorry, Master." Obadiah darted to the fence post and grunted as he heaved it off the ground.

Papa glared at Obadiah for a moment then addressed Riley. "You can fetch her before your Sunday meeting, and I'll have the papers ready."

"Thank you, sir."

Riley and Naomi sprinted toward the barn.

Obadiah plunked the post in the hole with more force than necessary.

Papa turned to America. "Looks like you bought them some time." He kissed the top of her head. "This won't change anything. There's no way he'll be able to come up with the rest."

"We'll see."

"Shouldn't you be getting ready for your young man? Go put on a proper dress before he gets here."

America cupped her hand over her mouth. She'd forgotten about Harland.

*****

William rode down West Main Street past the Fleming County Courthouse. The brick building looked regal with its white columns and bell tower. Other than the courthouse, Flemingsburg was a normal town with a few stores, a livery, a hotel, and half a dozen churches.

He rode to one of the brick churches and tied his horse to the hitching post. The parsonage sat next to the church, and he knocked on the door wishing he had more time to visit during this stop.

A gray-haired lady with a dark blue day dress answered the door. "William, oh it's so good to see you. Come in, boy."

William entered and hugged her. "It's good to see you too, Sister Martha. Where's Brother Charles?"

"He's out visiting members of our congregation. He'll be back soon." Martha motioned for William to sit at the oak table near the fireplace and poured him a cup of coffee. "How long can you stay?"

"Not long I'm afraid." William took a sip of coffee and wrapped his hands around the warm cup. "I couldn't resist stopping by to spend the night in a warm bed on my way to a revival I'm holding near Dover. Not to mention one of your fried chicken dinners."

Martha sat across from him. "I'm glad you came. I know you'll be here in a couple of weeks for camp meeting, but this gives us a little time to visit. Brother Charles and I haven't seen you since your father's funeral." She looked down. "I was sorry to hear about his loss."

William swallowed a gulp of coffee to keep his emotions tamped down. "Father and Mother thought highly of both of you. How are things faring at the church?"

Martha gave him a shrug. "You know Brother Charles. He likes to ruffle feathers, very much like you," she patted his hand, "but this town is better than most in Kentucky. There aren't many slave owners, and many of the townsfolk are abolitionists, so we don't have much trouble."

"I'm glad to hear it."

"What about you?" One side of Martha's mouth turned up. "You graduate and head for China in August. Have you met the right lady to marry and take along with you?"

William couldn't help the chuckle escaping his lips. Martha always was a matchmaker. "I thought I'd found the perfect lady. She also wants to be a missionary in China, and she'll also graduate in August."

Martha raised an eyebrow. "Thought you'd found her? Why don't you tell me a little about her? Why doesn't she meet your high standards?"

Heat rushed up William's spine at the rebuke. Martha was his mother's best friend and the only woman who could chastise him like his mother had. Both of them had often chided him for his judgmental attitude. "This is different. She has a major flaw I can't abide no matter how attracted I am to her."

"So, you are attracted to her?" The lilt in hear voice showed she wasn't going to let this drop until he told her the whole story. "What's her name?"

"America Leighton, and it's hard not to be drawn to her. She's a beautiful woman, but not only beautiful on the outside. The devotion she has for God lights her countenance."

Martha drank a sip of coffee. "Does she know you're interested in her?"

"I'm not." William kneaded the back of his neck. "I mean I was, but I wasn't going to tell her this soon. I didn't want to court anyone until graduation was closer. To tell the truth, until I met her, I had my heart set on remaining single for the same reasons the Apostle Paul listed in First Corinthians. It would be better to travel to China without a wife and family to worry about. I still believe it's the best course."

She raised an eyebrow. "Sounds like you fancy her to get this flustered."

"I'm not flustered." He cringed at his high-pitched tone. "It's better I don't marry."

"I see." Martha rested her arms on the table and gazed at him for a few moments before she said any more. "So, what is this horrible flaw? Does she keep her mouth open when she chews? Or maybe she has an annoying habit of sticking out her tongue when she's nervous."

He tugged at his collar as an image of Merry stuffing her carpetbag under the train seat flittered through his mind. "She does stick her tongue out, but I find the habit rather endearing."

"Only someone in love would find that endearing."

He cleared his throat and glared at her.

She ignored him. "If you don't mind her wayward tongue, what has your dander up?"

William leaned back in his chair. "She claims to be an abolitionist, but her father owns slaves."

Martha crossed her arms and gave him a glower making him half expect her to grab him by the ear and take him to the woodshed. "William Washington Woods. Did it ever even cross your mind I'm an abolitionist and my father owns slaves?"

"That's different." He hated the way he sounded, like a naughty schoolboy trying to defend his misdeeds. He took a breath and let it out to collect his thoughts. "She says she came to Kentucky this winter break to confront her father and try to get him to free his slaves, but as soon as she got off the train, she started ordering those slaves around like she was a spoiled princess. After what happened with my father, I can't allow myself to risk becoming too fond of her."

Martha patted his hand. "My dear boy, it's as obvious as the nose on your face you're already in love with her."

"I can't be." He placed his hands in his face.

Martha stood and placed her hand on his shoulder. "You're condemning her about things you couldn't possibly understand. Everyone you know is an abolitionist and supports what you're doing. Your father even died for the cause. It's different with Sister America. She's been raised in a slave holding family. For her to go to an abolitionist college like Oberlin says a lot."

"She may attend Oberlin, but she didn't end her ties with her family like you did. I don't completely trust her commitment to the cause."

"It's easy for you to judge. You're a man. It takes courage for her to be willing to face her father about his slaves. It took me years before I was able."

"Still you were willing to end your relationship with your family. I'm not sure she'd be so inclined."

Martha placed her hand on William's. "You don't know what it's like for a woman with no husband or father to provide for her. My father disowned me and sent me away with only the clothes on my back. If Charles hadn't married me, I would have been destitute. Sister America will have no recourse if she's thrown out."

"I never realized." William's throat thickened. "Do you really think Sister Merry's father would reject her if she goes against him?"

"I don't know, but surely the thought has crossed her mind. She needs your support and compassion, not your condemnation."

His cheeks burned. "I need to pray some more about it."

"You'd better pray quick, or you might be too late." Martha squeezed his hand. "If she graduates in August, she'll be looking for a husband to go with her to the mission field. From what you said, I don't think she'll have any problem finding suitors."

William shot a glance toward Martha. He never thought about

having any competition.

Chapter Eighteen

America led her horse, Red, and a grey mare to the front of the house and tied them to the porch rail before stepping onto the porch and opening the door. "Aunt Ruth."

Ruth hurried outside. "Is he here?"

"Not yet, but he should be shortly."

"It's a might cold to wait here on the porch."

"I don't want him coming inside." America plunked onto the porch swing.

Ruth sat beside her and wrapped a shawl around her head and the shoulders of her worn wool coat. "He seems like a fine gentleman."

America rolled her eyes. "Are you trying to marry me off too?"

"Don't you look at me that way, child. Your pa's bound to see you hitched, and you could do worse than Mr. Harland Boidae."

America looked away.

Ruth patted her hand. "Naomi and Riley stopped by. It was a fine thing you did for them."

"We still need to get the money, or they won't be together very long."

"Don't expect that'll happen. At least they'll have a couple of months."

"Haven't you heard? With God, all things are possible." She repeated William's words, but they rang hollow in her ears.

"You talking about the white man's God. Don't always work out that way with colored folk."

America swallowed. It was hard to argue with her point, although she hadn't had much luck with God answering her prayers lately either. "You'll see. God will make a way. I side-saddled the grey mare for you."

Ruth put her hands on her hips. "Miss Merry, there be no need for you to do all that. I could have got along."

Harland rode up on his spotted horse and dismounted. The man even wore a suit to go riding although this time it was riding attire. He wore a short brown jacket, a riding cap, and long black boots. He dressed the part of a rich, pompous slave owner.

"Good day, America." He perused her Turkish bloomers. "Am I early? I thought you'd be dressed by now."

"I am ready."

"Oh, I see. I hope it's not too cold. If you like, I could go to town and get my buggy?"

America strode to where she had tied the horses earlier. A breeze whipped her face. She shivered and shook off the chill. "I'll be fine. I dressed for the weather. Aunt Ruth's accompanying us as a chaperone."

Harland helped America mount and tossed a glance back at Ruth. "We'll keep it at a lope. It's only a mile. Your slave can follow on foot."

Heat rose up the back of America's neck. "She'll ride."

"You can't be serious. I am not riding with a Negro."

Heat flashed up America's back. "If she doesn't, I'm not going." She dismounted and led the horse toward the stable.

Harland raised his hands. "Fine, but she can keep her mount a respectable distance behind us."

America took in a short breath and climbed back onto Red. The slave owner was showing his true colors after all. She would go on this outing because she promised Papa, but she would let Mr. Harland Boidae know he had no chance of winning her. If he insisted on continuing with this, when Christmas came, they were through.

They rode to a clearing near the bottom of the hill at the bank of the Ohio River. At least Harland got one thing right. He had picked her favorite spot. From here, she could easily see the Ohio shore. Buildings lined the riverfront in Ripley, and the sign for the foundry was clearly visible. Further back, a brick house sat at the top of the hill. There was something about that home and the steps leading to it.

Harland flashed a disarming grin almost too big for his face. "I was beginning to think you didn't know how to smile."

"I was admiring the view."

"Then you approve of my choice of location."

She nodded.

"Why don't we take a walk by the river and let your father's slave stay here?"

"Perhaps it would be best." She could let him know her intentions before this went too far.

Ruth caught up with them, and they dismounted and secured their horses to a nearby spruce.

"Aunt Ruth," America said. "You stay here. We're going for a walk."

"Miss America, I can't abide it. The colonel told me to keep you in my sights."

"Girl, you going against what your mistress said?" Harland took a step toward Ruth. "Maybe you need a whipping."

America moved in front of her. "She's doing what her master told her." She turned to Ruth and held her hands. "I promise we won't go far, and we'll stay where you can see us."

Ruth pressed her lips together and nodded.

They strolled down the path leading to the riverbank. It would have been a pleasant walk if not for the company. The trees and foliage were mostly pine and spruce with a few hickory and burr oaks mixed in. The trail looked well used, but the brush blocked the view of the riverbank until they were almost upon it. The fragrance of pine and dried leaves in the air mixed with the scent of the river, but the fury she felt toward Harland after he threatened Ruth wouldn't let her enjoy it.

Harland's blue eyes gazed at her, like cold steel. They reflected light but contained no heat, no fervor.

She shivered and pulled her jacket in tighter. Kentucky winters arrived later and were less harsh than in the Western Reserve, but the nip in the air reminded her it would soon be here.

He took her hand in his, and it took everything within her not to pull it away. "I've asked your father for permission to court you. I've admired you since our first dance together at the church picnic, but when you decided to go away to college in Ohio, I kept my peace-- until now. When I heard you returned, I knew now was the time to speak."

She cursed the promise she'd made to her father. "I shall allow you to court me, but-"

A grin beamed across Harland's face. "This is wonderful. I hoped you'd say yes, that you felt the same. You don't know how long I've prayed for you to return home. I can admit it now. I've been fond of you for years. Your zest for life, your intellect and beauty, your commitment to God."

"Please, let me continue."

"I am going on. Please forgive me." His face reddened. "What did you want to say?"

It hadn't escaped her notice he was interested before she left Kentucky, but he never mentioned it, and the idea of him coming to call didn't set well. Besides, she felt compelled to go to Oberlin. She didn't know his feelings ran this deep. Most men showed passion in their gaze, but not Harland. Maybe the tragedy he suffered as a child caused him to mask his emotions. She pulled her hand away. "I must tell you the reason I'm agreeing to this."

"Yes, my dear."

Her tongue swiped her lips. "I don't have any affection for you, and even if I did, I would not yield to those feelings."

Harland's smile slipped. "I don't understand. Why?"

"I have the call to be a missionary. I want to return to Oberlin."

"Colonel Leighton said you weren't going back. He said you would enter into marriage as soon as you found someone suitable. I'd hoped it would be me."

"My papa refuses to let me finish my education. He wants me to stay here. I'm trying to change his mind, but even if I don't, I wouldn't allow you to woo me."

Harland's jaw clenched. "Colonel Leighton led me to believe you agreed to all this. If you feel this way, why did you come with me on this outing?"

America fixed her eyes on an eagle flying over the river toward the house on the hill. If only she could fly across the Ohio as easily. She wished she'd never crossed into Kentucky. "I made an agreement with him to allow you to court me for one month. He hopes you'll win my hand."

"Then there's hope."

"I shall never marry a man who own slaves."

Harland's mouth tightened into grimace. A few seconds passed. "I told you I don't agree with slavery, and I treat my slaves well." His soothing voice didn't cool the steel in his eyes.

"Like you treated Aunt Ruth? Wanting her to walk to the river while we rode? Then when she insisted on staying with us as my father ordered, you threatened to have her whipped."

Harland kept quiet for a moment longer than America expected before giving a half grin. "You're right. I behaved badly. I'm striving to change, but it's difficult. Negros are different than we are."

"Would it surprise you to know I went to school with coloreds? We even ate in the same dining hall and went to church meetings together. One black man in Oberlin, Mr. Langston, is a lawyer for white folks as well as coloreds. They're made in God's image just as we are."

Harland's mouth dropped open. "I can see why Colonel Leighton doesn't want you to return."

"Now you know why it would never work between us."

Harland shook his head. "A lawyer? Is his father white?"

America turned and marched to the clearing with Harland at her heels.

"I only meant to say... It's just God made whites more intelligent than coloreds. Oh, America, will you listen for a moment?"

She stopped, but nothing he could say would make any difference.

Harland motioned for her to sit with him on a felled tree. "I'm trying to grasp this. You must realize how shocking it is."

"Not in Oberlin."

"Does it make any difference I've planned to free my slaves within the next five years?"

America drew her hand to her mouth. Did it?

"I would've freed them earlier," Harland eyes darted to the right. "I just gained ownership of them a couple of years ago when my father became too ill to run the mill. He deeded his holdings to me. I didn't want to act hastily and leave these men and women destitute. That would be worse than the bondage they're under now."

"I appreciate you sharing this with me, but I'm called to mission work, not to become a mill owner's wife."

Harland placed her hand in his. "My future plans include more than owning a mill. I've been asked to run for a United States Senate seat next year. Imagine how I can help with the issue of slavery then."

America brushed some red leaves and pinecones aside with her foot.

"You may be wrong about what God wants for your life," Harland said. "Perhaps God's will is for you to stay here and assist me in ending slavery for good."

She stood and paced a few feet away. "No, you're wrong." A gust of wind stirred leaves onto the path. She wrapped her arms tight around herself to guard against the chill. "I'm glad you're running for the senate, and I wish you well in your endeavors to end slavery, but God plans for me to be a missionary."

The leaves rustled as Harland stepped behind her. "Changing the law and ending slavery in Kentucky may be the greatest missionary endeavor of all. You could still support missionary work as I do. Would you at least consider it?"

No! She took another step away. God called her to be a missionary, but if her father didn't change his mind... Could she have misread God's intentions like she had Harland's? Better to wait and see where this would lead. She turned to face him. "You still want to court me?"

Harland's smile allowed his full set of white teeth to show. "You're still as fiery and opinionated as you were when you left. Give me a month."

"I have no choice. I promised Papa."

"I want to hear more about your views of equality among the races. Perhaps we could converse on the matter during lunch."

America shrugged. Harland was a persuasive man.

*****

Joe dug a shovel into a pile of horse manure in a stall at the back of the barn. A noise echoed through the stall, he glanced up.

Riley took off his straw hat. "Sir, we need to talk."

Joe propped the shovel against the wall and wiped his hands on his trousers. "Speak your peace."

"Miss Leighton came up with a plan for me to have more time to buy Naomi's freedom."

"Did she now?" For a white woman, she never ceased to amaze him.

"Colonel Leighton's letting me take Naomi now if I pay him the money I already got. He's giving me two months to get the rest."

Joe snorted. "You ain't gonna get that money in two years, let alone two months."

"I know, but what else can I do?"

"You still willing to take off with her if you don't get it in time?"

"You know I am."

"When are you coming for her?"

"I sign the papers Sunday. Figured we'd jump the broom at church if it's all right with you?"

Joe placed his hand on Riley's shoulder. "You make sure you do what you have to. You keep my little girl safe."

"I will, sir. You have my word."

"Then you got my blessing." Joe grabbed the shovel.

Riley paused and looked at his feet.

"Something else you want to say?" Joe asked.

"It's about Bart."

"Yeah, what about him?"

"He came to me after church, told me what happened."

Joe dug the shovel into the pile of dung.

"He feels bad. He knows he done wrong, but he don't know what to do now. He needs a friend." Riley's expression turned from a humble Negro farmer asking for his girl's hand to the anointed preacher who delivered God's Word with power.

"That sorry excuse for a man needs a kick where the sun don't shine."

Riley snorted. "Yeah, that too."

"What do you want from me? He got himself into this."

"True, but Izzy and Todd are the ones suffering."

Joe flushed. He didn't like when the preacher's look was directed toward him. "At least he gets his belly full of meat every week. Should be enough for him."

"Maybe you could help them?"

"Too risky. His master would tear up these woods if they was to run off."

Riley crossed his arms and gave the sideways glare.

Joe glanced down at the dung he was standing in. The stench had a way of seeping into his pores. It would take days to get rid of it. "All right, but they'll have to wait 'til the river freezes. I ain't putting nobody in harm's way to fetch them."

Riley beamed and slapped him on the back.

Joe winced.

"Sorry. Forgot about your back. Are you gonna warn Colonel Leighton?"

"No, I ain't taking another beating to tell the master how some white man treats his slaves. He wouldn't listen to me no how."

"You're not gonna do nothing to protect that girl?"

"I'll pray for her, but I can't do no more. I got my own kin to fret about."

Chapter Nineteen

Saturday evening, America rode in the wagon with Joe and Ruth. At first, her father didn't want her to go, but she insisted. He agreed but only if Joe took her. He didn't want her out after dark without an escort. He wrote a pass for his slaves in case they ran into difficulty.

America had been looking forward to the Saturday evening prayer meeting. Before she left for Oberlin, she'd often joined Reverend and Mrs. Thornton and a few others on Saturday nights. This week, she had a lot to pray about.

Tomorrow Riley and Naomi would be married. They would have a great life together if she could find a way to help them raise the money, but how could they come up with the funds so soon?

Naomi wasn't the only thing troubling her thoughts. She missed Oberlin and longed to return. She'd learned about Oberlin College from Reverend and Mrs. Thornton. They had been graduates of the school, and Reverend Thornton had even helped persuade her father to let her attend. Hopefully he would talk to her father on her behalf again.

She also wanted to seek their counsel about Harland. It surprised her how much she enjoyed his company over the last couple of weeks. He had shared with her his plans to go to China on a mission's trip in a few years. She'd started to become fond of him when his zeal for a Kentucky free of slaves became evident, and she hoped he'd win the election for the US Senate. An abolitionist from Kentucky would further the cause.

His views had not yet become as liberal as her own on the issue, but he hadn't had the privilege of attending Oberlin and having a new world open to him as she had.

She remembered the first day of classes.

*****

America had stared in awe at Tappan Hall, the five-story brick building full of classrooms in College Park. She'd never been in a building so tall before. She'd hurried through the door to catch up with her new roommate, Lavena Falcon, and dropped her books on the floor.

Lavena reached down to help her pick them up. "We're going to be late for our first class." Lavena rushed toward everything. She even talked fast with that strange New York accent.

America stood and adjusted the stack of books. "We have time.

You're always in such a hurry."

"I want to get a seat in the front row. Imagine it, America. We'll be going to classes with men and taking some of the same courses."

"I hope I can keep up. We aren't as smart as they are. I don't want to look foolish."

"We are too. You need to rid yourself of provincial thinking. God created men and women as equals. Remember what Galatians says about there being no Jew or Greek, slave or free, male or female in the Kingdom of God?"

America gaped at Lavena. She'd never heard anything like this before. "But... but God created women to marry, have babies, and take care of the home."

"I thought you came to Oberlin because God called you to be a missionary."

"Yes." America climbed the stairs to catch up with Lavena who'd already reached the second-floor landing. "I... I planned to study so I could be a missionary's wife, so I could help my husband on the mission field. I never thought I might..."

"Are you going to ignore the verse in the Bible clearly saying women are equal with men?"

America's mind reeled. She'd never heard Bible interpreted like that before, but it did plainly say, in the Kingdom of God, there was no male or female. "You're confusing me."

Lavena stopped on the third-floor landing to wait for her to catch up. "What if you don't find a missionary to marry? Are you going to reject your calling because you can't find a man to hide behind? Maybe God wants you to go to the mission field alone."

"Shouldn't I look for the right husband to go with me?"

"If God wants you to marry a missionary, isn't He capable of bringing the right man along?"

"Yes, I suppose so."

"Then you don't have to help him, do you?" Lavena increased her pace again and climbed the fourth flight.

"No." America scampered to keep up. Why did her roommate have to walk so fast? She was glad her class wasn't on the fifth floor.

Lavena started down the hall. "I plan to never marry."

America stopped short. She tried to speak, but no words came out.

Lavena turned and gazed at America with one corner of her mouth turned up. "I'm devoting my life to helping slaves gain their freedom and securing property rights and the right to vote for women. I plan to become a female journalist and influence culture with the written word. If God brings a man along who will support those endeavors, I'll consider marriage, but I won't have children."

"You can't be serious."

"Oh, but I am. A whole new world is opening up. Consider there are choices for women we never had before, and allow God to lead you."

America leaned against the wall to steady herself and took a deep breath. She'd opened a door to a domain she'd never known existed. Had it been there all along? One thing was certain, she could never again pretend this new territory she'd wandered into didn't exist.

She followed Lavena into the classroom where Greek New Testament was held. Two black men sat at desks with their books open and papers, quills, and bottles of ink before them. She couldn't keep from staring at them. She knew Oberlin College allowed Negros to become students, but she'd assumed they'd be in a separate section in the back or maybe even have different classes.

She slipped into the seat at the desk next to Lavena and whispered, "I didn't know coloreds would be allowed to sit up front with us."

"They also eat with us and go to church with us," Lavena said. "Coloreds should be treated with the same respect as their white brothers and sisters. One reason I came to Oberlin is Father Finney believes God created all people equal."

America hadn't heard a word said during class that day. Her head had swirled with strange new concepts.

*****

America roused herself from her thoughts. She didn't want to journey to China for only a year as Harland had proposed. God had placed in her a desire to spend her life on the mission field. She'd allowed herself to daydream about working there alongside William, but she would go regardless. She had to find a way back to Oberlin. Perhaps Papa would listen to Reverend and Mrs. Thornton. She had to convince them to speak in her behalf again.

Joe helped her out of the wagon. "Would it be all right for me to take a ride while you and Ruth's at church praying?"

Her arm slightly above her wrist itched, and she reached down to scratch it. A big fat tick was embedded there. Ooh. Snarling up her nose at the disgusting bug, she squeezed it, pulled it out, and threw it on the ground. "That would be fine. You have the pass the colonel wrote out. Meet me back here in a couple of hours."

America looked inside the church. Nobody was there. She traipsed through the grass to the cabin and glanced back. Ruth lingered behind and whispered something to Joe. America rounded the corner to the front log house. She heard William's voice and froze.

"Brother Benjamin, it's good to see you again."

Her stomach fluttered, and she backed up a step. William Woods? Here?

Reverend Thornton spoke. "You too, Brother William. I was so sorry to hear of your father's passing. He was a good man who gave his life for the cause. I miss him."

Her face flushed. Why was he here, and why didn't Reverend Thornton mention he knew him?

"We all do. I'm glad you wrote me."

"I know your desire to carry on in your father's footsteps..."

She started to step out of the shadows.

"...and rescue slaves. I knew you would want to help."

She stopped and drew her hand to her mouth. Rescue slaves? Reverend Thornton and William? She stepped back and bumped into Ruth.

Ruth noisily cleared her throat.

"America." Reverend Thornton's eyes narrowed. "I didn't see you there."

"I didn't mean to eavesdrop." Her tongue swiped at her lips. "I went to the church first."

William's jaw twitched. "Sister Merry, how much did you hear?"

"Enough to know you two are in some plot to rescue slaves."

William threw Reverend Thornton a furtive glance.

"You're still trying to get yourself lynched, aren't you, Brother William?" She'd never been angrier at anyone in her life -- and more scared. "I can't believe you would bring Reverend Thornton in on your plans."

"America," Reverend Thornton said. "Brother William is here at my request."

William placed his hand on her arm and led her into the cabin. "We need to talk inside before anyone else hears."

"I'll stay out here on the porch, miss," Ruth said.

Reverend Thornton placed a hand on Ruth's shoulder. "It'll be okay."

Ruth nodded.

"Aunt Ruth?" America raised an eyebrow. "Do you know what's going on here?"

The slave nanny lowered her eyes.

"Maybe you best come too." America grabbed Ruth's arm and followed William and Reverend Thornton inside.

Slavery was wrong, a sin against God. In Deuteronomy, God

commanded them to hide fugitive slaves, but this was different. They were stealing slaves from their masters, and it looked like her slave nanny was a part of it. What they were doing was dangerous and against the law.

Chapter Twenty

Joe skulked into the barn and whispered, "Nancy, you there? It's Joe."

A young black woman barely seventeen scooted out from behind the hay stacks in the corner. "Thank God. That preacher said you'd come and fetch us, but I was afeared." She sniffed and wiped a tear from her eye.

Two young boys around five and three ran out and grabbed hold of her skirt. They stared at Joe with wide eyes.

Joe saw the fear in Nancy's eyes, wrapped his arms around her, and let her cry on his shoulder. "It be all right now. You got to be strong for your boys."

Nancy pulled back, wiped her face with a bandana, and blew her nose. "I wouldn't be trying this if the master weren't gonna be selling my boys from me. It's hard hiding out from the slave catchers, not sure who I can trust."

"We're only a couple miles from the Ohio. You'll be across before you know it."

"We come clear from Georgia. It's been near on two months since we ran off."

Joe touched her arm. "We got to hurry. I got to be back here within a couple of hours."

"What do we do?"

Joe let out a grunt as he lifted a board off the back of the wagon to reveal a hollow compartment. "It'll be cramped, but it ain't far."

"Mama, I'm afeared," the oldest boy said.

"It be all right, Micah." Nancy lifted him into the compartment. "It's just like we's playing a game of hide-go-seek like we did when the catchers was hunting, but you got to be quiet so they don't find us."

"I will, Mama."

"You're my big boy helping me with your little brother the way you done. You'll be fine, just fine. We all will."

Joe lifted the youngest boy up. The oldest boy crawled in, and Nancy squeezed in beside them.

After replacing the board, Joe covered the back of the wagon with horse blankets and climbed onto the front. "It won't be long now." He flicked the reins, and the horses trotted along the path to the river.

*****

William stroked his chin. Merry stood there, arms crossed, with fire in her eyes and a scowl on her face. She'd never looked more appealing. He wasn't sure if she was angry, scared, or shocked, probably a combination of the three, but she had to be dealt with before she told anyone else about their plans. She declared herself an abolitionist. He would tell her the truth and test her commitment to the cause.

It was a risk. If he was wrong, not only would his heart break in a way he hadn't expected, but he would endanger the Thorntons and every runaway slave expected to show up, not to mention Joe and Ruth. He let up a silent prayer.

Ruth propped herself against the wall. She looked like she'd crawl into it if she could. She had reason to be frightened. They risked prison, but if she or Joe were caught... He didn't even want to think of the danger they were in if Merry decided to expose them.

Benjamin spoke first. "America, sit down."

Merry eased into the chair by the fireplace, her gaze still fixed on William.

"Adela," Benjamin called to his wife who sat by the fire. "Make us some coffee please."

Adela patted Merry's shoulder as she passed and blew out a candle setting on the windowsill before filling the pot with water.

Benjamin sat beside Merry. William faced her and tried to decide how she would react to the truth. He hoped she would be the courageous woman Martha claimed she was, but she was a Southerner and a slave owner's daughter.

Merry turned to Benjamin. "What's going on here? Are you a part of the Underground Railroad?"

"Before I speak," Benjamin said, "I must have your word you won't repeat anything we say here, no matter how troubling."

"Troubling? A good word for it." Merry bit her bottom lip. "All right. No matter what y'all are plotting, I have no desire to see any of you arrested or worse. You have my word."

William released the breath he was holding. He didn't like the way the fire in her eyes made his knees wobble. His feelings for her complicated things.

Benjamin stood and strode to Adela's side. "Brother William, why don't you explain what's going on to America?"

"How much should I tell her?"

"All of it," Benjamin said. "I trust her with my life. Don't you?"

It seemed an odd question, as if Benjamin knew the affection William struggled with even though he'd never mentioned her. There was a bond between them from that day on the steps of First Church. Martha had been right. He loved her, even if he did have doubts.

He looked into Merry's blue eyes still boring through him, and the supper Adela fed him earlier soured in his stomach. "Ten years ago, Brother Benjamin worked as an assistant to my father when he attended Oberlin. He even lived with us a couple of years."

"Professor Woods?" America's features softened, and she touched his hand. "I'm sorry."

Grief choked out the words he wanted to say.

"I worked as a student teacher and research assistant," Benjamin said. William was grateful for giving him a moment to collect himself. "Professor Woods was a great man. Brother William is very much like him."

William's voice thickened. "Thank you. You could give me no higher praise." He cleared his throat. "Brother Benjamin is a conductor on the Underground Railroad. Surely you knew he opposes slavery."

Her gaze darted to Benjamin then back to him. "Of course, but he doesn't take an open stand from the pulpit. I never dreamed he would be so involved with the movement."

"He doesn't openly preach against it because he doesn't want anyone suspecting he works with Reverend Rankin."

Merry ran her hand across her mouth. "Reverend John Rankin? The abolitionist across the river?"

"Brother Benjamin hides slaves until he can conduct safe passage over the Ohio at night. The slaves make their way to Reverend Rankin's house on the other side where they'll seek shelter."

"The house on the hill?"

William wiped his hand through his hair. How did she know? "Yes, the house on the hill. It's visible to everyone. The slaves find it easily. Reverend Rankin hangs a lantern from his doorstep when it's safe to cross."

"What does Aunt Ruth have to do with any of this?"

Benjamin glanced over at Ruth, and she nodded. "Ruth and Joe let us know when the lantern's lit, and they use your father's wagon to transport escaped slaves to the river."

Merry turned stunned eyes to William. "Why did Reverend Thornton contact you? What do you have to do with all this? You don't live in Kentucky."

"No, I don't, but he knows I travel here during winter break as a circuit preacher."

Adela handed William a cup of coffee. He gulped it as he collected his thoughts. He still couldn't gauge her reaction. She was shocked, he could see, but would she accept the righteousness of their actions or turn on them? If only he knew for sure.

"January's the best time to cross," Benjamin said. "The river will freeze over in about a month. It's better when they can walk across."

Merry tilted her head toward William, and a loose strawberry blond curl fell into her face. He had the urge to tuck it back in but resisted. She set her coffee cup in her saucer, and it rattled.

"Everywhere I go to preach," William said, "I'm contacting slaves to let them know where the safe houses are, and if they find their way to Brother Benjamin's, they'll have a route of escape across the Ohio. I also let them know about the signal Sister Adela devised."

"Signal?"

Adela tilted her head toward the blown-out candle. "When it is safe, I place a lit candle in the right corner of the window."

Merry glanced toward the window. "That's why you blew it out when I came in. What if one of the slaves tell?"

"They won't," William said. "We're careful."

"It's so dangerous," Merry said. "What if they catch you?"

William gulped hot coffee. It burned going down his throat. "Sister Merry, you told me yourself, I'll probably be lynched for preaching abolition in the South. I can't die twice."

A groan escaped Merry's throat. "What about Uncle Joe and Aunt Ruth? I shudder to think what would happen to them."

Ruth sat beside Merry and took hold of her hands. "We done decided already, if we get caught, so be it."

Merry laid her head on Ruth's shoulder. "I don't understand. If you're going to put yourself in harm's way, why not cross the river yourselves?"

Ruth spoke softly in her ear. "We're doing what the good Lord wants. We be all right. Colonel Leighton's not bad for a master, but others need our help. We can do more staying put."

Merry drew away from Ruth and glanced over to Adela. "Can't you talk sense into them?"

"I support them in this." Adela placed a hand on her husband's cheek. "I help where I can. It's better to lose your life obeying God than pretend slavery doesn't exist and do nothing."

"Are they obeying God?" Merry shook her head, that blasted curl distracting him. "Brother William, I understand why you want to follow in your father's footsteps, but after what happened to him, shouldn't you consider the cost?"

William took a short breath, and a piece of him broke inside. This was what he feared most. If she wavered in her commitment to abolition and couldn't take a stand here, what good would she be on the mission field? "I thought you believed slavery to be a sin. On the train ride here, you told of more than one occasion where you've warned slaves when catchers were in Oberlin."

"That's different." Merry took a deep breath and puffed her cheeks out before slowing exhaling. "Scripture teaches us to give aide to fugitives, but this... We should be striving to change the law, but you're stealing slaves from their masters."

William reached for the Bible on the table and turned to a scripture his father read to him many times. The last time was before Father made that fateful trip to Virginia. The verse came alive to him then. God spoke almost audibly urging him to do everything in his power to free God's people from the bondage of slavery. "Sister Merry, read Luke Four, Verses Eighteen and Nineteen."

She read aloud. "The Spirit of the Lord is upon me, because he hath anointed me to preach the gospel to the poor; he hath sent me to heal the brokenhearted, to preach deliverance to the captives, and recovering of sight to the blind, to set at liberty..." Her voice faltered. "To set at liberty them that are bruised."

"Don't you see?" William pointed to the verse. "We must do all we can to preach deliverance to the captives and to set at liberty those bruised by the tyranny of slavery. How can I not obey my Lord in this just because my life might be in danger? What good would I be on the mission field if I can't stand for Him here? No matter what the law of man is, I'll choose to obey the law of God." He paused, waiting to hear Merry's answer. The piece of his heart she'd stolen depended on it.

*****

"We're almost there." Joe trotted the horses down the hill to the bank of the river. "Just a little further. You all right back there?"

Nancy's muffled voice came through the floor boards. "We'll make it."

"I know it. You a strong woman." He rolled the wagon behind a grove of trees and pulled up on the reins before climbing down and peering into the landscape across the river. Nobody there. The lantern hung from the house on the hill. Joe removed the plank from the back of the wagon. "Come on out."

Nancy squeezed out the opening and helped her boys down. The moonlight shone on the river where a raft approached them. She grabbed her sons and ran behind a rhododendron bush.

"No need to be afeared," Joe said. "He's gonna help you cross."

The chestnut brown man with a thin face and strong chin reached the bank and dragged the raft to shore. "You there, Joe?"

Joe ran up to him and gave him a bear hug. "Right on time."

The man laughed. "I always am."

"Come on out," Joe called

Nancy and her sons moved from around the bush.

"This be my friend, Mr. John Parker. He's a free man from Ripley, owns a foundry there. He'll help you and your boys cross and get you to the safe house. You'll be fine now."

Nancy threw her arms around Joe. "I'll never forget what you done. Thank you."

"You be safe now," Joe said.

John patted him on the back. "When are you and Ruth gonna cross?"

"We'll be staying put for now, but we might want you to give passage to our young'uns soon."

"Just say the word." John helped Nancy and her sons on the raft and pushed it from the shore. He dug the pole into the water to push the raft along.

Joe let out a sigh. It felt good helping folks like Nancy and her boys. When Naomi and Obadiah's time came, he prayed it would go this easy. At least nobody in Colonel Leighton's family suspected.

Chapter Twenty-One

America's stomach churned as she slid into the chair. "You're right. Oh God, forgive me for not doing all in my power... What can I do to help?"

"Nothing." William stood and peered out the window. "You need to stay out of this."

"Brother William," Reverend Thornton said. "Why so abrupt? America's ranch borders the river, and she could be of assistance writing passes for her father's slaves and helping in other ways."

"A moment ago, she believed we were in the wrong. Now she's pledging her help?" William faced America with the same judgmental glare he gave her at the train station when Ruth and Joe came for her. "You need to decide which side you're on."

America rubbed the puffy sore spot on her arm as she fought to hold her anger at bay. She wanted to wipe that insufferable holier-than-thou scowl off his face. He never lived in the South. His father was an abolitionist. He didn't know what it was like. "I'm trying to do what God wants."

"A moment ago, you accused us of going against God. Now you want to rush out and rescue slaves, and you say I'm going to get myself killed."

She stood and placed her hands on her hips. "Brother William, I've had enough of my papa ordering me around. I don't need you to start. You have no right to leave me out of this. I told you my concerns, and you answered them. Now, if I can be of assistance..."

"Of course you can," Mrs. Thornton said.

William pushed through the door and slammed it. America wasn't sorry to see him go.

Mrs. Thornton put her arm around her. "Why don't you tell us why you came to see us?"

America took a breath to calm herself and told the Thorntons the whole story, how her father forbad her to return to Oberlin, about her new suitor, and about Naomi.

"Harland is a kind man who is working toward freeing his slaves," America said. "I don't want to hurt him, but I must find a way back to Oberlin."

"What if your father doesn't change his mind?" Mrs. Thornton patted her hand. "What will you do then?"

A lump lodged in America's stomach. "I need to consider God may have other plans for me."

Reverend Thornton sat in the rocker facing America. "Do you really believe that?"

"I don't know." America rubbed her wrist. "The only thing I'm sure of is I have to do something to help Naomi. I couldn't bear being trapped here if I didn't do something to stop her from being sold."

"America." Reverend Thornton stared at his hands folded in his lap. "There's only so much you can do. You can't save the world."

"God sent me here." America shook her head trying to make sense of it. "I have to find a way."

"If what you're saying is true, you need to pray about it and do what God says no matter what. Trust Him to work it out."

America wrapped her hands around the warm coffee cup. "If Riley doesn't get the money in time, maybe Naomi could cross."

Reverend Thornton stared at her a moment longer than she expected. "Riley would want to go with her,"

She drank a sip of coffee and let the warmth of it dissipate the chill traveling up her spine. "He could meet her later."

Reverend Thornton's brow furrowed. "It's against the law for a Negro to travel to Ohio without his master's permission."

"Riley's a free man," America said. "He has the papers to prove it."

"Doesn't matter." Reverend Thornton's gaze fixed on her. "All that means is he doesn't have a master to sign the papers allowing him to leave Kentucky. It's common for free black men on their way to Ohio to be waylaid by slave catchers and sold into slavery."

America took another sip of coffee. "Then he could travel with her. I'm sure he'd be willing to sell his farm and leave Kentucky."

"We've talked some on it," Ruth said, "but Obadiah would need to go too."

America gaped at Ruth. "Why?"

"Naomi would be safe," Ruth said, "but if she takes off, the first thing Colonel Leighton would do is sell Obadiah on the auction block. Joe and me won't sacrifice one child for another. They'd both have to go."

"Papa would lose everything, and what about you and Uncle Joe?"

"Ruth," Reverend Thornton said, "would you mind waiting on the porch for a moment."

Ruth nodded, stepped outside, and closed the door.

Mrs. Thornton placed a hand on America's shoulder. "The only way to save them grief is for all of them to escape."

"I'd be willing to take them on," Reverend Thornton took a gulp of coffee and set his tin cup on the table. The metallic sound echoed. "If that's what you want, you'd need to consider the consequences to your family, and you'd have to persuade Joe and Ruth."

"We've already tried to convince them," Mrs. Thornton filled Reverend Thornton's cup. "They won't leave."

"Joe wouldn't hear of it." Reverend Thornton blew on the coffee and took a sip. "He's afraid of slowing them down. His back has been ailing him, and it's getting to the point where he struggles to do a day's work."

America drew her knuckles to her lips. "If Naomi and Obadiah escape, and Uncle Joe and Aunt Ruth don't go with them, Papa would beat them to try to find out where the others went. He'd sell them, probably to different masters to get enough money out of them. He'd have no choice if he wanted to save the ranch."

"What if Colonel Leighton finds out you've helped them?" Reverend Thornton set his cup on the table. "If he finds out you're the reason he's lost everything..."

America strayed to the window and looked out. William had marched up the hill to lean against an old apple tree and stew. She'd been so happy to see him when she'd heard his voice, and now she wished he'd never come. "You mentioned I might be of assistance to you. How?"

"Ruth and Joe risk a lot to come here and report to us about the lantern," Reverend Thornton said. "If they're stopped and questioned about why they're out, it might mean trouble, but if you visit with us once a week for prayer meeting, you could bring them along without any suspicion."

"Since they're your father's slaves," Mrs. Thornton said, "you could also write passes nobody would question."

"You need to consider the risks." Reverend Thornton's voice gained an edge to it. "If you're caught, you'll risk imprisonment like the rest of us, not to mention your father's wrath. Don't make this decision lightly."

America turned to face them. "I have a lot to pray about."

Chapter Twenty-Two

William leaned against an apple tree near the top of the hill overlooking the church and Benjamin Thornton's house. From here, he could see the light in the parsonage window and catch an occasional glimpse of Merry.

Benjamin had been close to him as he had been to his father, more like an older brother than an acquaintance, but he couldn't let his friend bring Merry into this. She didn't have any idea what she was getting into, and she could get hurt or killed. He wiped his hand through his hair. This was a cause worth dying for, both for him and those he worked with, but he wouldn't risk her life.

Clouds overshadowed the moon. William blew in his hands to warm them. America mystified him. Her father owned slaves, and she was a Southerner, but here she was willing to risk her life to become a rescuer. He'd never been prouder of her, but it was still hard to swallow she could change her opinions so easily. One minute, she was calling them thieves and criminals, and the next, she vowed to help them.

He had reason to guard his heart. After all, his father had been betrayed by a woman from the South. He remembered that bright day when clouds obscured his optimism and left him skeptical of the motives of anyone born south of the Ohio River.

*****

William had stepped into the telegraph office and nodded to Mr. Green, the telegraph operator. He'd been expecting a message from his father who'd taken a year off teaching at Oberlin to preach abolition in Virginia and rescue slaves.

After a few months in the South, Father had written him. He'd decided to marry again. William was happy for him. He'd been so lonely since William's mother died of consumption a year earlier. Father had wanted him to come to Virginia to meet Mrs. Murphy, a widow who shared their abolitionist views.

Mr. Green didn't give his usual cheerful greeting. He focused on the paper in his hand as he folded and creased it, his lips pressed together.

William leaned on the counter. "Did I get a telegram?"

"Yes." Mr. Green's voice choked up, and he set the creased note on the counter and slid it toward the edge. "Yes, you did. I'm sorry."

William's jaw tightened. He grabbed the paper, unfolded it, and read the words.

Father lynched–stop–caught stealing slaves–stop–no need to come–stop–sending body on next train–Mrs –Murphy.

He dropped the telegraph and crashed through the door. It was a sunny September day when he entered the telegraph office, the morning sun lighting the eastern sky. Now a fog enveloped him. He drifted down Professor Street past the mill. He remembered turning at Morgan Street but not much else. Something was wrong with the story. Why didn't Mrs. Murphy want him there?

He shuffled onto Epis Cemetery, his footsteps heavy, barely moving. His watery gaze focused on some of the names and dates on the tombstones. He reached his mother's grave and rubbed his eyes with his thumb and forefinger. *Rebecca Woods. Loving Wife and Mother. Born September 3, 1816. Died December 17, 1855.* The yellow chrysanthemums he planted still bloomed, life springing out of death.

His gut wrenched as if someone grabbed it and twisted, wringing the last drop of strength from him. He dropped to the ground next to her grave, the place where he would bury his father in a few days. Both parents gone in a year's time. No grandparents or siblings except for his aunt and uncle in Vermont. He was alone.

He pulled himself to his feet and wandered out of the cemetery. One foot in front of the other. A thud on the hard ground with each step. Down Morgan Street before turning on Main Street. Past houses and stores. People passing but he didn't pay them heed.

The sun shone from the west in his eyes. Morning had passed to mid-afternoon like the thud of his steps, thickly yet unnoticed. He reached College Square and leaned against the Historic Elm where the founders dedicated the land to God twenty-five years ago.

He never lived anywhere but Oberlin. Father moved here from Vermont soon after the college opened in 1833 and married Mother a year later. This had been William's whole life. Now nothing kept him here. One thing-- what he worked so hard for, what his father was so proud of since he heard the call from God-- earning his degree so he could go to China. All he had left was that and his devotion to the abolitionist movement.

A couple stood on the porch of the hotel to his left, huddled together, and laughed as if they had a secret. He raced past them and stopped in front of the bookstore. Strange he would end up here. The bell above the door rang as he entered.

Sister America Leighton glanced up from where she was stocking books on the shelf. "Can I help you?"

"No, I just wanted to look around." He cleared his throat. "My father helped Mr. Hanson start this bookstore. Father felt the college students needed a place like this. They would learn more if an abundance of books were available."

She set the books down and placed her hand on his arm. "I was in chapel when they announced Professor Woods' death. I'm sorry for your loss."

His voice cracked. "Thank you."

"If there's anything I can do... "

"No, thank you for your concern." A tear rolled down Sister Leighton's cheek. "I'll pray God will give you comfort."

"You're very kind." He left and meandered further down Main Street onto Lorain. He didn't know when he stopped to sit on the steps in front of First Church or how long he'd been there. Time seemed to be a concept beyond his grasp.

He buried his head in his knees and groaned. A hand clasped onto his. He looked up. Sister Leighton was praying for him. Her face, framed with strawberry blond curls, glowed as she cried out to God. The warmth of her hand spread through him, and he didn't feel quite so alone.

When the prayer ended, she sat there with him, not saying a word. He didn't know how long she was there, but her presence comforted him in a way he couldn't express.

Finally, she spoke. "Professor Woods is the reason I'm here at Oberlin. I've never known a more godly man."

"I don't understand." William gazed into Sister Leighton's eyes. They had the same tint of blue as Lake Erie. "Father's never mentioned you."

"He wouldn't have known." She bit her bottom lip. "I have the call to become a missionary, but my father doesn't approve of an unmarried woman traveling to China alone."

"China." His head jerked up. She was called to China as he was?

She nodded. "I've taken private lessons in Mandarin and studied the geography and culture, and I've worked hard to keep my grades up. A year ago, another professor told me this was a foolish flight of fancy. After all, I am only a lady. How can I go to the mission field without a husband? The same thing my father had told me in his latest letter. I'd almost decided to leave Oberlin and go back home."

Even through his fog of grief, he had compassion for her plight. Even if she did gain the credentials and support needed, it was doubtful she'd ever be assigned a task less mundane then mending clothes or mopping floors for the male missionaries. "What changed your mind?"

"Your father." She gave him a slight grin. "I was in his Pauline epistles class, and he mentioned Romans 12:1 in relation to Paul's determination to carry out God's mission."

William chuckled, then wiped his hand over his face, amazed this woman could make him smile at a memory of his father so soon after his death. "He was passionate about that passage."

"It changed my perspective completely," Miss Leighton said. "The call may be beyond me, but when I consider myself a living sacrifice to whatever God has for me, going to China alone or with a husband doesn't matter. I will go as an act of worship to my Lord and accept whatever may come."

He leaned forward staring into her sea blue eyes. A man could get lost in there as quickly as a ship could in the Great Lakes. Her gaze held such passion. There were few who comprehended the passage in such a personal way. She astounded him.

"Forgive me." Sister Leighton blushed. "I am rattling without any regard these recollections might be painful to you."

"Not at all. I have fond memories of my father teaching that passage." He placed his hands on his head as a wave of grief overwhelmed him.

Sister Leighton tilted her head toward him. "Will you be traveling to Virginia?"

"The telegraph said there was no need. They're sending him..." The muscle in his jaw twitched. "They're sending his body up here for burial. It will be at Wellington Station day after tomorrow. I don't know what to do. I have to find out what happened."

Tears welled in her eyes. "Don't make any decisions now. Take time to grieve. Wait until winter break. If you decide to investigate, you can do it then."

"Yes, I suppose so."

A month later, he had made the trip to Virginia. It took time to dig out the truth, but he'd found out all of it. Mrs. Murphy wasn't the abolitionist his father had thought. She turned out to be the mother of a man who earned his living catching slaves. She lied to Father to try to find out if he knew anything about Underground Railroad stations. She manipulated a couple of names out of him, and the men were arrested and jailed. When Father started to suspect, Mrs. Murphy's son and the town's vigilante group lynched him.

William had tried to get the sheriff to arrest the men, but he wouldn't. One of the local farmers said the sheriff was a part of it, but William couldn't prove anything. He'd finally accepted the fact there was nothing more he could do and had returned to Oberlin.

*****

The bond he had with Merry on the front steps of First Church had comforted him, and he spent the next few months asking around about her. Hope of a courtship stirred until a friend warned him her father owned slaves. He decided the best course of action was to forget about her, but she kept showing up around campus. She even ended up in a couple of his theology classes. No matter what he did, he couldn't avoid Merry. She drew him in with each timid glance, hesitant blush, and awkward smile. Pretending to ignore her didn't help. Even when she wasn't around, she invaded his thoughts.

When she showed up on the same train he was taking to Kentucky, he couldn't believe the coincidence. Was it by chance, or did God keep placing her in his path? During their conversation on the train, her passion for God and for the abolition of slavery convinced him to open his heart, but there was more.

Her zeal for abolition grew not from the way she was raised or because she decided it was a noble cause. She had the same compassion for the slaves and their plight as she showed William on the steps of First Church.

By the time they'd reached Maysville, he realized he was falling in love with her. He couldn't help risking his heart and life despite his distrust of so-called Southern abolitionists -- until he saw the way she treated Ruth and Joe.

Joe pulled the wagon up to the barn. Merry would be leaving soon. William climbed down the hill toward the house. Time to go back and face Benjamin. He owed him an explanation, and the truth was the only one he had.

Chapter Twenty-Three

Ruth stood at the barn waiting, and Joe raised an eyebrow. Reverend Thornton wasn't the kind to make colored folks stay outside in the cold. Ruth ran to the wagon before it came to a full stop.

He pulled up on the reins and climbed down. "What's wrong?"

"Miss Merry knows everything."

Air escaped Joe's lungs as if a tree branch had punched him in the gut. He said nothing for a moment while he tried to make sense of it. "How could she?"

"She overheard Reverend Thornton talking with that traveling preacher from Oberlin."

He wiped the back of his neck. "Dear Lord, what do we do now?"

"It'll be okay. She won't say anything."

"She's Colonel Leighton's daughter. She ain't gonna side with us over her own pa."

Ruth wrapped her arms around Joe. He leaned in to kiss the top of her head. He didn't have a choice now. They needed to get Naomi and Obadiah across before Miss Merry had a chance to tell.

"I believe her," Ruth said.

A throat cleared from behind him. "I do too."

Joe jumped at the sound of a man's voice and turned to see Brother Woods. "I didn't know you was there."

"I'm sorry," Brother Woods said. "I didn't mean to sneak up on you. I was taking a walk."

"I know Miss America well enough to believe she wouldn't betray us," Ruth said, "but, Brother Woods, you're the one who stormed out."

Brother Woods rubbed his foot across the yellow leaves on the ground. "Joe, do you really believe she'd run to Colonel Leighton?"

"She's white, ain't she?" Joe's jaw clenched. "I don't even know if I can trust you."

Brother Woods offered a hesitant smile. "You trust the Thorntons."

"They've proved they're good Christians. Most white folks don't live it."

"I can't argue with you there." Brother Woods gazed at the house. "Merry's proved she's a good Christian, hasn't she?"

Joe turned away. He tried to be the best slave he could to Colonel Leighton, not to please his master, but to please God, and what did it get him? He hated Colonel Leighton for selling his children. It rose up from his gut threatening to spread to every organ in his body, but he couldn't get away from the voice whispering in his ear. *Let it go.*

He didn't know if he could, but America wasn't the cause of this. If it wasn't for her, Riley wouldn't have the extra time to come up with the money. "So you want me to put my life in the hands of my master's daughter?"

Brother Woods nodded. "I can't answer for you, but I trust Sister Merry with my life."

Joe snorted. "Do you trust her with ours?"

"You'll have to decide for yourself."

Ruth placed a hand on Joe's arm. "I ain't ever known you not to listen to God. What's he telling you?"

"You already know that, woman." Joe let out a sigh. "All right. We'll wait."

"You've made the right decision." Brother Woods patted him on the back.

Joe winced.

Brother Woods stared at him. "What happened? Are you in pain?"

Joe waved away his concern. "My arthritis acting up is all." He wasn't about to tell the man he'd been whipped.

America stepped onto the porch, and Brother Woods started toward her. She turned her head away and strode past him. His jaw twitched. He opened his mouth, but he didn't say anything. He just watched her as she headed to the cart.

Joe helped Ruth into the wagon then gave America a hand.

America climbed in. "Joe, Ruth, I want you to know, no matter what I decide to do, your secret's safe with me. I'll never tell my papa about what you do here. Never."

Joe flicked the reins and prayed she was telling the truth.

*****

William strolled to the cabin, hands in his pockets.

Benjamin stepped out onto the porch, head tilted, eyes fixed on him. "Care to tell me what that was all about?"

He shrugged. "I don't want Sister Merry hurt."

"Neither do I, but you know there's risk to this."

William's voice rasped out as barely a whisper. "I love her."

Benjamin's eyes widened. "Oh. Does she know?"

"No." William pulled at his shirt collar.

"Tell her, man."

"I planned to when we return to Oberlin, but now... It's too dangerous. I might be arrested or killed at any moment."

"Sometimes I worry about Adela, but she's as committed to the cause as I am. It would be wrong for me to expect her to flee when I won't."

Williams crossed his arms. "What if you're lynched or shot?"

"We've talked about it some. She'll go live with her ma in Ohio if something happens. If truth be known, I'm not afraid of dying for the cause. I'll be in Heaven with my Lord." Reverend Thornton wiped his face with his hand. "Being thrown in Frankfort Prison gives me pause sometimes. I've heard stories about that place."

"Me too." William leaned against the rail and stared down the path Merry's wagon had taken. "How can I bring a wife into this?"

"After you graduate, you'll leave this behind."

"And go to the mission field where the danger increases."

Benjamin placed his hand on William's shoulder. "Have you forgotten? America's headed to the mission field as well. She'll go whether she has a husband or not. She's a determined woman."

"After the way I acted, she might not even want me to court her." William let out a sigh. "She's struggling with how far her commitment to the abolitionist movement will go. Sometimes I worry she won't have the courage to go through with it."

"Maybe it's time you learn a little more about America Leighton." Benjamin placed a hand on William's shoulder. "It's possible she's sacrificing a great deal more than you know."

Chapter Twenty-Four

America sat on the front bench waiting for church to begin and tried to suppress a yawn but failed. She hadn't slept much the previous night. The events of last evening reeled around in her mind until the rooster crowed. It was a struggle to stay awake through breakfast.

If she traveled this course, she would betray her father and maybe bring him to financial ruin. Would he ever forgive her? On the other hand, how could she forgive herself if she didn't do everything in her power to make sure Naomi escaped the auction block. There were thousands like her in the South being torn from their families every day.

She cast a furtive look toward the side door where William would enter and adjusted herself in the seat.

Papa grabbed hold of her hands. "Stop twiddling your thumbs."

She tried to rest her hands in her lap without moving them when another yawn caused her to cover her mouth. She loved Papa and wanted to please him. Was it obeying God to deceive her own father?

Her stomach had fluttered in excitement when she'd first caught sight of William the night before. He reminded her of Oberlin, the place she now considered home. She couldn't imagine never seeing it again.

More than views of abolition and equality stirred her desire to return. When she had learned Father Charles Finney was the president of the college, awe filled her. She knew of the revival services he preached back east. Some newspapers called him the founder of the Second Great Awakening. After listening to him in Chapel, she understood why. He prayed with a fervor that had swept the college campus.

During one incident over a year ago, she'd heard a buzzing noise. No bees or birds were around. She'd walked toward the student houses trying to find the source of the hum when it had grown louder. The windows to the buildings housing the students had been open, and the buzz of their prayers had filled the air.

William entered the side door and gave her a slight nod as he took his place beside Reverend Thornton. America strolled to the piano, and Reverend Thornton led them in song. William's bass voice resonated above the off-key crooning of the congregation as he sang the hymns in perfect harmony. His hands lifted and his eyes closed in heartfelt worship. It warmed her heart.

Soon the songs and prayers ended, and America took her seat beside her papa. Out of the corner of her eye, she caught Harland smiling at her but pretended not to notice.

William stepped in front of the congregation and cleared his throat. She wondered if he realized he always did before he began preaching. He looked inspirational standing there in his black preacher's suit. His eyes surveyed the congregation until they rested on her, and the dimple on his right cheek deepened. Maybe he wasn't angry with her after all.

Nothing attracted her more than a godly man, especially one with warm brown eyes with flecks of yellow and green in them and dimples indenting his cheeks hinting at a smile even when none was present. Harland was godly too and very charming and handsome. She was fond of him, but somehow, he didn't affect her the same way.

William didn't preach what America expected. She was sure he would decry the practice of slavery and encourage men like her father to release their slaves. Instead, his words pointed to her.

"I have heard it said among you, that you would take a stronger stand against the sin in your midst, against gambling, drunkenness, gossip, and slavery. I've heard you say I don't understand. That's the way things are here. I can't go against my family and community."

He gripped the sides of the pulpit. "Yet in Luke 14, Christ says, 'If any man come to me, and hate not his father, and mother, and wife, and children, and brethren, and sisters, yea, and his own life also, he cannot be my disciple.' Our parents deserve our honor, yet our love and devotion to Christ outweighs every other relationship."

Was that the choice she considered? Was she choosing between her father and Christ?

"You may deem this too great a cost, but remember what Christ sacrificed for us."

America let out a long exhale. She had no choice. If God didn't provide a way to ransom Naomi, she would find a way to lead all of her father's slaves to freedom.

*****

William had every intention of preaching against the evils of slavery, but he changed his message at the last moment. When he prayed for Merry at the anxiety bench at the end of service, he knew God had led him.

Benjamin told him how she stood up to her father, calling for him to free his slaves, and the indignities she had suffered as a result. She even considered helping her father's slaves to freedom knowing it would cause financial ruin and jeopardize her relationship with her family. William hoped he would be able to do the same in her situation.

He'd risked his life on many occasions, but he never had to go against his family. His father risked more for the cause than he had. Father's last words before they lynched him were a prayer for God to end slavery.

Maybe Benjamin and Sister Martha were right. It couldn't hurt to tell Merry of his love for her. She had courage and devotion with stubbornness mixed in, and when she had prayed for him, her great faith and compassion was unmistakable. He'd never known anyone who's prayers had such power to reach Heaven. They bored into his heart. She would be the kind of wife who would stay by his side no matter the fray.

William positioned himself outside so he could greet the parishioners as they left. This would ensure he had a chance to talk to Merry. Trying not to glance in her direction, he greeted each member of the congregation. The line dwindled until she was next. He reached out his hand to shake hers.

A gent stepped in front of him like he wasn't even there. "America, I'm so glad I caught up with you."

He'd noticed the man in the congregation earlier. The dandy wore a black frock jacket and trousers with a white stiff-collared linen shirt and a blue and red patterned silk vest and matching cravat. He finished the look with a walnut walking stick with a gold cobra handle and a top hat he'd now placed on his head.

The man took Merry's hand in his. "Could I call upon you this afternoon?"

William's throat grew dry. Had he waited too long? Who was this man?

Merry seemed to hear his unspoken question. "Brother William, may I introduce Mr. Harland Boidae? Harland is the leader of the missionary society for this county."

"Mr. Boidae, it's good to meet you." William gripped his hand tightly.

The dandy returned the strong grasp and flashed a grin too big for his face. "Likewise. You preached a fine sermon."

"Thank you." William disliked this man with the disingenuous smile. It no doubt hid his real intentions. "I'm studying to be a missionary." He said it in a boastful way, but he couldn't help himself.

Mr. Boidae's words dripped sweet with a hint of sarcasm. "Perhaps we could assist you with the funding when you're finished with school."

Not unless God wanted to teach him a lesson in humility. "Perhaps. It does help when those without the fortitude to go to the mission field provide the funding."

Mr. Boidae's smile turned into a smirk. "It's good those of us with the industry to earn the money can provide for you."

"What do you do for a living?"

"I own a mill."

"How many do you employ?"

"Four managers and a man to keep the books." Mr. Boidae removed his watch from his pocket and looked at it as if he were dismissing William from his presence. "I have all the laborers I need."

William wouldn't be discharged easily. "Slaves?"

Harland chuckled, and returned the watch to his pocket. "Yes, Reverend Woods, slaves."

William kept a plastered smile on his face as everything inside him churned.

"Harland, I won't be able to see you today," Merry said as if nothing was amiss. "I'm attending a wedding."

"I know of no wedding."

"It's later today at the African meeting. Papa sold Naomi to her intended."

"You mean that Negro preacher? America, it's not right for you to attend one of those meetings alone. Let me escort you."

"Thank you, but I need no escort."

"Since I'm courting you, I must insist."

William clenched his jaw. Merry courting this pompous-- he searched for a word he wouldn't have to repent over later-- slave owner?

Merry turned her head. "I appreciate your concern, but I'm going alone."

"It's not proper," Harland kissed her hand, "but I'll abide by your wishes, my dear. May I call upon you tomorrow?"

"Yes, you may," Merry said.

Harland tipped his hat, bowed slightly, and walked away.

"I can't believe..." William struggled to make coherent sounds. "Sister Merry, how could you allow yourself to be courted by a slave owner?"

"How dare you judge me? It's not like you've ever asked to court me. You have no idea what I'm going through." Merry stomped off.

William tapped his mouth with his fist. He took a couple of steps, then stopped. What good would running after her do? He'd made a mess of things. When he thought of her with that... that... The vein in his neck throbbed. He marched along the trail through the woods behind the parsonage. He had to get a hold of himself.

Courting? He knew he'd heard Mr. Boidae right. Merry suffered so much to go against her father. Why would she allow that slave owner to call on her?

He had only himself to blame. He should have told Merry his intentions long ago. The man probably plied her with gifts and poetry and turned her reasoning to mush. He'd find a way to bring her to her senses.

Chapter Twenty-Five

Colonel Leighton glanced at his pocket watch. He couldn't get rid of the dread lodging in his stomach that he wasn't doing right by Riley and Naomi. Giving false hope never did anyone any good, especially not the slaves. He agreed to this to please Merry, not for the extra money he'd pocket. It would be even harder for Naomi and her kin when the time came to sell her.

His decision to not tell Joe about the sale of Amos until the day of the auction was to make it easier on them. He shouldn't have blurted out he was selling Naomi too, but when Obadiah pitched a fit, he lost his temper.

Riley would never get the money in time. He was a poor dirt farmer. Where would he come up with four hundred dollars in the middle of winter? Letting them have that Negro wedding and pretending they'd be together was cruel. In two month's time, Naomi would be on the auction block in Maysville where she should have been yesterday.

Colonel Leighton strode to the fireplace and grabbed his pipe off the mantel. He tried to think of somebody to buy her who lived close by so her young Negro could still be near her, but with the financial panic, nobody around here was in the market.

The only two men who would have the funds and might be willing were Mr. Foster and Harland Boidae. He wouldn't sell her to Mr. Foster if he could help it. It was none of his business how other men treated their slaves, but he wouldn't subject Naomi to that, and asking Harland to buy her would complicate matters since the man was courting his daughter.

No, the auction in Maysville was his only choice. He would pray the way he did for Amos. God would find her a good master who'd take care of her.

Colonel Leighton filled the pipe with tobacco, packed it down, and lit it. There was a bright spot in this business. It would profit him considerably to sell Naomi and keep the four hundred greenbacks. He could buy more breeding stock and assure the success of the ranch. That might persuade Luke to stay on instead of taking Mr. Foster's offer.

He glanced at his pocket watch. Riley would be here soon. It might work for the best. Naomi might be with child by then. A pregnant slave would fetch more money.

A knock on the door signaled Riley's arrival. Colonel Leighton answered it and ushered him into the room. Riley took off his straw hat and held it in front of him. He wore a cheap plaid sack suit, probably the only one he owned. "Sir, I thank you kindly for giving me this chance."

Colonel Leighton drew a puff from his pipe. "I'm going to speak plain to you, boy. Then if you want to get out of this agreement, I'll let you."

Riley twisted his hat in his hands. "Please, sir, we made a bargain."

"This isn't right me giving you that girl and building false hope. There's more of a chance of a Republican becoming president than you getting enough money together to buy Naomi in time."

"Yessur." Riley brushed his hand over his hat and tried to straighten it. "I expect you're right."

Colonel Leighton stroked his beard. "You still want to go through with it knowing in two months I'm going to sell her at auction?"

"Yessur." The hat again became victim to Riley's wringing hands. "Even if we only got a short spell together, it'll be worth it."

"You'll be out a lot of money to have the girl for only a brief time."

"Yessur." The straw deformed through Riley's fingers.

The colonel had done his best to give the boy a chance to do the smart thing. He pointed to the note sitting on the writing desk. "Can you write your name?"

"Yessur." The corners of Riley's mouth turned up slightly as he stopped assaulting the abused hat.

Colonel Leighton let out a sigh, dipped the pen in the ink, and handed it to Riley. That's another reason Negros needed masters to take care of them. They didn't have any common sense.

*****

America rummaged through her trunk pulling out fancy dresses and laying them across the bed. Fine satin, silk, and velvet with hoop skirts and low-cut necklines would be out of place on the mission field. She had replaced them with cotton and wool day dresses when she'd left home to attend Oberlin.

She loved the freedom of not having to wear all those heavy undergarments and constraining corsets. Lavena had said one day women wouldn't be confined to long skirts. One day bloomer outfits would be commonplace. Imagine the freedom women would have then.

America pulled a blue velvet dress from the trunk. At least one of her fancy dresses would be put to good use.

"Choose one, Naomi, and it's yours."

"I couldn't." Naomi ran her hand across the material. "These be too fine for a slave."

America held the dress up to Naomi. "They're not too fine for my friend on her wedding day, and you're not a slave anymore. At least you won't be when Riley pays the rest of the note."

"I don't know."

America never planned to wear any of these dresses again except for her mama's wedding dress. She saved that one back for the day she would marry. Now she didn't even want to look at them. They reminded her she might never see Oberlin again. "At least pick one."

Naomi surveyed the dresses like a child picking out a piece of rock candy. She picked up a cream-colored dress with a yellow rose pattern and held it in front of her. "I do like this one."

"Try it on." America helped Naomi into the pantaloons and hoops and buttoned the dress in the back. She was skinnier than America was and didn't need the corset.

Naomi pranced in front of the full-length mirror and turned to admire herself. The cream color accented her bronze skin. America couldn't tell if she glowed more from the dress or because it was her wedding day.

A tear creased Naomi's cheek. "No matter what, I'll never forget this."

America heard a knock, opened the door, and invited Ruth to come into the room.

Ruth gaped at Naomi.

Naomi twirled. "Miss Merry gave it to me."

"Child, I never seen you looking prettier. Riley's downstairs. He signed the papers, and he's itching to take you to the church to jump the broom. Now don't you keep him waiting."

Naomi ran into Ruth's arms and hugged her before flitting down the staircase. America followed with a chuckle. Riley stood at the door beaming up at his bride.

At the bottom of the stairs, Papa grabbed Naomi's arm. "Girl, what are you doing in that dress?"

America pushed between them. "I gave it to her as a wedding gift."

He snorted. "She won't have it long. She'll be back in two months."

Riley wrapped an arm around Naomi and scooted her out the door without saying a word.

"Did you have to act like that?" America glared at her papa. "It's her wedding day."

He turned and poked the fire. "These slave weddings aren't binding. When she comes back, that so-called marriage will be done. After she's sold, she can jump the broom with some other Negro stallion owned by her new master."

America wanted to lunge at her father. She had defended him to Lavena and her other roommates at Oberlin and to William. She'd thought he was different, but he was the same as every other master who enslaved his fellow man.

She might not ever make it back to Ohio, but if she were trapped here, she would make sure every slave under his control would be freed no matter what she had to do to make it happen.

*****

Joe was brushing the dust out of his clothes when the door opened. He gazed up at Naomi and smiled. She was the prettiest thing he ever did see. The dress she was wearing was finer than anything black folks wore. He enveloped her in his arms and hugged her tight. He didn't want to let go.

Naomi pulled back and spun around. "Do you like it, Pa? Miss Merry gave it to me to wear for my wedding day."

"I ain't never seen nothing finer in all my born days." Joe wiped his face with a bandana. "Sure was nice of her to loan it to you and all."

Naomi kissed him on the cheek. "She said for me to keep it."

Joe extended his hand to Riley. "You gonna take care of my little girl?"

Riley shook it. "Yessir. I'll do whatever it takes."

"Then I reckon Naomi should know what she's getting into before she jumps the broom."

Naomi gave Joe her what-have-you-done-now look.

Riley wrapped his arm around Naomi's waist. "Your pa's got something to say."

"What are you two scheming?"

Joe wiped his hand over his face. "Sit down, child."

Naomi and Riley sank onto the bench at the table in the center of the room.

Joe sat across from them. "I already talked to Riley 'bout this. He goes along with it."

Naomi placed her hand in his. "Tell me, Pa."

"You ain't gonna be a slave no more. Riley and me are gonna try real hard to get together the money to buy your note, but if it don't work out..."

"I know you'll do your best. It'll be all right."

"Let your pa talk," Riley said.

"There's some things you don't know." Joe folded one hand over the other and drew them in front of his face. "Your ma and me help slaves escape over the river."

Naomi gasped.

"We never did feel the need for any of ours to go." Joe placed his hand on Naomi's. "Colonel Leighton's been good to us until he went and sold Amos. We didn't have time to get him across before the auction."

"What your pa's trying to say," Riley said, "is if we don't get the money in time, you and me are gonna cross."

"What about Pa, and Ma, and Obi?"

Joe cleared his throat. "We'll tell Obi when it gets closer to time. He can go too if he's a mind to."

Naomi's eyes watered. "You and Ma? You're going with us, aren't you?"

"No. We'll just slow you down. Better if too many ain't seen. Besides the cold gets into my back more every winter. The trip might be too hard for me."

"Pa..."

Joe kissed her on the forehead. "You'll have a good life with Riley. He's a God-fearing man, and he'll take care of you. I just wanted you to know you ain't got no call to fret. One way or another, you ain't gonna be taken away from him."

Naomi placed her hand on the side of his face. "I love you, Pa."

Joe wrapped his arms around her. "I love you too, child." He pulled back and winked. "You better get moving. You don't want to be late jumping the broom. Soon as your ma gets here, we'll be along."

Riley helped Naomi into his wagon, and they rode away.

Ruth arrived a few minutes later. "Did you tell her?"

Joe nodded and swallowed back the lump in his throat. No matter what happened, he'd lost his little girl forever, maybe the only son he had left too, and he still needed to decide what to do about America. It was weighing on him.

Chapter Twenty-Six

William prayed while waiting for the African church meeting to start. The church service would begin with Riley and Naomi's wedding ceremony which Benjamin would perform. William would deliver the sermon afterwards.

It was unusual for slaves to have church weddings, but then it was unusual for them to have their own meetings. Most slaves who were allowed to attend church sat in the loft and listened to a white preacher tell them how they should obey their white masters.

Benjamin changed everything by ordaining Riley as a minister of the gospel and assuring the church elders he would oversee the African church's meetings.

William wasn't as concerned about the church service as he was about who would be at the wedding. Merry would be there even if the snake courting her didn't like it. Maybe it would give him the chance he needed to convince her what Mr. Boidae was really like.

Colored people poured in, and Merry entered among them wearing her yellow dress. William had seen her in that dress often. It reminded him of sunflowers.

Naomi followed her through the door wearing a satin hoop dress. It wasn't the type of clothing a slave wore, even on her wedding day.

Maybe Merry had lent it to her. No, he'd never seen Merry wear anything fancy. She wore practical apparel, one of the things he admired about her. He didn't approve of the fancy silk and satin dresses with hoop skirts, the fashion of the day. He preferred practical dresses and rational clothing.

Bride and groom exchanged vows, and Benjamin pronounced them husband and wife. Riley and Naomi jumped the broom and kissed, and Riley whisked his bride away.

William took over from there preaching about the joy of the Lord surpassing all understanding and the freedom they had in Christ. Benjamin and Joe would contact the slaves about the freedom within their grasp. They would know who could be trusted.

The service ended, and William strode to the door and opened it. He wanted a chance to talk to Merry without her slave owning suiter around. The scent of wet leaves and crisp autumn air made its way inside.

After a few words with Adela Thornton, Merry sauntered to the exit and nodded to William.

"It was a fine wedding." William blurted out the words hoping to keep her from leaving.

Merry stopped. "Yes, Naomi made a beautiful bride." A colored family scooted behind her and out the door.

He stuck his hands in his pockets. "I'm glad you were here. I was afraid your beau would persuade you not to come."

She scrunched up the side of her mouth. "He's not my beau."

William pulled at his collar as he tried to make sense of her words. "Earlier he said–"

"I know what he said." Beams of light shone in her blue eyes as they gazed into his. "He is courting me, but he's not my beau."

William let out an audible sigh. She had to be the most confusing woman he'd ever met.

She chuckled. "I'm sorry. I know I'm being evasive. My father wants me to marry Mr. Boidae."

"Oh." She wouldn't, would she?

"I desire only to return to Oberlin." Merry tilted her head. "My papa forbids it."

William held his breath. A gust of wind blew yellow leaves through the doorway.

"I'm trying to change his mind." She offered a weak smile. "In the meantime, I gave my word I would give Mr. Boidae a month to woo me."

He blew out his elation. "I'm so relieved."

Merry wet her lips. "Why?"

"Well, with what you overheard last night, I thought..." He became flustered. "If you were serious about a slave owner, you might, you know..."

"You thought I might turn you in?" Her voice took on a tone of agitation. "That I might betray you?"

"No, you're twisting my words."

She darted through the door.

His face flushed. He spoke with power and clarity from the pulpit, but every time he said two words to her, he felt like a young boy pulling a girl's braids because he couldn't figure out the right words to say. He chased after her and called out. "I just hated to see you with someone like Mr. Boidae. You deserve better."

She spun back toward him. "Harland's a godly man. If I'm forced to stay in Kentucky, I might consider him a prospect. He is the leader of the Mason County Missionary Society, and he wants to do what's right."

"Do what's right? He's a slave owner."

"He recently acquired his slaves from his father." Her narrow chin jutted showing an indent he'd never noticed. "He plans to free them all within the next few years."

She was angry, but he couldn't let it drop. He had to give that braid one more tug. "He told you that?"

She crossed her arms. "Yes, and I believe him."

"Sister Merry, men lie to woo beautiful women. Have you considered he may be telling you what you want to hear?"

Storm clouds often warned of a tempest blowing in over Lake Erie. That danger appeared in Merry's glower now. "Earlier you thought I would betray you. Now you think Harland is lying. You, Brother William, seem to think all Southerners can't be trusted. You're wrong."

William opened his mouth but couldn't think of what to say. He rubbed his hand across the back of his neck. It was an opinion he had held, and he'd been wrong about her, but he knew Boidae's type. That dandy was a snake who would say whatever would give him the advantage.

He brushed his foot across yellow leaves on the ground in front of him. "It's a fault I'm trying to remedy. Please forgive me for misjudging you. I'm truly sorry."

The gale passed, the choppy waters dispelled, and her blue eyes again reminded him of Lake Erie on a calm day. She flashed him a smile brightening everything around him. "You're forgiven."

William motioned his hand toward the path. "May I escort you home?"

"I don't know." Merry thrust her tongue slightly between her lips. "I suppose it would be all right."

He offered her his arm. "It might help to talk about your troubles. I'm a good listener."

Merry paused for a moment before sticking her arm through his. "I'm dearly in need of a friend. I miss my roommates at Ladies Hall in Oberlin. I usually talked things over with them when I was troubled."

"How many roommates do you have?"

"Only six. I know others have more, but we have one of the smaller rooms at Ladies Hall. They've become my sisters in every sense of the word."

William nodded. "The fellowship there is rare." He stopped at a felled tree. "Would you like to sit and tell me about it?"

Merry sat beside him on the tree trunk. Her hand brushed his and chills ran through him.

"I took a strong stand with my father about slavery. I told him it was a sin, and he needed to free his slaves." She let out a noisy sigh. "It didn't go well."

William placed his hand on Merry's. He wanted to draw her hand close to his mouth. "How did he react?"

"With a trip to the woodshed."

He blinked. He didn't know how to answer the indignity she must have suffered.

"There's more." Merry's hands fidgeted in her lap. "Papa won't allow me to return to Oberlin. He wants me to marry. Did Reverend Thornton tell you the situation between Riley and Naomi?"

"Yes," William said. "If Riley doesn't get another four hundred dollars together by the end of January, Colonel Leighton's going to take Naomi back and sell her."

"He needs the money for a mortgage on the ranch. I tried to persuade him to sell some horses instead, but he won't listen." A tear fell down her cheek.

He wiped it with his thumb. "What will you do?"

"If Riley doesn't get the money, I'll help my father's slaves escape to Ohio, all of them. I've talked to Reverend Thornton about it."

"Sister Merry." William swallowed back the guilt forming a lump in his throat. How could he have doubted her commitment? "The colonel's wrath is sure to rage against you. You can't walk to Oberlin alone."

Merry shrugged. "I only know I must obey God."

He'd do whatever it took to help her. "I must tell you something." His eyes met hers. "I've grown fond of you. When we return to college, I'd like to call on you."

"Why tell me now?" She glanced away. "It's too late. I see no way of making it back to Oberlin."

Chapter Twenty-Seven

The wind rustled the yellow leaves underfoot as William walked along the path beside Merry. A cardinal chirped trying to stifle the quiet permeating the woods. William struggled to think of something to say, but the words stuck in the back of his throat.

He'd never considered marriage a part of God's plan for his life, then she'd shown up on those church steps. Maybe God's hand was in this. His calling made a normal life precarious, but Merry shared his desire, to share the Gospel overseas, and she stood ready to sacrifice everything for the kingdom of God. He couldn't imagine going back to Oberlin or to China without her.

They stopped as a deer crossed the path. William couldn't get the awareness of her out of his mind. Her skirt brushed against his pant leg. She stood so near, he could smell the lye in her freshly washed hair. His breathing grew rapid and his pulse raced. He leaned a little closer wanting to touch her lips with his. The deer dashed into the woods, and Merry resumed her pace along the path. He'd missed his chance -- again.

They approached the clearing where her two-story brick house stood. It wasn't as extravagant as the plantation homes he'd seen, but it hinted at an affluence brought about by slave labor. He gazed into her blue eyes and could almost feel the refreshing mist of Lake Erie on his face. He always felt that way around her, somehow revived and uplifted.

Merry smiled. "Thank you for walking me home and for listening. I value your friendship."

Friendship? The word hit him as if a herd of horses had stampeded his heart. "You're welcome. About what I said earlier..." He cleared his throat. "Forgive me for being so forward."

"Not at all. If I were to return to Oberlin, your proposal of courtship would be most welcome."

William squared his shoulders. "May I speak freely once more?"

A wind gust blew red and orange leaves around her yellow dress. "Please do."

"If I could help you get back to Oberlin, would you allow it?"

She blushed and lowered her eyes. A squirrel ran across the path and darted up an oak tree.

"I assure you my only intention would be your safe return to Ohio," he stammered. "We would travel by train, and I would behave as a gentleman."

The leaves crackled under her feet as she took a few steps toward the house. "My roommate, Lavena, is right about a lot of things." She stopped and waited for William to catch up with her. "Fathers and husbands are allowed to keep daughters and wives in bondage as they do their slaves. The way my father is holding me prisoner in Kentucky, it's not right. I'm glad Oberlin allows women the freedom to choose their own paths."

Most men didn't approve of Oberlin's liberal approach toward women. Some of the professor's wives even tried to limit their opportunities saying it was important to remain ladylike, but in William's home, his mother was a member of the Ohio Women's Rights Association and attended state suffrage conventions in Akron and Massillon. She said the speeches made by Sojourner Truth inspired her the most.

His father insisted his mother, who was learned in a great many things, be treated with respect. He could still hear his father's voice. *You'd be wise to listen to your mother. God blessed her with more intelligence and common sense than most professors I've known.*

Merry's tongue swiped her lips. "I assume you don't approve of the school's progressive stance?"

"You assume wrong. I was thinking about my mother." The muscle in his jaw twitched. "She passed two years ago." He stared at orange leaves swirling at Merry's feet. "Consumption."

"I'm sorry."

He cleared his throat. "My mother was a progressive woman, and my father approved of her suffrage and abolitionist activities. He believed a husband, as the head of the home, had a duty to encourage his wife to achieve her full potential as she pursues God's plan for her life."

Merry tilted her head. "Do you agree with your father?"

"I do."

"I'm hoping my papa will relent as the time to depart approaches." She touched his arm. "I don't want to hurt him by running off, but if he doesn't change his mind, could we talk more of this?"

William opened his mouth to reply when he caught a glimpse of Colonel Leighton standing on the porch, arms crossed, with a look in his eyes every bit as dangerous as Merry's earlier tempest.

"America, get in the house." The colonel barked the order.

"I'm sorry. I must go." Merry brushed past him and through the door without another word.

"My daughter has a beau who's a fine match for her. You'd do wise not to vie for her affections. Good day, sir." Colonel Leighton marched into the house and shut the door a little harder than needed.

*****

America bristled as her father grabbed her arm.

His jaw jutted. "What is wrong with you, girl? Allowing a man to escort you unchaperoned. I taught you better."

"Papa, please." She pulled away. "He's a student at Oberlin. He was accompanying me as a friend only."

"Is that another thing they teach you at Oberlin, to be alone with men?"

"I'm sorry." Heat traveled up her spine. "I was wrong."

Papa flashed her a quizzical look followed by a slight grin. "I'm relieved you admit it. I was beginning to think you've turned your back on everything I've taught you."

"You taught me well. We only differ on one issue."

"Not only one I should think." Papa motioned to the settee. "Come and sit with me. We're going to settle this rift between us."

America sat next to her father by the fireplace. She wished it were so easy. "What issue do we differ on other than slavery?"

"The way a proper lady should act."

Her face flushed. "How could you say such a thing, Papa? I've always acted decently."

Papa took her hands in his. "I'm talking about the role of a lady in society. I'm your father. As such, I must guide you the way I see fit until such time as I pass the role to the man to whom I give your hand in marriage."

"I'm an adult, Papa. Surely I should have some say in the decisions made in my behalf."

"You mean well." Papa packed his pipe and lit it. "The female anatomy isn't suited to make wise choices. You proved it when you took off to Oberlin and didn't come home for years. If that's not bad enough, you allowed those abolitionist rebels to influence you. Your behavior has shown me you need my guidance."

"But, Papa --"

"Don't interrupt. Now, you shun the prospect of a union with a fine gentleman so you can go to heathen lands alone." He drew in a puff from his pipe and let it slowly out of his mouth and nose. His voice gained a calm melodic tone. "It may be God has placed the desire for missionary work within you to be a support to your husband as he funds these endeavors, but you won't even consider it."

America blew out a breath and looked at the mantel. Only five figurine horses left. She hoped another one wouldn't succumb to the argument. "I agree Harland is a good man, and under other circumstances, I would welcome his attentions, but I can't consider matrimony with him when I'm called to the mission field."

"You believe it to be the case." He set his pipe on the table and rubbed his palms against his thighs. "Consider this. When I, your father, try to tell you otherwise, you won't listen. Are you following God when you shun those He's given in authority over you?"

She tried to keep her voice as calm as his. "I came home for a visit, not to stay. I've been supporting myself for over three years now with my employment at the college bookstore. I may be a woman, but I'm not addled. I know what God told me to do, and I know my own mind."

"I never said you were addled." Papa let out an audible sigh. "When I was in the US Calvary, I didn't always agree with what my commanding officer ordered, but I obeyed as a good soldier does. You want to serve God, yet you're not willing to obey orders and let Him work things out."

The start of a headache was coming on, and she rubbed her temples. "Papa, I need to go upstairs and rest. My head hurts."

He nodded. "We'll finish this later."

She climbed the stairs to her bedroom. Nothing had changed. If she obeyed her father and married Harland, she would have a good life, but she would never fulfill her calling. If she took William's offer to return to Oberlin, she'd give up her family for an uncertain future.

William's declaration of feelings for her had taken her by surprise. She'd wanted a courtship with him since they prayed on the steps at First Church, but she resigned herself to the fact he didn't feel the same. He always seemed to disapprove of her.

Her fondness for William confused her. She couldn't deny it, but at the same time, the man could get her dander up faster than anyone she'd ever known. Even if she did care for him, she needed to marry somebody who had compassion for her and her situation, who wouldn't judge her for wanting to compromise occasionally for the sake of peace. It had become obvious William wasn't that man.

The constant turmoil caused her head to hurt. She wet a cloth and placed it on her forehead. It tired her having to stand up to her father and, it seemed at times, to everyone. At this point, she wished she could give in, even on the issue of slavery, to relieve the guilt and anguish she felt about displeasing Papa.

William could never understand no matter how much she admired him. He didn't retreat when there was a fight. Instead, he frequently ran to the skirmish. She'd always dreamed of marrying a man who had her papa's blessing, not someone she would run off with in the middle of the night. Maybe she should talk to Papa about William.

America let out a sigh as she lay on her bed and pulled the quilt her mother had made over her. So tired. He wouldn't listen to her about William any more than he did about slavery, or Naomi, or Oberlin.

Why did William wait so long?

Chapter Twenty-Eight

America tried to focus on Harland's words as she sat beside him on the settee in the parlor, but her mind kept going back to what William had said earlier.

Harland cleared his throat. "America, did you hear me?"

"I'm afraid I was preoccupied."

His smile slipped. "Perhaps I should come back when I have your full attention."

"I'm sorry." She blinked. "I have a bit of a headache."

"Are you all right?"

"I'm fine." She squinted to keep the light the fireplace gave out from hurting her eyes. "I'm listening now."

A grin came across his face as he handed her a letter. "It's from the missionaries we support in China. Their school has twenty students, and the whole village is now serving God."

America scanned the paper. The letters blurred. She blinked and read it again. "Oh Harland, this is wonderful. God is truly doing a work there."

"One day, we can travel to China and see for ourselves." He lowered his eyes. "Forgive me. I'm being presumptuous. I know your desire is to return to Oberlin."

"I'm not promising anything, but..."

Harland leaned in.

"I'm considering the possibility God may want me here."

His face lit up.

She rubbed her temples. "I haven't decided yet."

"I'm praying God helps you make the right choice even if it means I might lose you. My desire is for you to obey God."

Her hands trembled. "Do you mean that?"

"With all my heart." He placed her hand in his. "It's not the only thing troubling you, is it?"

"No."

He rubbed her hand between his fingers. "Tell me about it."

"It's Naomi." She pinched her nose to keep her eyes from watering. "If Riley doesn't get the money to buy her note from my father by the end of January, she'll be sold in the slave auctions. Papa needs the money to pay the mortgage."

Harland patted her hand. "How much does he need?"

"Four hundred dollars." She let out a sigh. "It might as well be four thousand."

He stood and headed to the door of the kitchen. "I'll speak to your father. Stay here."

America called after him. "It won't do any good."

*****

Colonel Leighton sat near the kitchen door reading a book. From this angle, he could see Harland and Merry without invading on their privacy or eavesdropping on their conversation.

Harland headed to the kitchen door. The colonel stood. He hadn't expected the visit to end this soon. If Merry had turned Harland away by pestering him with her idiotic notions, he'd give her a talking to.

"Sir." Harland adjusted the collar on his grey frock suit jacket. "May I speak with you alone?"

"Of course." Colonel Leighton motioned to the kitchen table where they sat across from each other. "What's wrong? Did my daughter say something?"

"America told me of the situation with Naomi."

Colonel Leighton stroked his beard. He wasn't sure whether to be angry she would burden someone with a family matter or to be pleased she felt close enough to Harland to share her concerns.

"I have a proposition to make," Harland said.

"Go on. I'm listening."

"I'd like to buy Naomi's note from you for the four hundred you require from Riley."

Colonel Leighton raised his eyebrow. "Why would you want to do that? You don't need another slave."

The politician smile crossed Harland's face. "Your daughter is very persuasive."

"I don't know." The colonel held in his gratification at this development. "I'd lose money on the deal. If Riley doesn't pay in time, I'd keep his money and my slave."

"Come now. I'm doing this as a favor to America. You don't expect me to take a loss?"

The man was shrewd. He'd make a fine provider for America. "All right, I'll sign the note over to you, but if Riley were to come up with the money after the deadline, would you still sell Naomi to him?"

"I don't know." Harland drew his knuckle to his lips. "I might if the price were right, or I might give her to America as a wedding gift if America were to agree to marry me."

"Do you intend to ask her?"

"I do, with your permission."

"It's a little soon. At this point, I doubt she'll say yes."

Harland's smile widened. "Leave it to me. Women don't know what they want. They need to be guided. She'll come around." He stopped at a mirror by the door to straighten his blue and red silk cravat before he ambled back to the parlor.

Colonel Leighton sat in the chair where he could see the couple unimpeded. He should have been relieved. He was assured of having enough to pay off the mortgage, Naomi was safe from the auction block, and Harland wanted to marry his daughter.

Something in his gut stirred. Harland acted so sure of himself. Harland being a slave-owner still came between them. Even if the colonel approved, Merry had strong ideals she wouldn't dismiss lightly. She should be wooed into matrimony, not coerced.

*****

Harland walked into the room, stood over America, and smiled.

"Well," she said. "Are you going to tell me what happened?"

His grin grew wider. "I did it."

"You did what?"

He sat in the chair beside her. "I bought the note on Naomi. Riley has all the time in the world to buy her freedom now."

She flew into his arms.

Harland held her for a moment then leaned back. He moved his face closer to hers, and right before their lips touched, he cleared his throat and released his hold. "I'd better go."

He headed to the door and grabbed his coat off the hook and his hat and gloves from the foyer table. "I'll never forget this." Her voice thickened. "Thank you."

He put on his coat and gloves, then grabbed his walking stick. "May I call on you tomorrow?"

"Yes, of course." She opened the door, and a breeze blew in chilling her.

He stepped out into the wind as red leaves swirled around his feet. She kept the door open as she watched him ride away on his spotted horse. He was such a kind man. Why couldn't she feel more than a growing friendship and fondness for him? It would be so much easier if she could love him the way she did William.

Her strong attraction toward William had brought her nothing but grief. There was no point on dwelling on the relationship they would never have. She couldn't betray her father and run off with him. Even if she did, he would never see her as anything more than a slave owner's daughter.

Harland was different. He understood. He knew what it was like to live in Kentucky where slavery was commonplace, and yet, he allowed God to change his heart and his views. Surely, paying for Naomi's note proved such. He didn't judge her or jump to conclusions like William did. She could relax around him.

She could grow to love him, she was sure of it.

*****

Joe and his family entered Riley's cabin. Naomi stood by the fireplace with a yellow scarf tied around her head and a stained apron secured around her waist stirring a pot of stew. When the master gave the family the evening off, she insisted they come by for supper.

Naomi glanced up and ran into her father's arms. She smelled like fresh baked bread. Joe held onto her for a moment before releasing her.

She darted back to the pot over the fireplace. "Supper will be laid out soon."

"Do you need some help?" Ruth tied an apron around her waist.

A knock at the door sounded, and Riley answered it. Harland Boidae stepped inside.

"Mr. Boidae," Riley said with the syrupy sweet voice he used with white folks. "Can I help you with something?"

Mr. Boidae chuckled and removed his gloves and hat. "Yes, boy, you can take good care of my property."

Obadiah's hands balled into fists, and Joe placed a hand on his son's shoulder to remind him to keep his peace.

"What do you mean, sir?" Riley asked. "I ain't got no property of yours."

Mr. Boidae pointed toward Naomi with his cobra walking stick. His stance matched that of a snake ready to strike. "Not yet, but come the end of January, your pretty little Negress becomes mine." He pulled a paper out of his coat pocket. "This is Naomi's note. You signed it, didn't you?"

"Yeah, but..." Riley's nostrils flared. "That's Colonel Leighton's note, sir. Where'd you get it?"

Mr. Boidae stepped closer and leered at Naomi like she would be his next meal. Joe stepped in front of his daughter. Obadiah moved to his side.

"Sir, I done asked you where you got that note." The sweetness in

Riley's voice flattened and took on an edge of fear.

"I bought it from Colonel Leighton." Mr. Boidae's eyes continued to wander down Naomi's body. "Paid four hundred for it. A bargain if I say so myself. America was so vexed about her, she about begged me buy the note." He grinned. "Said she'd do anything."

"Mr. Boidae." The syrup in Riley's voice was gone now. "I'm inviting you to leave my home now."

Mr. Boidae snorted. "Oh, I'll leave, boy. I'll be back come January twenty-second." He slipped his gloves on his hands and tipped his hat. "That pretty little thing is well worth waiting for." He chuckled as he left.

Obadiah slammed the door shut behind him.

Naomi collapsed into Riley's arms.

"Don't fret." Joe wiped the back of his neck with his hand. "You'll be gone before Mr. Boidae comes knocking again."

Obadiah charged a couple of steps toward Joe. "What do you mean gone?"

"Hush," Ruth said. "You keep your peace and listen to your pa for once."

Obadiah opened his mouth. His eyes darted from Joe to his ma before slumping onto the bench by the table.

Ruth nodded to Joe.

Joe gave her a sideways grin before facing his son. "Obi, your ma and me help slaves cross the river. If we can't raise the money to keep your sister from being sold, we need you to cross with her and Riley come mid-January."

A glint appeared in Obadiah's eyes. "All this time." He shook his head. "All this time, Pa, bowing and scraping to the colonel, and you been doing this?"

"Yeah." Joe held his breath. Obadiah's anger got the better of him at times. Joe wanted to show Obi he still had the wherewithal to take care of him if need be.

"You could have trusted me." Obadiah flung toward him and gave him a bear hug while keeping his arms away from the lashes on Joe's back. "I could have helped, Pa. I could have..." He buried his face in his pa's shoulder. "I'm sorry. I figured you was just scared. I didn't know."

Joe patted his son's back. "It be all right, Obi. It be all right."

Obadiah lifted his head. "When the time comes, I'll get them over safe or die trying."

"I know you will."

Emotion choked the words out of the air.

Riley delivered the preacher look. "What about Bart and Izzy?"

Joe cleared his throat. "What about them?"

"You ain't gonna leave them in his grasp, are you?"

Ruth set her hand on his arm. "What's going on?"

Joe looked up to Heaven. Must be the Good Lord's timing for all of it to see the light of day. "Mr. Boidae's forcing himself on Izzy. Bart let him have his way with her for some extra meat and such. Todd saw them."

Ruth pulled her hand to her mouth. "What about Miss Merry? Are you gonna warn her?"

"Ain't I got enough worries what with Naomi and the other colored women in his clutches? I can't be sticking my neck out for some white woman. Besides, if it weren't for the master's daughter, Mr. Boidae wouldn't have his hands on Riley's note."

Ruth crossed her arms. Riley's glare bore into Joe until he let out a groan and stormed out of the cabin slamming the door behind him.

He sprinted up the hillside. His back hurt, and he collapsed in the dirt.

Lord, I know you want me to forgive Colonel Leighton and warn him, but I can't. He's the one who forced his daughter into that snake's arms. "Master's getting what he deserves."

"Miss Merry's not."

Joe spun toward his son's voice.

Obadiah gave him a shrug. "Miss Merry's been good to Naomi, to all of us. She don't treat us like Colonel Leighton or Luke. She acts like we as good as her. It ain't right to let her fall in Mr. Boidae's hands if we can do something about it."

"I figured you hated the master."

Obadiah sat in the grass next to Joe. "I don't hate him. I can't bear what he do to us, how he treats us like we's nothing. It makes me mad we can't do what we want like free folks. What I hated more than anything is the way I figured you was afeared of him. Made me ashamed."

Joe stared at the apples on the ground.

"Now I know. You got to warn him, Pa. You can't let this go on."

"He won't listen. Don't matter I've served him well for years. He'll take a white man's side over me any day."

"Pa." Obadiah gave him a dimpled half grin like he used to when he was little. "Where's your faith you always jabbering about?"

The boy was right. Joe knew what he needed to do, but the colonel didn't help Amos or Naomi when he could have. "You get on back. I'll be there directly."

Obadiah nodded and made his way down the hill.

Joe threw an apple against the tree. He wouldn't get any thanks for warning his master. All he could expect would be another beating. He still hadn't recovered from the last one, and it made his back ache worse than ever. Probably wouldn't do America no good anyhow.

No, I won't do it. Lord, you're asking too much

.

Chapter Twenty-Nine

Joe sat at the table with his head propped in his hands. He'd never known a more stubborn woman. Ruth wouldn't let it drop.

She grabbed tin plates off the shelf. "You need to tell her."

"Woman, I ain't gonna do it. Master don't care about selling our children off. Why should I care about his?"

"She's been good to Naomi. You know."

He shook his head and let out a groan. "Let it be. He ain't gonna hurt her none. He's got a hankering for black women. Lots of slave owners do. It don't mean they treat their wives bad."

Ruth turned her back to him. "Brother Woods is leaving soon."

"What's he got to do with anything?"

Ruth dished out food from the pot hanging over the fireplace and banged the plate in front of him. "He's who she should be marrying. Naomi will be all right. She's gonna cross over, but what about America? She'll be stuck with that white turd."

Joe stared at the stew on his plate. It wasn't often his wife used that kind of talk. "Can't I have one meal in peace, woman?"

Ruth plunked down on the bench across the table from him. "I ain't gonna say no more, but how are you planning on getting peace with your Maker?"

He didn't want to let her know he was wondering the same thing.

*****

William swung his ax into another log. He wanted to do something to help Benjamin, but the real reason he chopped wood was to keep his mind off the waiting. He couldn't keep it up much longer. The sun had already set, and clouds obscured the full moon. The lantern provided some light, but it was foolish chopping wood at night. He set the ax down and rubbed his arms. "Are you sure she's coming?"

Benjamin grabbed pieces of the log and threw them in the wood box. "She said she'd be here."

"You don't think her father suspects anything."

A rustling sounded as the wagon with Merry, Joe, and Ruth came up the path.

"Reverend Thornton," Merry said through panted breath. "I'm sorry we're late. Harland wanted to attend the prayer meeting with me."

William's chest tightened. "How did you get away without him?"

"I didn't have to. Papa insisted he leave. Harland's been at the house to visit every day, and Papa felt we'd spent enough time together this week."

Benjamin nodded. "Let's go inside. We can talk there."

Joe turned away and strode to the barn. Ruth chased after him and whispered something in his ear.

William stared at them for a moment trying to figure out what was going on. He'd never seen them have cross words with each other before. He trailed Brother Benjamin and Merry into the house.

Merry removed her cloak. "The lantern at Reverend Rankin's house is lit, and nobody is lurking around the river. I gave Joe an overnight pass."

"Thank you," Benjamin said, "but if there's a hint of trouble, don't take any chances."

"I shouldn't have any difficulty," Merry said. "I've been more receptive to my father's wishes."

William twisted his mouth. "What's that supposed to mean?"

"If you must know, I'm considering staying in Kentucky and marrying Harland."

"You can't be serious." Heat rose up the back of William's neck. "You would throw away your calling on that... scoundrel."

"How dare you call him such a thing?"

"I can think of some other things to call him, but I couldn't say them in front of a lady."

"Harland is a fine gentleman. My father has made his decision concerning Oberlin. I must consider this is what God would have me do."

"What about Naomi?" William took a step toward her. "A week ago, you were willing to go against your father to make sure she and your other slaves were freed, but now you're considering marrying a slave owner. I don't suppose she matters."

"You don't know what you're talking about." Merry's glare reflected hurt more than anger. "Harland paid Naomi's note off so Papa wouldn't sell her. He's trying to help."

"He gave her freedom, just like that?" William flexed his hands into fists at his sides. He wished Boidae had been there right then.

"No, not just like that." Merry rubbed her temples. "Riley still has to pay Harland, but now he has time to come up with the money."

"Sister Merry, he's doing it to impress you. If he really cared, he'd have set her free. Now he can use her to buy your affections, and it looks like it's working."

Merry spun and stomped out the door.

William darted outside in time to watch her running down the path out of view. He sensed Benjamin's glare before he looked over his shoulder to confirm it. His father once gave him that look when he caught him stealing a book from the store. He was about ten at the time, and he wasn't sure he'd make it to eleven.

Benjamin pointed his finger at him. "She has risked losing her father for the cause. You, of all people, should understand her, and you accuse her of allowing a man to buy her affections? What's wrong with you?"

William picked up the ax near the chopping block. "She's made her choice. I don't have to be happy about it." He swung the ax. Pieces of the log flew in the air.

"There's something not right about this." Benjamin stared down the path Merry had taken. "I'm worried about her."

"To hear her talk, he's an abolitionist."

Benjamin's brow furrowed. "He's lying to her, no doubt, but is attacking her character the way to warn her of his intentions?"

William swung the ax.

*****

America had never been so angry in her life. She sat up straight and held her hands in her lap to keep from creating a spectacle by storming out of church in the middle of the sermon. How dare William? God's discipline indeed, as if she didn't know what he was up to. She'd never met a man like him before, a man who would use the pulpit for his own means. She couldn't wait for church to end.

Service was dismissed. She turned to Harland who had taken to sitting beside her a week earlier. "Could you call on me later? There's something I need to do first."

Harland bowed slightly. "Of course."

He was a gentleman, unlike others. She strode out of the church toward the path leading to the river. She reached the edge of the woods, something rustled behind her. She spun around. William had chased after her. She folded her arms and waited for him.

William tripped and fell on the muddy ground with a thud. He pulled himself up and flashed a sideways grin. "I wanted to talk to you."

America kept her tone stern. "Are you all right?"

"Yes." He tried to brush the mud and leaves off his black suit, but he only smeared it, making the suit look worse. "Only my pride is hurt, and perhaps it's something needing to be brought down."

She couldn't argue, but she still planned to give him a good going over if he dared... "You obviously want to say something. Go ahead."

At least he had the good graces to look sheepish. "Sister Merry."

"You may go back to calling me Sister Leighton. I'll return to Brother Woods."

The muscle in William's jaw twitched. "Sister Leighton, I'm sorry for what I said last night. I know how deeply you care about the slaves in your father's charge. No matter my misgivings about Mr. Boidae, I had no right to say what I did."

She had thought of many things he might say and how she would answer him, but she didn't expect an apology. "What about the message you delivered today?"

His Adam's apple bulged. "I assure you it was preached to me first by Brother Benjamin the moment I lost my temper and said those horrible things to you. The Holy Spirit also corrected me last night while I wrote my notes for today's sermon. Please forgive me."

"You're wrong about Harland too."

William looked at the ground. "No, I'm not."

America let out a long sigh. "You confuse me." Her anger waned, and she wanted to hold on to it a bit longer. "One moment, you're asking me to sneak off to Oberlin with you, and the next, you're accusing me of compromising my principles for a smooth-talking slave owner. Why did you act in such a manner?"

"You don't know?"

"Of course, I don't know. Do you really think so little of me?"

His eyes pressed shut then opened wide. "You talked about marrying Mr. Boidae and staying in Kentucky. My jealousy got the better of me."

"Jealousy?"

"I'm in love with you."

Her knees wobbled. "You have a strange way of showing it."

"Nevertheless, I am. Will you forgive me?"

She cupped her hands over her eyes. The sun shined too brightly for a cold day like today. Her head throbbed, a drum pounding with an admonition to obey her father and marry Harland.

Maybe if he'd told her before they left for Kentucky. "I forgive you, Brother William."

A dimple appeared on William's right cheek. "Thank you, Sister Merry."

"I haven't decided what I'm going to do yet, but I don't see how I can run off like a fugitive slave. I can't betray my father."

He kneaded the back of his neck. "You need to decide today. I have to leave for another church tomorrow."

"Oh." She rubbed her temples. The headache was getting worse.

"When will you be back?"

Green flecks darted across William's eyes as he gazed into hers. "Unless you decide now to listen to reason, I won't be back. I know you care for your father, but surely you can't stay here and marry a slave owner just to please him. I thought God called you to be a missionary."

"He did." A gust whipped her cloak against her. "At least I thought He did, but maybe God has different plans for me. Harland is a good man, and he plans to free his slaves. Think of the good I could do as a US Senator's wife. I need to at least consider the possibility."

"Nonsense. You used to be an intelligent woman. Have you lost all your senses? Have you become one of those timid ladies who obey a man's every command? Maybe you want to spend the rest of your life having dinner parties with smug politicians."

Heat surged through her. "How dare you? You have no call to order me around as if I were one of your slaves." She stomped her foot.

"I can't abide watching you throw away your life and your calling on that man." William's voice caught. "There's something wrong about him. I know it."

She rubbed her eyes. "If you want to leave, maybe you'd better do so."

He took a step toward her and held out his hands. "Sister Merry, please reconsider. Say there's a chance you'll change your mind, and I'll stop by here before I return to Oberlin. I'll take you back only as a friend if you want, but you can't stay here and marry that man."

Snowflakes fell from the sky. "Don't bother." Her head pounded, and she thought she might swoon. "I won't run off without my father's blessing with a man who thinks so little of me." The white flakes were too bright.

William's shoulder's sagged. "Then if you've made your decision, there's nothing I can do."

She closed her eyes tight then forced the open. "You're wrong about Harland. He's a good man, and he loves me."

"I hope it's not too late when you find out his true colors." Some flakes stuck to his hair. "Would you like me to escort you home?"

"I don't think it would be wise."

"Then this is good-bye."

A lump caught in her throat. "Yes, I'm afraid so."

William stuck his hands in his pockets and sauntered up the path to the church. Snow began to cover it making the sun reflecting off him brighter. She half expected him to glance back, but he didn't.

She wanted to run after him, to stop him.

She squinted and shielded her eyes. What good would it do? She wouldn't go against her father.

Chapter Thirty

Harland mounted his horse and headed to the Leighton Ranch. He chuckled at America's gullibility at believing he would free his slaves when they were married. He didn't expect their relationship to move this fast. She'd be easy to control.

She even trusted him when he said he inherited his slaves from his father. Before his father had taken to his bed, they'd only had three slaves left. His father had gone on some kind of religious crusade and had freed the rest of them. Harland worked hard to increase the slave force with suitable female mill workers. He'd even traveled as far as Lawrence County to obtain some at a bargain price. They were cheaper than paid labor, and more profitable, especially when he bred them, a task he enjoyed.

A year ago, Harland's father had grown so debilitated he couldn't get out of bed. The doctor had said he wouldn't last a year. Father had lay in his bed, awake for a change, with a look of fear in his eyes. His skin had grown pale with a yellowish hue. He had blinked and struggled to pull himself into a sitting position.

Harland had plastered a sympathetic expression on his face to hold his frustration in check. The man was useless. "Father, you need to get your affairs in order. I'll run the mill for you and see your needs are taken care of, but you need to deed your assets to me."

"You're my son, my only child." His father's voice had choked up. "I would think you'd have some sadness about hearing I might die."

Harland hadn't known how to respond. Father's rigid principles and abuse had been the reason Mother killed herself. "Do you want everything you've worked for your whole life to collapse?" He had set the papers on the bed and had dipped a pen in the inkwell sitting on the night table. "I've talked to a lawyer, and he drew up the necessary papers. All they need is your signature."

Father had slumped into the pillow behind him. "Promise me no more of your shady dealings."

Harland had laid his hand over his heart. "I give my word."

Father had set the pen on the paper before him. "One more thing."

Harland had held in his disgust and placed his hand on Father's shoulder. "Anything."

"I've purposed in my heart to free all of my slaves since I've repented of the practice. Vow here on my deathbed you'll free Bart and Izzy, and their boy."

"I'll do it."

Harland had let out a sigh of relief when Father had signed the paper. A barmaid from Lexington who had nowhere else to go cared for his father's needs so he wouldn't have to see the man. Her desperation guaranteed her loyalty. He had no intention of fulfilling any of the promises he made since he now had what he came for, especially not freeing the slaves.

America's constant prattle about abolition reminded Harland of his father, but once she was his wife, he would take her in hand until she submitted to his will. Marrying Colonel Leighton's daughter would guarantee his election to the United States Senate.

He would have wooed her even if she'd been homely to get her father's endorsement, but at least she was fair to look at. Her wardrobe needed revised. She frequently clothed herself in those common day dresses like any dirt farmer's wife, not to mention that ridiculous bloomer outfit she wore when they went riding.

When she became his wife, he'd burn those bloomers and wool frocks. He'd buy her the finest satin and velvet hoop skirt dresses with ruffles and frills, and corsets to decrease her waistline along with suitable undergarments, attractive bonnets, and a new cloak. It wouldn't be proper for a senator's wife to dress so plain, and no bride of his would ride a horse astride like a man. A side-saddle and a new riding outfit would be his wedding gift to her.

Once she was properly outfitted, America would make a fine spouse. She would impress the voters and men of stature. Even her abolitionist views could work to his favor. He'd be able to play both sides of the fence, guaranteeing the anti-slavery vote as well as the vote of slave owners.

He gazed in the mirror and straightened his tie. With his new suit, he made a dashing figure she wouldn't be able to resist. Today he would propose to America with Colonel's Leighton's blessing, and today she would say yes.

Chapter Thirty-One

Harland entered the parlor and greeted Colonel Leighton with a grin outshining the silver tray Ruth had recently polished. "Could we talk?"

Colonel Leighton motioned to the chairs in front of the fireplace. "I wanted to speak to you as well. You've been over here quite a bit lately for a man who isn't betrothed."

"I agree." Harland leaned in toward the colonel. "I'd like your permission to ask for America's hand in marriage today."

The colonel scowled. "She might give you the mitten. She may have a more favorable opinion of you than she did at first, but she still insists she won't marry a slave-owner."

"I know." Harland ran his hand through his blond hair. "I've told her it's only a matter of time before I free my slaves."

The colonel raised an eyebrow. He was astonished Harland would make such a foolish business decision, even if it was out of love for Merry. "My daughter's a stubborn woman. Do you think that will satisfy her?"

Harland gave a half shrug. "May I be honest with you?"

"If you want my daughter's hand, I expect it."

"I do plan to eventually free my slaves." Harland widened his grin. "However, I did lead America to believe I might do it a little sooner than is prudent."

Colonel Leighton stroked his beard. He didn't like the idea of Harland lying to her even though he understood why.

"I plan to tell her the truth." Harland made eye contact with Colonel Leighton without so much as a blink. "She's so headstrong when it comes to abolition, I wanted to let her get to know me first."

The colonel returned a probing gaze of his own. "You need to tell her everything before you ask for her hand. I won't have you start your lives together in a lie."

"I'm sorry I deceived her." Harland glanced down. "I'll make it right."

Colonel Leighton shook Harland's hand. "Then you have my blessing." A sense of relief spread over him. Once America was safely married to a man like Harland, he wouldn't worry about her so much.

*****

America looked in the mirror one last time before Harland was due to arrive. Dark puffy circles lined her eyes. She'd felt unusually warm, and Papa was convinced she had the ague, but it was just nerves causing her frequent headaches.

The time she promised her father would conclude in a week, but she decided not to end the courtship. Harland proved himself to be a Christian gentleman, and she was fond of him. She had felt an uneasiness around him, but that could be explained. No doubt her feelings for William and William's dislike for Harland affected her.

William was as wrong about him as he'd been about her. No evidence in Harland's behavior gave her any cause for concern other than him owning slaves, and he'd made a commitment to free them.

A nudging inside urged her to pray about Harland's intentions, but what good would it do? Listening to God's direction about returning home got her in this situation. Now she was trapped with no way of escape – like the Negros who prayed for deliverance.

She rubbed her temples. The start of another headache? She hoped not. Her thoughts jumbled. She would never be a missionary as Harland's wife, but maybe being a senator's wife would give her a venue to further the kingdom of God in a way she never could have by traveling overseas.

"America." Papa's voice bellowed out from downstairs. "Harland's here."

"I'll be down presently." Her stomach churned, and she placed her arm over it. *Lord, give me peace about this or deliver me from it.*

She descended the stairs and nodded a greeting toward Harland. The staircase wobbled, and her balance almost faltered. She rubbed her sore neck and leaned against the railing to keep from falling.

Harland's eyes crinkled. "I wish to ask you something. I've already spoken to your father."

America licked her dry lips. There'd be no deliverance, no rescue, no prayer breaking through the fog to reach God on her behalf. "Go ahead."

Harland lowered to one knee and took her hand in his. "Will you marry me?"

A metallic taste assaulted her mouth as she tried to choke out the words, but they wouldn't come. A dread swept over her in waves, threatening to drown her. She struggled to breathe.

"It seems I've left you speechless," Harland said. "I suppose that's a normal reaction. I love you, and I intend to do everything in my power to make you happy. I know we'll have a wonderful life together." He rose and embraced her.

America smelled the foul odor of his cigar and gagged. She pushed on his chest and pulled away from him.

"I didn't mean to take liberties with you." Harland's gaze chilled her. "Since we're betrothed, an embrace in your father's house is permissible, don't you think?"

She forced out the words. "I never answered you."

His steel blue eyes narrowed. "I've been presumptuous. It's just I'm so excited about our life together." He grinned and tilted his head. "I plan to free my slaves and tear up the note on Naomi as a wedding present to you, and for our honeymoon, we'll sail to China and see the missions I help support. I know I'm being extravagant, but I can't help it. I'm a man in love."

So hot. Her head hurt. Thoughts spun in circles. She tried to latch on to one as she wiped the sweat off her brow.

Papa shook Harland's hand. "I'm happy for both of you."

Luke kissed her on the cheek. "So am I."

Wait. Luke's not here. He's with Virginia.

Her brother hugged her and whispered in her ear. "I've never known you to cower to the colonel's demands so easily. You're betraying your calling for a slave owner." He pulled away, but he wasn't Luke anymore.

William raised his judgmental eyebrow at her and faded away.

What else was she supposed to do? Papa wasn't going to change his mind and let her return to college. Marrying Harland was her only choice.

Harland wrapped his arm around her. "I thought I'd have to do some mighty fine wooing to win this lady's heart. I couldn't believe she consented so easily."

Did she consent? She couldn't remember.

"You've made yourself a fine match," Papa said. "I can tell my Merry's never been happier by the blush on her cheeks."

America raised her hand to her face. So hot. The floor rose to meet her.

*****

Master Leighton carried his daughter to the settee.

Mr. Bodai took hold of her hand. "She seemed all right a moment ago. Maybe it was the excitement."

Joe swallowed as he grabbed a blanket and covered her. It was all he could think to do. It scared him to see her look so pale.

"She's been complaining of headaches lately." The master felt her head. "She's burning up with fever. Harland, help me get her to her bed."

Mr. Bodai took America in his arms. She stirred, moaned something Joe couldn't understand, and dropped her head against Bodai's chest.

Master turned to Joe. "Take my horse and get Doctor Adams. Tell him to hurry." Joe was almost out the door before the master finished speaking. He ran to the barn and saddled Colonel Leighton's favorite stallion as fast as he could. Master had to be worried. He'd never let Joe ride this horse before. Joe finished with the bridle, then mounted and galloped up the hill toward Dover.

He had some repenting to do, but there wasn't time now. If America died, Naomi and Ruth would never forgive him. He should have warned her. She had to be all right. He arrived and tied the horse to the hitch post in front of the doctor's house before pounding on the door.

The doctor's wife answered with a toddler propped on her hip. "Joe, what do you want?"

"I need the doctor, ma'am." He panted to calm his breathing. "Colonel Leighton's daughter took ill. He sent me to fetch Doctor Adams."

"Oh." Mrs. Adams set the child on the floor. "He's not here."

"She's real sick." Joe tried to keep the panic from rising to his throat.

"He's up the road about a mile checking on a patient," Mrs. Adams said. "You can wait in the barn. He'll be back shortly."

"She's bad off, ma'am. Could I go fetch him?"

Mrs. Adams steepled her forefingers together against her mouth. "I suppose it's needful. You take the road west, and it'll be the third farm you pass."

Joe tipped his hat. "Thank you, ma'am." He mounted the stallion and rode to the house Mrs. Adams described. He jumped off the horse, and knocked.

A man he'd never seen before answered. "Yeah, boy, what you want?"

"I need Doctor Adams, sir."

"He's busy." The man closed the door before Joe could say a word.

Joe paced in front of the house. He dared not knock again. He pulled his coat tighter and glanced at the snow clouds hovering over him.

Ruth was right about one thing. Miss Merry should be jumping the broom with Brother Woods, not Mr. Boidae. Now Brother Woods didn't even know she was ailing all because Joe had held onto his unforgiveness, and after he told Obadiah no good comes from it.

Even if he told Colonel Leighton the truth about Mr. Boidae now, what good would it do? *Lord, I done wrong.* Where was that doctor?

Doctor Adams walked out the door with his bag in hand.

Joe ran up to him. "Doctor Adams, sir, Colonel Leighton sent me to fetch you. His daughter took ill."

Doctor Adams climbed into his buggy. "America Leighton? I didn't know she was back from Ohio."

"Yessur, she is. She up and swooned, and she's burning up."

"You ride on ahead, boy. Tell your master I'll be there soon."

Joe nodded, mounted the horse, but he didn't head back to the ranch. There was one stop he needed to make first. He rode hard to the Thornton's home.

As soon as Reverend Thornton opened the door, Joe rushed into the house. "Sir, we gotta talk."

Reverend Thornton's eyes widened. "Of course, Joe. What happened?"

"It's Miss Merry. She's powerful sick. Colonel Leighton sent me to fetch the doctor. He's on the way, but I'm afeared."

The reverend grabbed his coat. "I'll go pray with her straight away."

"Wait," Joe said. "There's more."

Reverend Thornton motioned to the table. "Why don't we sit down and you can tell me about it."

"No time." Joe swallowed the lump in his throat. "Miss Merry is fixing to jump the broom with Mr. Boidae. I figured you might know how to get a hold of Brother Woods and get him back here."

"I believe she's making the wrong choice too, but she's a grown woman. She can choose who she wants to marry."

Joe took a deep breath and told Reverend Thornton the truth about Mr. Boidae and how he didn't say anything to Colonel Leighton or America. "This is all my fault. If I'd told her before Brother Woods left..."

Reverend Thornton placed his hand on Joe's shoulder. "I'll post a telegram to William. It may be a few weeks before he gets the message though. In the meantime, you best get back to the house."

Joe nodded and headed to the door.

"Joe."

He stopped.

"Colonel Leighton doesn't need this turmoil while he's fretting about his daughter's health. Don't say anything until America gets well. Maybe by then, William will be back. If he's not, I'll go with you to warn the colonel."

Joe's voice thickened. "Thank you, sir." Miss Merry just had to be all right.

Chapter Thirty-Two

William caught a glimpse of the church nestled in Hidden Fork on the shore of Cumberland River in southeastern Kentucky. It would be nice to lay on a soft bed instead of the hard ground. He hated sleeping outside in the cold. Even when he did doze, thoughts of Merry being wed to that slave owner disrupted his rest.

When he had held the revival services in Flemingsburg last week, Brother Charles and Sister Martha both had admonished him not to give up. Charles told him about how he had to fight for Martha when her father had threatened to disown her if she continued speaking out against slavery. Martha told him she almost gave in to her father's wishes, and if Charles hadn't been there supporting her, she might not have had the courage to stand up against him.

They didn't understand. Merry didn't have the mettle Martha had. Instead of standing up to her father, she bowed to his wishes. She would soon be a slave owner's wife. At least he found out in time what kind of a woman she was.

He marched to the small log cabin behind the church and knocked. At least here, he wouldn't have to defend himself like he had with Charles and Martha. He could recover from the blow to his heart and try to forget Merry without anyone accusing him of allowing pride and unforgiveness to cloud his judgement.

The door inched open. A Kentucky rifle stuck through the opening. "What's your business here?"

His heart raced. "Sir, I'm Brother William Woods from Oberlin. I was expected."

The thin man opened the door wide and set the rifle down. "I'm sorry, Brother Woods. I'm Reverend Keller." He shook William's hand. "Please, come in."

William stepped inside, let out a deep breath to release the tension. The warmth from the blazing fire in the hearth on the far wall spread through him. His fingers and toes burned in complaint for leaving them in the cold for too long.

"Reverend Keller, about what just happened--"

"I'm sorry about the gun." The preacher wiped his hand over his scraggly beard. "Please come sit by the fire." His voice seemed almost pleading.

William gave a curt nod and handed his coat, muffler, and gloves to Mrs. Keller. Sitting on the dirt floor, he removed his boots and wiggled his feet and hands in front of the blaze.

"We'll get you something to eat." Mrs. Keller's hair was tied in a tight knot, making her face look severe, but her sparkling brown eyes and smile lines suggested she laughed often, although maybe not much lately. "Are you hungry?"

William's stomach growled as if on cue. "Yes, ma'am."

Everyone started working at once. Reverend Keller reached up and grabbed cups from a high shelf, but he moved stiffly, like a man twice William's age instead of only a few years older.

A thin girl around six with big brown eyes and hollow cheeks set plates on the table. Her faded pink calico dress was a little too short. Her older sister, probably about eight years old, with a dress made of burlap, cut a loaf of bread into slices. Neither girl wore shoes.

Mrs. Keller wiped her hands on a stained apron covering her faded black dress and dished out some stew.

Reverend Keller winced as he poured water into the tin cups. "Please sit, eat. There's not much game in the woods this winter, but..." He wiped the back of his neck with his hand.

"Squirrel stew," Mrs. Keller said. "It's not much, but it's filling."

William nodded. "Thank you, ma'am."

"These are our girls," Reverend Keller said. "Molly and Mary. The baby's Andrew."

Keller's daughters greeted William and sat at the table with their parents. After the blessing, they ate as if they hadn't had a meal in days. William wondered if it might not be true. The stew had squirrel meat and potatoes, but not much else. The bread wasn't buttered, so he doubted they had a cow or enough money to buy cream to churn.

William scanned the one room cabin. The table and wooden benches were the only furniture other than a set of shelves where kitchenware was kept and the cradle where their infant son slept. The patchwork quilts and straw mattresses by the fireplace indicated they slept on the floor. At least they had a well-banked fire. Wood was plentiful in Kentucky for anyone industrious enough to chop it.

William finished eating everything on his plate. He could have eaten more, but he was given the largest portion, and he didn't want to embarrass them with the request. The meal did take the edge off his hunger. He leaned back and patted his belly. "A fine meal, Mrs. Keller. I thank you."

"I was glad to do it." She cleared the dishes. "We've been looking forward to your visit. When you were late, we feared the worst."

"He's here now." Reverend Keller stood and leaned against the wall with his arms crossed. "God is good."

"Reverend Keller." William rubbed his hand across his chin. "About the gun..."

"I'm sorry as I can be." He nodded his head toward the children. "We'll talk in a bit. Why don't we take a walk over to the church where you'll be preaching Sunday?"

William nodded, slipped his boots on, and bundled up in the coat and muffler he'd discarded earlier. He couldn't help but notice Reverend Keller's wool jacket was threadbare in places and had a hole at one of the elbows.

They closed the door behind them and strode to the church about a hundred yards away. As soon as they got inside, William faced Reverend Keller. "You have some explaining to do. Do you greet all visitors with a gun in hand?"

Reverend Keller slunk onto a bench in the back. "You don't know what we've been through. I'll do whatever it takes to protect my wife and young'uns."

William placed a hand on Reverend Keller's shoulder and felt him bristle. He removed his hand. "You know why I'm here. I have the money from the Western Reserve Abolitionist Mission Society, and I've been instructed to help however I can, but I'll have to give them a report, and when you greet me at the door that way—"

"There's no excuse for it?"

"What's going on?"

Reverend Keller let out an audible sigh. "Things were going well. The antislavery church the mission sent me to start had grown into a nice size congregation. As I told the mission society, we deny fellowship to any slave owners who attend, and I denounce slavery from the pulpit."

"I know. What's changed?"

"The abolitionist stance wasn't that hard to take at first. Most of the folks in this area don't even own slaves. A few families did repent and free them."

"Also good news, but it doesn't explain the gun."

Reverend Keller's shoulders slumped low as if he didn't know the heaviness of the weight he'd been carrying until that moment. "A couple of years back, a hail storm wiped out all the crops. Last year, when folks started getting back on their feet, a tornado swept through and wiped out another year's planting. When the financial crisis hit, the bank went under, and them who did have something held back lost it all."

"Sounds like the people here are having a hard time."

Keller nodded. "A few months ago, a group of men moved into the area saying they were going to start a coalmine here. You can imagine how excited everyone was with the railroad needing all the coal it can get. Then the men began an association calling themselves the Society to Preserve Order. That's when they showed their true colors. They're a secessionist group blaming abolitionists in the North for the financial panic."

Reverend Keller stood and stretched like he was trying to shift the load to make it manageable. "It wasn't so bad at first. They spoke against me and requested I be removed from the pastorate. They claimed I distributed abolitionist material and was trying to incite rebellion. I do confess to distributing the pamphlets in violation of the law, but I would never advise anyone to rise up in violence against their masters."

"The missionary society wouldn't have assigned you a church if they didn't believe you to be a pacifist."

"Some defended me, but most..." Reverend Keller strummed his fingers against his leg. "The president of this society is an important man. He's the owner of the mine. Most of the men around here have joined the association."

William lowered his voice. "This still doesn't explain the gun."

Reverend Keller walked to the Franklin stove at the front of the church, keeping his back to William. "I've never threatened anyone with a firearm. I always thought I'd die first, but these men have become a mob. They burned down some free Negros' homes. Any colored who protested was dragged to the nearest tree and whipped. They even lynched a couple of them for being uppity."

He turned toward William and sunk onto a nearby bench. "It's not just coloreds. They threatened some in the church if they don't renounce their membership. Members of the society bought out the General Store and the Grain and Feed; they won't sell to church members. There are only a few left who haven't asked to be removed from the rolls."

Reverend Keller rested his hands on his knees and lowered his head. "Then last night..." The strumming began again, starting with his index finger, moving to his pinkie, then back again. "They came to the house and dragged me outside. Said I was guilty of spreading treasonous propaganda and trying to promote an uprising of slaves. They tied me to a tree and gave me ten lashes."

William's jaw clenched. "They whipped you?"

Reverend Keller nodded. "My wife tried to stop them. They held her back, said unless I allow slave owners to take membership in the church, it will be worse next time."

"What will you do?"

A sob escaped Reverend Keller's throat. "I don't know."

"I can see why you took to firearms." William sat beside Reverend Keller. "I'm sure the mission society will understand, but are you sure it's wise to stay under these circumstances?"

"What happens if I leave? My church will be at this mob's mercy. I have to stay and confront this evil."

"Have you talked to the law?"

"There's no law around these parts. Now the community is looking to the Society to keep the peace."

"I'll help however I can." William handed Reverend Keller the sack he had attached to his belt. "This should be a good start."

Reverend Keller emptied the bag on the pew and counted the money. His voice choked up. "I didn't expect this much. We might even be able to buy freedom for a few more slaves."

"You need to use some of this to support your wife and children. The mission society expects it."

"I know, but I can do so much good with it."

"After you buy what you need."

"Agreed." The corners of Reverend Keller's mouth turned up slightly. "Last week, I stood in the middle of town and announced we'd have a guest preacher from Oberlin on Sunday, and you'd be preaching against slavery. Everyone's talking about it. We should have a full house, especially after what happened yesterday."

William's heart raced. He again would be preaching abolition in a church that might have him lynched for it, but unlike Merry, he wouldn't compromise with evil. "It should be an interesting meeting."

Chapter Thirty-Three

America heard voices and tried to open her eyes, but the light caused her pain, and she closed them tight. She tried to focus on what the men were saying.

"There's no way to be sure, but she should be getting better by now. If it were influenza... Did she act peculiar before she fainted?"

"What do you mean?" She recognized her father's voice.

"Did she act confused or unusually docile or irritable, you know, act out of character?"

So hot. She tried to push the covers off, but something pulled them back.

"She was agitated when I told her she couldn't return to Oberlin, but that was weeks ago."

"Anything more recent."

"She's had a few headaches lately, but otherwise, she's been fine. She even agreed to marry Harland Boidae before she swooned."

Harland, that couldn't be right. Harland owned slaves. Wait, he bought Naomi. He was going to free her. She pulled her hand to her forehead. Head hurt, so hot. Why so hot? "Papa." The sound of her voice frightened her. She could barely hear it rasp out. So weak.

"I'm right here, Merry."

She forced her eyes open to see Papa hovering over her. "Where's William? I need to... can't leave... don't go..."

"Who's William?" The man who spoke earlier came into focus. The doctor.

"That circuit preacher from Oberlin, William Woods I think his name is, but he's been gone for over a week now."

"It must be the fever talking," the doctor said.

"You said it could be influenza," Papa said. "What else might it be?"

"Has she had any bug or tick bites recently?"

"Not that I know of."

The tick. "Papa..." She struggled to speak.

"What else?" Papa asked.

"Brain fever."

Papa's face went white, and he plunked onto the bed beside her.

"I don't..." She tried focus on the words wanting to reassure him. "It's not... not... brain..." So tired.

*****

Harland rode his spotted horse on the path through the woods. It wasn't fair. Everything he wanted was within his grasp when America had to take ill, and it didn't look like she was getting better any time soon. He would have to keep sitting at the bed of a sick woman until something happened. He didn't even do that for his father. It was pathetic.

What if she died? All this trouble for nothing. Oh, he'd still have Colonel Leighton's support, but it would be difficult to be elected to the US Senate without a wife like America at his side. He couldn't risk marrying another woman too soon without losing Leighton's backing.

He pulled up the reins and dismounted near the slave quarters. Todd, the son of that wench he liked to use, stepped out the door of one of the cabins.

Harland grinned. When Todd had walked in on him and Izzy, the boy had lunged at him before his ma and pa pulled him back. Harland hadn't done anything to him at the time. He was too busy showing Izzy's husband what happens when you don't guard the door like you're told.

Todd should have gotten a beating then, but it wasn't too late. He'd teach him his lesson now. He grabbed Todd by the arm and yanked him toward the barn.

"What's wrong, master? What'd I do?"

"Shut up! I'll teach you to respect your master, boy, and not to interfere with my amusement."

Todd's eyes widened, but he didn't say any more. Good. He should be scared. By the time Harland got through with the boy...

They reached the barn, and Harland tied the boy to a post. He took off his frock coat, vest, and cravat, and folded them neatly on a hay bale. He'd have Izzy clean the straw off them later. He grabbed the whip and swung hitting whatever he could as Todd screamed out.

Harland allowed the energy to shoot through him and brought the whip down over and over. He loved the power beating the slaves gave him, but he had to stop before he wanted to. If he whipped the boy much longer, Todd would pass out and wouldn't feel the pain.

Harland grabbed his walking stick and raised it above his head. The fear in Todd's eyes fed his zeal, and he swung it down on Todd's legs. The blood-curtailing cry took the edge off his fury.

The gold cobra cut into the boy's foot, and blood gushed out all over Harland's shirt and trousers. They were ruined. He went to grab the handkerchief out of his jacket pocket. Blood on his hands. Blazes. He couldn't get to his handkerchief without ruining the jacket.

He grabbed his walking stick and swaggered out of the barn toward the pump. Izzy ran toward him, and he grabbed her arm. "Get in the barn, and see to that brat of yours."

*****

Colonel Leighton sat in the rocker at America's bedside with only a small candle lighting the room. He didn't want the light from a lantern to disturb her sleep. Luke and the slaves went to bed hours ago. He might as well keep the vigil since, if he retired, he would lay awake staring at the ceiling. He hadn't been sleeping much these past couple of weeks.

Brain fever? What would he do if his little girl died? He remembered when her mother, Elizabeth, came down with cholera. She was gone within hours.

America looked so much like her mother with her strawberry blond curly hair and blue eyes, but the resemblance didn't end with looks. She inherited her mother's fiery personality. When Elizabeth believed she was in the right, she wouldn't yield to his arguments.

He'd been pleased when Merry tempered that stubbornness and agreed to marry Harland. Doctor Adams asked if she'd had a change in personality lately, if she'd become docile. Maybe her change toward Harland was a sign of the brain fever.

Her abolitionist views and her stubborn rebellion went too far, but a part of him was a little disappointed she gave up so easily. He wanted what was best for her, but he hadn't intended for her to go against what she believed was right.

Lord, is she right? He didn't know what to think anymore. *Thou shalt also consider in thine heart, that, as a man chasteneth his son, so the Lord thy God chasteneth thee.* The verse Brother Wood's used in his sermon two weeks ago took hold of him. At the time, the colonel had dismissed it as not pertaining to him, but Brother Woods had warned those who believe they are above reproach need God's chastening the most.

 Maybe this was God's discipline. Did God strike Merry down to punish him?

Merry stirred and murmured. He felt her forehead. So hot. He dipped a cloth in the water basin beside her bed and wiped her face with it.

She groaned louder. "William..." Unintelligible moans. "William, don't leave. Please, help me." More groans. "William, I love you."

Colonel Leighton pulled back and slunk into the chair. Was she in love with William Woods? Why hadn't she said anything? He had worried about her going to the mission field alone. Maybe God had brought her the right man to marry, a man who studied to be a missionary, and he'd ruined it by pushing her into Harland's arms.

Chapter Thirty-Four

William stood at the front of Reverend Keller's church and cleared his throat. Keller had been right. The church filled to capacity with men, some with handguns or rifles, many standing in the back. He couldn't get away from the impression the circus had come to town, and he was the main attraction.

He delivered his sermon on the evils of slavery, and he had to admit, they listened politely. There were no heckles or noise of any kind, but he scanned the faces and saw no response.

Trudging on, he ended the sermon with a plea for Reverend Keller. "As you know, the Society to Preserve Order had your preacher flogged. This is intolerable," a roar moved through the crowd, "and they plan to do it again if he doesn't relent and allow slave owners to take membership. I implore you now to do what is right."

He walked over to Reverend Keller. "I stand with the man of God against the mob who would beat him. Who will join me?"

Nobody moved. William glared at each man in the congregation. Some looked down. Others returned his gaze. One man's eyes darted from William to Reverend Keller. His face flushed, and beads of sweat covered his brow. William thought for a moment he might step forward, but the coward strode out of the building.

The muscle in William's jaw twitched. "This sermon is concluded. Thank you for coming." He marched out ahead of the crowd.

"Brother Woods, wait." Reverend Keller's voice trailed behind him.

William kept walking. He needed to get away. The silence of the good Christian men in this village threatened to choke him with their hypocrisy.

No doubt what Reverend Keller said was true. These people did renounce slavery and help free Negros. They probably congratulated themselves on how much more enlightened and spiritual they were than their neighbors, but when it came time to risk their safety by standing with their pastor against the mob, they shrank back.

Just as Merry had cowered before her father.

What was worse, the members of the society saw them do it.

William spent that afternoon trying to reason with Reverend Keller as they sat at the wooden table drinking coffee. "Think of your wife and children, man. They're in danger too."

Reverend Keller tapped the pattern with his fingers on the table. "Don't you think I know that? I can't withdraw from my calling as a missionary in the South if I run at the first sign of opposition."

"First sign?" William banged his fist on the table. "If anyone in Hidden Fork would support you, I'd say go ahead, but they aren't willing to put themselves in danger. Your work here is over. You've done what you could."

"Should I stop because I stand alone?"

"There are others who need you." William blew out his frustration. "A month ago, I left a group of Christians who stood against the tyranny of slavery and were removed from their church. They are sorely in need of clergy. You could go there."

"Where is this congregation?"

"In the mountains north of here. Lawrence County."

"I'll consider it after I pray. I won't leave because there's danger, but if God directs me there, I'll go."

Glass shattered as a rock crashed through the window. Flickering lights from torches and shouts filled the air. "Keller, come on out here. You need another whipping."

Mrs. Keller let out a whimper and grabbed her girls close to her. "Don't go, Abe, please."

Reverend Keller started to the door.

William placed a hand on his chest to stop him. "I'll talk to them. If I tell them you're leaving..."

"I don't know that yet."

"I can tell them you're considering it. It might buy you time."

Keller nodded his head.

William squared his shoulders and strode through the door to face the vigilantes. He peered through the darkness at the flickering light from the torches they carried. There were about ten of them, five dressed in suits, the others in work clothes.

Two men stood in front. One farmer loomed a full foot above William. He had to be as tall as Joe and was every bit as muscular. The other man stood beside him wearing a suit. He had a well-trimmed gray beard and looked like he belonged in a bank, not as the leader of a mob.

The large man spoke. "Where's Keller?"

"Men, there's no need for this." William held his hands up in a sign of surrender. "Reverend Keller is thinking about leaving town for another pastorate."

The large man raised the whip in his hand stepped forward. "Good. We can help him make up his mind."

The man wearing the suit shook his head, and the large man stepped back.

The suited man stroked his beard. "Aren't you the preacher who tried to get the folks in this town to side with Keller?"

William swallowed and nodded.

"Do you stand with him now?"

"Yes, sir, I do."

The man smirked. "Then you won't mind joining him."

The crowd laughed.

"Wait," Reverend Keller called from the doorway. "Leave him alone. It's me you're after."

The man in the suit raised his voice. "It's not just you, Keller. We're after any abolitionist rebel trying to cause trouble in these parts, and it looks like we found ourselves two."

The crowd pressed around William and Reverend Keller and grabbed them. William struggled to free his arms, but there were too many men. He half-walked and was half-drug and tied to one of the maple trees near the side of the house.

One man tore William's shirt off. The draft of cold air on his back caused a shiver to go through him. He clenched his jaw waiting for the first lash to strike.

A swish sounded behind him, and the whip struck. He'd never felt such pain. His back was on fire. He ground his teeth to brace himself for the next lash. And the next. A groan came from his throat, and he tried to keep from crying out. When the eighth strike fell, he wailed. He couldn't keep his composure for the next two.

One of the men took out a knife, and panic lodged in William's throat. The man grabbed his hands roughly and cut the ropes holding him to the tree. He stood for a moment, then his legs collapsed under him. His face slammed in the ground. He coughed and spit out the dirt making its way in his mouth.

How did the slaves endure this treatment? He struggled to lift his head and spied Reverend Keller lying in a pile of red leaves near the tree he'd been tied to. The man didn't move, and William feared he might be dead.

The large man who whipped them lifted Keller's head by his hair. He let out a moan.

"Can you hear me?" the man said.

Keller nodded.

"Good, you and that agitator you brought here better be gone by Saturday. We're giving you four days. If we see you after that, we'll bring a couple of ropes and have a necktie party."

*****

Keller's daughters lay in their straw mattress with wide eyes watching while Mrs. Keller used a cloth dipped in a basin of water to wash the blood off her husband's back. He didn't let out any groans, but he bit his lower lip and grimaced occasionally. The younger daughter, Mary, let out an occasional whimper.

William's jaw tightened. No child should be subjected to seeing her father horsewhipped.

Mrs. Keller poured honey on Reverend Keller's wounds and laid clean cloths on them. He let out a sigh.

She retrieved hot water from the kettle on the fireplace grate and more cloths from her rag basket and strode to William's side. Every inch of him hurt, but Reverend Keller's pain had to be worse. He hadn't recovered from his last beating before being subjected to this one.

She dabbed the wet cloth across William's back, and he groaned. It might as well been a hot knife washing off his blood with the pain it caused. How did Keller remain silent through this?

William tried to hold still, but he couldn't keep from squirming and wincing. Mrs. Keller applied the honey to his back. The sweet fragrance filled his nostrils as the honey cooled the burning sensation. Then she laid cloths on his back, and the pain jabbed at him all over again. He grabbed hold of the blanket under him and bunched it in his fists to keep from crying out again. Slaves endured far worse beatings than this. He shuddered at the thought.

Mrs. Keller washed her hands in the basin. "I'm finished."

William let out the breath he was holding and released the assaulted blanket. It still hurt like the dickens, but the honey and dressing eased the worst of it.

He gingerly turned toward the tenacious preacher. "Have you had enough? Do you plan to stay here until they lynch you?"

Mrs. Keller gasped.

William pulled himself into a sitting position. "Not one member of that congregation will lift a finger to stop it."

"I know."

"Well, man, there's another congregation who needs you. Are you going to let them down because of your stubborn pride?"

"You're right, Brother Woods." Reverend Keller nodded to his wife. "It's time to move on."

"We need to get out of here as soon as we can," William said. "They'll be back on Saturday. It will only give us a couple days to rest, but we need to be out of here by Friday."

"Christmas Day," Mrs. Keller said. "I don't know if my husband will be able to travel by then."

"He'll have to be. We have no choice."

Chapter Thirty-Five

"It's been three weeks, and she's not getting any better." Colonel Leighton tried to hold back the panic in his voice.

"It's time to accept your daughter is most likely going to die," Doctor Adams said. "Even if she survives, she might not be the same."

"I won't accept it." He turned to the fireplace and rested his hands on the mantel. "She's going to make it. You hear me?"

"If the fever doesn't break soon..." Doctor Adams cleared his throat. "I'll do what I can. Another treatment might help."

Colonel Leighton nodded but couldn't bring himself to turn around. He was afraid of the expression he'd see in Doctor Adam's eyes. She had to recover, if not for him, then for Harland.

Three weeks ago, when Harland asked for her hand in marriage, the colonel was beginning to doubt the man, but Harland had been so attentive and caring since Merry's collapse. He hadn't missed one day stopping by to see her. Most days he'd sit and read to her from the Bible. She slept through it, but Harland said it was all right. She knew he was there.

It still disturbed the colonel whenever Merry cried out, it was William's name she called, not Harland's. At least Harland had never been nearby when she stirred.

It didn't matter who she wanted to marry if she didn't live through this. Colonel Leighton folded his arms on the mantel and buried his face in them.

Lord, please.

*****

America lay under the covers with her eyes closed. She'd been awake for a while, but the effort it would take to open her eyelids didn't seem worth it. Snuggling under the warm blankets felt good.

Her head ached but not as bad as before. She could almost think without a fog muddling her brain. She didn't remember much after she fainted, broken images of hot and cold and of people hovering over her, Aunt Ruth, Papa, the doctor. Harland.

Harland was there every time she woke up. Or was she dreaming? It was hard to tell which images were real. William. He hadn't been there. He went away, left her. Warned her. He'd help her get to Oberlin.

He left her.

Harland asked her to marry him. It all came back to her now. Harland would free his slaves as a wedding gift, and he bought Naomi's note. He would take her to China to be a missionary. No, not to be a missionary. To observe mission work. She'd never be a missionary now. A warning. "Harland."

"I'm here, dear," Harland said.

Her eyes popped open. Harland held her hand and smiled.

"Thank God." Ruth darted to the bed and felt America's forehead. "Fever's broken. I'll fetch the colonel."

"Aunt Ruth," America rasped out. "Water."

Ruth poured water in a glass and held it up to America's mouth. It felt good going down her parched throat. Ruth set the glass down and left her alone with Harland.

He stroked her hair. "I was so worried."

"How long?"

"How long have you been like this?"

She nodded.

"Two weeks and two days. You scared us. The doctor feared it might be brain fever. He tried packing you in ice to get your fever down and applied leeches to suck out the poison. Nothing worked. Thank God you're better now." His eyes widened. "You remember me, don't you? The doctor said you might be confused."

"Harland." She forced out the words. "We're getting married. Going to China."

"I love you."

She couldn't answer.

Harland's ice blue eyes darted. "You rest. We'll talk when you feel up to it."

Doctor Adams and Papa rushed into the room. The doctor laid his hand on her forehead. "The fever's broken. I need to do an examination. Everyone out but Ruth."

America spent the next hour being prodded, poked, and asked meaningless questions like her name, her brother's name, and the year she was born. When Doctor Adams sat in the chair beside her and leaned back, she felt totally drained.

Doctor Adams smiled. "It looks like you're going to be all right. Ruth, send the others in."

Harland, Papa, and Luke stepped into the room. America was surprised to see Luke. She couldn't recall him being there before. He must have been. He said something before she fainted or did she dream it? She needed to talk to him, ask him about the warning. No, William had warned her.

Luke told her she gave in too easily. Gave in about what?

Everyone had their backs to her. She strained to hear what the doctor told the men. "As far as I can tell, she's fine. I still think it was brain fever, but the leeches must have worked in time. Other than the twitch in her right eye, she doesn't show any signs of brain damage. Either way, she needs bed rest for at least another week. She'll be a little confused at first, but in a few days, she should remember everything. When she feels up to it, you can let her do anything she wants, but you need to keep a close watch on her. If she acts erratic, or if the fever returns, send for me right away."

"Thank you, doctor," Papa said.

Doctor Adams left, and the men, once again hovered around her bedside.

Brain fever? No wonder she was so muddled. She'd be better in no time. She had to be. She'd missed Christmas and tomorrow would start the new year. The river was probably frozen by now, and Reverend Thornton and Joe would need her help rescuing slaves.

She raised herself up. "May I talk to Luke alone?" Even that small movement took all her energy, and she fell back into the pillow.

Papa guided Harland and Ruth out of the room.

Luke sat on the bed next to her. "I'm glad you're doing better."

"Me too." She tried to clear her mind. "You said something when I took ill or was I dreaming?"

*****

Joe rested his hands on his knees as he sat in his cabin by the fireplace next to Reverend Thornton. He thanked God he'd be able to tell Colonel Leighton about Mr. Boidae soon. Ruth didn't want to wait, but she agreed to let him be the one to own up to it.

Ruth handed Reverend Thornton a cup of coffee.

"I'm glad you stopped by," Joe said. "Miss Merry's fever broke."

"Good to hear." Reverend Thornton took a sip. "Has Harland been around?"

"Every day. I don't know how he has time to beat up on his slaves with as much as he's lingering around Miss Merry." Joe wiped his face with his bandana. "You heard about Todd?"

Reverend Thornton glanced at his feet. "Riley told me."

"Preacher, that boy's gonna be crippled for the rest of his life. Izzy says Mr. Boidae beat him with his walking stick."

Thornton crossed his arms. "He's telling his neighbors the boy got caught in one of the spinning machines at the mill." He cleared his throat. "How soon before they can travel? We need to get them away from that monster."

"I don't know," Joe said. "A couple of weeks, maybe a month."

"We'll give America time to gain her strength, but then we need to do what we can to protect her. Are you still willing to go to Colonel Leighton with me?"

Joe nodded. "I'm willing to do whatever it takes to make things right, but I'd feel a whole lot better if Brother William would get here so he can take her back to Ohio."

"I sent a telegram to Lawrence County weeks ago, but he hasn't answered. At this point, I'm not sure he's coming.

*****

The blanket wrapped around William did little to keep the wind from sending chills through him. His breath came out in white puffs, and his fingers stung from the cold. He flicked the reins urging the horses to increase their speed as they pulled the wagon. It wouldn't be long now.

His back still ached, but he had offered to drive the horses. Reverend Keller wasn't up to it after two beatings in two weeks. Mrs. Keller had propped mattresses and blankets in the back so her husband could be comfortable.

The wagon hit another rut, and Keller groaned. "Sorry." He tried to avoid the next one, but he hit the one beside it and heard another grimace. The path through the mountain had been filled with these furrows.

"Ma," Mary, the youngest girl, said. "How much longer?"

"Girls, it's time to walk," Mrs. Keller said. Every time the girls got antsy, she would insist they get some exercise.

Mary and Molly climbed down from the wagon. "But it's cold," Mary said.

"You be minding me, girl."

"Yes, ma'am."

The children didn't mind the cold as much as William even though they would occasionally whine about it. He suspected it was because of the warm coats, gloves, hats, and fur lined boots he'd insisted Mrs. Keller buy the girls with the money he'd given them.

Mr. Keller objected at first, but he wasn't in good enough shape to argue about it for long. When they stopped at the outpost store at the next town, William sent Mrs. Keller and the girls into the store first and then chided the reverend for not taking care of his family the way the Bible said, and Keller had relented.

"Ma, could I ride with Brother Woods for a spell?" Molly, the oldest, said.

Mrs. Keller nodded and Molly climbed up beside William.

A strong wind whipped through the trees, and William pulled the blanket tighter. Soon they'd be in front of a blazing fire and having one of Mrs. Price's home-cooked meals. William's mouth watered. It would be great to have something other than squirrel and rabbit, their fare since being on the trail.

The game had been scarce this year. He was used to severe winters it Northern Ohio, but this was a cold winter even by Ohio's standards. He couldn't wait to sink into a warm tick feather mattress instead of the cold ground with only a campfire for heat.

"Can I take the reins for a spell, Brother Woods?" Molly asked. "You look tuckered."

William winked at the eight-year-old. "May be a little much for you on these mountain passes."

Mrs. Keller walked beside the wagon holding the baby in a sling in front of her. "Now Molly, don't you go pestering Brother Woods. I should be the one driving the wagon."

"She's fine." William said. "Besides, I already told you five times, you have a husband and children to tend to. I'll drive the wagon."

Mrs. Keller scowled, but she didn't say any more.

William tugged one of Molly's braids "Tell you what. You go ahead and drive a spell, and I'll stay here in case you need help."

Molly flashed a grin and grasped the reins. "You'll see. I can do it."

William leaned back in his seat but stayed alert. They traveled along the path by Big Sandy River for another hour before he could make out the shape of the cabin in the distance. Big snowflakes fell from the sky, a few at a time at first, then hard enough to shroud their path ahead. "I'll take it from here, Molly."

He drove the wagon up to the cabin and climbed down. A sharp pain shot through his back. He grimaced and clenched his jaw until it passed then marched to the door and pounded.

Cal opened it and smiled. "It's good to see you, Brother Woods. Come in."

"I have company."

Cal glanced past him. "Anyone you bring is welcome."

William strode to Reverend Keller's side and helped him down. Keller groaned.

Cal hurried to the wagon and gave William a hand. "This feller ailing some?"

"Yes." William panted as he led Reverend Keller to the chair next to the fire. He clenched his jaw to keep from moaning. The weight caused his lashes to remind him he also was in pain. "Could we talk?"

"Course," Cal said. "We can leave this man and his family to be tended by the women folk while we go out to the barn."

William didn't look forward to braving the cold or a long walk. It wasn't far, maybe a hundred feet, but right now it seemed further than the gold mines of California. Sweat poured down his face by the time he entered the barn. He took in a short breath to cover the grimace escaping his throat.

Cal didn't notice or pretended not to. "Emma gave birth while you were gone, a healthy son. We named him William Price."

"Congratulations. I'm honored you would name him after me." William leaned against the stall gate. "How are things going with Reverend Hull and the rest?"

"Not bad," Cal said. "He and his cohorts still try to cause a ruckus on occasion, but they know they can't get nowhere with it. More than half the folks around here are attending church in our barn. We stand together, and Reverend Hull knows he's met his match."

"Good."

"The men folk got together and voted. We're gonna build a proper church come spring, and we won't allow slave owners to be members. We're still praying for a man of God who preaches the Word and don't hold to slavery. You interested?"

"I told you, I'm going back to Oberlin." A sharp pain shot up William's back, and he tried to keep his breath steady. "The man I brought with me is looking for an anti-slavery congregation."

"You don't say. Well, let's go in and jabber with him some more."

William took a step, let out a yelp, and fell to one knee.

Cal helped him up. "So you gonna tell who beat the tar out of you and the preacher in there?"

"Yeah." William pressed his lips together until the worst of it passed. "Are you going to let me sit in front of the fire and have a cup of hot coffee first?"

Cal nodded, and they headed for the cabin.

William told the Price family about confronting the town and about the beatings they received. He took a sip of coffee. It felt good going down his throat and warming his insides. The fire and blankets were doing their job of thawing him out. Even with the spasms coursing through his back, he felt better.

"Brother Woods," Granny Price said. "I thank ye for bringing us the man of God and his family."

Cal faced Keller. "You'll stay, won't you?"

Reverend Keller nodded. "I believe God directed us here."

Cal shook his hand. "It's done then."

"Brother Woods, you're gonna stay and winter with us," Mrs. Price said. "You need time to heal up."

"I appreciate that, ma'am. I was hoping you'd offer."

"A telegram arrived while you were gone." Cal handed him the paper.

William lifted an eyebrow. Benjamin Thornton was the only one who knew where he was. He opened and read it.

William Woods-stop-America sick-stop-fell ill after HB proposed-stop-She's in danger-stop-She needs you-stop-Come back soon. Benjamin Thornton.

A heaviness gripped his chest. Cal and Reverend Keller kept talking, murmuring he couldn't decipher, as the world around him faded from view. So, Harland proposed, and now she was sick. He wiped his hand across the lettering. Even if she was in some kind of danger, what could he do about it? She'd made it clear she didn't love him. Was he supposed to go crawling back hoping when she recovered so she could add humiliation to the thrashing she gave his heart last time?

He crumbled the note and stuffed it in his pocket. Let her intended husband take care of her now. He was done with her.

Chapter Thirty-Six

America fought to make sense of the flood of memories from before she took ill. Luke sat by her bed holding her hand.

She forced a weak smile. "Before I collapsed, you said I was giving in too easily. About what?"

"I wasn't here when you came down with this. I was at Virginia's house. Don't you remember?"

"Yes." *Parts of it.* "I saw you, at least I think I did."

Luke's brow furrowed. "It was the fever."

"You said something about me giving in too easily and turning my back on my calling."

"Sis, I said nothing." Luke leaned forward. "I do admit, I was surprised you agreed to marry him."

"What do you mean?"

"You said you would never marry a slave owner. You made a wise decision changing your mind. Harland is a man of means. He'll take good care of you." He shrugged. "I just didn't think you would."

"Harland's going to free his slaves." The memories came back to her in waves, some rushing to shore, others receding before she could catch hold of them.

Luke raised an eyebrow. "He told you he would?"

America struggled to remember. Why else would she agree to marry him? "Yes, I remember him saying it. Why?"

"It's hard to believe. He needs those slaves to work the mill. He must have at least twenty. Freeing them would be foolhardy, and he's a shrewd man."

America had to talk to Harland as soon as she could to know which memories were real and which were sandcastles waiting to be washed away by the ocean's swell. She closed her eyes and laid her head back.

"You're tired, Sis. We'll talk later."

She wanted to sleep but not yet. "Could I talk to Harland alone?"

"I'll get him." Luke exited the room.

Drowsiness overtook her.

America woke to find the doctor and her papa at her side. She scanned the room. "Where's Harland?"

Papa touched her cheek. "You've been asleep for a day and a half. Harland was at your side until about an hour ago. I made him get some rest. He wouldn't leave, so I allowed him to use the guest room."

"Am I getting worse?"

"No, child." Doctor Adams confident smile reassured her. "Don't you fret. You've been through a lot. Your body needs rest. You'll be able to stay awake longer as you recover."

"I thought maybe I'd had a relapse."

"I'm here to give you another treatment." Doctor Adam's held up the jar of blood-sucking leeches.

America snarled her nose. "They're disgusting."

"Don't take on like that, missy." Doctor Adam's set the jar on the table. "Most likely, they saved your life."

"Papa?"

Her father stepped to her side. "Right here, Merry."

"Could you tell Harland I want to see him when he wakes?"

"Of course." Papa's face looked drawn.

"Tell him to wake me if I'm asleep."

Papa nodded and started out the door. "I'll tell him now."

"Thank you." Hopefully, the leeches would help. She needed a clear head when she talked to Harland.

*****

Harland's voice called America's name, and she opened her eyes. Her stomach churned, and she fought to come out the of the drowsiness swarming around her.

"You awake?" Harland placed his hand on her forehead. "Your father said you were asking for me, that you wanted me to wake you."

"Yes, I did." Her muscles ached, but she rose to a sitting position anyway. She was still so weak, but she needed a clear head for this conversation.

"I hated to do it." Harland stuffed a pillow behind her back. "You looked so peaceful lying there. I've been fretting ever since you came down with this fever. If I lost you, I don't know what I would do."

"I'm fine." She shook herself to clear the fog. These declarations of love weren't making this any easier. "We need to talk."

Harland sat in the chair beside her bed and leaned forward. "This sounds serious."

"It is." America twined her fingers together. "It's about the conversation we had before I collapsed."

"When I asked you to marry me, and you said yes?"

She shook her head. She didn't remember saying yes. "Before that. Did you say you would free your slaves as a wedding gift?"

Harland took her hand in his and smiled. "That's what I said."

"Did you mean it?"

He blinked, but his eyes never left hers. "With all my heart."

America let out a sigh of relief. "Are we going to China for a honeymoon?"

"I'd go anywhere in the world with you."

She closed her eyes. "Thank God. I thought I might have heard wrong."

"I'll promise you the world, my dear, if you consent to be my wife. You belong to me. I need you more than you can imagine."

Now she knew Harland would release his slaves, and she could rest easy. She could count on that memory being true. Everything would be okay.

She opened her eyes to see him sitting there staring at her with a grin like a cat gives a mouse he's toying with before he devours it. The hair on the back of her neck prickled.

Being sick had caused her to forget something. Something important.

*****

William's chest tightened like a tree had fallen on it. It happened every time he prayed. Thoughts of Merry crowded him.

He pulled out the telegraph he'd stuffed in his pocket and smoothed out the page. America's in danger. Benjamin couldn't have meant the sickness she came down with. There had to be something else, but what?

Danger. Benjamin used the word danger. Maybe the underground railroad stop had been discovered. No, they would all be in danger, not just Merry.

Cal sat beside him. "You look like you're carrying the weight of the world on your shoulders. Last time I checked Scripture, God told us He'd carry our burdens."

"I've tried praying. The burden gets heavier."

"You want to tell me what's wrong?"

William shrugged and handed Cal the telegram.

Cal read it. "Who's America?"

"A lady from Oberlin. I made the mistake of declaring my love to her. She decided to marry someone else."

Cal placed his hand on William's shoulder. "So, you ignored the telegraph?"

"She made her choice."

"Who's HB?"

"Harland Boidae."

Cal gasped "Harland Boidae? You left her in his clutches."

The air left William's lungs. "You know Boidae?"

"I've met him." Cal wiped his hand across his mouth. "It happened over a year ago. Did you know Reverend Hull is friends with him?"

"No, I didn't. Maybe you better tell me all you know about him."

"Like I said, he visited about a year and a half ago. He was looking to buy some female slaves for his cotton mill. Reverend Hull said he might find some meeting his fancy here. Now I don't know all that happened, some of it's just stuff I heard. Anyway, them who wanted to sell female slaves brought them by the parsonage so he could have a gander. There were about six young girls, none of them older than sixteen. He took one out to the barn to check out the merchandise."

"Oh, dear Lord." William wondered how he was able to speak in a room with no air.

"You want to hear the rest," Cal said.

He nodded.

"Gus wanted to sell a slave girl he owned. A pretty little twelve-year-old with bright eyes. I think her name was Zola or Zona, something like that. He brought her pa along thinking maybe Boidae would be interested in him too. She was the one Boidae took to the barn."

He placed his hand over his mouth. He wanted to vomit.

"Her pa objected and tried to punch Boidae in the mouth. Gus and Horace held Zona's pa back while Boidae grabbed the girl, dragged her away, and... well, you know. Boidae decided to buy Zona, and her pa went crazy. He lunged at him and tried to kill him. Gus and Horace about beat Zona's pa half to death. They held him for the circuit judge. He was convicted of attempted murder and sentenced to hang. Boidae did the honors of yanking the horse out from under him."

William's hands trembled. "I left America with him."

"Reverend Hull preached the next Sunday about how justice had been done. Inside my gut, I knew something wasn't right. If I'd been Zona's pa, I would have done the same thing even if I hanged for it."

"Oh, God, forgive me." The muscle in his jaw twitched. "I can't stay. I have to get back to Mason County straight away."

Cal placed his hand on his shoulder. "I'll go with you."

William shook his head. "You have your family and your new son to take care of."

"Do you think any of my kin would cotton to me sending you off to take care of Boidae on your own? Granny would clean my plow. Jack and Hugh will keep an eye on them while I'm gone."

"Thank you."

"We'll leave at first light."

William nodded. He didn't think he'd get any sleep tonight. He was right. Most of the night, he tossed and turned listening to the howl of the wind accusing him. He'd allowed his wounded pride to put Merry in danger.

At some point, he dozed. The rooster crowed, and he shivered and pulled the blankets tightly to him wiping his groggy eyes. The air had turned frigid.

America.

He climbed out of bed, forced his eyes open, and let out a groan. The chill hanging in the air bore into him, and he dressed as quickly as he could. He hadn't trusted Harland from the start. He should have tried harder to persuade Merry.

At least he was getting an early start. Cal owned good horses. They could keep up a fast trot for hours without having to slow down and rest. They could be back in Dover within a couple of days, maybe even sooner.

He climbed down the ladder from the loft.

Cal gave a waving gesture and took a sip of coffee. "About time you woke. I've been up for hours."

William glanced at the door. Supplies were already bundled there. "You should have woken me. We need to leave as soon as I eat breakfast."

Emma poured William a cup of coffee. The blazing fire and the warm substance calmed the piercing cold inside him.

"We're not going anywhere today," Cal said.

William swallowed. "What do you mean?"

"Maybe you better take a look outside."

He stepped to the window, wiped the frost off of it with his sleeve, and peered through it at the vast white landscape. A storm had dumped two feet of snow the night before, and it was still coming down. He couldn't see the barn even though it was only a hundred feet away. Cal was right. He wouldn't be going anywhere until the storm passed. He'd never forgive himself if they didn't reach Merry in time.

Chapter Thirty-Seven

America couldn't stop fidgeting while the doctor examined her. She'd done the required week of bed rest. She'd read two books, visited with Aunt Ruth, Naomi, and Papa, and discussed wedding plans with Harland, but she was restless and eager to get up and moving again.

During her visits with Reverend and Mrs. Thornton, Papa, Luke, or Harland were always around. She hadn't been able to talk to them about how the slave rescues were going.

Doctor Adams packed his medical bag. "You've recovered faster than I've anticipated. I see no reason to keep you in your bed."

"Thank you." Finally. America was sure if she had to spend one more day of bed rest, she would die of boredom.

"You're welcome. Don't overdo it or that twitch in your eye will get worse. If you tire, sit and rest."

"I will. I promise."

"I'll make sure she does." Harland scooted to her side and took her hand.

She appreciated his presence there, but enough was enough. He smothered her with his concern. She resisted the urge to pull her hand away.

The doctor turned to Papa standing by the door. "If she displays any symptoms of intense agitation or hysteria, send for me right away."

Papa shook his hand. "How long before that twitch goes away?"

Doctor Adams let out a sigh. "She's fortunate that's all she has. Most likely, it will always be there."

"It's not bad." America offered a weak smile. She never considered herself a vain woman, but she stared at that twitch in the mirror several times since she'd recovered. It made her look like an imbecile, and to think it would haunt her the rest of her life... She wished it didn't disturb her so much. It was silly to worry about such a superficial thing when it could have been much worse, but still... "I hardly notice it, and except for when it waters, I can see clearly. Doctor Adams is right. God has blessed me."

"Of course, dear." Harland smiled. "Even with the twitch, you're still a beautiful woman."

"Harland," Papa said. "Would you see the doctor out?"

Harland's eyes darted to America and then to her father. He nodded and left the room.

"It's not proper for him to be in your bedchamber since you've recovered." Papa opened the bedroom door and bellowed into the hallway. "Ruth."

A moment later, Ruth entered.

"Help your mistress dress, and escort her down the stairs. Merry, I'll tell Harland you'll be down momentarily." Papa left.

Ruth pulled a dress and undergarments out of the trunk, and poured some water in the basin. "I expect you'll want to wash up first."

"Yes." America removed her nightgown and washed. Her muscles quivered, but she planted a plastered smile on her face to keep from showing it. Ruth had become a mother hen, and she was tired of being doted on. "How are Naomi and Riley?"

"They doing fine, fretting some with January already here. Riley didn't get the money together, so they'll have to cross the river soon."

America sat on the edge of the bed. "What do you mean? Harland bought her note so he could free her."

"No, miss, she's not free unless Riley pays it off. Come two weeks from now, Mr. Boidae's planning to come fetch her."

"You've got it wrong." She lifted her arms so Ruth could pull the dress over her head. "Harland's planning to free her."

Ruth adjusted the dress. "He came to Riley's before Christmas and told him about buying the note. He'll fetch her January twenty-second if we don't pay up."

America's eye twitched, and she wiped it with her handkerchief. "Nonsense. I'm sure this is all a misunderstanding. I'll check with Harland."

"Don't!" Ruth fumbled buttoning the dress. Her fingers slipped off the buttons. "You'll be wasting your breath, and I don't abide you getting on that man's bad side."

"What's wrong?"

Ruth buttoned the last button, and started smoothing the sheets on the bed. "Nothing at all. I was just speaking out of turn is all. It'll all work out. No reason for you to bother Mr. Boidae." She fluffed the pillows.

America grabbed Ruth's hand. "He told me he'd free her. I'll talk to him about it."

"There's no need."

"Don't fret. It'll be all right." America looped her arm in Ruth's and made her way to the hallway. She held her breath as she struggled down the stairs to meet Harland. She was glad for Ruth standing at her side to steady her.

She tried to smile at Harland. What Ruth said made no sense. He gave his word to free Naomi, but he did go to Riley's. Something he said gave them the wrong impression.

Harland stood at the foot of the stairs smiling up at her until she reached the bottom. He took her arm and escorted her to the yellow chair by the fireplace. "I'm so glad you're better."

"Thank you." She eased into the chair. "I appreciate your concern during my illness."

Harland's grin slipped a bit. "Surely, more than concern. When I saw you lying there, helpless, I was so afraid. Thank God he answered my prayers." He took her hand in his. "I don't know what I would have done without you."

America swallowed hard. Ruth had to be mistaken about him, but she had to be sure. She pulled her hand away. "Harland, I have something I need to discuss with you."

Harland glanced at her hand with a scowl, nodded, then plastered a smile on his face. "Of course. Is there something wrong? You know you can talk to me about anything."

America glanced down and let out a sigh. Might as well say it straight out. "When you said you would free your slaves on our wedding day, did you mean you would release Naomi as well?"

Harland's smile slipped. "I paid four hundred dollars to buy her papers from Colonel Leighton. I expect Riley to live up to his side of the agreement."

"You promised to release all your slaves on our wedding day, did you not? Surely, you meant her as well?"

"You don't understand." He patted her hand. "Four hundred dollars is a lot of money -- money I didn't intend to spend. I'll allow Riley to keep Naomi in his possession, but I plan to be paid."

A sigh of relief escaped her. "Then you don't intend to take her away from Riley?"

"No, whatever gave you that idea? We'll work out something."

"Thank God. From what I heard, I thought--"

"What did you hear?" An edge entered his voice.

"It's nothing really."

Harland glared at her with those ice blue eyes of his.

America took a deep breath and slowly exhaled while she tried to form her words. It frustrated her that her thoughts were still foggy, but something seemed wrong. She couldn't seem to narrow it down. "Did you tell Riley you would come for Naomi if he didn't pay by the deadline."

"Who told you that?" His voice had a tinge of anger in it. "Your slaves?"

Her eye twitched, and she dabbed it with her handkerchief. Why was he so angry? "Did you go to Riley's house?"

"How could you take the word of a Negro over mine? You consented to be my wife, and now, you're calling me a liar?"

"Please, I'm not trying to upset you." She furrowed her forehead and raised her hands in a conciliatory gesture. "I'm not accusing you of anything." The hair on the back of her neck prickled. She had to know. "I only want the truth. Surely as your fiancé, I deserve to know."

He leaned back, but those eyes stabbed at her like icicles. "I did go to Riley's house, but it was before you accepted my proposal and before I agreed to free my slaves."

America flushed as her thoughts scrambled. "I'm sorry. I should have known." Why wasn't she relieved now that he told her what happened?

"Yes, you should have." He pointed a finger in her face to match his pointed glare. "Is this the way our marriage is going to be? You'd rather believe I would deceive you based on the word of slaves than trust your future husband? I thought better of you."

She shivered, but not with shame or embarrassment. A disquiet enveloped her seeming to squeeze life out of her with each breath. "It won't happen again."

America excused herself saying she was tired and returned to her room. It didn't make sense. Why would he go to Riley's at all when he supposedly bought his note to help her save Naomi? She fell on her knees beside her bed.

Lord, I don't know what to believe. Reveal Harland's true intentions to me.

*****

Colonel Leighton was curious. Reverend Thornton and Joe looked so serious as he led them into the parlor. He offered Reverend Thornton a seat. Joe stood near the wall.

"Colonel Leighton," Reverend Thornton said. "Joe and I need to talk to you concerning Mr. Boidae."

"Go on," Colonel Leighton said.

"Mr. Boidae has been lying to you and your daughter, sir," Reverend Thornton said.

The colonel loaded his pipe with tobacco. "How so?"

"First," Reverend Thornton said, "he's told America he plans to free his slaves and allow Naomi to stay with Riley. I know for a fact he has no such intention."

Colonel Leighton let out the breath he was holding. "Reverend Thornton, my daughter allows her abolitionist views to rule her reason.

Harland did tell her a few white lies to appease her, but he assured me he rectified the matter and was upfront with her about his deceptions before he proposed."

"There's more," Reverend Thornton said. "Joe, tell him what Mr. Boidae did to his slaves."

So that was it. Joe had some foolish notion about something that was none of his concern. "Go ahead, Joe." Colonel Leighton strode to where the whip hung on the wall, leaned back, and crossed his arms. "Why don't you tell me about how a white man treats his slaves?"

Joe glanced down. "Yessur, he forced himself on a slave woman he owns. When her son walked in on them, he whipped her husband for not guarding the door. Later, he took that snake head stick of his and beat their boy half to death with it. The boy's a cripple now."

Colonel Leighton's mouth grew dry. "You sure, Joe?"

"Yessur, I ain't never lied to you."

The colonel stuck his pipe in his mouth but didn't relight it. Joe told the truth. He knew it deep inside. He wondered at discerning something so profoundly in the core of his being yet not grasping it until it was brought to light. Something was wrong with Harland.

"I checked out the story when Joe came to me," said Reverend Thornton. "Every word is true."

"This is intolerable. For a man who claims to be a Christian to treat his slaves in such a manner..." The vein in his forehead pulsed. "I thank you, Reverend, for bringing it to my attention. I'll do what needs done. You go on upstairs to see America. I'll be up presently."

Reverend Thornton nodded and climbed the stairs.

Colonel Leighton glowered at Joe. "How long?"

"What do you mean?"

"How long have you known about Harland Boidae without telling me? How long have you waited while I allowed that snake to court my daughter?"

Joe's shoulders slumped. "Almost two months."

The colonel's mouth gaped open. He couldn't believe his slave would betray Merry like this after all she tried to do for them. It astonished him more than the disclosure of what Harland had done. He always thought better of Joe. "Why? I've taken good care of you and your family. I haven't dealt with you harshly. Why would you allow this to go on without saying something?"

Joe's Adam's apple bulged. "I done wrong."

"You done wrong all right." Colonel Leighton grabbed the whip off the wall. "Before we take care of this, I want to know. My daughter's treated you better than anyone around these parts, and she's done all she could to keep me from selling Naomi, and you don't say a word while that snake comes to court her?"

"Does it matter? I still got a beating coming."

"Yes, it matters. Merry says you're a good man, a God-fearing man, and up 'til now, I wouldn't say different. You won't get in any more trouble than you're in now if you tell me. I just want to know."

"I got my reasons." Joe's chin quivered. "They ain't good enough."

Colonel Leighton crossed his arms and glared at Joe with the whip dangling from his right hand. He didn't have any plans to move until Joe owned up to all of it.

"I was mad, pure and simple." Joe's body hunched over with the admission. "I figured I'd get a beating if I talked bad to you about some white man. I'd liked to say I was afeared, but the truth of it is I was just plain mad."

"I can't imagine why you'd be angry with Merry. She's never done anything to harm you."

Joe was a big man, but at that moment, his stature diminished, the guilt he bore under managing to take several inches off his height. "You sold my son away from me, and then you sold my little girl's note to Mr. Boidae. It wasn't about America, but I wanted you to hurt for your little girl the way I hurt for mine. This was all about getting back at you."

The colonel gasped.

Joe squared his shoulders, and his giant build returned. "The Good Lord's been troubling me about it 'til I made peace with Him, and now, I want to make it right with you. I'm asking your forgiveness. I reckon you'll still put that whip to good use, and I'm fine with it, expected it, but I'm powerful sorry. That's why I told you all of it now."

Colonel Leighton rarely procrastinated when it came to taking care of unpleasant business, but a sliver of light seeping past his defenses had shaken him. He set the whip back on the hook. "You go on back to your cabin. We'll take care of this later."

Chapter Thirty-Eight

Colonel Leighton leaned against the wall in Levi Boidae's kitchen and strummed his fingers against it. He had never been close to Harland's father. They were neighbors, that was all. He hadn't visited the man since he took to his bed almost two years ago. He knew he should, it was the Christian thing to do, but life had a way of delaying good intentions.

Levi was not Colonel Leighton's favorite person. Before Mrs. Boidae died, she and Harland often showed up at church with bruises and the occasional black eye. That was the only time he ever remembered seeing Gertrude Boidae. Levi kept a tight rein on his family.

Colonel Leighton wanted to knock some sense into Levi back then. The memory of Elizabeth's death was so fresh in his mind. For a man to abuse his wife in such a way when she could be taken away at any moment was beyond comprehension.

Then Gertrude committed suicide, and all he could do was offer his condolences. Levi had been a broken man afterward, going through the motions of life, running his business, taking care of his son, but never drawing out of his own world. His world became the mill.

Two years ago, Levi surprised everyone when he visited the anxiety bench and changed in his demeanor. He even set about freeing his slaves and making things right with people he had cheated in the past, but a few months later, he took to his bed and refused to see anyone who tried to call on him, even Doctor Adams and Reverend Thornton.

Harland handled all of the tragedy in his life well. Colonel Leighton had admired that about him, but now, he wasn't so sure. Maybe this had affected Harland in a way that stayed hidden. Before Colonel Leighton confronted Harland, he had to know how bad it was.

Eva, the nurse, came back into the room. The girl was young, about twenty, and pretty. Her coloring suggested she might have some Negro or Indian blood in her, and she wore her clothing in a scandalous manner. Her blouse was unbuttoned further than it should have been. She was barefoot, and her skirt was short enough to easily show her ankles. She talked too loud and pranced around in a crude manner implying she might have been a barmaid or strumpet.

"Mr. Boidae doesn't want to see you," she said.

Colonel Leighton crossed his arms. "Ma'am, I'm not going anywhere until I see Mr. Boidae."

Eva twisted her hair falling loose around her shoulders. She was so common, she didn't have the decency to pin it up. She touched his arm. "It's best if you go."

He jerked his arm away and stepped toward the hallway. He wouldn't let this trollop stop him.

Eva ran to the hallway entrance and blocked it with her body. "He doesn't want to see you. You're not going in there."

Colonel Leighton stroked his beard. He had never assaulted a woman, and he wasn't about to start now, even one as crude as this nurse. He didn't like it, but he'd have to resort to bribery. He pulled five silver dollars from his pocket and placed them on the table. "I'm going to see Boidae now. Move aside and you'll be paid for your trouble, but I'm not leaving until I see him."

Eva twisted her hands together. "You promise you won't tell? Mr. Harland can't find out ever."

He raised his right hand as if taking an oath to reassure her. "I promise."

Eva darted to the table and grabbed the coins. "He's in the room to the right."

Colonel Leighton strode to the bedroom. He hesitated at the doorway to prepare himself. He doubted that nurse did much to take care of Levi. The stench would most likely assail him the moment he entered the room. He inched the door open.

The room was sparsely furnished with a table holding a pitcher of water, a bed, a chest, and a chamber pot. A blazing fire on the wall between the bedrooms kept the room warm. Instead of the unpleasant odor he expected, the aroma of soap and crisp freshly laundered linens filled his nose. The drapes were pulled back allowing light to enter the room.

Levi lay under the yellow patch quilt looking as if breathing were too much of a strain for him. His face looked swollen, and his complexion had a grayish cast.

A book with a ribbon marking its place rested on the seat of the rocking chair. Could it be that crass girl knew how to read? Surely Levi didn't have the strength to read to himself.

Colonel Leighton set the book on the table and sat in the rocker. "Hello, Levi. It's me, Beauregard."

"Beau Leighton? You came to visit me?" Levi's voice sounded weak, but he was alert. "The only person I ever see is Eva."

"I'm sure Harland takes good care of you."

Levi grunted. "Eva takes care of me. If it were up to Harland, I'd be long gone."

Colonel Leighton ignored the statement. At least Harland made sure his father was well cared for. There was more he wanted to know. "I decided a visit was long overdue since we'll be family soon."

"What do you mean?"

"Harland and my America are getting married." The colonel studied Levi to gauge his response. "Didn't he tell you?"

Levi's mouth opened, and he tried to prop himself up. "No!" He coughed until mucus came up from his throat. Colonel Leighton handed Levi a spittoon and propped pillows behind him.

"They can't," Levi said when he recovered. "You have to stop it."

The muscle in his neck corded. "What do you mean, stop it?"

Levi's head flopped back on the pillows as if he didn't have the strength to hold it up. "You can't blame him. It's my fault. I've asked God to forgive me, but it's too late to help him. Too late."

"Stop rambling, man." He had a strong urge to grab Levi by the shirt and shake him no matter how sick he was. "If you know something, for the sake of my daughter, tell me."

"He doesn't know right from wrong. I don't know how to explain it. He'll do anything, say anything, if it gets him what he wants. He pretends he's a good man, a Christian, but most of what he says is a lie." Levi coughed again. "I don't even think he knows the truth anymore. He's evil, I tell you, evil."

The vein in Colonel Leighton's forehead throbbed. "How can you say that about him? He's your son."

Levi let out a sob. "Don't you think I know that? Finding his mother swinging from a rope when he was little did something to him. I didn't help matters. I treated Gertrude and Harland harshly... I hurt them. When she died, I escaped in my own grief, barely paying attention to the boy except when he did wrong, then I showed him no mercy. I treated Harland worse than the slaves. It did something to him. There was one time I caught him catching the cat's tail on fire. Then there was the time I found his dog hung by the neck from the rafters in the barn. He denied doing it, but I knew it was him. He's not right in the head."

Cold fingers climbed up his spine.

"He hasn't come to see me since he took over the mill." Levi's voice lowered. He barely had the strength to utter the words. "If it weren't for Eva, I'd be alone. I begged her to fetch Reverend Thornton, but she won't. She's says Harland would know. She's afraid of him, and I don't blame her. The boy's as savage as a meat ax."

The colonel's mouth had gone dry. He wet his lips before he spoke, but his voice cracked. "Is there something I can do for you?"

"Eva takes good care of me. She's a real angel, treats me like I'm her pa." Levi coughed. "There is one thing."

"Just name it."

"Could you make sure she's taken care of when I'm gone, maybe find her another job? I worry about her."

"I'll do what I can."

Levi grabbed his hand. "You protect your daughter. Don't you let Harland near her, you hear?"

Colonel Leighton nodded and walked back into the kitchen. Eva wiped her eyes with her sleeve.

"Eva."

She stepped back against the wall. "Yes, sir."

He held his palms up. "It's okay. I won't tell anyone you let me see him. I give my word."

She let out a sigh and plunked into the chair. "Thank you, sir."

"I'm going to send Reverend Thornton by." Colonel Leighton dropped another silver dollar on the table. "You let him see Mr. Boidae."

Her lips pursed. "If Mr. Harland finds out? You don't know what he's like."

Colonel Leighton wiped a tear from her cheek with his thumb. "Nobody's going to find out. You're under my protection now."

"I tried my best."

The fear in her eyes touched a chord of sympathy in him. "Do you know the horse ranch by the river five miles east of here?"

She nodded.

"That's my ranch." He stepped to the door and placed his hand on the latch. "When Levi's gone or if Harland finds out you tried to help him, come get me. I'll give you all I can." He stepped out onto the porch and kneaded the knot in the back of his neck. It was worse than he ever could have imagined.

Chapter Thirty-Nine

America rested on the settee in the parlor beside her father. He had propped her up, wrapped her in blankets, and asked Ruth to fix her a cup of tea.

Papa cleared his throat. "I want to talk to you about your engagement to Harland."

"Let me speak first." America swallowed a sip of tea. "I need to say something before I lose my courage."

He stroked her hair like he used to when she was a little girl. "Have we grown so far apart you have to summon your courage to speak to me?"

The whiff of his pipe tobacco smelled so much better than Harland's cigars. "Promise you'll listen to me before you say anything?"

He reached down to kiss her on the forehead. "I love you, Merry. You're my child. When you were sick, and I thought I might lose you..." His brow furrowed. "You say your peace, I'll listen."

Her eyes watered up, and her right eye twitched. She didn't want to cry in front of him, but she couldn't help it. It'd been so long since she'd felt close to him.

Papa handed her his handkerchief and placed his arm around her.

She wiped her eyes and rested her head on his shoulder. "I can't marry Harland."

"That's what --"

"Papa, you promised you'd listen." She could hear her father's heartbeat. She held her breath waiting for him to say more, but he didn't. "I don't love him. I never have. I just wanted to please you. I feel uneasy around him. I prayed about it, and I know God doesn't want me to go through with this. I'm giving him the mitten."

Papa rubbed his hand in circles across her back. "I pushed you into this. I'm sorry."

"There's more." She swiped her lips with her tongue. "I have a fond affection for another man. I didn't realize it until shortly before I became ill, but I'm in love with someone else."

"William Woods, the preacher from Oberlin?"

She glanced up. How did he know? "Yes."

"Does he feel the same way?"

She nodded. "I've messed everything up. He left because I told him I was going to stay in Kentucky and marry Harland. He won't be back."

"This is all my fault." Papa took her teacup and set it on the parlor table. "I wanted you to find a husband to take care of you, and I forced you into the clutches of an evil man."

America rose up. "William is not evil. He's the most godly and principled man I've ever known."

Her father's eyes darted away. "I wasn't speaking of William. Harland is not the man he represents himself to be."

America splayed her hand across her chest. She was almost afraid to say, "Go on."

"He's forced himself on at least one of his female slaves, and he crippled her son. Even if you loved him, I wouldn't allow this wedding to take place."

America drew her hand to her mouth. "He has Naomi's note."

"I know." Papa stroked the side of her face. "I'll do what I can for Naomi, but right now we need to get you out of this engagement."

"How did you find out?"

"Joe and Reverend Thornton told me earlier this morning. Joe had known for almost two months and didn't say anything."

"Another reason slavery is wrong. He didn't tell you because he was afraid it would end up with him getting a beating."

Papa's Adam's apple bulged. At least he didn't argue the point. Maybe it was progress.

"Harland's coming over this afternoon." A weight lifted from her. "I'll end it with him then."

"No, you won't."

"You said --"

"I will not allow that man near you." Papa stood and strode to the fireplace. "I'll talk to Mr. Harland Boidae alone."

*****

Harland Boidae hated being out on a cold day like today, but he had to persuade Colonel Leighton and America he was the devoted fiancé. It was a relief she was doing so well. He feared she would die on him or wake up crazy as a loon and ruin all his plans. He'd have to put up with that irritating eye twitch, but it could have been worse.

This might work out to his advantage. He'd never seen her so timid as she was when he accused her of calling him a liar. If the fiery America came to the forefront again, he could control her with feigned outrage and persuade her the brain fever had muddled her thinking. He wouldn't have to lay a hand on her.

The marks always showed.

America's condition wasn't the only encouraging report he got this week. Eva told him his father grew weaker every day. The devil would have that man before the snow melted, maybe even this week.

Harland dismounted in front of the Leighton home and smiled at his good fortune. Soon Levi Boidae would die, and with America at his side, his political plans were set.

He knocked on the door, and when Ruth answered it, pushed his way inside. Colonel Leighton stood at the fireplace smoking his pipe, his brow furrowed and his stance that of a military man, not a rancher. The man appeared angry, but Harland couldn't imagine why.

Harland strode to the fireplace and extended his hand. "Good day, sir." Colonel Leighton didn't shake it. "Is something wrong? America hasn't had a relapse?"

"Sit down." It sounded more like a command than an invitation.

He complied and forced a smile.

The colonel spoke in soft menacing tones. "I assure you my daughter is well and concurs with the decision I've made concerning you."

Harland worked to keep his voice conciliatory. "What decision is that?"

"I'm going to be upfront with you, sir." The vein in Colonel Leighton's neck pulsed. "There will be no wedding between you and my daughter. I won't have it. Furthermore, you will have no more dealings with her or I'll have you horsewhipped."

The muscles in Harland's stomach tightened. "But... May I ask why?"

"You've represented yourself as a Christian and a gentleman, but the jig is up. You are neither. You, sir, are the worst kind of scoundrel."

Heat rushed through Harland's veins, but his future depended on not losing his temper. "I don't know what you're referring to, sir. It's obvious someone has been spreading malicious lies about me. I can't imagine what they said or why you would believe them."

Colonel Leighton set his pipe on the fireplace mantel. "Fine, if you insist. You had relations with one of your slaves, a woman called Izzy, and you cruelly abused her son with punishment no Christian slave owner should inflict."

"You're wrong. Todd got caught in one of my spinning machines. It was an accident. Who told you these lies?" Harland held down the panic rising in his gut.

"It came from three reliable sources."

"You won't even tell me the names. You're going to believe some Negros over me?"

Colonel Leighton's eyes narrowed. "The fact you believe your slaves are the only ones privy to this convinces me even more of your guilt, but no. There are others who know of your villainy."

Sweat beaded Harland's forehead. He tried to hold the tone of his voice down, but it came out loud and shrill. "Are you calling me a liar?"

"Yes, sir, I am."

"Get America down here." Harland took a few steps toward the staircase. "She'll believe me. She knows I'm an honorable man."

The colonel treaded to the staircase and blocked it. "No! You are never to see Miss Leighton again."

Harland's fingers curled into a fist as he struggled to think of something to gain control. "It would be in your best interests to allow this wedding."

Colonel Leighton's hands fisted at his sides. "Never."

"Oh, you'll concede my claim to her. You wouldn't want your neighbors to know your daughter had improper relations with me before she grew ill, even before our engagement. I'm ready to do the right thing by her. I hate to soil her reputation, but if you don't –."

The pain in Harland's jaw struck just before the floor rose to greet him. The taste of blood assailed his mouth. He pulled himself to a sitting position, blinked his eyes, and rubbed his chin. He glared up at Colonel Leighton. The man stood over him, pistol pressed against his forehead.

The colonel spoke in a quiet rage. "You will not say one word about America, or I'll let everyone know your activities of late and make sure your political aspirations are at an end. Mark my words. A man who treats his slaves like that in these parts won't be elected to dogcatcher let alone the US Senate. Leave my home." He pulled back the hammer. "Now!"

Harland tried to shake off the fog and marched out the door, his face hot and numb. "This isn't over. I mean to have her as my wife."

Colonel Leighton called out after him. "You come by here again, and I'll shoot your hide full of buckshot." He threw Harland's gray wool overcoat into the snow and slammed the door behind him.

Harland brushed off his crumpled burgundy suit and shook out his coat before mounting his horse and galloping away. This wasn't over. No woman had the right to refuse him, especially not one whose illness left her with a deformity. He would marry America and make Colonel Leighton pay for what he'd done.

<h1 style="text-align:center">Chapter Forty</h1>

America pulled the loose string on the sleeve of her dress while she sat on the edge of her bed waiting. She wanted to sneak to the top of the staircase to try to overhear the conversation, but she was afraid Harland would see her. She started to the door when it opened.

Papa entered the room, his shoulders tense.

"What happened?"

He paced like a mountain cat. "You don't need to fret. I've ousted him from the house. He won't be back."

"Something's still troubling you."

Papa stopped and placed her hands in his. "I don't want to disturb you with this after you've only recently recovered."

America swallowed the lump in her throat. "I'll fret about it more if you don't tell me."

He gazed into her eyes until she glanced away. "I want you to know, whatever happened, I love you, and I'll stand by you. He's an evil man. I could see how he could seduce an innocent woman with his charms."

Her mouth dropped open as a chill spread through her.

Papa looked down. "He's impugning your honor, says you two have to get married."

"You don't believe I would... I never gave myself to him in any way. We haven't even kissed."

Papa let out an audible sigh. "I'm so relieved. I didn't want to believe him, but you wouldn't be the first lady to be caught in an evil man's snare. I needed to hear the truth from your lips."

America's cheeks warmed. "How did you respond to those filthy lies?"

"I showed him to the door." Papa chuckled. "After he pulled himself off the floor."

"You hit him?"

He nodded. "I also warned him of the consequences should he spread rumors about you. He has his own reputation to consider."

America threw her arms around his neck. She'd never been prouder. "I've made a mess of things. If only I hadn't sent William away."

He pulled her in tight. "If he's worthy of you, he'll be back."

"He thinks I've made my choice. He won't interfere. The only way is to return to Oberlin so I can undo some of the damage I've caused."

"No." Papa pulled away and took hold of her arms. "I almost lost you, first to illness, and then to that snake. I won't let you return to Oberlin alone. It's too dangerous."

"Papa --"

"Unless things are worked out between you and William before you leave and I have assurances he'll look after your safety, you'll stay home with me."

"I'm not afraid."

"I am."

America tapped her fist on her mouth. The great Colonel Leighton didn't intimidate easily. If he had concerns, then there was reason for them. "Papa, what about Naomi? Harland still holds the note on her."

"I've been pondering on that."

America widened her eyes.

"Don't give me that look. Naomi has been in my household all her life. I may have felt the need to sell her, but I don't want her mistreated."

"Then you'll buy her back?"

"I can't." Papa shrugged. "I used the money to pay the mortgage."

"Can't you do anything?"

Papa stroked his beard. "The law is clear. If Riley doesn't come up with the money to buy her note by two weeks from Friday, Harland can take legal possession of her. There's nothing I can do."

Since they were talking so freely, America decided to risk a little. "Riley has an offer for his farm. He could come up with half. Maybe if you sold Red and another couple of horses, just until Riley can get the rest of the money..."

"I don't think I could sell the horses in time." Papa patted her hand. "I'll try."

"One more thing."

"Yes."

"I'd like to go to prayer meeting Saturday. I haven't been out of the house for weeks, and I feel stronger."

"I don't know." Papa paused.

She delivered a pleading gaze.

"All right, as long as you ride in the wagon with Joe and Ruth, I can't see the harm. I'll let Joe take a rifle in case he runs into trouble."

America kissed her father on the cheek. She needed to make arrangements for Naomi and Riley's escape in case Papa didn't persuade Harland to give him an extension.

*****

Harland stood at the window rubbing his bruised jaw. Colonel

Leighton dismounted with a volcano revolver in hand. The man had sand, he'd say that much for him. Harland stepped onto the porch and aimed his Kentucky long rifle at the colonel. "You dare show up here?"

Colonel Leighton raised his handgun. "I fought in the cavalry for ten years before settling here. I was the best marksman in my division. Do you really want to do this?"

Harland paused. If it would further his cause, he would shoot that smug look off Colonel Leighton's face, but now was not the time. He lowered the rifle and propped it against the side of the house. "What do you want?"

Colonel Leighton holstered his gun and stepped onto the porch. "Business. I want to buy back the note on Naomi."

"The pretty slave America was fretting about?"

"Naomi. I'll give you four hundred, same price you gave me."

Harland rubbed his hands together. It looked like he had something Colonel Leighton wanted, and after all the shock about him bedding his slaves. "Make a bargain with Riley. If he pays by the due date, I guess I won't have a choice."

"I'll need a little more time."

"Well, I don't know. America begged me to buy her, said she'd do anything I want–anything."

Colonel Leighton grabbed the collar of Harland's coat. "Shut your filthy mouth!"

Harland grinned. "I can see why you want that pretty little Negress, being widowed for so many years. She'll warm a bed fine." He stared Colonel Leighton down. It wouldn't take much to get the man to blow. He enjoyed toying with him. "She's not for sale."

"Come, man. This is business. You don't need another slave. Name your price."

"I do need her. I plan to use her for breeding." Harland grabbed his rifle. "Now get off my land."

The glare Colonel Leighton shot Harland was as deadly as the revolver in his hand. "I'll be back, you mark my words." He mounted his horse and rode away.

Harland leaned against the house and let out a deep gratifying sigh almost to the point of humming. There weren't many who got the better of Colonel Beauregard Leighton. Only two weeks until the note came due.

Chapter Forty-One

William followed Cal's lead down the mountain. Fresh snow covered icy patches along the path. Rock formations lined with embankments of snow and huge icicles loomed overhead with the warning they could give way at any moment. An occasional crackling followed by an icicle breaking further convinced William of the danger.

The men plodded the horses at a slower pace to make sure their footing held. A landslide of white from a tree branch above them plunged to the path behind them.

They'd taken the pass over the mountains against Cal's advice. He didn't want to risk coming this way with the ice storms they'd been having. He warned William the shortcut wouldn't help if they had trouble, but William didn't give up easily. He'd already wasted enough time.

They rode on to where the path narrowed, and William glanced over the edge at the drop-off. Jagged rocks and trees covered in white lined the precipitous descent to the valley below. His gut churned, and he forced himself to look at the path ahead. When he kept his eyes on Cal, he felt safer. Cal had been through these mountains enough times, although maybe not in these conditions.

William placed his gloved hands under his armpits to keep them warm. Even with the snow gear they'd brought, he couldn't keep his fingers from getting numb without keeping them close to his body.

A crackling sounded and some rocks the size of large hail fell and bounced off the gorge bringing down a torrent of snow. Cal's mare backed up as more rocks plummeted toward them. The horse lost her footing, and slid on a patch of ice. She tried to right herself and, with a screaming whinny, tumbled down the hill at least thirty feet to the bottom where a patch of trees stopped her fall.

William dismounted and ran to the edge. Cal rolled down the knoll covered with snow and stopped on a flat spot about half way down near half a dozen pine trees. If this had happened a few feet earlier near the slope...He climbed down, careful to make sure his footing was secure, and holding onto the fir trees along the way to keep his balance. He reached the trees where Cal lay and knelt beside him.

Cal groaned and lifted himself up.

William let out a breath. "Are you all right?"

"I think so." Cal gingerly got to his feet and brushed himself off. "Where's my horse?"

Further down the hill, the mare struggled to get to her feet only to fall again.

"It doesn't look good." William sighed. This meant a trek to the bottom. "You stay here."

He hiked to the bottom of the ravine as fast as the icy conditions allowed. The horse's front right leg was shattered, a bone stuck out of the skin. A groan from the animal told William all he needed to know. He helped Cal to the path above before pulling his rifle from his scabbard. He trekked down to the mare, set his jaw, and pulled the trigger.

They made camp and started a fire to give Cal the chance to catch his breath. Thank God he wasn't hurt. He could have easily broken his neck.

"I don't know what to say," Cal said. "I should have seen those rocks falling."

"You know these mountains. If something like this happened to you, what chance would I have getting through without you? I'm glad you came along."

Cal's eyes fixed on the mountains to the east of them. "We should have gone on the road around the hills. It would have been safer."

William stared at his feet. "It would have added a week to the trip."

Cal gulped his coffee. "It's gonna take a might longer now."

"I know."

*****

Harland hid in a grove of trees. The clouds covering most of the stars made his hiding place ideal. If there was anything he could find, he'd see it from here. After Colonel Leighton dared threaten him at his own house, a question wormed into his mind. What happened every week at the Saturday night prayer meeting attended only by his wayward fiancée?

Harland had offered to accompany America on a number of occasions, but each time, she made a flimsy excuse why he shouldn't come. The reverend never announced the meetings or invited anyone to attend them. It was odd they didn't want anyone there.

America was such a staunch abolitionist, and Reverend Thornton had Northern sympathies. What if they were involved in stealing slaves? Harland couldn't wait to discover for himself what they were up to. He'd found this hiding spot the day before and had arrived at dusk, tied his pony a hundred feet away, and waited.

That was a couple of hours ago, and there was no sign of anyone. It was a cold night, and he blew into his hands to warm them. He looked at his pocket watch. She had only recently recovered from her illness. Maybe her father wouldn't allow her out on her own yet.

She'd be here by now if she was coming. He let out a heavy sigh and shuffled toward where he'd tied his pinto. Horses whinnied, and he spun around. A lantern flickered along the path to the house. The wagon rolled closer occupied by America and a couple of her slaves.

Harland's heart beat faster in anticipation.

America and the older slave woman hiked to the house and knocked on the door. Reverend Thornton stepped onto the porch.

They greeted each other, but he couldn't hear what they were saying. He cranked his neck to get a better look, but nothing out of the ordinary happened. This wasn't getting him anywhere. Maybe it was just a prayer meeting. He could afford to wait a few minutes longer to make sure.

The big slave, Joe, pulled the wagon next to the barn, but that didn't help. He was probably going to loosen the straps on the horses and let them munch on some hay while they were waiting. Joe got out, but instead of attending to the horses, he headed to the barn door, and called inside. "Zed, you can come on out."

A black man and woman left the barn and timidly looked around. America's slave pointed to the back of the wagon and removed a board covering a hollow place.

Harland swallowed the shout of glee forming in the back of his throat. He relished the thought of swooping down on them and making his hand sticky with their blood, but he held back. That wasn't why he was here.

He glanced at the porch. Mr. and Mrs. Thornton and America watched it all. There could be no doubt every one of them was in on stealing slaves and transporting them across the river. He had what he'd come for. America was now his to do with as he willed.

He almost stepped out from his hiding place to confront them but stopped short. This was too good to act now. He'd savor it for a while longer. Before he was finished with them, Colonel Leighton would hand his daughter over on a silver platter.

The big man covered the hollow part of the wagon with a board and covered the back with blankets before driving away toward the river.

Harland skulked to his horse he had tied deeper in the woods. He'd wait until the right time to use this information. America would marry him with Colonel Leighton's blessing unless he wanted his daughter to end up in prison.

He chuckled. It might be more enjoyable to see the fear in her eyes, twitch and all, if he were to haul her into court in chains. He'd relish the anguish on the colonel's face if he decided on that course. It might be worth it.

Harland rode into the night. This was better than he'd ever expected.

*****

William walked ahead of his bay gelding and allowed Cal to ride. Cal had insisted he wasn't hurt, but William knew better. The horse trotted down a gully. Cal winced and caught hold of his ribs. It wasn't the first time.

The knot in William's gut grew every day. He yearned to move faster. This trip should have taken two days, and it had already been a week. The snowstorm would delay them another two weeks... If he hadn't been so stubborn and had gone the long way like Cal wanted, they would be there by now. The muscle in his jaw twitched. If he'd left when he first got the telegram, he would have made it before it snowed. His pride caused this delay, not the weather. He'd never forgive himself if something happened to Merry.

At least they were out of the mountains. The foothills were easier to navigate than the narrow path through the Appalachians.

Wolves howled echoing through the hills. The bay Cal was now riding whinnied. They sounded close.

A gray wolf with white fur framing its face stepped out of the trees onto the path. William halted, and the mare stirred and tugged at her reins. William grabbed the reins tighter to keep the horse calm.

The wolf stared at William with clear yellow eyes, challenging him. William edged toward his rifle secured to the horse. The wolf tilted its head, gave him one more glare, and loped into the trees.

"If that don't beat all," Cal said. "I've never seen a wolf act like that before."

"Me either."

They hiked on in silence until the sun began to set.

"We better make camp." William helped Cal onto a nearby rock. "This looks like a good place. I need to get wood for the fire. Are you going to be all right?"

Cal nodded and sucked in heavy breaths.

The echo of wolves' howls pierced through William. He removed the mare's saddle, poured her some water, then tied her reins with a double knot to a nearby tree. The bay twitched and shook her mane. It wouldn't do them any good if their only horse spooked and took off.

They needed a campfire, but he didn't want to leave Cal in his current condition. Instead he gathered twigs near the campsite. He gathered brush, made a fire pit, and opened a can of beans.

Cal grabbed his side and wrapped a blanket closer around him.

William dished him out some food. "You've been favoring that side since the accident."

"I'll be all right. I don't want to be slowing you down any more than I already have."

"What happened wasn't your fault." William swallowed hard. "It was mine. I should have listened to you and gone the safer way." He poked the fire with a branch. "We need more wood." He stood and turned.

A gray wolf with a white face like the one on the trail stood at the edge of the clearing not more than twenty feet away growling and bearing its teeth. Its yellow eyes glowed in the firelight.

William grabbed the .58-caliber rifled musket.

The horse whinnied and pulled at her restraints.

Cal shouted from behind him. William turned, and his heart skipped a beat. Seven wolves, all gray with various white markings, surrounding them. Where did they all come from? They bared their teeth, growled, and darted in and out. One rushed in toward the horse.

William clenched his jaw, took aim, and fired. The wolf nearest the horse whimpered, took a step, and fell leaving a pool of red blood in the snow. He tossed the rifle and ammo to Cal, grabbed a branch intended for the fire, and lit it. Swinging the torch around them in a circle, he kept the wolves at bay. They weaved in and out, trying to find an opening.

Another wolf loped toward Cal as he fumbled to load the musket. The wolf lunged, and Cal fired. The animal landed in the snow with a thud and twitched, the ground around him turning red.

The remaining wolves bared their teeth, still weaving in and out, making it harder for William to keep them away with the one flaming branch he held. He moved closer to Cal. The wolves loped around them in a circle and approached from different directions.

*****

America told Reverend and Mrs. Thornton the events of the last few days. "I'm more relieved than upset about Harland being out of my life, but I'm heartbroken about William." She swallowed hard to keep her voice from choking up. "I love him."

Mrs. Thornton brown eyes watered. "I'm so sorry."

America turned toward Reverend Thornton. "Is it possible for you to get word to him?"

Reverend Thornton looked at his feet. "I telegraphed him when you became ill over a month ago. If he was coming, he would have been here by now."

America clutched her stomach to hold in the sobs. Ruth embraced her, and she cried into her nanny's shoulder.

It was too late. Some things couldn't be fixed.

*****

Six wolves baring teeth closed in from different directions. William swung the lit tree branch around one side then the other. Wolves crisscrossed looking for an opening.

Cal rammed another bullet into the musket and fired, killing another wolf.

William swung to his right side. The mare jerked and almost knocked him down. "Easy girl."

Two wolves to Cal's left thrust toward him as he reloaded.

William turned in time to singe one wolf and sent him whimpering away. The other darted back.

The three on the other side closed in. Cal fired again hitting his mark. The remaining three growled and scurried into the woods.

William wiped his brow. "I need to light more fires."

Cal nodded.

He gathered brush and used his bowie knife to cut off dry limbs from a nearby tree, and lit four fires surrounding them. When he had assured himself the campsite was secure, he dropped to the ground and gave himself a moment to draw in some deep breaths.

Cal moaned and slumped against the rock. Blood gushed from his head.

Chapter Forty-Two

Joe wiped his brow and placed another log on the chopping block outside the barn as the master strode toward him.

"We need to talk," Colonel Leighton said.

Joe nodded and set the ax down. In a way, he was relieved. Waiting for the beating had been bearing down on him. Best to get it over with.

"I tried to buy Naomi's note," Colonel Leighton said, "figured I could sell a couple of horses, but Mr. Boidae won't hear of it. I've done all I can. I'm sorry."

Joe's knees weakened, and for a moment, he forgot to breath. "I'm out to sea." If the sun had exploded in the sky, it wouldn't have surprised him more. "You done that for me?"

Colonel Leighton cupped his hands over his mouth and blew into them. "It was the least I could do."

"What about the whipping?"

Colonel Leighton shook his head. "Joe, I've been considering a few things. You and your family have served me well, and I might not have treated you fairly by selling your children. I still don't hold to America's views about slavery. You Negroes are better off with a master to see to your needs, but I can understand why you were angry."

Joe swallowed. "Then you forgive me."

The colonel crossed his arms. "I'm working on it, but it's hard to swallow you put my girl in danger. Even so, there's nothing I can do about Naomi." His brow furrowed. "Unless Riley can get hold of some money, a week from Friday, she'll belong to Boidae, and there's not a thing I can do to stop him." He rubbed his hand over his forehead, turned, and walked back to the house.

Joe would never have believed the master could have changed this much in such a short spell. The only hope for Naomi now was to cross the Ohio this Saturday. He'd tell Riley to be ready.

At least he wouldn't lose his remaining child. Obadiah had decided to stay and help with the rescues. He'd turned into a fine man.

Joe heard a clang in the barn, grabbed the ax, and darted around the opening in time to see Bart picking up the shovel he knocked over.

"What are you doing here?" Joe glanced back to make sure nobody saw.

Izzy and Todd scooted out from the stall they'd been hiding in. Todd used a wooden crutch and dragged his bandaged foot behind him.

Bart shrugged. "I know you said two weeks, but I got weary of waiting."

"Well, you're gonna have to." Joe looked back one more time then closed the barn door and bolted it. "Todd's not up to traveling yet, and it's needful for some others to cross first. They ain't gonna be able with Mr. Boidae and his men on the lookout. Get on back to your master."

"Can't do it. We left last night. He knows we're gone by now. We ain't gonna have another chance."

Joe wiped the back of his neck with his hand. "You beat all. Why can't you ever do like you're told?"

Izzy placed her hand on Joe's arm. "It's my fault. I couldn't stomach being with master one more night, not after what he did to Todd. I just couldn't. I begged Bart to do something. For once, he listened."

Joe let out a short breath. The deed had been done. He had to help them. "You hide here 'til nightfall. I'll get you to the safe house, but you're just gonna have to wait a few days to cross. I ain't gonna take the chance with Mr. Boidae's men combing the woods for you."

"Thank you," Izzy said. "God bless you."

Riley and Naomi were going to have to wait to cross the river. He wouldn't risk them traveling with Bart and Izzy. The smaller the group, the easier to hide. They wouldn't have much time to spare. Maybe they could slip away after church Sunday night.

He should have insisted they cross before now, but Naomi wanted to give Miss America a chance to work it out how they might stay. Joe hoped they hadn't waited too long.

*****

Harland adjusted in the saddle of his mount on the hill overlooking Reverend Thornton's house. From here, he had a clear view with the pine trees and brush impeding anyone seeing him.

Three of his men scoured the area near the river for his escaped slaves, but he doubted they'd find them. It was more likely they'd show up here. They'd wait a couple of days to cross figuring things would die down a little. Most likely it'd be Saturday during those weekly prayer meetings.

A wagon with Colonel Leighton's big Negro and America's slave nanny rode up to the barn. The big slave pulled a wooden plank off the wagon. Izzy, Bart, and their boy scurried into the barn.

Harland tugged on his bottom lip with his thumb and forefinger. America wasn't with them. Now he'd have to wait. Better to take a chance of losing a few slaves than risk losing his leverage over her.

He was getting tired of Izzy anyway. She was getting old, almost thirty, and no matter how hard he tried, he couldn't breed her. It was obvious she was barren. He had planned to sell her at auction Saturday anyway.

Next week, he'd have a new slave to warm his bed. He licked his lips as he conjured up an image of Naomi in his mind. She was every bit as pretty as the slave girl he'd bought in Lawrence County, Zona, the one who'd died birthing her baby. He could afford to be patient.

*****

William led his gelding as he inched down the foothill. He doubted Cal would ever take a trip with him again. Cal slumped in the saddle, his head wrapped with bandages made from William's shirt. The bite marks hadn't gone into his skull far, but he needed a doctor.

A white column resort hotel was nestled in the valley near the bottom of the hill. The frozen riverbanks behind the hotel had docks where travelers kept their boats in the summer.

William led the horse along the road leading to the entrance. A sign, *Esculapia Resort*, gave him a sigh of relief. They'd wandered upon the biggest mineral springs in the country, and only a few hours' ride from Dover.

Maybe staff remained there during the winter months. If not, he'd break in and get Cal settled before he rode to Vanceburg to get the doctor. He could worry about paying for the damages later.

He pounded on the door. No answer. He pounded a few more times. Nothing. There was no choice. He picked up a rock and raised his arm to throw it through the window.

The door opened. A large woman in her forties pointed a shotgun at him. "What do you think you're going to do with that, young man?" She spoke in a heavy German accent. A large woman, she wore her blond hair in a tight bun accentuating her light raised eyebrows, narrow nose, and high cheekbones. Her piercing blue eyes glared, and her Nordic features inspired trepidation.

William dropped the rock and gave her a sheepish grin. "I'm sorry, ma'am. I didn't know anyone was home."

"So you decided to break in, did ya?"

"Yes... I mean no... My friend. He's hurt."

The woman looked around him at Cal. "Why didn't you say so?" She lowered the shotgun. "Bring him in."

William rushed back to the horse and helped Cal into the hotel. As he led Cal through the foyer, he gaped at the luxurious surroundings. A grand piano sat in the middle of the room. Mirrors and paintings lined the walls. Clusters of sofas and cushioned chairs gave space for visiting among the guests. Oriental rugs covered the wood-paneled floor. At the far end sat a desk made out of cherry where guests registered.

The woman stood at the entrance of the hallway beside the desk. "Follow me."

William allowed Cal to lean on him as they followed her through the hallway.

She stopped at the third door to the right and unlocked it. "You sure are lucky you caught me here. Name's Mrs. Baum. Mr. Baum owns the resort. My husband and I normally stay in Maysville over the winter, but this year, we decided to winter here. He rode to Vanceburg for supplies."

"No luck about it," William said. "God directed us to you."

Mrs. Baum opened the door to the bedroom. "Well, I don't believe in all that prayer truck. God's too busy with the problems of the world to worry about us." She used a wedge to tighten the ropes on the four-poster rope bed in the center of the room.

William pulled back the heavy gold curtains hanging from the canopy and helped Cal into the bed. Cal sunk into the feather mattress.

Mrs. Baum lit the lantern on the cherry dresser and started kindling in the fireplace against the wall. "It'll be nice to have some company other than Mr. Baum around. It gets lonely around here in the off-season. Mr. Baum's a fine man, but he doesn't like to talk much, mostly grunts and nods."

William took in the surroundings. On the wall opposite the fireplace, an eight by eight pane window afforded guests a view of the river. Green and yellow swirled wallpaper covered the walls. A sitting area with two cushioned chairs and a sofa surrounded the fireplace. A screen with a painting of a deer standing at the edge of a river blocked off the area with the chamber pot, wash basin, and mirror. Mrs. Baum must have given them one of the best rooms.

William pulled Cal's boots off his feet, helped him out of his coat, and covered him with the feather comforter.

"You better get going," Cal said. "I'll be all right now."

"Not until I get a doctor and make sure."

Cal propped himself up. "You need to get to America."

Mrs. Baum fluffed up a pillow and placed it behind Cal's head. "Sounds like this boy's hurt worse than he thinks. Doesn't even know what country he's in."

"America is the name of a lady I'm going to see," William said.

"Oh," Mrs. Baum said. "Guess I need to learn when to keep my thoughts to myself. Mr. Baum always says I talk too much."

"Not at all," William said. "I'm grateful to you. Do you know where I could find the nearest doctor?"

Mrs. Baum put her hand to her mouth. "Now let me see. There's a doctor in Maysville. He's good. He treated Mr. Baum when he broke his leg last summer. My husband was trying to fix a hole in the roof. He got the ladder out and climbed up, but when he got near the top, the rung broke, and he came tumbling down. The doctor set his leg. It took him most of the summer to heal. He's doing fine now. I told him he's too old to be climbing on roofs. He needs to hire a young man to help around here."

William's stomach knotted. He resisted the urge to try to hurry her along. "Are there any closer, ma'am?"

"Well, there's a doctor in Vanceburg. I never met him, but folks there say he's all right. He's a little young for my tastes. Doctors should be older, don't you know?"

"Yes, ma'am, I suppose so. How do I get to Vanceburg?"

"Take the road north about five miles," Mrs. Baum said. "When you come to the fork, Vanceburg's to the right. Maysville's to the left. It'll take time to get there, maybe an hour by horseback. You should wait until morning."

William turned to Cal. "I'll be back as soon as I can."

Cal slumped back into the pillow. "At least go to see America after you get the doctor. Don't waste time coming back here."

"Do you want Granny Price to use her cane on me?" William teased as much to ease his own mind as to make Cal feel better. "If I leave without making sure you're okay, she'd hunt me down."

Cal chuckled and closed his eyes. "Yep, I expect so."

*****

William rode to Vanceburg as if wolves were still chasing him. When he arrived, he trotted down Main Street hoping to spot a sign showing him where the doctor lived. A man stepped out from a house, and William rode up to him. "Could you direct me to the doctor?"

The man gave directions, and William soon stood pounding at the door of a small white house in the middle of town.

A pregnant woman in her early twenties answered. "Yes, may I help you?"

"I need the doctor," William said. "My friend's been attacked by a pack of wolves."

"Oh, my. Bring him in."

"I left him at the resort. He was ailing too much to ride farther. If the doctor could come with me..."

The woman's brow furrowed. "That is a problem. I'm Doctor Murphy's wife, but he's not here right now."

William ignored the urgency rising from his gut. "Mrs. Murphy, pleased to meet you. Could you tell me when the doctor will be back?"

"I don't rightly know. He's making his rounds. He'll be back when he's done."

"If you could tell me where he is, I could go fetch him."

"Won't do you much good. He could be at half a dozen farms outside of town. You'll probably end up missing him. Why don't you come into the doctor's office? I'll make you a cup of coffee while you wait. You look like you've had a time."

He glanced down at his clothes. Dirt and leaves stuck to his trousers, and blood stained his coat, Cal's blood. He caught a whiff and scrunched his nose. The mixture of the stench of a drenched dog, body odor, and smoke clung to him. "All right, ma'am. Thank you."

He followed Mrs. Murphy to a small room heated by a box wood stove in the corner and slunk into one of the two chairs sitting near it. Mrs. Murphy excused herself and slipped into the hallway.

William leaned back in the chair. Now that he sat still, his eyelids grew heavy. It would be dark soon. Even if the doctor got there in time to go to the resort tonight, William would most likely have to wait until tomorrow to travel to the Leighton Ranch.

He strummed his fingers on the arm of the chair. Where was Doctor Murphy? He closed his eyes a minute, opened them, closed them again.

Harland drug Merry into the barn. She struggled to get away.

"William," she called out. "William, save me. Where are you?"

"He'll never make it in time." Harland laughed and hissed as his face turned into the head of a cobra.

William's eyes shot open. It was dark out. The sun had gone down. A cup of coffee sat on the parlor table beside a flickering candle. He took a sip, but it was lukewarm. He must have been asleep for at least an hour.

Voices from the hallway came closer. Mrs. Murphy and a young man, barely twenty-five, stepped into the room.

The man extended his hand. "I'm Doctor Murphy. I hear you've had a time."

"Yes, sir," William said. "My friend and I've been on the trail for two weeks now. He fell off his horse when it slipped on some ice, then we were attacked by wolves."

Doctor Murphy's eyes widened. "Wolves? Must be quite a story. You can tell it to me on the way to the resort." He kissed his wife on the cheek. "Don't wait up. I'll stay the night there."

William told the doctor his adventures on the trip back. He'd have to wait until morning to get to Merry. During a quiet spell, a stab of guilt struck him for being so impatient to leave. Cal wouldn't be lying in there hurt if he hadn't been so stubborn. His shoulders hunched. His stubbornness and pride had caused so much pain.

Lord, forgive me. Heal Cal, and take care of Merry. I put them in your hands. It wasn't the first prayer he uttered.

After examining Cal and wrapping his stomach, Doctor Murphy mixed powder in a glass of water Mrs. Baum poured and had Cal drink it. The doctor stood and motioned for William to step into the hall.

"He's got a cracked rib near as I can tell," Doctor Murphy said. "The powder should help some with the pain. The bite marks aren't deep, and there's no infection. He won't be able to travel for about six to eight weeks, but he should be fine. By then the weather will be better for traveling anyway."

William let out his breath. "Thank you, Doctor Murphy. I'm sorry for bringing you out this late."

"No problem at all. I don't mind spending the night here."

"Mr. Woods." Mr. Baum's voice startled William. He didn't realize the gruff German man with the same heavy accent as his wife was behind him. "Come into the foyer."

William followed Mr. Baum into the front room and sat in the chair across from him. Mr. Baum was as stern and direct as Mrs. Baum was friendly and talkative. Although Mr. Baum was a few inches taller than his wife, they both matched each other in formidable facial features.

"I'll come to the point," Mr. Baum said. "Your friend needs care for the next two months, and my wife and I are glad to help. Mr. Price said you have somewhere you have to be, ya?

"Yes, sir."

"We need to make arrangements before you go."

"Thank you, sir. I'm afraid I don't have much money on me, but I could give you a promissory note."

"It won't do. I could wallpaper this room with the promissory notes given to me. None of them were paid." Mr. Baum crossed his arms across his massive chest. "I charge quite a bit for one of those rooms, but I do understand the circumstances. It being winter, I wouldn't have guests anyway, but you will pay me for my trouble."

"I don't know what to do. I'm willing to pay whatever you require, but I don't have the funds on me right now."

"I need some work done around here, and free labor helps me as much as hard cash."

William's gut twisted. Another delay. "How much labor?"

"You work hard for me tomorrow, and we'll call it even."

It was more than fair. Mr. Baum could have asked for a lot more, but tomorrow was Saturday. After doing the required chores, even if William was so tired he could hardly stay in the saddle or had to ride in the dark, he would leave. He wouldn't wait any longer.

Chapter Forty-Three

Joe stood outside Riley's cabin door, swallowed the lump in his throat, and knocked.

The door swung open, and Naomi threw herself into Joe's arms. "Pa, I'm so happy to see you. I wasn't sure you'd be by before we crossed."

Joe pulled back and squared his shoulders. "I'm needing to talk to you and your man about your crossing."

Naomi gazed into his eyes. "Come on in, and sit by the fire. It's cold out there."

Joe came into the cabin and shook Riley's hand before sitting across from him at the table.

Naomi poured them coffee. "We're ready to go."

Joe swallowed a gulp of his coffee and forced out the words. "You can't leave tonight."

Riley stood. "Why not? I ain't got the money, and Mr. Boidae will be coming for her soon."

He stared into his coffee cup. "You'll have to wait."

"We can't," Riley said. "He'll be by in six days."

Naomi placed her hand on his arm. "Hear Pa out. He knows what's best."

Riley eased back in his seat and drew his fist to his mouth. "Go ahead."

Joe nodded. "Bart and Izzy came to me a few days ago. Mr. Boidae's men are all over looking for them. They're crossing tonight. It'd be too dangerous for you to cross too. At least wait until tomorrow night."

Riley strummed his fingertips on the table. "We can't let that man get his hands on Naomi."

"We got time," Joe said. "Not much, but some. Obadiah's gonna come by tonight. It'll make me feel better knowing he's close if Mr. Boidae tries to get my little girl before the note's due."

Riley's hand flattened on the table making a thud. "You reckon he'll do that?"

"I don't know what the snake will do." Joe wiped the back of his neck with his hand. "Either way, the law will side with a white man over us. I wish I could figure on something, but we just gotta leave it in the Good Lord's hands."

"Pa," Naomi said. "No matter what happens, I know you're doing what you think best."

Joe swallowed. He had done his best, but was it enough?

*****

William sat in the chair beside Cal's bed as the sun started to set. "I'm all done with the chores here. I'm leaving soon."

Cal propped up on his pillow and grabbed his side. "Are you sure you shouldn't wait until morning? It's already getting dark."

"I have to get there tonight. Don't ask me why, but I do."

"If God's telling you to go, you'd better get a move on."

William glanced at the floor. "I'm leaving for Oberlin next week. I might not get back this way."

"I thank you for all you've done. You've been a good friend."

William flashed a grin. "You mean like taking you on a trip where you fell down a ravine, got your horse killed, and broke a rib, and if that's not enough, you got attacked by wolves just cause I didn't have enough sense to go the way you said?"

Cal snorted. "Yeah, I owe you, but I was thinking more about you bringing us the truth and helping us find a new pastor. Reverend Keller seems like a right fine man."

"He is."

"You make sure you keep in touch. Post me a letter, and tell me what happens."

"I will." William rubbed his hand across his chin. "Cal?"

"Yeah."

"I'm proud to call you my friend."

"You better get going. Stand here jawing all night, and you might be too late."

William nodded. He hoped he wasn't already.

*****

Five men on horseback rode toward the wagon. America made out one of the horses in the moonlight. It was Harland's spotted stallion. She wrapped her arms around herself to keep from trembling. She wanted to tell Joe to go faster, but there was no way a wagon could outrun a man on horseback.

Joe pulled up on the reins and stopped the wagon beside the river's edge. He set the rifle on his lap and covered it with a blanket. The men surrounded them with Harland in the front.

Harland tipped his hat, a scowl replacing his customary smile. "What are you doing out at this time of night?"

"Just taking Miss Merry to prayer meeting, sir," Joe said.

"Prayer meeting's the other way," Harland said.

"Not that's it's any of your concern," America said. She hoped Harland didn't hear the catch in her voice. "I asked them to take me on a ride by the river before we went to the church."

Harland scanned the landscape. "Have you seen anyone out here?"

"No sir," Joe said. "We surely ain't."

America glanced toward the frozen river. The lantern hanging from the house on the hill shone brightly. "Why?"

Harland still diverted his attention to look around. "Three of my slaves took off a few days ago, but I'll find them."

America swallowed trying to moisten her dry mouth.

"Maybe you'd best get to your prayer meeting," Harland said.

Joe tipped his hat. "Yes sir." He pulled on the reins and directed the horses to turn toward the church. "Straight away."

Harland called after them. "See you go right there."

Joe called back. "Yes sir."

Nobody said anything until the wagon had ridden over the hillside out of Harland's view.

America glanced back. "What are we going to do?"

"We're gonna do what we told him," Joe said. "We're gonna head to prayer meeting. We'll tell Reverend Thornton the lantern's lit, but Mr. Boidae's men is looking for them slaves."

America held her arm across her waist. "He won't stop until he's searched every part of this county. What if he catches them trying to cross?"

"It's in the Lord's hands," Ruth said. "We got to do what we can and leave the rest to Him."

Every sound in the night grew louder. An owl hooted. A noise in the bushes, probably a raccoon or a deer.

America tried to convince herself they weren't being followed, that Harland didn't suspect, but the noises fed her imagination. Leaves rustled. She turned to see a deer dart into the trees.

More rustling and the hoot of an owl. She peered into the woods trying to see an image or a glimpse of something. Nothing but trees, bushes, and shadows caused by the moonlight.

A bright night.

She tried to decide if it was a good thing or not.

It wasn't only the noises. America couldn't shake the feeling someone was watching them.

*****

Harland nodded to his men. "We have them now. This will be where they try to cross. Tom, you and your men stay with me."

Tom, a young broad-shouldered man with a stern look on his face and a cleft in his chin, nodded.

"Jake, follow them to the house. Don't let yourself be seen."

Jake was in his thirties with a grizzled face matching his temperament. "I won't."

"Let the men go off with the slaves," Harland said. "We'll catch up with them here. After they leave, make sure the women don't leave that house, especially America. If she gets away, you'll answer to me."

Jake licked his lips and smiled showing his rotten teeth. "I'll keep them there if I have to hogtie them."

Harland placed his hand on his rifle. "You keep her alive and her beauty and purity intact or you'll answer to me, but whatever you have to do short of that..."

Jake nodded and rode off.

Harland smiled to himself. Tonight, he would have his revenge.

Chapter Forty-Four

Reverend Thornton's cabin came into view. The wagon rolled up beside it, and America didn't wait for Joe to help her down. She ran to the door and pounded. Reverend Thornton answered the door, and she rushed in. Ruth and Joe entered behind her.

Mrs. Thornton wrapped a comforter around America's shoulders. "Come sit by the fire. I fixed us some hot coffee."

Reverend Thornton blew out the candle in the window and placed his finger to his mouth. "Have your coffee. I'll be back." He put on his coat and slipped out the door.

America shivered but not from the cold. Fear caused more chills than the frigid weather. She cupped her hands around the coffee cup and listened to her own heartbeat as she waited.

Reverend Thornton came in and bolted the door, something she'd never seen him do and parked himself on the bench across from them. "I thought I might have heard something when you rode up, but it must have been the wind. Nobody's there."

"Are you sure?" America's stomach muscles tightened like a wedge tightened the ropes on a bed. "I thought I heard it too."

Reverend Thornton shrugged. "Probably just a deer or a squirrel. Don't fret." His smile didn't convince her. It didn't quite reach his eyes. "Now tell me, is the lantern lit?"

Joe nodded. "Yeah, but Master Boidae's got men combing the woods for his escaped slaves. Might not be good to go out tonight."

Reverend Thornton's jaw tensed. "No choice."

"Why do you have no choice?" The wedge in America's stomach tightened another notch. "Harland won't give up."

"We can't wait," Reverend Thornton said. "We have to get Bart's family away tonight. We can't keep them hidden for long. That man will tear up this countryside until he finds them."

"I'd best get going then." Joe headed to the door.

"I'm going with you this time." Reverend Thornton grabbed his coat off the hook. "Ruth, don't stick around waiting this time. Take my buggy and get America home safe."

"I'll get her there." Ruth reached over and placed a hand on Joe's cheek. "You be careful."

Joe kissed her with urgency and passion. "Woman, I got you to come home to. I ain't planning to be nothing but careful."

Ruth placed her hand on America's arm. "Come on, Miss Merry.

Let's leave the men folk to do what they got to do."

Reverend Thornton took Mrs. Thornton in his arms. "As soon as Ruth and America leave, you bolt the door and don't open it until I return."

Mrs. Thornton hugged Reverend Thornton. "I have a bad feeling about this. Please, don't go."

"You worry too much. I'll be fine."

"You be careful, you hear."

"I love you." He touched her cheek and walked out. Joe followed him and closed the door.

Ruth turned to America. "I'll hitch the buggy."

America started toward the door. "I'll help you." Her knees weakened, and she collapsed to the floor.

Ruth and Mrs. Thornton hurried toward her and helped her up.

"Are you all right?" Mrs. Thornton asked.

"I'm fine. I just... America felt shaky, and her eye twitch and watered. She knew she should hurry home, but she didn't think she could manage it. All the events of the last few weeks came rushing in on her. "Let me finish my coffee before we leave."

Mrs. Thornton nodded. "Don't take too long. You heard what Benjamin said."

"I just need a few minutes." She sat at the table and sipped her coffee until she felt steady enough to rise. "Thank you, Mrs. Thornton. I'm ready to go now."

"You be careful." Mrs. Thornton took America's cloak from the hook and wrapped it around her shoulders.

"You stay here and rest. I'll hitch the buggy now." Ruth headed toward the door.

The door crashed open, and a man busted through pointing a navy revolver with an eight-inch barrel in Ruth's face. "You're not going anywhere."

The wedge in America's stomach clenched her muscles taut. "What is this? What do you think you're doing?"

The man with a chiseled face and dark eyes scowled. "You ladies make yourselves comfortable. I'm here to see you stay put." He looked familiar like she'd seen him before.

The mill. He worked for Harland. Her fear gave way to indignation. "How dare you accost ladies in their own home? When my father, Colonel Leighton, hears about this, you'll rue the day you were born."

"Miss Leighton, I don't take orders from your father. I answer to Mr. Boidae, and he told me to keep you here. Do as you're told, and nobody gets hurt."

America crossed her arms and gave him what she hoped was a defiant glare, but her eye twitched. "What if we refuse?"

The man pointed the pistol toward Ruth and Mrs. Thornton. "Then I'll insist. Mr. Boidae told me not to hurt you, but he didn't say anything about them."

"There's no need." Mrs. Thornton placed her arm around America's shoulder and guided her to the table. "We're not going to try anything."

"You sure aren't," the man said. "Now sit in them chairs."

America took her place beside the other women but jutted her chin. She wouldn't let him think he got the better of her. "What's your name?"

"Jake."

"Do you really want to face Colonel Leighton or maybe go to prison because of Harland Boidae? Is he worth it?"

Jake grunted. "He pays good. Besides, you best be fretting about yourself. Mr. Boidae's not a man you want to cross."

America rested her arm over her stomach. "You can't spend the money in jail."

"You can't keep jabbering if you're dead." Jake stroked her face with the back of his hand.

She cringed and pulled away from his touch. "You're making a mistake."

"Shut your mouth before I shut it for you."

She should be scared, but she was too angry and worried about the others. She heard a voice in her spirit. *Pray.*

She prayed for the safety of the escaped slaves, and the men helping them. God would answer her prayers, but she couldn't shake the feeling His answer might be no.

Something was about to go wrong.

*****

Joe pulled the wagon to a stop at the top of the hill overlooking the Ohio River. He cocked his head and listened to the rustling of the trees. The sound stopped. Probably the wind.

He and Reverend Thornton removed the wood plank hiding the others. Bart and Izzy crawled down from the wagon.

"Come on, Todd." Joe sat on the edge of the wagon. "Climb on my back. I'll carry you for a spell."

"I'll carry him." Reverend Thornton sat next to Joe. "You don't need the extra weight."

Todd wrapped his arms and legs around Reverend Thornton.

Joe stood and peered into the dark trying to make out images.

Nothing there. If anyone were, he'd see them from here, but with the brush and trees, they wouldn't have the same advantage. Maybe it was his imagination running wild.

An owl hooted, and Joe startled. He chuckled at his foolishness and traipsed down the hill toward the river. He sprinted to catch up with the others. They'd already made it half way down.

Another rustling from behind, and he gazed into the night a third time. "Someone's back there."

Reverend Thornton stopped and tilted his head. "Are you sure, Joe? Maybe it's an animal."

Joe exhaled a visible breath. "I'm sure."

"What we gonna do?" Izzy grabbed Joe's arm. "I can't let him beat my baby again. He liked to have killed him last time."

"What if we get caught?" Bart scratched his behind. "Maybe we ought to go on back. He might not whip us too bad if we beg him for mercy."

"When did you ever know Master Boidae to show mercy?" Izzy placed her hands on her hips and glowered at her husband. "Maybe you can offer Todd up to him to whip, and me to warm his bed. He might show you mercy then."

Bart's eyes bulged. "I'm afeared, Izzy." He glanced back.

"Go on back if you want, you worthless piece of--"

"Stop." Joe wiped his face with his bandana. The frigid wind battered him, but sweat still beaded his brow. "They ain't close enough to see us. Not enough cover. They might be loping around waiting for us to get to the river."

Reverend Thornton steepled his forefingers to his mouth. "We could distract them. I could lead them off while you get the slaves across."

"We ain't slaves," Izzy said. "We ain't never gonna be a white man's slave no more. You hear?"

"Izzy, hush." Bart looked around, afraid of being overheard. "Let 'em study on what we gonna do."

"We're almost to the river now," Joe said. "Might work, but one man ain't gonna lead them nowhere."

Reverend Thornton raised his eyebrow. "What are you thinking?"

"I'm going with you," Joe said. "Better chance that way. Izzy and Bart can make it with Todd."

"They'll catch us," Reverend Thornton said. "It's almost certain. I might go to jail, but you..."

Joe shrugged his shoulders. "Can't be helped."

Reverend Thornton placed a hand on Joe's shoulder. "You're a good man."

Joe nodded, but Reverend Thornton was the good man here. He was a white man with all the privileges, but he was willing to risk everything. Joe was just a slave. Even if he died, he didn't lose much, and he gained a place in Abraham's bosom where he wouldn't have to fret no more about what some white man could do to him. He'd be free.

"Izzy, Bart." Reverend Thornton pointed to the riverbank. "You and Todd find a good spot to hide. When they take after us, you make your way across and get to the brick house on the hill. There are stairs leading the way. They'll take care of you."

Izzy kissed Joe's cheek. "Thank you."

"Reverend Thornton done most of it."

Izzy gave Reverend Thornton a wary look.

Joe understood. It was hard to trust white folk, but it wasn't right. The reverend risked a lot for them.

Bart took Todd from Reverend Thornton and carried him on his back as they made their way to the riverbank and hid in some brush.

Joe gazed at the path ahead. "You ready?"

"Ready, Joe." Reverend Thornton began running.

Joe ran after him along the Ohio River leading the men as far from the hiding place as they could. The thunder of hoof beats soon followed. Their pursuers no longer tried to remain hidden.

Joe glanced at the riders still a ways back. It had worked. They were all chasing after him and the reverend. He breathed heavy, and his heart thumped as his footsteps sounded on the hard, cold path.

The sound of the approaching horses grew louder. Soon they were upon them and four men on horseback including Mr. Boidae circled them and pointed rifles in their direction. The chase was over.

Joe collapsed on the ground and let up a silent prayer for courage.

"Where are they?" Mr. Boidae growled the question as he and his men dismounted.

Reverend Thornton raised his hands. "Who?"

"You know who." Mr. Boidae pulled Joe up by his coat. "We saw you with them."

"Mr. Boidae, sir," Joe said. "I ain't seen nobody out here but you."

A whip lashed across Joe's back. Pain coursed through him, and he yelped. One of Boidae's men raised the whip and brought it down again.

"You have no right," Reverend Thornton said. "This man doesn't belong to you."

"He's the piece of dung helping my slaves run off," Harland said. "That gives me the right. Tom, take the good reverend here to the sheriff in Maysville. I'll deal with this one myself."

Reverend Thornton's eyes widened, and he took a step back. "What slaves? You've got this all wrong. We were out looking for a runaway horse." His voice sounded shaky.

Two men grabbed him. "It's Colonel Leighton's horse, and Joe's his slave. You'll answer to him." He struggled as they tied his hands. "You're making a mistake." They dragged him to a horse. His voice pleaded as they rode into the night. "The colonel will be furious with you."

The man with the whip brought it down again, and Joe cried out.

"Now, boy." Mr. Boidae said. "You gonna tell me what I want to know or is my man here gonna beat you half to death?"

Joe tasted something metallic in the back of his throat and tried to swallow. His parched throat threatened to choke him.

He lifted his head and stared Mr. Boidae straight in the eye.

"I ain't telling you nothing."

Chapter Forty-Five

William wasn't sure of the reaction he'd get if he knocked on Colonel Leighton's door at ten o'clock at night. He wasn't the man's favorite person, and the late hour might not be the best time to change a father's opinion, but he felt compelled to proceed. He rapped hard on the wood panel.

Colonel Leighton and Luke opened the door fully dressed holding rifles and handguns. William gulped.

"Brother Woods," Colonel Leighton said. "What are you doing here?"

"I came to see about Merry," William said. "I heard she was ill."

"That was weeks ago," Luke said.

William brushed the snow off the step with his foot. "I tried to make it earlier."

"I don't give a fig about that. Merry was supposed to be home over an hour ago." Colonel Leighton raised an eyebrow. "Do you know where she is?"

"No, sir. Can I help you look for her?"

Colonel Leighton nodded. "We're getting saddled up now." He strode out to the barn as William and Luke followed behind. "She was headed to Reverend Thornton's for a prayer meeting with two of my slaves. I haven't heard from any of them since."

William's jaw hardened. If they'd been caught helping slaves escape...

Colonel Leighton saddled his black stallion. "We've had a problem with Harland Boidae. The engagement is off."

William squelched the urge to ask questions about what happened. There'd be time for that later.

"We're trying Reverend Thornton's first," Luke said. "If she's not there, we'll be paying Boidae a visit."

William understood now why it was so urgent for him to get here tonight. He let up a silent prayer of thanks. Even with all the delays, it looked like he arrived just in time.

*****

Jake sat on a chair by the door. His chin lowered to his chest. He'd closed his eyes a few times, jerked, and repositioned himself before beginning to nod off again. This time, his eyes closed without the jerk, and a low murmuring snore came from his throat.

America nudged Mrs. Thornton and Ruth. This might be their only chance. She stood and skulked toward the door. After three steps, Jake stirred. She froze and waited, but he never opened his eyes. She held her breath and took another step.

Footsteps sounded on the porch. Ruth dashed in front of America, and Jake shot up out of his chair and pointed his gun at them. The door crashed open, and Harland burst in.

Two men followed him dragging Joe through the doorway. At least it looked like the big-hearted giant. His face was bruised and swollen. His left eye set twisted in the socket with blood dripping from the corner of it. Blood gushed from his nose, now an inch further to the left than it once resided. His shirt hung on him in shreds giving no protection to the torn flesh on his back. The men dropped him on the floor.

Ruth let out a cry and knelt at his side. "Joe."

He rose gingerly until he was in a sitting position. "It be all right, darling." His voice sounded weak. "Don't fret. It's ain't as bad as it looks."

America beat Harland's chest. He grabbed her arms and held them.

She struggled to break free. "How dare you? This is Colonel Leighton's slave, not yours, and when he hears about how you accosted me, there will be no place for you to run."

"Shut up!" Harland pushed her against the wall and slapped her.

Joe rose to his feet faster than she thought possible considering his condition and sprang to her side.

Harland pointed a revolver in his face.

"Now, America." Harland tilted his head toward Joe. "I didn't want to threaten your slave in front of you, but you need to listen."

She struggled to push out the words. "You have no right."

"You'll learn when we marry. I like your fire, sweetheart, but only to a certain point."

At that moment, America knew his ice blue eyes didn't hide what was inside Harland. Evil cast a haze of steel over them. His eyes revealed his soul.

"All of you." Harland pointed the gun toward Joe, Ruth, Mrs. Thornton, and then toward America. "You worked with that no-account preacher to help my slaves run off."

She shook her head.

"Don't deny it. I followed you to Thornton's house. I know what all of you've been doing, but I figured I'd keep my peace about it, but then, sweetheart..." He touched her face.

She cringed, disgusted by the feel of his hand.

He continued. "You had to go and break our engagement and steal away my slaves."

"We didn't." The words rang untrue even in her ears.

"Like I said, I had you followed. My men here will testify under oath. The question now is what are we going to do about all this?" Harland laced his fingers, considering the possibilities. "Thornton's been arrested, and my men gave Joe a good beating."

America stared at the cobra head of Harland's walking stick covered in blood.

Joe flashed her a furtive glance and shook his head.

"I should give Ruth a whipping too," Harland said, his voice eerily calm, "but I'll leave her to Colonel Leighton. If you agree to marry me, I'll let them go back to their master. He can decide how to punish them. Except for Thornton's wife. Wouldn't be right for her not to join her husband in prison."

America lunged toward Harland. "I'll never marry you."

Harland grabbed her by the arm and slapped her. "I'll teach you to go against your future husband." He grabbed the whip from Tom.

"No." Joe charged at Harland. The gun fired.

America's ears rang, and she pulled away. Red splatters sprayed her skirt. Joe stayed erect for a moment gazing at the hole in his middle then dropped to the ground, blood squirting out of his chest.

Ruth screamed. "Joe." She covered his body with hers and wailed.

"Don't cry." Joe made a gurgling sound as he touched Ruth's hair with his hand. "I'm about to be a free man."

Harland pointed the gun at America.

America placed her hand over her mouth and gagged. She rasped, "They'll hang you for this."

Harland snorted. "Maybe it's time you learned the facts of life, sweetheart. I shot a Negro stealing my slaves. No jury in Kentucky would convict me."

*****

Colonel Leighton rode up to the Thornton house with Luke and Brother Woods at his side. A gunshot blast thundered through the night air.

The colonel jumped down from his horse into a dead run for the door. Brother Woods and Luke wasted no time joining him. Brother Woods crashed through first. Colonel Leighton and Luke were right behind with rifles pointed.

Colonel Leighton's military training took over, and he assessed the situation in less time than it took a heart to beat.

Joe lay on the floor rasping and gurgling with blood rushing out of his chest. Ruth, covered in Joe's blood, held his head and sobbed. Mrs. Thornton stood stoic by the fireplace.

Colonel Leighton dealt with the immediate danger of Harland and rough-hewn men pointing handguns at the ladies first. The colonel threw his rifle to Luke and grabbed Harland by the neck. Harland's eyes widened in fear as he pressed a revolver against his temple.

Harland dropped his gun to the floor and raised his hands. "It's not how it looks." He nodded to the other men, and they did the same.

"Luke, cover them. If they even twitch, shoot to kill."

Luke propped a rifle to his shoulder. "Yes, sir."

America pressed against the far wall, her eye twitching, her cheek bruised, tears running down her face. She was splattered with blood, but she didn't look wounded. Thank God. Brother Woods ran to her side.

Colonel Leighton knelt by Joe and pressed a handkerchief against his chest to try to stop the bleeding. "We'll get you help. Just lie still."

America whimpered behind him. "He tried to whip me. Joe stepped in front of me." She pointed at Harland. "He shot him."

"Sorry... didn't warn..." Joe rasped out through the gurgles. "Forgive."

Colonel Leighton dropped the military commander tone, and his voice thickened. "You saved my little girl's life."

Joe's hand dropped to the floor.

Ruth buried her face in Joe's shoulder. "Don't you die on me."

"Don't... Crossing first... other side... I... love." The gurgling stopped, and Joe's lifeless eyes remained open.

"No." Ruth gasped for air.

Colonel Leighton closed Joe's eyes. Heat rose to his neck as he turned and pointed his revolver in Harland's face. "Give me one reason I shouldn't shoot you dead right now."

"Father, no." Luke placed his hand on the colonel's arm. "Let the law handle it."

A malevolent grin crossed Harland's face. "The law's not going to do a thing to me. Every one of these people, your slaves, the preacher and his wife, even your own daughter, were stealing slaves on a regular basis. They helped three of mine get away tonight. I caught them in the act. Reverend Thornton's already in custody. If you have me arrested, I'll see to it your daughter goes to Frankfort Prison."

Colonel Leighton cocked the gun. "I'll see you dead first." He aimed at Harland's mouth as twisted, pressed lips replaced the man's smile. Might be worth it to get rid of that smile permanently.

"You're lying," Luke said. "She may be an abolitionist, but she doesn't steal slaves."

"Merry, did you..." The muscle in Colonel Leighton's neck corded. "Were you a part of this?"

America nodded her head and buried her face in William's shoulder.

Luke sputtered. "What were you thinking? How could you?"

"Stop!" Colonel Leighton grabbed Luke's shoulder. "Just stop." He holstered the gun and tried to calm his breathing. "Boidae, I'm going to take my family and slaves home now. We'll work this out tomorrow."

Harland resumed his cocky smile. "Sounds fine to me. I'm sure we can come to terms to keep your daughter's name out of it. What should I do with the preacher's wife?"

America called out. "Papa, please."

"You have her husband in jail," Colonel Leighton said. "Isn't that enough for one night?"

"Acceptable. I can always have her arrested later." Harland straightened the creases out of his suit and motioned to his men. "Let's leave them be for now. Colonel Leighton, I'll stop by tomorrow evening to work out an arrangement, and I will have satisfaction."

Chapter Forty-Six

America kept hold of William's arm as he drove the wagon to the ranch. She didn't want to let him go, almost afraid she might lose him again. Papa and Luke followed on horseback with William's bay in tow.

Ruth rode with Joe's body, holding his head in her lap and stroking his hair. She hadn't uttered a sound since he died except an occasional heave coming from her gut.

The wagon pulled up to the house and stopped.

A numbness covered America's thoughts, and she fought to escape it. She was in the heart of a cave with no way to process time or distance. Everything was cold, dark, empty. No tunnel, no way out. "Papa, I need to tell you what happened."

Papa helped her down from the wagon. "I want to hear it, but not now. Luke, find Obadiah and tell him about his pa. Have him get his sister and Riley over here. Ruth needs them."

"Obi's at Riley's." Ruth's voice sounded flat.

Luke's emerald eyes glowed in the moonlight. "If they hadn't been stealing slaves, there wouldn't be anything to get through."

"Luke!" Papa had reverted into his military tone. "Do as I say. Better yet, don't tell Obadiah anything. Have him get Naomi and Riley over here as soon as he can. I'll let them know what happened."

Luke twisted his mouth like he wanted to say more, but he didn't. He rode down the path in full gallop.

"Woods," Papa ordered. "Help me get Joe into the kitchen. We'll prepare his body there."

William nodded and marched to the wagon.

Papa patted Ruth's hand and helped her down. His voice softened. "We'll bury him in the family plot in the morning. Don't you fret about a thing. I'll take care of this."

Ruth had a glassy look to her eyes as she gazed beyond him.

"Merry, get Ruth inside the house, and fix her a cup of tea."

America wrapped her arm around Ruth and escorted her into the parlor while William helped her father move Joe's body. Ruth ambled at a dreadfully slow pace, but America kept hold of her arm. "Just a little further."

They reached the kitchen entrance. The door was open. Her father and William laid Joe's body on the table. America blinked her eyes to keep the tears from flowing.

Ruth's gaze clouded over, and she stopped.

"Everything will be all right." America reached over and closed the door to block the view. She grabbed Ruth's elbow. "Just a bit more." She nudged Ruth on.

They reached the sitting area in front of the fireplace. Ruth sunk to the floor without saying a word. America wished she'd cry or say something. She seemed like all the tragedy happening was beyond her ability to grasp, and instead of grieving, she bolted the door of the cave to keep the sorrow from destroying her.

America knelt beside her. "I'm going into the kitchen to fix you a cup of tea. I won't be long. Will you be all right?"

Ruth pressed her lips together and nodded.

America wiped her twitching eye and stepped into the kitchen. She paused for a moment at the doorway. She'd never seen a dead body being prepared for burial before. She held her breath and stepped through.

Joe's body lay on the large wooden table. All of the clothes had been stripped off and the lower portion was covered with a sheet. William and Papa washed the blood off his face and chest. The water in the basin turned crimson.

America stepped back and brought her hand to her stomach. Not being able to look, she turned away. He died to save her. Maybe if she didn't look at him, she could pretend it hadn't happened.

She filled the teakettle with water. Her hand trembled as she set it on the stove. She tried to strike the flint to light the kindling but fumbled. She couldn't get her fingers to work.

William stepped beside her and lit the stove.

She could feel his breath on her neck, but she couldn't look at him. "You came."

"I won't ever leave you again." William leaned in toward her ear. "You have my word."

"Maybe you never should have left her in the first place," Papa said.

William's voice cracked. "No, I shouldn't have."

"Time to hash things out later." Papa moved to the back door. "I'll be out back waiting for Obadiah. He needs to hear this from me first before he sees his father sprawled out on our kitchen table. William, take Merry out to the front porch, before you finish here. She needs some air." He closed the door behind him.

William held out his arm to escort her through the parlor. They passed Ruth crumpled in front of the fireplace, but she never stirred.

They reached the porch, and America leaned against the railing as if she needed it to hold her up.

William touched her shoulder. "I'm so sorry, Merry."

She turned and gazed into his dark eyes appearing as storm clouds gathering to sweep her away. "I'm sorry too. I gave you little choice."

He wrapped his arms around her and pulled her body tight against him." I... I love you." He kissed her.

She wrapped her arms tight around his neck and surrendered to the tempest. She was drowning but didn't want to come up for air. She moved her lips away and let her head lean against his chest. Their heartbeats pounded together in her ears. "I love you too."

He pulled back. "This time, I'll stay and fight for you. I'll keep you safe."

*****

Colonel Leighton stood outside. The clouds obscured the moon and stars, but the light shone with vivid intensity as if it were noon. He didn't know if he could bear the brightness. He wiped his eyes with his fingers and thumb.

The cold wind whipped through him, but it didn't chill him the way Joe's death had. Joe had been nothing but a servant, a slave, and yet Joe turned out to be the better man. If it weren't for him, God knows what Harland would have done to Merry.

He could see it now. To take a man and enslave him and to consider him nothing more than property was immoral. He had sinned. *Lord, forgive me.* He leaned against the house and buried his head in his arms. He had been wrong, so very wrong. He didn't know how to make amends for what he'd done. Joe was dead. He couldn't bring him back.

Clutching his stomach, he doubled over, and retched. When he recovered, a figure in the shadows moved toward him.

"Colonel Leighton," Obadiah said as he drew closer. "I came straight away like Luke said. Naomi and Riley will be here directly. What's this all about?"

"There's no easy way to say this." Emotion flooded the words as he forced them out. "Harland Boidae caught your pa and ma and my daughter rescuing slaves. He meant them all harm. When he went after Merry..." He cleared his throat. "Your pa stepped in the way and protected her. Boidae shot him. He's dead."

Obadiah grabbed the colonel's shirt. "No! It can't be. You're lying." He buried his head in Colonel Leightons shoulder and wailed.

"I'm sorry, son." He patted Obadiah's back as the muscles in his neck knotted. "Your pa's body's in the kitchen. Your ma's in the parlor. She needs you."

Riley and Naomi rode up in a wagon. Obadiah stepped back and wiped his face on his sleeve. Riley helped Naomi down.

"What's wrong?" Riley asked.

"It's Pa." Obadiah's voice took on a gravely tone. "He's dead."

Naomi's knees gave out, and Riley caught her before she hit the ground.

"I'm sorry," Colonel Leighton said. "Naomi, your pa died a hero. He saved my daughter's life."

Naomi buried her face in Riley's chest and sobbed.

Colonel Leighton placed his hand on her shoulder. "I'll take care of everything. Don't you fret. I owe it to your pa."

*****

The sun shone brightly on the winter day they buried Joe. William thought it appropriate since Joe truly did let his light shine in this dark world. For a slave funeral, it was well attended. His master, Colonel Leighton, wore his military dress uniform. America stood at his side. Joe's family, Ruth, Obadiah, Naomi, and Riley, were there. One son, Amos, was absent, but if he could have been there, he would.

Adela had come out. She and Benjamin thought a lot of Joe, but considering Benjamin's trial was scheduled for the next day, he didn't expect her.

John Parker, a free black man William had met once, attended. He owned a foundry in Ripley and was the first Negro to get a US patent. William couldn't imagine how they'd met or why he would risk coming to Kentucky for Joe's burial. Reverend John Rankin from Ripley was also there.

A group of about twenty Negros came to pay their respects, some free, some slave. Riley told him Joe had helped many of them in his lifetime. More probably would have come if their masters had allowed it. Then there were all the slaves Joe helped escape to freedom. They were there in spirit.

Luke was the only member of the colonel's family absent. He refused to attend "some rebel slave's burial" and had gone to Virginia's instead.

William helped Obadiah and Riley shovel dirt on top of Joe's body. Ruth stayed with Naomi at her side holding her hand and watched until the last shovel full was packed down tight. Ruth fell to her knees on top of the grave and wailed. The sound pierced through him.

"The funeral is over," Riley said. "Thank you for coming."

Colonel Leighton stood at attention and saluted Joe's grave. He turned to Obadiah. "Take your mother to the cabin and keep her there.

Naomi, Riley, you stay there too. I'll let you know when I take care of things with Mr. Boidae."

"Yes, master," Obadiah said. "I'll see they stay put 'til you call."

Obadiah and Riley wrapped arms around Naomi and Ruth and led them down the path.

"William, Merry," Colonel Leighton said. "We have some talking to do."

William's jaw clenched as he followed Merry and Colonel Leighton into the parlor. He sat beside Merry on the settee.

Colonel Leighton sat across from them. "Merry, you don't know how relieved I am you're all right, but we still have things to take care of, and I have some decisions to make. No matter what you've done, I know you'll be truthful with me, but I need to know it all now before Harland shows up."

Merry looked at her hands, and a tear slid down her cheek. She told her father everything except William's involvement.

Colonel Leighton took Merry's hands in his. "Is that all of it?"

"No." The words came out of William's mouth before he realized it, but he couldn't let Merry shield his part in it. "I was involved in the slave rescues too, sir. I've been a friend of Benjamin Thornton's for many years as was my father. I've helped him on numerous occasions, and I knew Merry's part in this."

Colonel Leighton stood and leaned against the fireplace hearth with his arms crossed. "You knew, and yet you did nothing to protect my daughter from this affair? You allowed her to be involved in this lawless plot?"

Heat rose to William's neck. "I tried to dissuade her, but she insisted on going forth."

"Do you love my daughter?"

He glanced over to Merry and gave a half smile. "Yes, sir, I do."

The vein in Colonel Leighton's brow pulsed. "Merry told me you believed Harland to be a dangerous man."

"I knew something wasn't right. I didn't know what."

"You left her with a man you believed to be dangerous, and you involved her in a conspiracy that could have got her killed?"

William rested his hands on his knees. He couldn't think of anything to say to excuse what he'd done.

"Papa," Merry said. "I told William I planned to marry Harland. What else could he do?"

"Merry, stop." William gazed at his hands folded in his lap. "Your father is right. After getting you involved in all of this, I did nothing to protect you. I could have come back earlier. Benjamin contacted me when you took ill, but I didn't because my pride was hurt."

He stood and faced Colonel Leighton. "I have no excuse, sir. I was wrong."

Colonel Leighton placed his hand on his revolver. "You need to leave my house now before I do something I'll regret."

America grabbed her father's arm. "Papa, no."

"America, this man is not worthy of your affections, not because he's an abolitionist, but because he didn't place your safety above his ego." He turned to William. "Are you leaving?"

"Yes, sir." William pulled at his collar. "For now, but I'll be back. I won't leave her again."

"Mr. Woods, you're not welcome in my house."

William paused for a moment, but he didn't blame Colonel Leighton for being angry after what he'd done. He'd figure something out. He had to. He treaded out the door.

Chapter Forty-Seven

As soon as the door closed behind William, Colonel Leighton squared his shoulders and prepared for the onslaught from his daughter.

"Please, Papa, you can't do this." America stood and grabbed hold of his arms. "I love William. It's not right you would keep him from me."

He kissed her on the top of her head. "You need to trust me."

America threw her hand in the air and stormed over to the settee. It was an hour before she calmed down enough for him to try to reason with her, but before he had a chance, Luke marched into the house.

"I saw Harland on the trail," Luke said. "He'll be here soon."

"America," Colonel Leighton ordered. "Get upstairs, and stay there until I send for you."

"This concerns me too," America said. "Shouldn't I be here?"

"Can't you just do as you're told?" Luke crossed his arms. "Why do you always have to make things worse?"

She glared at Luke. "Why are you so all-fired mad?"

Luke took a couple of steps toward her. "If you hadn't been involved with abolitionist criminals, Father wouldn't have to be negotiating with a madman to get you out of trouble."

She wrapped her arms around herself. "You have no right."

"If it were up to me, I'd let Harland haul you to jail along with our rebellious slaves."

"Luke!" Colonel Leighton snapped. "You keep your tongue or I'll send you up with her." A knock pounded on the door. "America, upstairs now."

She climbed the stairs and slammed her bedroom door.

Colonel Leighton winced. With everything happening, he'd forgotten to talk to her about how to close a door.

Luke headed to the entrance.

"Remember," Colonel Leighton said. "Let me do the talking."

Luke nodded and let Harland inside.

Harland dressed for the occasion. He'd discarded his blood-stained clothes from the night before and wore his black frock suit, white starched collars, and red silk vest and cravat. He completed the look with that insufferable grin on his face.

When Harland spoke, his voice had a lilt to it. "Are you ready to come to an agreement?"

Colonel Leighton gave a disheartened shrug and stared at the floor. "It appears I have no choice." Better to let Harland think he had the upper hand for now. The man was so sure of himself.

"Good." Harland marched into the parlor, leaned against the fireplace, and crossed his arms with his smirk in place. "Here are my terms. You tell the law Joe was working for Reverend Thornton helping my slaves escape, and you give your daughter to me in marriage. In return, I won't mention America, Mrs. Thornton, or Ruth's parts in this."

"That won't do." Colonel Leighton kept his voice calm as he filled his pipe with tobacco.

"Which part?"

"I'll never allow you to marry my daughter." He packed it down.

"You'd rather have her go to jail?"

He lit the pipe and took a drag. "Anything would be preferable to her being imprisoned in a marriage to you."

"Suit yourself." Harland started to the door.

Colonel Leighton waited until Harland's hand was on the knob. "Wait, I haven't told you my terms."

Harland stopped and turned, his eyes cold. "Go ahead."

Colonel Leighton waited a moment longer before speaking. Let Harland worry a little. "No Christian man would tolerate the way you treat your slaves. If word got out, it would lose you the election. Especially if I were to run against you."

Harland's smiled slipped, and his eyes widened. "I might weather the storm and still be elected."

"Come now. I have a lot of friends in this state." Colonel Leighton tramped his pipe and relit it. "It's not just the slaves. You accosted my daughter and Mrs. Thornton. I may not be able to have you convicted in a court of law, but if word got out the way you treated those ladies, even if they were proved to be slave rescuers, your defeat would be certain. Is marrying America worth that?"

A moment's silence filled the air before Harland spoke again. "What do you propose?"

"Keep your peace about the women's involvement. I'll let the law know Joe helped the preacher steal your property when you killed him. If you pay me fair market price, I'll drop my claim to Joe."

Harland's hands formed fists. "How much?"

"Naomi's note will do it."

The wickedness in Harland's heart showed through his glower. His fingers fisted around his cobra head cane. He swung it at the yellow vase on the table near the door, and glass shattered on the wood floor.

Colonel Leighton set his hand on his revolver. "That vase cost ten dollars."

Harland shook his head. He seemed to be at a loss to know what to do or say. He pulled Naomi's note and a ten-dollar gold piece out of his pocket and slapped them both on the table. "I require one thing more if I decide to release America from any blame in this."

"What?"

"Not only your silence." Harland grinned, but it was tight, forced, "but your support. You campaign for me and support me in my bid for office, and I won't bother America or the others again. I'll settle for Reverend Thornton going to prison."

Colonel Leighton drew in a drag from his pipe. "Come man, surely you don't expect me to support your bid to office after all this. I won't do it."

"You will if you want my cooperation." Harland took a step forward and pointed his finger at the colonel's chest. "If I'm defeated, there'll be no reason for me to keep silent. I'll see to it America's reputation is soiled beyond repair, and I'll have her hauled to prison."

As a young man in the cavalry, Colonel Leighton climbed the ranks to become an officer and then a colonel because he had an innate sense of which battles were worth fighting. As much as he hated supporting Harland, the election and the power coming from it was what the man lusted after. If Colonel Leighton were to fight this, he would lose every other victory.

"It appears I have no choice." The colonel drew close to Harland's face and grabbed the collar of his jacket. "Know this, if I ever see you near my daughter or my slaves again..." He stepped back and calmed his breathing. It wouldn't help to lose control. "You'll find out what it feels like to be on the other end of the whip."

Harland extended his hand. "Then we have an agreement."

Colonel Leighton ignored the hand and opened the front door. "Get the blazes out of my house." When Harland left, the colonel slammed the door.

He stood with his eyes closed for a moment to get rein on his emotions. "Luke." He turned to face his son. "Get the slaves and Riley and bring them back here. We have one more thing to take care of."

Luke looked like he wanted to say something, but he didn't. He followed orders. Colonel Leighton needed to spend time with his son as soon as this was over. He could understand why Luke was angry. He's the one who taught him his attitudes toward slavery.

Watching Joe die for America had changed the colonel in a way he couldn't put into words. God revealed the truth, and he could never go back to what he believed before yesterday. Somehow, he had to show Luke or he'd lose him.

*****

America lifted her skirt and ran down the stairs when her father called, anxious to find out what happened.

"Everything's all right." Papa wrapped his arms around her. "Mr. Boidae and I came to an agreement."

"Thank God."

"Luke will be here soon with Ruth, Naomi, and Riley. I'll tell you the rest then."

The door opened, and Luke entered. Obadiah followed him supporting Ruth on his arm. Riley and Naomi trailed after them. They stood before Papa staring at the ground waiting for him to speak. America could swear she heard their heartbeats. She didn't blame them. As always, their future and their lives depended on their master.

Papa handed Riley an envelope. "I got this from Boidae. Naomi's note. I figured you'd want to be the one to tear it up."

Riley's eyes widened. He held the note in his shaky hands, staring at it as if it he was holding a rattler. His mouth worked as if he wanted to say something, but no words came out. A grin crossed his face, and he ripped the note, and then ripped it again, and threw it in the fireplace. He tenderly embraced Naomi, his shoulders shaking.

America swiped at the tears forming in her eyes.

Papa held up another envelope. "These written papers give every one of you your freedom."

A lightness came over America. She could float away on the slightest gust of wind. She had never been prouder of her father.

"Father." Luke wiped his hand across the back of his neck. "You can't. You'll ruin us. We'll lose everything."

"It's done," Papa said. "I have an obligation to Joe to take care of his family, and I intend to keep it."

"You don't have to give them their freedom to do that." Luke's voice bellowed. He paced to the fireplace and back. "If Joe hadn't been stealing slaves, he wouldn't be dead. This is his fault, and America's."

Papa snapped his fingers. "Enough."

Luke strode toward the fireplace and back a couple more times then let out a noisy sigh. "Father, if you do this, I'll take the job at the Foster Plantation."

"Think this through." Papa placed a hand on Luke's shoulder. "I understand why you're angry, but you'll be turning your back on running this ranch and raising horses. Is it worth giving up everything you love?"

"I can't abide staying here and watching this." Luke pulled away from him. "I swear if you throw away everything we've worked for, I'll never set foot in this house again. I mean what I say."

"You would turn your back on me, your own father?"

"You're going against everything you've ever taught me and for what, a few slaves?" Luke's emerald eyes glared at his father. "Think of what you're doing."

"Luke, I love you." Papa let out a deep breath, "but Merry's right about a lot of things. Maybe if I'd seen that before, it wouldn't have come to this."

Luke tramped toward the door. "I won't be back."

America grabbed his arm. "Luke, please."

He scowled at her, pushed her hand aside, and stormed out of the house knocking the table over on his way out.

The door slammed behind him.

"Oh, Papa." America swiped her tongue across the back of her teeth. "I'm sorry."

Papa hugged her. "It'll be all right. He needs time to think this through. He'll be back. You'll see."

She leaned her head into his shoulder. No matter what he said, they both knew Luke wouldn't return. Her brother was too entrenched in his attitudes toward slavery. Papa had given up his only son to make things right.

Her father stepped back, gave her a reassuring nod, and turned to Obadiah. "You're free to go, all of you. I won't lift a finger to stop you, but if you stay and help me build up this ranch, I'll provide your lodging and food as I've always done. I can't afford to pay you, but I'll give you a couple of foals when we breed the horses. A couple of foals a year ought to be enough for your services."

Obadiah glanced over to Ruth. She nodded her head. "We'll stay. Thank you, master."

"You can call me Colonel Leighton. I'm your employer, not your owner."

Obadiah stared at the whip on the wall. "Can you still use your whip on us?"

Papa grabbed it off the wall and threw it in the fireplace. The oil rope crackled in the fire.

"You got yourself a deal, sir," Obadiah said.

Papa reached out his hand.

Obadiah looked at him warily before shaking it.

Papa turned to Riley. "If you want to try ranching, I'll offer you the same agreement. I'll need the extra help with Luke gone. Might be easier than trying to make a go of your farm?"

"Naomi and me will study on your offer some," Riley said. "I'll let you know."

"One more thing." Papa cleared his throat. "I know who bought Amos. As soon as we get this ranch earning money again, the first thing we'll do is buy his freedom."

Ruth let out a sob.

America wiped the tears forming in her eyes. God had done the impossible. If only He would do the same for her.

Papa would never agree to her returning to Oberlin or marrying William. She'd done what she came to Kentucky for, but she'd never be able to graduate or go to the mission field with the man she loved. A profound sadness swept over her. The cost was worth it, but she still grieved for what she had lost.

Chapter Forty-Eight

William held Adela Thornton's hand as they sat in the back row of the frigid courtroom. The small box stove in the corner of the room near the front didn't give enough heat to warm the whole room.

A judge's bench and witness seat were at the front by the stove. The courtroom wasn't large, only three rows of chairs with an aisle between them. It seated a total of maybe twenty people. The rows were full but not with many onlookers. For the most part, defendants sat waiting to be called before the judge. Guards stood at every row, but Benjamin had not yet arrived.

A sheriff escorted Benjamin in and led him to the front row. He looked frazzled and unkempt and had cuffs around his wrists, but he managed a thin smile when he glanced their way.

The bailiff stood. "All rise for the honorable Judge Buckingham."

Everyone stood, and the judge made his way behind the bench. "You may be seated. Benjamin Thornton, remain standing."

The courtroom bustled as everyone found a seat except Benjamin.

The judge looked at the paper in front of him. "Reverend Benjamin Thornton, you're charged with stealing three slaves owned by Mr. Harland Boidae. How do you plead?"

"Guilty, your honor. Furthermore, I would do it again."

Adela gasped.

Judge Buckingham leaned forward. "Very well. That you, a man of the cloth would do such a thing, would steal property from members of your congregation, makes this offense worse. From what I can see, you show no remorse for your actions. Do you have anything to say before I pass sentence to convince me not give you the full measure the law allows?"

"I answer to a higher law." Benjamin's shoulders squared. "The law of God who will one day end the practice of slavery if He has to tear apart this great nation to do it. I would rather suffer imprisonment by the hands of men than suffer at the hands of an angry God as this great state of Kentucky will if they don't repent and renounce the sin of slavery."

William resisted the urge to shout amen despite worrying about his friend. Benjamin's prophecy sealed his fate.

Judge Buckingham pounded his gavel. "Enough! I sentence you to eighteen years at the Frankfort State Prison starting now."

"No!" Adela drew her hand to her mouth.

The sheriff grabbed Benjamin's arm.

Adela ran up to him. "Wait, can we see him before you take him away?"

"Meet me in the back room. You can each have five minutes with him." The sheriff escorted Benjamin to the small room off the hallway outside the courtroom.

William led Adela there. She leaned against him, struggling to stay on her feet.

The sheriff marched out of the room. "The wife can go first. You wait here." Adela entered, and the sheriff locked the door from the outside.

William paced the floor waiting for his turn. He had a lot to pray about. Not only Benjamin but Merry as well. If only he had left when he first received the telegram. He could have been there for her when she needed him. Maybe Joe wouldn't have had to give his life to save her.

He wouldn't make the same mistake again. He had two tickets for the train to Oberlin dated two days from now in his coat pocket. She would be on that train with him or he wouldn't leave.

The sheriff unlocked the door, and Adela staggered out and sank into a nearby chair. She wiped her eyes with her handkerchief and gave a forced smile.

William laid a hand on her shoulder before going through the door. When he entered, he shivered. This room made the courtroom feel warm in comparison. It had one small window giving very little light, with bars on it, and no glass protecting it from the wind. William sat at the small wooden table with two chairs, the only furniture in the room. Benjamin was chained to the chair he sat in.

William heard the sound of the lock turning behind him. He leaned forward and gave his friend a bear hug.

"We don't have much time," Benjamin said. "Adela's taking the train to Ravenna, Ohio where she grew up. Her ma and a maiden sister still live there. She doesn't want to leave me, but I made her promise. The train leaves in the morning, and I need you to get her on it."

"I give my word, but is there anything else I can do for you?"

"I knew the risks. How's Joe? Is he all right?"

"Your wife didn't tell you?"

Benjamin's Adam's apple bulged. "No, she said she didn't want to spend our last few minutes talking about other people."

William laid his hand on Benjamin's shoulder. "He died protecting America from Boidae."

Benjamin lowered his head and released a groan from his throat.

William waited a moment until Benjamin recovered from the news.

"Riley told me Colonel Leighton stopped that snake from having anyone else arrested, and gave Joe's family their freedom. He even got Naomi's note back and let Riley tear it up."

"Colonel Leighton's a good man," Benjamin said. "He was just blind to the injustice of slavery. There are a lot like him in the South. They can't get past what they've been taught and believed their whole lives. I shudder to think what it will take to put an end to it."

"I've misjudged him just as I did Merry."

"How are things between you and her?"

William shrugged. "I love her, and she loves me. She forgives me for deserting her when she needed me most."

Benjamin raised an eyebrow. "But..."

"Colonel Leighton told me to leave and never come back."

"Because you were involved with the slave rescues?"

"No." William swallowed back the lump in his throat. "It's because I allowed my pride to stop me from returning to protect her."

"You'll find a way. You have to." Benjamin grabbed hold of William's arm. "Get her out of the South. God's judgment is coming, you mark my words."

"I'll do whatever I have to."

"Good." Benjamin leaned back. "Our time's about up. Tell Ruth I'm sorry about Joe, but he's crossed over. She can take some comfort in that. Tell her he was the finest Christian man I've ever known."

"Why did you confess?"

"Because, according to man's law, I'm guilty."

"You knew they'd send you to Frankfort."

A rueful grin came across Benjamin's face. "I feared being sent to that place for years, but now, I have peace about it. God goes before me in the presence of my enemies. It may be God's sending me into the greatest mission field I've ever known. He'll see me through this."

The door opened. "Time's up," the sheriff said.

"Get Adela and America away from here," Benjamin said. "You give your word?"

"I do." It wouldn't be easy, but he intended to do whatever he had to do to keep his promise.

Chapter Forty-Nine

William turned the handle on the door and crept inside the Leighton home. He couldn't make anything out in the darkness. If only it were a full moon tonight. He waited for a moment in the foyer to allow his eyes to adjust as he slipped off his boots.

He crept through the parlor and up the stairs and winced when a step creaked. He paused a moment in case someone stirred then, rubbing his palms on his pants, started up again. When he reached the top step, he let out the breath he was holding.

Now all he had to do was make it to the last bedroom to the right without waking anyone. Naomi had told him that's where America slept when she drew the layout of the house for him. He shivered and prayed God would help him. Did God answer the prayers of men sneaking into houses in the middle of the night? He hoped so.

He passed the first door without incident, but upon approaching the second room, he heard a scuffle and muffled footsteps and rushed to the alcove.

Standing against the wall hoping the shadows would hide him, he listened to the door open. He tried not to make a sound and rested his hand on his chest. His heartbeats sounded loud enough to wake the dead.

Colonel Leighton, dressed in bedclothes, carried a candle as he turned away from William and headed for the stairs. He descended the staircase into the shadows.

William sunk to the floor. He didn't know whether to wait for the colonel's return or if he should try to dart into Merry's room.

He had to try. When Colonel Leighton came back, he would be facing William's direction. He wouldn't be able to escape the colonel's gaze again.

Dashing to Merry's door, he turned the doorknob and slipped into the room. It was dark, but he dared not light a candle. He didn't want to alarm Merry and cause her to scream. In the blackness, he could make out the shadow of a bed and headed to it. Once there, he covered Merry's mouth.

Even in the dark, he could see her eyes open wide. "Shhh, it's all right. It's me."

Pain struck him in the back of his head as he sank to the floor.

*****

"William!" America threw off her covers, lit a candle, and knelt at his side.

He held the back of his head as he crouched by the bed, shuddering, trying to shake away the fog.

She kept her voice low hoping her father hadn't heard the commotion and sputtered her words through gritted teeth. "What are you doing here?"

He groaned. "What did you hit me with?"

"A brass candlestick holder." She rushed to the pitcher on the nearby chest and dipped a handkerchief in it. She knelt at his side and dabbed the lump forming on his head. "Why are you here?"

"I wanted to talk to you." William gingerly pulled himself to his feet and sat on the edge of the bed.

"In the middle of the night? In my bedchamber? I can't believe you of all people, a preacher, a man of God..." America looked at her nightgown and flushed. She grabbed the robe from the foot of her bed and slipped it on.

He grinned then winced as if the act pained him. "I'm sorry I scared you."

"You should be. What if Papa heard?"

"He's downstairs."

She let out her breath. "He must be having one of his midnight snacks." They might have a half hour before he came back. She glared at William. "So why did you sneak into my room? What's so important?"

He shook his head again. "I came to take you back to Oberlin."

She sat next to William. "Papa will never agree to it."

He leaned forward and kissed her.

Her heart fluttered as she moved from the bed and pulled the robe in tighter. "I don't know what to do. Papa was so wonderful. He forced Harland to give him Naomi's note and gave it to Riley to tear up, then he freed his slaves. Luke blew up, but Papa told him he'd been wrong about slavery."

"He won't change his mind about Oberlin or me?"

She shook her head. "I don't want to hurt him."

William stepped to her side and stroked her hair. She allowed the touch to comfort her.

"We have no choice," he said. "I'm taking you with me to Oberlin. We're leaving tonight."

"You really are trying to get lynched, aren't you?"

The dimple in his right cheek showed in the candlelight. "I've got it all worked out."

A knock on the door made her jump. "Quick, under the bed."

He scurried to the floor and rolled under the mattress and ropes holding it.

"Just a moment." She tossed the cloth she'd used on William's head into the basin on the dresser and opened the door.

Papa stood in the doorway. "Are you all right? I heard something."

America rubbed her hand across her mouth. She hated lying to her father. "I woke with a start. I thought I saw a man hovering over me." She allowed a slight smile as she pictured William on the floor after she clobbered him.

"You must have had a bad dream." Papa scanned the room. "With all you've been through, I'm surprised you haven't had more."

"I guess so."

"Would you like to talk about it?"

America bit her lower lip. "No, not tonight. I'm all right now."

"Good-night, Merry. I love you." Papa kissed her on the forehead and withdrew closing the door behind him.

She didn't bother to say anything, worried her father might hear. William quietly scooted out from under the bed.

They sat still, America in the rocking chair and William propped on the chest at the foot of her bed, for an hour without a word waiting to make sure her father had fallen asleep. Finally, she dared whisper. "I'll pack my bag."

"Pack light," William said.

She threw a few essentials in her carpet bag. Glancing at her trunk, she decided to take one thing, her mother's wedding dress. After tonight, she'd never be able to return to retrieve it. "I'll write Papa a note, let him know what I'm doing."

William grabbed the bag out of her hand. "There's another way. Wake him up. Tell him you're leaving with me. He might not like it, but at least he'll have a chance to say goodbye."

America rubbed her hand across her bottom lip. Things were better between her and her father, and she hated to whisk off in the middle of the night without a word, but he would stop her. This was the only way. "I'll write the note."

William nodded.

She dipped her pen in the ink and paused. What could she say? She kept it short.

I love you, Papa, but I'm going back to Oberlin with William. I hope you understand.

Love, Merry.

She blinked her eyes. "Wait in the hallway. I'll get dressed."

William creaked open the door and skulked to the alcove.

America dressed quickly and slipped out the door.

He kissed her again, and tingles ran through her as his lips pressed against her. He motioned for her to follow him.

A lump formed in stomach. She carefully placed her foot on each step of the staircase. When she made it halfway down, a floorboard creaked.

William held onto her hand, and they made it to the bottom. They headed for the foyer.

Papa stepped in front of the door and lit a lantern.

Chapter Fifty

William shifted his weight from foot to foot. He didn't know what to say.

Colonel Leighton's glower directed toward him flicked in the lantern light. "You have some explaining to do, Mr. Woods."

There was nothing to do but acknowledge the corn and hope Colonel Leighton wasn't the kind to enjoy a good tar and feathering. "Yes, sir, I do."

"Papa! It's not his fault. I'm going back to Oberlin. He's just helping me."

William winked at her. "Maybe you better let the men folk talk. Why don't you wait upstairs?"

"The men folk?" America gave him the look she'd obviously inherited from her father.

"Merry," Colonel Leighton barked. "Upstairs."

America marched to her room and slammed the door loud enough for them to hear.

"She has a bad habit of slamming doors lately," the colonel said.

William rubbed his head where the candlestick holder had hit him. "Colonel Leighton, could we sit down? After I've said my peace, if you want me arrested, or horsewhipped, I won't resist. I probably deserve it."

"You beat all, you know that." Colonel Leighton stroked his beard. "All right, but if you don't give me straight answers about why you're sneaking my daughter out of my house in the middle of the night, I'll fill you full of buckshot, and no jury will convict me."

Merry was wrong. William didn't have to worry about being lynched. He was going to be shot by an irate father. "Fair enough. I'm in love with Merry, and I'm going to marry her as soon as we graduate."

"Do you think whisking her away without a word is the way to gain my approval?"

William thought about it for a moment. It had seemed the best way at the time, but he could see now it may not have been the wisest course of action. He'd made a mess of things again. "No, sir. I was wrong. I should have come straight to you."

"You sure as blazes should have. You didn't stand by Merry and protect her before. Why don't you tell me why in Sam Hill I should trust you with my daughter now before I knock you clean to Sunday!"

William glanced at his feet. "I was wrong before, there's no getting around it, but I want to protect her now." He made eye contact with the colonel hoping he'd see his sincerity. "I'll never leave her again. You know she'll be safer away from here, and I won't travel to Oberlin without her. If you don't allow her to leave, I'll stay here and forego my education until I can prove myself to you."

"If you feel that way, why didn't you come to me?"

"I should have." William swallowed. "When you told me you wouldn't permit me to see her again, I didn't know what else to do."

"I wanted to see what kind of mettle you were made of. I knew if you loved my daughter, you'd be back. Does Merry know you want to marry her?"

"I think so, but I haven't officially asked her yet."

Colonel Leighton lit his pipe. "If I allow you to take Merry away, you'll ask her before you leave this house. I want to make sure her future's provided for. She's not going off to some heathen mission field alone."

"Yes, sir. I'd be honored to have her for my wife."

"When do you plan on leaving for China? I have a reason for asking."

"Right after the wedding," William said. "I already have the money for the trip, and the American Missionary Society has approved my application. I'll receive my ministerial license when I graduate, so I won't have to wait."

"If you get her out of the country that soon, I can run against Harland for the United States Senate. I won't have to worry about that snake having Merry arrested." Colonel Leighton took a drag on his pipe. "Some businessmen in Maysville have been after me to do it for years. They'll support my campaign."

"What a relief. This country would be in real trouble if a man like him ended up in government."

"I imagine it's happened before. I wouldn't be surprised if our current president is very much like him."

"Colonel, one thing's bothering me. I thought you shook hands with Harland and agreed to support him in his bid for office. I didn't take you as someone who would go back on your word."

"As far as I'm concerned, the arrangement I made with him is a devil's bargain I didn't agree to or shake on. I merely allowed him to think what he wanted for the time being. I have no intention of living up to it as soon as I'm assured my daughter is safe from his grasp." Colonel Leighton narrowed his eyes and delivered a pointed glare toward William. "Not that I need to explain my morals to a man sneaking in my house in the middle of the night."

William flushed. "Point taken."

"There is something I intend to shake on with you. I don't want you dragging my Merry into any more dangerous slave rescues."

"You have my word. As of this moment, no more slave rescues." He didn't think it necessary to tell Colonel Leighton this was his last school break before graduation anyway. He wouldn't have another opportunity to rescue slaves if he wanted to.

Colonel Leighton extended his hand. "Son, you take care of my little girl or you'll rue the day you ever saw me."

*****

America paced back and forth in her room. What could be happening? If Papa did anything to hurt William... She wanted to reserve that for herself. Men folk indeed, and after he espoused agreement with women's issues.

She looked out the window. The sun peaked over the hills allowing a sliver of yellow light, but the sky looked ominous. Dark snow clouds with a red hue signaled another winter storm brewing. She recited part of the rhyme she'd learned as a little girl.

"Red sky in the morning, sailors take warning." Not the best weather to travel in.

Papa opened the door. "Come downstairs, Merry."

She followed him down the staircase. William waited at the bottom. At least Papa hadn't killed him or thrown him out.

William took her hand in his and knelt on one knee. "America, will you marry me?"

Tears came to America's eyes. What had Lavena said when she first went to Oberlin? *If God wants you to marry a missionary, He'll bring the right man along.* He had surely done so. "Yes, but not until graduation."

William took her in his arms and kissed her.

Papa cleared his throat.

William stepped back and gave a sheepish grin.

"You go with him, Merry," Papa said. "Go to Oberlin and then to China, and don't ever come back here. Trouble's brewing here, and I want you away from it. William promised he'd protect you, and I believe him."

The tears flowed down her face, and she hugged her father. Pipe tobacco. She'd miss that smell. "I love you, Papa."

"I love you too. Make sure you write me at least once a month. Don't you ignore my letters like you did before." He took her in his arms. "If you ever need me, you telegraph. I'll come straight away."

Papa picked up Merry's bag and handed it to William. "Take care of her."

"I will, sir. You can count on it."

*****

America felt a nudge and struggled to open her eyes. She'd fallen asleep on the long train ride home. She smiled at William and looked out the window. Wellington Station came into view, just ten short miles from Oberlin.

She thought about the home she'd left. She'd miss her papa, Ruth, Naomi, and Obadiah, and she'd miss Joe. She shut her eyes against the threatening tears. When she opened them again, William smiled at her and squeezed her hand.

She'd probably never see Kentucky again, but it wasn't home anymore. Her home was with William. Papa was right. A storm was brewing, and only God knew where it would end.

The End

About the Author

Tamera Lynn Kraft has always loved adventures. She loves to write historical fiction set in the United States because there are so many stories in American history. There are strong elements of faith, romance, suspense and adventure in her stories. She has received 2nd place in the NOCW contest, 3rd place in the TARA writer's contest, and is a finalist in the Frasier Writing Contest.

Tamera been married for thirty-nine years to the love of her life, Rick, and has two married adult children and three grandchildren. She has been a children's pastor for over twemty years. She is the leader of a ministry called Revival Fire for Kids where she mentors other children's leaders, teaches workshops, is a children's ministry consultant and children's evangelist, and has written children's church curriculum. She is a recipient of the 2007 National Children's Leaders Association Shepherd's Cup for lifetime achievement in children's ministry.

You can contact Tamera online at her website: *http://tameralynnkraft.net*

www.ingramcontent.com/pod-product-compliance
Lightning Source LLC
Chambersburg PA
CBHW070604170726
48291CB00003B/694